ELECTION DAY 2084

A Science Fiction Anthology on the Politics of the Future

ELECTION DAY 2084

A Science Fiction Anthology on the Politics of the Future

edited by

ISAAC ASIMOV AND MARTIN H. GREENBERG

Prometheus Books

700 East Amherst St. Buffalo, New York 14215

Published in 1984 by
Prometheus Books
700 East Amherst Street
Buffalo, New York 14215

Printed in the United States of America

Library of Congress Catalog Card No. 84-42794
ISBN No. 0-87975-258-0 cloth
0-87975-270-x paper

Acknowledgments

"Franchise," by Isaac Asimov, copyright © 1955 by Quinn Publishing Co., copyright renewed © 1983 by Isaac Asimov, is reprinted by permission of the author.

"Death and the Senator," by Arthur C. Clarke, © 1961 by Street & Smith Publications, Inc., is reprinted by permission of the author and his agents, Scott Meredith Literary Agency, Inc., 845 Third Ave., New York, NY 10022.

"Committee of the Whole," by Frank Herbert, copyright © 1965 by UPD Corporation, is reprinted by permission of Kirby McCauley, Ltd.

"Political Machine," by John Jakes, copyright © 1961 by Ziff-Davis Publishing Co., is reprinted by permission of the author.

"The Children of Night," by Frederik Pohl, copyright © 1964 by UPD Corporation, is reprinted by permission of the author.

"2066: Election Day," by Michael Shaara, copyright © 1956 by Street & Smith Publications, Inc., copyright renewed, is reprinted by permission of the author and the author's agents, the Scott Meredith Literary Agency, Inc.,845 Third Ave., New York, NY 10022.

"On the Campaign Trail," by Barry N. Malzberg, copyright © 1975 by Roger Elwood, originally appeared in *Future Corruption* and is reprinted by permission of the author.

"Hail to the Chief," by Randall Garrett, copyright © 1962 by Street & Smith Publications, Inc., is reprinted by permission of the author and his agents, the Scott Meredith Literary Agency, Inc., 845 Third Ave., New York, NY 10022.

"A Rose by Other Name . . . ," by Christopher Anvil, copyright © 1960 by Street & Smith Publications, Inc., is reprinted by permission of the author and his agents, the Scott Meredith Literary Agency, Inc., 845 Third Ave., New York, NY 10022.

"Beyond Doubt," by Robert A. Heinlein, copyright © 1941 by Fictioneers, Inc., and copyright 1968 by the author, is reprinted by permission of Blassingame, McCauley and Wood.

"Frank Merriwell in the White House," by Ward Moore, copyright © 1973 by UPD Publishing Corporation, is reprinted by permission of the author's agent, Virginia Kidd.

"Hail to the Chief," by Sam Sackett, copyright © 1954 by Columbia Publications, Inc., is reprinted by permission of Forrest J. Ackerman, 2495 Glendower Ave., Hollywood, CA 90027.

"Polity and Custom of the Camiroi," by R. A. Lafferty, copyright © 1967, 1970 by R. A. Lafferty, is reprinted by permission of the author and the author's agent, Virginia Kidd.

Contents

Introduction

ISAAC ASIMOV

We who read science fiction are used to dealing with the advance of technology. We read of spaceships and new weapons and unusual devices of all kinds that amuse and astonish us, and we are ready to accept them because we know well that in a million years of history modern man and his immediate ancestors have steadily advanced in technology. From the use of fire and the first chipped pebbles we have advanced to the hydrogen bomb, the laser, and the computer — and the end is surely not yet.

We are less used to dealing with the advance of social devices. We don't often think of that. We expect the evolution of machinery. But do we often think of the evolution of the concept of justice, for instance? And yet social devices evolve as well.

Consider elections.

The ancient Athenians had a unique variety of election, one that no one else ever used, before them or since, as far as we know, and one that they themselves used for only a century. They voted, in times of crisis, not on whom to elect to office, but on whom to exile for ten years — how to secure social peace by getting rid for a while of a man too likely to prove dangerous. They voted by scratching a name on a piece of pottery (an *ostrakon*) and we still speak of "ostracism" as a result.

The Romans during the third and fourth centuries often elected emperors by having each of various legions proclaim its commander and then march on Rome. The legions would argue out the matter by battle and the winning commander found he had won the election as well, winning a term that lasted until assassination.

That was such a popular form of election and so wasteful that in medieval Europe a system was devised whereby election to the rule of a kingdom (or a duchy or, for that matter, a manor) was made automatic by the establishment of rules of inheritance based on things like legal marriage, order of birth, and so on. This frequently established an incompetent as ruler but at least it did so in peace.

But suppose we consider our own country and our own customs. We elect presidents and other high officials according to a system defined by our Constitution, which has been in existence for nearly two centuries. We follow the Constitution as closely now as we did at the start, so has there been room for change?

You bet there has. In the first place, there have been amendments to the Constitution. The Twelfth Amendment (1804) directed a vote for both a president and vice-president, instead of for president only, with the man who finished in second place becoming vice-president. The Seventeenth Amendment (1913) allowed people to vote directly for their senators, instead of having senators chosen by the state legislatures.

To begin with, voting was restricted to white males of 21 years and over, but the Fifteenth Amendment (1870) permitted black males to vote as well, the Nineteenth Amendment (1920) permitted women to vote, the Twenty-fourth (1964) forbade any limitation of the right to vote by reason of failure to pay a poll tax, and the Twenty-sixth (1971) lowered the voting age from 21 to 18.

Some changes in voting took place without any tinkering with the Constitution. To begin with, many states had property qualifications for voting, so that only solid, responsible citizens who owned land and had a "stake in the country" could vote. This made it certain that the government would be of the well-to-do, by the well-to-do, and for the well-to-do — but it did not last. Little by little, state by state, property qualifications were removed.

Thus all the changes in voting qualifications over the past two centuries have been in the direction of universal suffrage, which idealists like me consider a good thing, even when a majority, out of sheer stupidity, votes for the wrong person.

Even when neither the Constitution nor the law changes, customs may. For instance, the electoral college was chosen according to the whim of the individual states — by election or by appointment by the state legislature. Each state chose a number of electors equal to the sum of the senators and representatives they possessed in Congress, and those electors gathered and voted for president, consulting only their own wills.

Little by little that changed. Different sets of electors are chosen for each candidate contesting the election, and the people, without knowing or caring who those electors are, then vote in each state for this candidate or that. The appropriate set of electors in each state, and it is they who have been *really* elected, will then eventually vote for president. It is *still* their constitutional right *even today* to vote for whomever they please, for Mickey Mouse, if they wish; but, with very, very few exceptions, they now act as puppets, voting for the man who gained the majority in their state. Nevertheless, Americans do *not* vote for president, but for electors, whose names they do not even know. What's more, it is possible (and has even sometimes happened) that large majorities in some states are overridden by narrow majorities in other states and the candidate with a minority vote in the nation as a whole is elected president with a majority of the electoral vote. It may also be that a candidate with a narrow majority in the nation as a whole may win it in many states and end with a "landslide" vote in the electoral college and act as though it was really a landslide.

Then how about the process of nomination? At the start, nominations were put through by various factions in Congress, meeting in "caucus." State legislatures might nominate some "favorite son" from their own state, and all might battle it out. It was not until 1844 that the "Anti-Masonic party" (one of the small parties that periodically appear on the scene and fade after a while) held a national convention to decide on their nominee, and that device caught on and spread.

The quadrennial conventions were so full of hoopla and were such exciting events that it was difficult to realize there is absolutely nothing in the Constitution prescribing them, nor any law, either. They are nothing but custom.

In the twentieth century, primaries began to come into fashion. In this state or that, members of a given party got together and voted on the nominee. This would send various numbers of delegates to the national convention who were pledged to vote for this candidate or that.

Primaries have grown so numerous now that the national convention has lost almost all its meaning. There are no longer "favorite sons" (when did you last hear that phrase used?) and no longer any horse-trading; nor are there numerous ballots marking a stubborn refusal to horse-trade, such as the 103 at the Democratic convention of 1924.

Conventions gather with the delegates already committed and with some particular candidate already assured of a majority and of the nomination. One ballot suffices, and the only excitement is that of the party platform and the choice of the vice-president. However, the party platform is always a pious fraud that no one (not even the most foolish voter) takes seriously, and the vice-presidential choice is invariably dictated by the presidential nominee. Traditions may continue — like the electoral college — but they will have less and less meaning and attract less and less interest, and will finally conduct their rubber-stamp proceedings in silence.

Consider the changes that have taken place in our own generation since 1950. The expansion of the primary system has increased the length of a campaign until now the United States suffers the confusion and expense of a virtually perpetual presidential campaign. It wearies us all and decreases the desire to participate.

Consider television, which has horrendously increased the expense of a campaign and put a premium on jackasses who can smile and who have "charisma" and who are "Great Communicators," all at the expense of ability and of issues.

Consider the "momentum" created by the multiplicity of polls and the bandstanding phenomenon by which those who the polls say are in the lead actually gain the lead — because there are always people who vote for the leader, just as there are people who buy best-sellers because they are best-sellers and thus keep them best-sellers.

Consider the skilled public-relations firms, hired by those candidates with enough money for it, who manipulate the minds of the public to the point where there is scarcely any meaning in voting.

Consider the computers and the exit polls that announce the victors in an election even while people are still voting.

Well, then, what may we expect of elections in the future? What further changes will take place?

I began by saying that science fiction deals with the future evolution of social devices less often than with the evolution of technology — but it doesn't ignore the former entirely. Here in this anthology we have a generous selection of stories by skilled science-fiction writers who present us with other societies in which elections and office-holders must take into account all sorts of things we need not consider today.

Come, then, and help elect high officials in strange societies and under strange conditions.

Franchise

ISAAC ASIMOV

Science fiction is, among other things, a literature of alternatives.
It is altogether appropriate then, for Isaac Asimov to suggest an
alternative way of choosing the president of the United States.
And given the mixed record of achievement of those elected to
high office, who's to say he's wrong? — M.H.G.

Linda, age ten, was the only one of the family who seemed to enjoy being
awake.

Norman Muller could hear her now through his own drugged, unhealthy
coma. (He had finally managed to fall asleep an hour earlier but even then
it was more like exhaustion than sleep.)

She was at his bedside now, shaking him. "Daddy, Daddy, wake up. Wake
up!"

He suppressed a groan. "All right, Linda."

"But, Daddy, there's more policemen around than any time! Police cars
and everything!"

Norman Muller gave up and rose blearily to his elbows. The day was
beginning. It was faintly stirring toward dawn outside, the germ of a miserable gray that looked about as miserably gray as he felt. He could hear Sarah,
his wife, shuffling about breakfast duties in the kitchen. His father-in-law,
Matthew, was hawking strenuously in the bathroom. No doubt Agent Handley was ready and waiting for him.

This was *the* day.

Election Day!

To begin with, it had been like every other year. Maybe a little worse,
because it was a presidential year, but no worse than other presidential years
if it came to that.

The politicians spoke about the guh-reat electorate and the vast elec-
tuhronic intelligence that was its servant. The press analyzed the situation
with industrial computers (the New York *Times* and the St. Louis *Post-*

11

Dispatch had their own computers) and were full of little hints as to what would be forthcoming. Commentators and columnists pinpointed the crucial state and county in happy contradiction to one another.

The first hint that it would *not* be like every other year was when Sarah Muller said to her husband on the evening of October 4 (with Election Day exactly a month off), "Cantwell Johnson says that Indiana will be the state this year. He's the fourth one. Just think, *our* state this time."

Matthew Hortenweiler took his fleshy face from behind the paper, stared dourly at his daughter and growled, "Those fellows are paid to tell lies. Don't listen to them."

"Four of them, Father," said Sarah mildly. "They all say Indiana."

"Indiana *is* a key state, Matthew," said Norman, just as mildly, "on account of the Hawkins-Smith Act and this mess in Indianapolis. It—"

Matthew twisted his old face alarmingly and rasped out, "No one says Bloomington or Monroe County, do they?"

"Well—" said Norman.

Linda, whose little pointed-chinned face had been shifting from one speaker to the next, said pipingly, "You going to be voting this year, Daddy?"

Norman smiled gently and said, "I don't think so, dear."

But this was in the gradually growing excitement of an October in a presidential election year and Sarah had led a quiet life with dreams for her companions. She said longingly, "Wouldn't *that* be wonderful, though?"

"If I voted?" Norman Muller had a small blond mustache that had given him a debonair quality in the young Sarah's eyes, but which, with gradual graying, had declined merely to lack of distinction. His forehead bore deepening lines born of uncertainty and, in general, he had never seduced his clerkly soul with the thought that he was either born great or would under any circumstances achieve greatness. He had a wife, a job and a little girl, and except under extraordinary conditions of elation or depression was inclined to consider that to be an adequate bargain struck with life.

So he was a little embarrassed and more than a little uneasy at the direction his wife's thoughts were taking. "Actually, my dear," he said, "there are two hundred million people in the country, and, with odds like that, I don't think we ought to waste our time wondering about it."

His wife said, "Why, Norman, it's no such thing like two hundred million and you know it. In the first place, only people between twenty and sixty are eligible and it's always men, so that puts it down to maybe fifty million to one. Then, if it's really Indiana—"

"Then it's about one and a quarter million to one. You wouldn't want me to bet in a horse race against those odds, now, would you? Let's have supper."

Matthew muttered from behind his newspaper, "Damned foolishness."

Linda asked again, "You going to be voting this year, Daddy?"

Norman shook his head and they all adjourned to the dining room.

By October 20, Sarah's excitement was rising rapidly. Over the coffee, she announced that Mrs. Schultz, having a cousin who was the secretary of an Assemblyman, said that all the "smart money" was on Indiana.

"She says President Villers is even going to make a speech at Indianapolis."

Norman Muller, who had had a hard day at the store, nudged the statement with a raising of eyebrows and let it go at that.

Matthew Hortenweiler, who was chronically dissatisfied with Washington, said, "If Villers makes a speech in Indiana, that means he thinks Multivac will pick Arizona. He wouldn't have the guts to go closer, the mushhead."

Sarah, who ignored her father whenever she could decently do so, said, "I don't know why they don't announce the state as soon as they can, and then the county and so on. Then the people who were eliminated could relax."

"If they did anything like that," pointed out Norman, "the politicians would follow the announcements like vultures. By the time it was narrowed down to a township, you'd have a Congressman or two at every street corner."

Matthew narrowed his eyes and brushed angrily at his sparse, gray hair. "They're vultures, anyway. Listen —"

Sarah murmured, "Now Father —"

Matthew's voice rumbled over her protest without as much as a stumble or hitch. "Listen, I was around when they set up Multivac. It would end partisan politics, they said. No more voters' money wasted on campaigns. No more grinning nobodies high-pressured and advertising-campaigned into Congress or the White House. So what happens. More campaigning than ever, only now they do it blind. They'll send guys to Indiana on account of the Hawkins-Smith Act and other guys to California in case it's the Joe Hammer situation that turns out crucial. I say, wipe out all the nonsense. Back to the good old —"

Linda asked suddenly, "Don't you want Daddy to vote this year, Grandpa?"

Matthew glared at the young girl. "Never you mind, now." He turned back to Norman and Sarah. "There was a time I voted. Marched right up to the polling booth, stuck my fist on the levers and voted. There was nothing to it. I just said: This fellow's my man and I'm voting for him. *That's* the way it should be."

Linda said excitedly, "You voted, Grandpa? You really did?"

Sarah leaned forward quickly to quiet what might easily become an incongruous story drifting about the neighborhood. "It's nothing, Linda. Grandpa doesn't really mean voted. Everyone did that kind of voting, your grandpa, too, but it wasn't *really* voting."

Matthew roared, "It wasn't when I was a little boy. I was twenty-two and I voted for Langley and it was real voting. My vote didn't count for much, maybe, but it was as good as anyone else's. *Anyone* else's. And no Multivac to—"

Norman interposed, "All right, Linda, time for bed. And stop asking questions about voting. When you grow up, you'll understand all about it."

He kissed her with antiseptic gentleness and she moved reluctantly out of range under maternal prodding and a promise that she might watch the bedside video till 9:15, *if* she was prompt about the bathing ritual.

Linda said, "Grandpa," and stood with her chin down and her hands behind her back until his newspaper lowered itself to the point where shaggy eyebrows and eyes, nested in fine wrinkles, showed themselves. It was Friday, October 31.

He said, "Yes?"

Linda came closer and put both her forearms on one of the old man's knees so that he had to discard his newspaper altogether.

She said, "Grandpa, did you really once vote?"

He said, "You heard me say I did, didn't you? Do you think I tell fibs?"

"N—no, but Mamma says everybody voted then."

"So they did."

"But how could they? How could *everybody* vote?"

Matthew stared at her solemnly, then lifted her and put her on his knee.

He even moderated the tonal qualities of his voice. He said, "You see, Linda, till about forty years ago, everybody always voted. Say we wanted to decide who was to be the new President of the United States. The Democrats and Republicans would both nominate someone, and everybody would say who they wanted. When Election Day was over, they would count how many people wanted the Democrat and how many wanted the Republican. Whoever had more votes was elected. You see?"

Linda nodded and said, "How did all the people know who to vote for? Did Multivac tell them?"

Matthew's eyebrows hunched down and he looked severe. "They just used their own judgment, girl."

She edged away from him, and he lowered his voice again. "I'm not angry at you, Linda. But, you see, sometimes it took all night to count what everyone said and people were impatient. So they invented special machines which could look at the first few votes and compare them with the votes from the same places in previous years. That way the machine could compute how the total vote would be and who would be elected. You see?"

She nodded. "Like Multivac."

"The first computers were much smaller than Multivac. But the machines grew bigger and they could tell how the election would go from fewer and fewer votes. Then, at last, they built Multivac and it can tell from just one voter."

Linda smiled at having reached a familiar part of the story and said, "That's nice."

Matthew frowned and said, "No, it's not nice. I don't want a machine telling me how I would have voted just because some joker in Milwaukee says he's against higher tariffs. Maybe I want to vote cock-eyed just for the pleasure of it. Maybe I don't want to vote. Maybe—"

But Linda had wriggled from his knee and was beating a retreat.

She met her mother at the door. Her mother, who was still wearing her coat and had not even had time to remove her hat, said breathlessly, "Run along, Linda. Don't get in Mother's way."

Then she said to Matthew, as she lifted her hat from her head and patted her hair back into place, "I've been at Agatha's."

Matthew stared at her censoriously and did not even dignify that piece of information with a grunt as he groped for his newspaper.

Sarah said, as she unbuttoned her coat, "Guess what she said?"

Matthew flattened out his newspaper for reading purposes with a sharp crackle and said, "Don't much care."

Sarah said, "Now, Father—" But she had no time for anger. The news had to be told and Matthew was the only recipient handy, so she went on, "Agatha's Joe is a policeman, you know, and he says a whole truckload of secret service men came into Bloomington last night."

"They're not after me."

"Don't you see, Father? Secret service agents, and it's almost election time. In *Bloomington.*"

"Maybe they're after a bank robber."

"There hasn't been a bank robbery in town in ages. . . . Father, you're hopeless."

She stalked away.

Nor did Norman Muller receive the news with noticeably greater excitement.

"Now, Sarah, how did Agatha's Joe know they were secret service agents?" he asked calmly. "They wouldn't go around with identification cards pasted on their foreheads."

But by next evening, with November a day old, she could say triumphantly, "It's just everyone in Bloomington that's waiting for someone local to be the voter. The Bloomington *News* as much as said so on video."

Norman stirred uneasily. He couldn't deny it, and his heart was sinking. If Bloomington was really to be hit by Multivac's lightning, it would mean newspapermen, video shows, tourists, all sorts of—strange upsets. Norman liked the quiet routine of his life, and the distant stir of politics was getting uncomfortably close.

He said, "It's all rumor. Nothing more."

"You wait and see, then. You just wait and see."

As things turned out, there was very little time to wait, for the doorbell rang insistently, and when Norman Muller opened it and said, "Yes?" a tall, grave-faced man said, "Are you Norman Muller?"

Norman said, "Yes," again, but in a strange dying voice. It was not difficult to see from the stranger's bearing that he was one carrying authority, and the nature of his errand suddenly became as inevitably obvious as it had, until the moment before, been unthinkably impossible.

The man presented credentials, stepped into the house, closed the door behind him and said ritualistically, "Mr. Norman Muller, it is necessary for me to inform you on the behalf of the President of the United States that you have been chosen to represent the American electorate on Tuesday, November 4, 2008."

Norman Muller managed, with difficulty, to walk unaided to his chair. He sat there, white-faced and almost insensible, while Sarah brought water, slapped his hands in panic and moaned to her husband between clenched teeth, "Don't be sick, Norman. *Don't* be sick. They'll pick someone else."

When Norman could manage to talk, he whispered, "I'm sorry, sir."

The secret service agent had removed his coat, unbuttoned his jacket and was sitting at ease on the couch.

"It's all right," he said, and the mark of officialdom seemed to have vanished with the formal announcement and leave him simply a large and rather friendly man. "This is the sixth time I've made the announcement and I've seen all kinds of reactions. Not one of them was the kind you see on the video. You know what I mean? A holy, dedicated look, and a character who says, 'It will be a great privilege to serve my country.' That sort of stuff." The agent laughed comfortingly.

Sarah's accompanying laugh held a trace of shrill hysteria.

The agent said, "Now you're going to have me with you for a while. My name is Phil Handley. I'd appreciate it if you call me Phil. Mr. Muller can't leave the house any more till Election Day. You'll have to inform the department store that he's sick, Mrs. Muller. You can go about your business for a while, but you'll have to agree not to say a word about this. Right, Mrs. Muller?"

Sarah nodded vigorously. "No, sir. Not a word."

"All right. But, Mrs. Muller," Handley looked grave, "we're not kidding now. Go out only if you must and you'll be followed when you do. I'm sorry but that's the way we must operate."

"Followed?"

"It won't be obvious. Don't worry. And it's only for two days till the formal announcement to the nation is made. Your daughter — "

"She's in bed," said Sarah hastily.

"Good. She'll have to be told I'm a relative or friend staying with the family. If she does find out the truth, she'll have to be kept in the house. Your father had better stay in the house in any case."

"He won't like that," said Sarah.

"Can't be helped. Now, since you have no others living with you — "

"You know all about us apparently," whispered Norman.

"Quite a bit," agreed Handley. "In any case, those are all my instructions to you for the moment. I'll try to co-operate as much as I can and be as little of a nuisance as possible. The government will pay for my maintenance so I won't be an expense to you. I'll be relieved each night by someone who will sit up in this room, so there will be no problem about sleeping accommodations. Now, Mr. Muller — "

"Sir?"

"You can call me Phil," said the agent again. "The purpose of the two-day preliminary before formal announcement is to get you used to your position. We prefer to have you face Multivac in as normal a state of mind as possible. Just relax and try to feel this is all in a day's work. Okay?"

"Okay," said Norman, and then shook his head violently. "But I don't want the responsibility. Why me?"

"All right," said Handley, "let's get that straight to begin with. Multivac weighs all sorts of known factors, billions of them. One factor isn't known, though, and won't be known for a long time. That's the reaction pattern of the human mind. All Americans are subjected to the molding pressure of what other Americans do and say, to the things that are done to him and the things he does to others. Any American can be brought to Multivac to have the bent of his mind surveyed. From that the bent of all other minds in the country can be estimated. Some Americans are better for the purpose than others at some given time, depending upon the happenings of that year. Multivac picked you as most representative this year. Not the smartest, or the strongest, or the luckiest, but just the most representative. Now we don't question Multivac, do we?"

"Couldn't it make a mistake?" asked Norman.

Sarah, who listened impatiently, interrupted to say, "Don't listen to him, sir. He's just nervous, you know. Actually, he's very well read and he always follows politics very closely."

Handley said, "Multivac makes the decisions, Mrs. Muller. It picked your husband."

"But does it know everything?" insisted Norman wildly. "Couldn't it have made a mistake?"

"Yes, it can. There's no point in not being frank. In 1993, a selected Voter died of a stroke two hours before it was time for him to be notified. Multivac didn't predict that; it couldn't. A Voter might be mentally unstable, morally unsuitable, or, for that matter, disloyal. Multivac can't know everything about everybody until he's fed all the data there is. That's why alternate selections are always held in readiness. I don't think we'll be using one this time. You're in good health, Mr. Muller, and you've been carefully investigated. You qualify."

Norman buried his face in his hands and sat motionless.

"By tomorrow morning, sir," said Sarah, "he'll be perfectly all right. He just has to get used to it, that's all."

"Of course," said Handley.

In the privacy of their bedchamber, Sarah Muller expressed herself in other and stronger fashion. The burden of her lecture was, "So get hold of yourself, Norman. You're trying to throw away the chance of a lifetime."

Norman whispered desperately, "It frightens me, Sarah. The whole thing."

"For goodness' sake, why? What's there to it but answering a question or two?"

"The responsibility is too great. I couldn't face it."

"What responsibility? There isn't any. Multivac picked you. It's Multivac's responsibility. Everyone knows that."

Norman sat up in bed in a sudden access of rebellion and anguish. "Everyone is *supposed* to know that. But they don't. They—"

"Lower your voice," hissed Sarah icily. "They'll hear you downtown."

"They don't," said Norman, declining quickly to a whisper. "When they talk about the Ridgely administration of 1988, do they say he won them over with pie-in-the-sky promises and racist baloney? No! They talk about the 'goddam MacComber vote,' as though Humphrey MacComber was the only man who had anything to do with it because he faced Multivac. I've said it myself—only now I think the poor guy was just a truck farmer who didn't ask to be picked. Why was it his fault more than anyone else's? Now his name is a curse."

"You're just being childish," said Sarah.

"I'm being sensible. I tell you, Sarah, I won't accept. They can't make me vote if I don't want to. I'll say I'm sick. I'll say—"

But Sarah had had enough. "Now you listen to me," she whispered in a cold fury. "You don't have only yourself to think about. You know what it means to be Voter of the Year. A presidential year at that. It means publicity and fame and, maybe, buckets of money—"

"And then I go back to being a clerk."

"You will *not*. You'll have a branch managership at the least if you have any brains at all, and you *will* have, because I'll tell you what to do. You control the kind of publicity if you play your cards right, and you can force Kennell Stores, Inc., into a tight contract *and* an escalator clause in connection with your salary *and* a decent pension plan."

"That's not the point in being Voter, Sarah."

"That will be your point. If you don't owe anything to yourself or to me — I'm not asking for myself — you owe something to Linda."

Norman groaned.

"Well, don't you?" snapped Sarah.

"Yes, dear," murmured Norman.

On November 3, the official announcement was made and it was too late for Norman to back out even if he had been able to find the courage to make the attempt.

Their house was sealed off. Secret service agents made their appearance in the open, blocking off all approach.

At first the telephone rang incessantly, but Philip Handley with an engagingly apologetic smile took all calls. Eventually, the exchange shunted all calls directly to the police station.

Norman imagined that, in that way, he was spared not only the bubbling (and envious?) congratulations of friends, but also the egregious pressure of salesmen scenting a prospect and the designing smoothness of politicians from all over the nation. . . . Perhaps even death threats from the inevitable cranks.

Newspapers were forbidden to enter the house now in order to keep out weighted pressures, and television was gently but firmly disconnected, over Linda's loud protests.

Matthew growled and stayed in his room; Linda, after the first flurry of excitement, sulked and whined because she could not leave the house; Sarah divided her time between preparation of meals for the present and plans for the future; and Norman's depression lived and fed upon itself.

And the morning of Tuesday, November 4, 2008, came at last, and it was Election Day.

It was early breakfast, but only Norman Muller ate, and that mechanically. Even a shower and shave had not succeeded in either restoring him to reality or removing his own conviction that he was as grimy without as he felt grimy within.

Handley's friendly voice did its best to shed some normality over the gray and unfriendly dawn. (The weather prediction had been for a cloudy day with prospects of rain before noon.)

Handley said, "We'll keep this house insulated till Mr. Muller is back, but after that we'll be off your necks." The secret service agent was in full uniform now, including sidearms in heavily brassed holsters.

"You've been no trouble at all, Mr. Handley," simpered Sarah.

Norman drank through two cups of black coffee, wiped his lips with a napkin, stood up and said haggardly, "I'm ready."

Handley stood up, too. "Very well, sir. And thank you, Mrs. Muller, for your very kind hospitality."

The armored car purred down empty streets. They were empty even for that hour of the morning.

Handley indicated that and said, "They always shift traffic away from the line of drive ever since the attempted bombing that nearly ruined the Leverett Election of '92."

When the car stopped, Norman was helped out by the always polite Handley into an underground drive whose walls were lined with soldiers at attention.

He was led into a brightly lit room, in which three white-uniformed men greeted him smilingly.

Norman said sharply, "But this is the hospital."

"There's no significance to that," said Handley at once. "It's just that the hospital has the necessary facilities."

"Well, what do I do?"

Handley nodded. One of the three men in white advanced and said, "I'll take over now, agent."

Handley saluted in an offhand manner and left the room.

The man in white said, "Won't you sit down, Mr. Muller? I'm John Paulson, Senior Computer. These are Samson Levine and Peter Dorogobuzh, my assistants."

Norman shook hands numbly all about. Paulson was a man of middle height with a soft face that seemed used to smiling and a very obvious toupee. He wore plastic-rimmed glasses of an old-fashioned cut, and he lit a cigarette as he talked. (Norman refused his offer of one.)

Paulson said, "In the first place, Mr. Muller, I want you to know we are in no hurry. We want you to stay with us all day if necessary, just so that you get used to your surroundings and get over any thought you might have that there is anything unusual in this, anything clinical, if you know what I mean."

"It's all right," said Norman. "I'd just as soon this were over."

"I understand your feelings. Still, we want you to know exactly what's going on. In the first place, Multivac isn't here."

"It isn't?" Somehow through all his depression, he had still looked forward to seeing Multivac. They said it was half a mile long and three stories high, that fifty technicians walked the corridors *within* its structure continuously. It was one of the wonders of the world.

Paulson smiled. "No. It's not portable, you know. It's located underground, in fact, and very few people know exactly where. You can understand that, since it is our greatest natural resource. Believe me, elections aren't the only things it's used for."

Norman thought he was being deliberately chatty and found himself intrigued all the same. "I thought I'd see it. I'd like to."

"I'm sure of that. But it takes a presidential order and even then it has to be countersigned by Security. However, we are plugged into Multivac right here by beam transmission. What Multivac says can be interpreted here and what we say is beamed directly to Multivac, so in a sense we're in its presence."

Norman looked about. The machines within the room were all meaningless to him.

"Now let me explain, Mr. Muller," Paulson went on. "Multivac already has most of the information it needs to decide all the elections, national, state and local. It needs only to check certain imponderable attitudes of mind and it will use you for that. We can't predict what questions it will ask, but they may not make much sense to you, or even to us. It may ask you how you feel about garbage disposal in your town; whether you favor central incinerators. It might ask you whether you have a doctor of your own or whether you make use of National Medicine, Inc. Do you understand?"

"Yes, sir."

"Whatever it asks, you answer in your own words in any way you please. If you feel you must explain quite a bit, do so. Talk an hour, if necessary."

"Yes, sir."

"Now, one more thing. We will have to make use of some simple devices which will automatically record your blood pressure, heartbeat, skin conductivity and brain-wave pattern while you speak. The machinery will seem formidable, but it's all absolutely painless. You won't even know it's going on."

The other two technicians were already busying themselves with smooth-gleaming apparatus on oiled wheels.

Norman said, "Is that to check on whether I'm lying or not?"

"Not at all, Mr. Muller. There's no question of lying. It's only a matter of emotional intensity. If the machine asks you your opinion of your child's school, you may say, 'I think it is overcrowded.' Those are only words. From the way your brain and heart and hormones and sweat glands work, Multivac can judge exactly how intensely you feel about the matter. It will understand your feelings better than you yourself."

"I never heard of this," said Norman.

"No, I'm sure you didn't. Most of the details of Multivac's workings are top secret. For instance, when you leave, you will be asked to sign a paper swearing that you will never reveal the nature of the questions you were asked, the nature of your responses, what was done, or how it was done. The less is known about the Multivac, the less chance of attempted outside pressures upon the men who service it." He smiled grimly. "Our lives are hard enough as it is."

Norman nodded. "I understand."

"And now would you like anything to eat or drink?"

"No. Nothing right now."

"Do you have any questions?"

Norman shook his head.

"Then you tell us when you're ready."

"I'm ready right now."

"You're certain?"

"Quite."

Paulson nodded, and raised his hand in a gesture to the others.

They advanced with their frightening equipment, and Norman Muller felt his breath come a little quicker as he watched.

The ordeal lasted nearly three hours, with one short break for coffee and an embarrassing session with a chamber pot. During all this time, Norman Muller remained encased in machinery. He was bone-weary at the close.

He thought sardonically that his promise to reveal nothing of what had passed would be an easy one to keep. Already the questions were a hazy mishmash in his mind.

Somehow he had thought Multivac would speak in a sepulchral, superhuman voice, resonant and echoing, but that, after all, was just an idea he had from seeing too many television shows, he now decided. The truth was distressingly undramatic. The questions were slips of a kind of metallic foil patterned with numerous punctures. A second machine converted the pattern into words and Paulson read the words to Norman, then gave him the question and let him read it for himself.

Norman's answers were taken down by a recording machine, played back to Norman for confirmation, with emendations and added remarks also taken down. All that was fed into a pattern-making instrument and that, in turn, was radiated to Multivac.

The one question Norman could remember at the moment was an incongruously gossipy: "What do you think of the price of eggs?"

Now it was over, and gently they removed the electrodes from various portions of his body, unwrapped the pulsating band from his upper arm, moved the machinery away.

He stood up, drew a deep, shuddering breath and said, "Is that all? Am I through?"

"Not quite." Paulson hurried to him, smiling in reassuring fashion. "We'll have to ask you to stay another hour."

"Why?" asked Norman sharply.

"It will take that long for Multivac to weave its new data into the trillions of items it has. Thousands of elections are concerned, you know. It's very complicated. And it may be that an odd contest here or there, a comptrollership in Phoenix, Arizona, or some council seat in Wilkesboro, North Carolina, may be in doubt. In that case, Multivac may be compelled to ask you a deciding question or two."

"No," said Norman. "I won't go through this again."

"It probably won't happen," Paulson said soothingly. "It rarely does. But, just in case, you'll have to stay." A touch of steel, just a touch, entered his voice. "You have no choice, you know. You must."

Norman sat down wearily. He shrugged.

Paulson said, "We can't let you read a newspaper, but if you'd care for a murder mystery, or if you'd like to play chess, or if there's anything we can do for you to help pass the time, I wish you'd mention it."

"It's all right. I'll just wait."

They ushered him into a small room just next to the one in which he had been questioned. He let himself sink into a plastic-covered armchair and closed his eyes.

As well as he could, he must wait out this final hour.

He sat perfectly still and slowly the tension left him. His breathing grew less ragged and he could clasp his hands without being quite so conscious of the trembling of his fingers.

Maybe there would be no questions. Maybe it was all over.

If it *were* over, then the next thing would be torchlight processions and invitations to speak at all sorts of functions. The Voter of the Year!

He, Norman Muller, ordinary clerk of a small department store in Bloomington, Indiana, who had neither been born great nor achieved greatness would be in the extraordinary position of having had greatness thrust upon him.

The historians would speak soberly of the Muller Election of 2008. That would be its name, the Muller Election.

The publicity, the better job, the flash flood of money that interested Sarah so much, occupied only a corner of his mind. It would all be welcome, of course. He couldn't refuse it. But at the moment something else was beginning to concern him.

A latent patriotism was stirring. After all, he was representing the entire electorate. He was the focal point for *them*. He was, in his own person, for this one day, all of America!

The door opened, snapping him to open-eyed attention. For a moment, his stomach constricted. Not more questions!

But Paulson was smiling. "That will be all, Mr. Muller."

"No more questions, sir?"

"None needed. Everything was quite clear-cut. You will be escorted back to your home and then you will be a private citizen once more. Or as much so as the public will allow."

"Thank you. Thank you." Norman flushed and said, "I wonder—who was elected?"

Paulson shook his head. "That will have to wait for the official announcement. The rules are quite strict. We can't even tell you. You understand."

"Of course. Yes." Norman felt embarrassed.

"Secret service will have the necessary papers for you to sign."

"Yes." Suddenly, Norman Muller felt proud. It was on him now in full strength. He was proud.

In this imperfect world, the sovereign citizens of the first and greatest Electronic Democracy had, through Norman Muller (through *him!*), exercised once again its free, untrammeled franchise.

Death and
the Senator

ARTHUR C. CLARKE

The author of such landmark works as *Childhood's End* (1953), *The City and the Stars* (1956), *2001: A Space Odyssey* (1968), *Rendezvous with Rama* (1973) and *The Fountains of Paradise* (1979) hardly needs an introduction, but it is worth noting that Arthur C. Clarke (b. 1917) is also an outstanding short-story writer. Along with Robert A. Heinlein and one of our other editors, he is one of science fiction's "Big Three," and the winner several times over of the most important awards in the field.

In "Death and the Senator" he examines the ever-important issue of the public vs. the private interest.

Washington had never looked lovelier in the spring; and this was the last spring, thought Senator Steelman bleakly, that he would ever see. Even now, despite all that Dr. Jordan had told him, he could not fully accept the truth. In the past there had always been a way of escape; no defeat had been final. When men had betrayed him, he had discarded them — even ruined them, as a warning to others. But now the betrayal was within himself; already, it seemed, he could feel the labored beating of the heart that would soon be stilled. No point in planning now for the Presidential election of 1976; he might not even live to see the nominations. . . .

It was an end of dreams and ambition, and he could not console himself with the knowledge that for all men these must end someday. For him it was too soon; he thought of Cecil Rhodes, who had always been one of his heroes, crying "So much to do — so little time to do it in!" as he died before his fiftieth birthday. He was already older than Rhodes, and had done far less.

The car was taking him away from the Capitol; there was symbolism in that, and he tried not to dwell upon it. Now he was abreast of the New Smithsonian — that vast complex of museums he had never had time to visit, though he had watched it spread along the Mall throughout the years he had been in Washington. How much he had missed, he told himself bitterly, in his relentless pursuit of power. The whole universe of art and culture had remained almost closed to him, and that was only part of the price that he had paid. He had become a stranger to his family and to those who were once his friends. Love had been sacrificed on the altar of ambition, and the sacrifice had been in vain. Was there anyone in all the world who would weep at his departure?

Yes, there was. The feeling of utter desolation relaxed its grip upon his soul. As he reached for the phone, he felt ashamed that he had to call the office to get this number, when his mind was cluttered with memories of so many less important things.

(There was the White House, almost dazzling in the spring sunshine. For the first time in his life he did not give it a second glance. Already it belonged to another world—a world that would never concern him again.)

The car circuit had no vision, but he did not need it to sense Irene's mild surprise—and her still milder pleasure.

"Hello, Renee—how are you all?"

"Fine, Dad. When are we going to see you?"

It was the polite formula his daughter always used on the rare occasions when he called. And invariably, except at Christmas or birthdays, his answer was a vague promise to drop around at some indefinite future date.

"I was wondering," he said slowly, almost apologetically, "if I could borrow the children for an afternoon. It's a long time since I've taken them out, and I felt like getting away from the office."

"But of course," Irene answered, her voice warming with pleasure. "They'll love it. When would you like them?"

"Tomorrow would be fine. I could call around twelve, and take them to the Zoo or the Smithsonian, or anywhere else they felt like visiting."

Now she was really startled, for she knew well enough that he was one of the busiest men in Washington, with a schedule planned weeks in advance. She would be wondering what had happened; he hoped she would not guess the truth. No reason why she should, for not even his secretary knew of the stabbing pains that had driven him to seek this long-overdue medical checkup.

"That would be wonderful. They were talking about you only yesterday, asking when they'd see you again."

His eyes misted, and he was glad that Renee could not see him.

"I'll be there at noon," he said hastily, trying to keep the emotion out of his voice. "My love to you all." He switched off before she could answer and relaxed against the upholstery with a sigh of relief. Almost upon impulse, without conscious planning, he had taken the first step in the reshaping of his life. Though his own children were lost to him, a bridge across the generations remained intact. If he did nothing else, he must guard and strengthen it in the months that were left.

Taking two lively and inquisitive children through the natural-history building was not what the doctor would have ordered, but it was what he wanted to do. Joey and Susan had grown so much since their last meeting, and it required both physical and mental alertness to keep up with them. No sooner had they entered the rotunda than they broke away from him, and scampered toward the enormous elephant dominating the marble hall.

"What's that?" cried Joey.

"It's an elephant, stupid," answered Susan with all the crushing superiority of her seven years.

"I know it's an effelant," retorted Joey. "But what's its name?"

Senator Steelman scanned the label, but found no assistance there. This was one occasion when the risky adage "Sometimes wrong, never uncertain" was a safe guide to conduct.

"He was called — er — Jumbo," he said hastily. "Just look at those tusks!"

"Did he ever get toothache?"

"Oh no."

"Then how did he clean his teeth? Ma says that if I don't clean mine . . ."

Steelman saw where the logic of this was leading, and thought it best to change the subject.

"There's a lot more to see inside. Where do you want to start — birds, snakes, fish, mammals?"

"Snakes!" clamored Susan. "I wanted to keep one in a box, but Daddy said no. Do you think he'd change his mind if you asked him?"

"What's a mammal?" asked Joey, before Steelman could work out an answer to that.

"Come along," he said firmly. "I'll show you."

As they moved through the halls and galleries, the children darting from one exhibit to another, he felt at peace with the world. There was nothing like a museum for calming the mind, for putting the problems of everyday life in their true perspective. Here, surrounded by the infinite variety and wonder of Nature, he was reminded of truths he had forgotten. He was only one of a million million creatures that shared this planet Earth. The entire human race, with its hopes and fears, its triumphs and its follies, might be no more than an incident in the history of the world. As he stood before the monstrous bones of Diplodocus (the children for once awed and silent), he felt the winds of Eternity blowing through his soul. He could no longer take so seriously the gnawing of ambition, the belief that he was the man the nation needed. *What* nation, if it came to that? A mere two centuries ago this summer, the Declaration of Independence had been signed; but this old American had lain in the Utah rocks for a hundred million years. . . .

He was tired when they reached the Hall of Oceanic Life, with its dramatic reminder that Earth still possessed animals greater than any that the past could show. The ninety-foot blue whale plunging into the ocean, and all the other swift hunters of the sea, brought back memories of hours he had once spent on a tiny, glistening deck with a white sail billowing above him. That was another time when he had known contentment, listening to the swish of water past the prow, and the sighing of the wind through the rigging. He had not sailed for thirty years; this was another of the world's pleasures he had put aside.

"I don't like fish," complained Susan. "When do we get to the snakes?"

"Presently," he said. "But what's the hurry? There's plenty of time."

The words slipped out before he realized it. He checked his step, while the children ran on ahead. Then he smiled, without bitterness. For in a sense, it was true enough. There *was* plenty of time. Each day, each hour could be a universe of experience, if one used it properly. In the last weeks of his life, he would begin to live.

As yet, no one at the office suspected anything. Even his outing with the children had not caused much surprise; he had done such things before, suddenly canceling his appointments and leaving his staff to pick up the pieces. The pattern of his behavior had not yet changed, but in a few days it would be obvious to all his associates that something had happened. He owed it to them — and to the Party — to break the news as soon as possible; there were, however, many personal decisions he had to make first, which he wished to settle in his own mind before he began the vast unwinding of his affairs.

There was another reason for his hesitancy. During his career, he had seldom lost a fight, and in the cut and thrust of political life he had given quarter to none. Now, facing his ultimate defeat, he dreaded the sympathy and the condolences that his many enemies would hasten to shower upon him. The attitude, he knew, was a foolish one — a remnant of his stubborn pride which was too much a part of his personality to vanish even under the shadow of death.

He carried his secret from committee room to White House to Capitol, and through all the labyrinths of Washington society, for more than two weeks. It was the finest performance of his career, but there was no one to appreciate it. At the end of that time he had completed his plan of action; it remained only to dispatch a few letters he had written in his own hand, and to call his wife.

The office located her, not without difficulty, in Rome. She was still beautiful, he thought, as her features swam on to the screen; she would have made a fine First Lady, and that would have been some compensation for the lost years. As far as he knew, she had looked forward to the prospect; but had he ever really understood what she wanted?

"Hello, Martin," she said, "I was expecting to hear from you. I suppose you want me to come back."

"Are you willing to?" he asked quietly. The gentleness of his voice obviously surprised her.

"I'd be a fool to say no, wouldn't I? But if they don't elect you, I want to go my own way again. You must agree to that."

"They won't elect me. They won't even nominate me. You're the first to know this, Diana. In six months, I shall be dead."

The directness was brutal, but it had a purpose. That fraction-of-a-second delay while the radio waves flashed up to the communications satellites and back again to Earth had never seemed so long. For once, he had broken through the beautiful mask. Her eyes widened with disbelief, her hand flew to her lips.

"You're joking!"

"About *this?* It's true enough. My heart's worn out. Dr. Jordan told me, a couple of weeks ago. It's my own fault, of course, but let's not go into that."

"So that's why you've been taking out the children: I wondered what had happened."

He might have guessed that Irene would have talked with her mother. It was a sad reflection on Martin Steelman, if so commonplace a fact as showing an interest in his own grandchildren could cause curiosity.

"Yes," he admitted frankly. "I'm afraid I left it a little late. Now I'm trying to make up for lost time. Nothing else seems very important."

In silence, they looked into each other's eyes across the curve of the Earth, and across the empty desert of the dividing years. Then Diana answered, a little unsteadily, "I'll start packing right away."

Now that the news was out, he felt a great sense of relief. Even the sympathy of his enemies was not as hard to accept as he had feared. For overnight, indeed, he had no enemies. Men who had not spoken to him in years, except with invective, sent messages whose sincerity could not be doubted. Ancient quarrels evaporated, or turned out to be founded on misunderstandings. It was a pity that one had to die to learn these things. . . .

He also learned that, for a man of affairs, dying was a fulltime job. There were successors to appoint, legal and financial mazes to untangle, committee and state business to wind up. The work of an energetic lifetime could not be terminated suddenly, as one switches off an electric light. It was astonishing how many responsibilities he had acquired, and how difficult it was to divest himself of them. He had never found it easy to delegate power (a fatal flaw, many critics had said, in a man who hoped to be Chief Executive), but now he must do so, before it slipped forever from his hands.

It was as if a great clock was running down, and there was no one to rewind it. As he gave away his books, read and destroyed old letters, closed useless accounts and files, dictated final instructions, and wrote farewell notes, he sometimes felt a sense of complete unreality. There was no pain; he could never have guessed that he did not have years of active life ahead of him. Only a few lines on a cardiogram lay like a roadblock across his future — or like a curse, written in some strange language the doctors alone could read.

Almost every day now Diana, Irene, or her husband brought the children to see him. In the past he had never felt at ease with Bill, but that, he knew, had been his own fault. You could not expect a son-in-law to replace a son, and it was unfair to blame Bill because he had not been cast in the image of Martin Steelman, Jr. Bill was a person in his own right; he had looked after Irene, made her happy, and fathered her children. That he lacked ambition was a flaw — if flaw indeed it was — that the Senator could at last forgive.

He could even think, without pain or bitterness, of his own son, who had traveled this road before him and now lay, one cross among many, in the United Nations cemetery at Capetown. He had never visited Martin's grave; in the days when he had the time, white men were not popular in what was left of South Africa. Now he could go if he wished, but he was uncertain if it would be fair to harrow Diana with such a mission. His own memories would not trouble him much longer, but she would be left with hers.

Yet he would like to go, and felt it was his duty. Moreover, it would be a last treat for the children. To them it would be only a holiday in a strange land, without any tinge of sorrow for an uncle they had never known. He had started to make the arrangements when, for the second time within a month, his whole world was turned upside down.

Even now, a dozen or more visitors would be waiting for him each morning when he arrived at his office. Not as many as in the old days, but still a sizable crowd. He had never imagined, however, that Dr. Harkness would be among them.

The sight of that thin, gangling figure made him momentarily break his stride. He felt his cheeks flush, his pulse quicken at the memory of ancient battles across committee-room tables, of angry exchanges that had reverberated along the myriad channels of the ether. Then he relaxed; as far as he was concerned, all that was over.

Harkness rose to his feet, a little awkwardly, as he approached. Senator Steelman knew that initial embarrassment — he had seen it so often in the last few weeks. Everyone he now met was automatically at a disadvantage, always on the alert to avoid the one subject that was taboo.

"Well, Doctor," he said. "This is a surprise — I never expected to see *you* here."

He could not resist that little jab, and derived some satisfaction at watching it go home. But it was free from bitterness, as the other's smile acknowledged.

"Senator," replied Harkness, in a voice that was pitched so low that he had to lean forward to hear it, "I've some extremely important information for you. Can we speak alone for a few minutes? It won't take long."

Steelman nodded; he had his own ideas of what was important now, and felt only a mild curiosity as to why the scientist had come to see him. The man seemed to have changed a good deal since their last encounter, seven years ago. He was much more assured and self-confident, and had lost the nervous mannerisms that had helped to make him such an unconvincing witness.

"Senator," he began, when they were alone in the private office, "I've some news that may be quite a shock to you. I believe that you can be cured."

Steelman slumped heavily in his chair. This was the one thing he had never expected; from the first, he had not encumbered himself with the burden of vain hopes. Only a fool fought against the inevitable, and he had accepted his fate.

For a moment he could not speak; then he looked up at his old adversary and gasped: "Who told you that? All my doctors—"

"Never mind them; it's not their fault they're ten years behind the times. Look at this."

"What does it mean? I can't read Russian."

"It's the latest issue of the USSR *Journal of Space Medicine*. It arrived a few days ago, and we did the usual routine translation. This note here—the one I've marked—refers to some recent work at the Mechnikov Station."

"What's that?"

"You don't *know?* Why, that's their Satellite Hospital, the one they've built just below the Great Radiation Belt."

"Go on," said Steelman, in a voice that was suddenly dry and constricted. "I'd forgotten they'd called it that." He had hoped to end his life in peace, but now the past had come back to haunt him.

"Well, the note itself doesn't say much, but you can read a lot between the lines. It's one of those advance hints that scientists put out before they have time to write a full-fledged paper, so they can claim priority later. The title is: 'Therapeutic Effects of Zero Gravity on Circulatory Diseases.' What they've done is to induce heart disease artificially in rabbits and hamsters, and then take them up to the space station. In orbit, of course, nothing has any weight; the heart and muscles have practically no work to do. And the result is exactly what I tried to tell you, years ago. Even extreme cases can be arrested, and many can be cured."

The tiny, paneled office that had been the center of his world, the scene of so many conferences, the birthplace of so many plans, became suddenly unreal. Memory was much more vivid: he was back again at those hearings, in the fall of 1969, when the National Aeronautics and Space Administration's first decade of activity had been under review — and, frequently, under fire.

He had never been chairman of the Senate Committee on Astronautics, but he had been its most vocal and effective member. It was here that he had made his reputation as a guardian of the public purse, as a hardheaded man who could not be bamboozled by utopian scientific dreamers. He had done a good job; from that moment, he had never been far from the headlines. It was not that he had any particular feeling for space and science, but he knew a live issue when he saw one. Like a tape-recorder unrolling in his mind, it all came back. . . .

"Dr. Harkness, you are Technical Director of the National Aeronautics and Space Administration?"

"That is correct."

"I have here the figures for NASA's expenditure over the period 1959–69; they are quite impressive. At the moment the total is $82,547,450,000, and the estimate for fiscal '69–'70 is well over ten billions. Perhaps you could give us some indication of the return we can expect from all this."

"I'll be glad to do so, Senator."

That was how it had started, on a firm but not unfriendly note. The hostility had crept in later. That it was unjustified, he had known at the time; any big organization had weaknesses and failures, and one which literally aimed at the stars could never hope for more than partial success. From the beginning, it had been realized that the conquest of space would be at least as costly in lives and treasure as the conquest of the air. In ten years, almost a hundred men had died — on Earth, in space, and upon the barren surface of the Moon. Now that the urgency of the early sixties was over, the public was asking "Why?" Steelman was shrewd enough to see himself as mouthpiece for those questioning voices. His performance had been cold and calculated; it was convenient to have a scapegoat, and Dr. Harkness was unlucky enough to be cast for the role.

"Yes, Doctor, I understand all the benefits we've received from space research in the way of improved communications and weather forecasting, and I'm sure everyone appreciates them. But almost all this work has been done with automatic, unmanned vehicles. What I'm worried about — what many people are worried about — is the mounting expense of the Man-in-Space program, and its very marginal utility. Since the original Dyna-Soar and Apollo projects, almost a decade ago, we've shot billions of dollars into space. And with what result? So that a mere handful of men can spend a few uncomfortable hours outside the atmosphere, achieving nothing that television cameras and automatic equipment couldn't do — much better and cheaper. And the lives that have been lost! None of us will forget those screams we heard coming over the radio when the X-21 burned up on re-entry. What right have we to send men to such deaths?"

He could still remember the hushed silence in the committee chamber when he had finished. His questions were very reasonable ones, and deserved to be answered. What was unfair was the rhetorical manner in which he had framed them and, above all, the fact that they were aimed at a man who could not answer them effectively. Steelman would not have tried such tactics on a von Braun or a Rickover; they would have given him at least as good as they received. But Harkness was no orator; if he had deep personal feelings, he kept them to himself. He was a good scientist, an able administrator — and a poor witness. It had been like shooting fish in a barrel. The reporters had loved it; he never knew which of them coined the nickname "Hapless Harkness."

"Now this plan of yours, Doctor, for a fifty-man space laboratory — *how* much did you say it would cost?"

"I've already told you — just under one and a half billions."

"And the annual maintenance?"

"Not more than $250,000,000."

"When we consider what's happened to previous estimates, you will forgive us if we look upon these figures with some skepticism. But even assuming that they are right, what will we get for the money?"

"We will be able to establish our first large-scale research station in space. So far, we have had to do our experimenting in cramped quarters aboard unsuitable vehicles, usually when they were engaged on some other mission. A permanent, manned satellite laboratory is essential. Without it, further progress is out of the question. Astrobiology can hardly get started —"

"Astro what?"

"Astrobiology — the study of living organisms in space. The Russians really started it when they sent up the dog Laika in Sputnik II and they're still ahead of us in this field. But no one's done any serious work on insects or invertebrates — in fact, on any animals except dogs, mice, and monkeys."

"I see. Would I be correct in saying that you would like funds for building a zoo in space?"

The laughter in the committee room had helped to kill the project. And it had helped, Senator Steelman now realized, to kill him.

He had only himself to blame, for Dr. Harkness had tried, in his ineffectual way, to outline the benefits that a space laboratory might bring. He had particularly stressed the medical aspects, promising nothing, but pointing out the possibilities. Surgeons, he had suggested, would be able to develop new techniques in an environment where the organs had no weight; men might live longer, freed from the wear and tear of gravity, for the strain on heart and muscles would be enormously reduced. Yes, he had mentioned the heart; but that had been of no interest to Senator Steelman — healthy, and ambitious, and anxious to make good copy. . . .

"Why have you come to tell me this?" he said dully. "Couldn't you let me die in peace?"

"That's the point," said Harkness impatiently. "There's no need to give up hope."

"Because the Russians have cured some hamsters and rabbits?"

"They've done much more than that. The paper I showed you only quoted the preliminary results; it's already a year out of date. They don't want to raise false hopes, so they are keeping as quiet as possible."

"How do you know this?"

Harkness looked surprised.

"Why, I called Professor Stanyukovitch, my opposite number. It turned out that he was up on the Mechnikov Station, which proves how important they consider this work. He's an old friend of mine, and I took the liberty of mentioning your case."

The dawn of hope, after its long absence, can be as painful as its departure. Steelman found it hard to breathe and for a dreadful moment he wondered if the final attack had come. But it was only excitement; the constriction in his chest relaxed, the ringing in his ears faded away, and he heard Dr. Harkness' voice saying: "He wanted to know if you could come to Astrograd right away, so I said I'd ask you. If you can make it, there's a flight from New York at ten-thirty tomorrow morning."

Tomorrow he had promised to take the children to the Zoo; it would be the first time he had let them down. The thought gave him a sharp stab of guilt, and it required almost an effort of will to answer: "I can make it."

He saw nothing of Moscow during the few minutes that the big intercontinental ramjet fell down from the stratosphere. The view-screens were switched off during the descent, for the sight of the ground coming straight up as a ship fell vertically on its sustaining jets was highly disconcerting to passengers.

At Moscow he changed to a comfortable but old-fashioned turboprop, and as he flew eastward into the night he had his first real opportunity for reflection. It was a very strange question to ask himself, but was he altogether glad that the future was no longer wholly certain? His life, which a few hours ago had seemed so simple, had suddenly become complex again, as it opened out once more into possibilities he had learned to put aside. Dr. Johnson had been right when he said that nothing settles a man's mind more wonderfully than the knowledge that he will be hanged in the morning. For the converse was certainly true — nothing unsettled it so much as the thought of a reprieve.

He was asleep when they touched down at Astrograd, the space capital of the USSR. When the gentle impact of the landing shook him awake, for a moment he could not imagine where he was. Had he dreamed that he was flying halfway around the world in search of life? No; it was not a dream but it might well be a wild-goose chase.

Twelve hours later, he was still waiting for the answer. The last instrument reading had been taken; the spots of light on the cardiograph display had ceased their fateful dance. The familiar routine of the medical examination and the gentle, competent voices of the doctors and nurses had done much to relax his mind. And it was very restful in the softly lit reception room, where the specialists had asked him to wait while they conferred together. Only the Russian magazines, and a few portraits of somewhat hirsute pioneers of Soviet medicine, reminded him that he was no longer in his own country.

He was not the only patient. About a dozen men and women, of all ages, were sitting around the wall, reading magazines and trying to appear at ease. There was no conversation, no attempt to catch anyone's eye. Every soul in this room was in his private limbo, suspended between life and death. Though they were linked together by a common misfortune, the link did not extend to communication. Each seemed as cut off from the rest of the human race as if he was already speeding through the cosmic gulfs where lay his only hope.

But in the far corner of the room, there was an exception. A young couple — neither could have been more than twenty-five — were huddling together in such desperate misery that at first Steelman found the spectacle annoying. No matter how bad their own problems, he told himself severely, people should be more considerate. They should hide their emotions — especially in a place like this, where they might upset others.

His annoyance quickly turned to pity, for no heart can remain untouched for long at the sight of simple, unselfish love in deep distress. As the minutes dripped away in a silence broken only by the rustling of papers and the scraping of chairs, his pity grew almost to an obsession.

What was their story, he wondered. The boy had sensitive, intelligent features; he might have been an artist, a scientist, a musician — there was no way of telling. The girl was pregnant; she had one of those homely peasant faces so common among Russian women. She was far from beautiful, but sorrow and love had given her features a luminous sweetness. Steelman found it hard to take his eyes from her — for somehow, though there was not the slightest physical resemblance, she reminded him of Diana. Thirty years ago, as they had walked from the church together, he had seen that same glow in the eyes of his wife. He had almost forgotten it; was the fault his, or hers, that it had faded so soon?

Without any warning, his chair vibrated beneath him. A swift, sudden tremor had swept through the building, as if a giant hammer had smashed against the ground, many miles away. An earthquake? Steelman wondered; then he remembered where he was, and started counting seconds.

He gave up when he reached sixty; presumably the soundproofing was so good that the slower, air-borne noise had not reached him, and only the shock wave through the ground recorded the fact that a thousand tons had just leapt into the sky. Another minute passed before he heard, distant but clear, a sound as of a thunderstorm raging below the edge of the world. It was even more miles away than he had dreamed; what the noise must be like at the launching site was beyond imagination.

Yet that thunder would not trouble him, he knew, when he also rose into the sky; the speeding rocket would leave it far behind. Nor would the thrust of acceleration be able to touch his body, as it rested in its bath of warm water—more comfortable even than this deeply padded chair.

That distant rumble was still rolling back from the edge of space when the door of the waiting room opened and the nurse beckoned to him. Though he felt many eyes following him, he did not look back as he walked out to receive his sentence.

The news services tried to get in contact with him all the way back from Moscow, but he refused to accept the calls. "Say I'm sleeping and mustn't be disturbed," he told the stewardess. He wondered who had tipped them off, and felt annoyed at this invasion of his privacy. Yet privacy was something he had avoided for years, and had learned to appreciate only in the last few weeks. He could not blame the reporters and commentators if they assumed that he had reverted to type.

They were waiting for him when the ramjet touched down at Washington. He knew most of them by name, and some were old friends, genuinely glad to hear the news that had raced ahead of him.

"What does it feel like, Senator," said Macauley, of the *Times*, "to know you're back in harness? I take it that it's true—the Russians can cure you?"

"They *think* they can," he answered cautiously. "This is a new field of medicine, and no one can promise anything."

"When do you leave for space?"

"Within the week, as soon as I've settled some affairs here."

"And when will you be back—if it works?"

"That's hard to say. Even if everything goes smoothly, I'll be up there at least six months."

Involuntarily, he glanced at the sky. At dawn or sunset—even during the day time, if one knew where to look—the Mechnikov Station was a spectacular sight, more brilliant than any of the stars. But there were now so many satellites of which this was true that only an expert could tell one from another.

"Six months," said a newsman thoughtfully. "That means you'll be out of the picture for '76."

"But nicely in it for 1980," said another.

"*And* 1984," added a third. There was a general laugh; people were already making jokes about 1984, which had once seemed so far in the future, but would soon be a date no different from any other . . . it was hoped.

The ears and the microphones were waiting for his reply. As he stood at the foot of the ramp, once more the focus of attention and curiosity, he felt the old excitement stirring in his veins. What a comeback it would be, to return from space a new man! It would give him a glamour that no other candidate could match; there was something Olympian, almost godlike, about the prospect. Already he found himself trying to work it into his election slogans. . . .

"Give me time to make my plans," he said. "It's going to take me a while to get used to this. But I promise you a statement before I leave Earth."

Before I leave Earth. Now, there was a fine, dramatic phrase. He was still savoring its rhythm with his mind when he saw Diana coming toward him from the airport buildings.

Already she had changed, as he himself was changing; in her eyes was a wariness and reserve that had not been there two days ago. It said, as clearly as any words: "Is it going to happen all over again?" Though the day was warm, he felt suddenly cold, as if he had caught a chill on those far Siberian plains.

But Joey and Susan were unchanged, as they ran to greet him. He caught them up in his arms, and buried his face in their hair, so that the cameras would not see the tears that had started from his eyes. As they clung to him in the innocent, unself-conscious love of childhood, he knew what his choice would have to be.

They alone had known him when he was free from the itch for power; that was the way they must remember him, if they remembered him at all.

"Your conference call, Mr. Steelman," said his secretary. "I'm routing it on to your private screen."

He swiveled round in his chair and faced the gray panel on the wall. As he did so, it split into two vertical sections. On the right half was a view of an office much like his own, and only a few miles away. But on the left —

Professor Stanyukovitch, lightly dressed in shorts and singlet, was floating in mid-air a good foot above his seat. He grabbed it when he saw that he had company, pulled himself down, and fastened a webbed belt around his waist. Behind him were ranged banks of communications equipment; and behind those, Steelman knew, was space.

Dr. Harkness spoke first, from the right-hand screen.

"We were expecting to hear from you, Senator. Professor Stanyukovitch tells me that everything is ready."

"The next supply ship," said the Russian, "comes up in two days. It will be taking me back to Earth, but I hope to see you before I leave the station."

His voice was curiously high-pitched, owing to the thin oxyhelium atmosphere he was breathing. Apart from that, there was no sense of distance, no background of interference. Though Stanyukovich was thousands of miles away, and racing through space at four miles a second, he might have been in the same office. Steelman could even hear the faint whirring of electric motors from the equipment racks behind him.

"Professor," answered Steelman, "there are a few things I'd like to ask before I go."

"Certainly."

Now he could tell that Stanyukovitch was a long way off. There was an appreciable time lag before his reply arrived: the station must be above the far side of the Earth.

"When I was at Astrograd, I noticed many other patients at the clinic. I was wondering—on what basis do you select those for treatment?"

This time the pause was much greater than the delay due to the sluggish speed of radio waves. Then Stanyukovitch answered: "Why, those with the best chance of responding."

"But your accommodation must be very limited. You must have many other candidates besides myself."

"I don't quite see the point—" interrupted Dr. Harkness, a little too anxiously.

Steelman swung his eyes to the right-hand screen. It was quite difficult to recognize, in the man staring back at him, the witness who had squirmed beneath his needling only a few years ago. That experience had tempered Harkness, had given him his baptism in the art of politics. Steelman had taught him much, and he had applied his hard-won knowledge.

His motives had been obvious from the first. Harkness would have been less than human if he did not relish this sweetest of revenges, this triumphant vindication of his faith. And as Space Administration Director, he was well aware that half his budget battles would be over when all the world knew that a potential President of the United States was in a Russian space hospital . . . because his own country did not possess one.

"Dr. Harkness," said Steelman gently, "this is *my* affair. I'm still waiting for your answer, Professor."

Despite the issues involved, he was quite enjoying this. The two scientists, of course, were playing for identical stakes. Stanyukovitch had his problems too; Steelman could guess the discussions that had taken place at Astrograd and Moscow, and the eagerness with which the Soviet astronauts had grasped this opportunity—which, it must be admitted, they had richly earned.

It was an ironic situation, unimaginable only a dozen years before. Here were NASA and the USSR Commission of Astronautics working hand in hand, using him as a pawn for their mutual advantage. He did not resent this, for in their place he would have done the same. But he had no wish to be a pawn; he was an individual who still had some control of his own destiny.

"It's quite true," said Stanyukovitch, very reluctantly, "that we can only take a limited number of patients here in Mechnikov. In any case, the station's a research laboratory, not a hospital."

"How many?" asked Steelman relentlessly.

"Well—fewer than ten," admitted Stanyukovitch, still more unwillingly.

It was an old problem, of course, though he had never imagined that it would apply to him. From the depths of memory there flashed a newspaper item he had come across long ago. When penicillin had been first discovered, it was so rare that if both Churchill and Roosevelt had been dying for lack of it, only one could have been treated. . . .

Fewer than ten. He had seen a dozen waiting at Astrograd, and how many were there in the whole world? Once again, as it had done so often in the last few days, the memory of those desolate lovers in the reception room came back to haunt him. Perhaps they were beyond his aid; he would never know.

But one thing he did know. He bore a responsibility that he could not escape. It was true that no man could foresee the future, and the endless consequences of his actions. Yet if it had not been for him, by this time his own country might have had a space hospital circling beyond the atmosphere. How many American lives were upon his conscience? Could he accept the help he had denied to others? Once he might have done so— but not now.

"Gentlemen," he said, "I can speak frankly with you both, for I know your interests are identical." (His mild irony, he saw, did not escape them.) "I appreciate your help and the trouble you have taken; I am sorry it has been wasted. No—don't protest; this isn't a sudden, quixotic decision on my part. If I was ten years younger, it might be different. Now I feel that this opportunity should be given to someone else—especially in view of my record." He glanced at Dr. Harkness, who gave an embarrassed smile. "I also have other, personal reasons, and there's no chance that I will change my mind. Please don't think me rude or ungrateful, but I don't wish to discuss the matter any further. Thank you again, and good-by."

He broke the circuit; and as the image of the two astonished scientists faded, peace came flooding back into his soul.

Imperceptibly, spring merged into summer. The eagerly awaited Bicentenary celebrations came and went; for the first time in years, he was able to enjoy Independence Day as a private citizen. Now he could sit back and watch the others perform—or he could ignore them if he wished.

Because the ties of a lifetime were too strong to break, and it would be his last opportunity to see many old friends, he spent hours looking in on both conventions and listening to the commentators. Now that he saw the whole world beneath the light of Eternity, his emotions were no longer involved; he understood the issues, and appreciated the arguments, but already he was as detached as an observer from another planet. The tiny, shouting figures on the screen were amusing marionettes, acting out roles in a play that was entertaining, but no longer important — at least, to him.

But it was important to his grandchildren, who would one day move out onto this same stage. He had not forgotten that; they were his share of the future, whatever strange form it might take. And to understand the future, it was necessary to know the past.

He was taking them into that past, as the car swept along Memorial Drive. Diana was at the wheel, with Irene beside her, while he sat with the children, pointing out the familiar sights along the highway. Familiar to him, but not to them; even if they were not old enough to understand all that they were seeing, he hoped they would remember.

Past the marble stillness of Arlington (he thought again of Martin, sleeping on the other side of the world) and up into the hills the car wound its effortless way. Behind them, like a city seen through a mirage, Washington danced and trembled in the summer haze, until the curve of the road hid it from view.

It was quiet at Mount Vernon; there were few visitors so early in the week. As they left the car and walked toward the house, Steelman wondered what the first President of the United States would have thought could he have seen his home as it was today. He could never have dreamed that it would enter its second century still perfectly preserved, a changeless island in the hurrying river of time.

They walked slowly through the beautifully proportioned rooms, doing their best to answer the children's endless questions, trying to assimilate the flavor of an infinitely simpler, infinitely more leisurely mode of life. (But had it seemed simple or leisurely to those who lived it?) It was so hard to imagine a world without electricity, without radio, without any power save that of muscle, wind, and water. A world where nothing moved faster than a running horse, and most men died within a few miles of the place where they were born.

The heat, the walking, and the incessant questions proved more tiring than Steelman had expected. When they had reached the Music Room, he decided to rest. There were some attractive benches out on the porch, where he could sit in the fresh air and feast his eyes upon the green grass of the lawn.

"Meet me outside," he explained to Diana, "when you've done the kitchen and the stables. I'd like to sit down for a while."

"You're sure you're quite all right?" she said anxiously.

"I never felt better, but I don't want to overdo it. Besides, the kids have drained me dry — I can't think of any more answers. You'll have to invent some; the kitchen's your department, anyway."

Diana smiled.

"I was never much good in it, was I? But I'll do my best — I don't suppose we'll be more than thirty minutes."

When they had left him, he walked slowly out onto the lawn. Here Washington must have stood, two centuries ago, watching the Potomac wind its way to the sea, thinking of past wars and future problems. And here Martin Steelman, thirty-eighth President of the United States, might have stood a few months hence, had the fates ruled otherwise.

He could not pretend that he had no regrets, but they were very few. Some men could achieve both power and happiness, but that gift was not for him. Sooner or later, his ambition would have consumed him. In the last few weeks he had known contentment, and for that no price was too great.

He was still marveling at the narrowness of his escape when his time ran out and Death fell softly from the summer sky.

Committee
of the Whole

FRANK HERBERT

Frank Herbert (b. 1920) is the author of *Dune* (1965; "soon to
be a major motion picture") and its four sequels. These works,
while important, have overshadowed his other excellent work,
which includes such outstanding novels as *The Dragon in the Sea*
(1956), *The Eyes of Heisenberg* (1966), *The Santaroga Barrier*
(1968), and *The Dosadi Experiment* (1977).

His short fiction is even less known, and it is a pleasure to
bring you "Committee of the Whole," a story that carries the concept of balance of power to its logical conclusion.

With an increasing sense of unease, Alan Wallace studied his client as they
neared the public hearing room on the second floor of the Old Senate Office
Building. The guy was too relaxed.

"Bill, I'm worried about this," Wallace said. "You could damn well lose
your grazing rights here in this room today."

They were almost into the gantlet of guards, reporters and TV cameramen before Wallace got his answer.

"Who the hell cares?" Custer asked.

Wallace, who prided himself on being the Washington-type lawyer —
above contamination by complaints and briefs, immune to all shock — found
himself tongue-tied with surprise.

They were into the ruck then and Wallace had to pull on his bold face,
smiling at the press, trying to soften the sharpness of that necessary phrase:

"No comment. Sorry."

"See us after the hearing if you have any questions, gentlemen," Custer
said.

The man's voice was level and confident.

He has himself over-controlled, Wallace thought. Maybe he was just joking . . . a graveyard joke.

The marble-walled hearing room blazed with lights. Camera platforms had been raised above the seats at the rear. Some of the smaller UHF stations had their cameramen standing on the window ledges.

The subdued hubbub of the place eased slightly, Wallace noted, then picked up tempo as William R. Custer — "The Baron of Oregon" they called him — entered with his attorney, passed the press tables and crossed to the seats reserved for them in the witness section.

Ahead and to their right, that one empty chair at the long table stood waiting with its aura of complete exposure.

"Who the hell cares?"

That wasn't a Custer-type joke, Wallace reminded himself. For all his cattle-baron pose, Custer held a doctorate in agriculture and degrees in philosophy, math and electronics. His western neighbors called him "The Brain."

It was no accident that the cattlemen had chosen him to represent them here.

Wallace glanced covertly at the man, studying him. The cowboy boots and string tie added to a neat dark business suit would have been affectation on most men. They merely accented Custer's good looks — the sunburned, windblown outdoorsman. He was a little darker of hair and skin than his father had been, still light enough to be called blond, but not as ruddy and without the late father's drink-tumescent veins.

But then young Custer wasn't quite thirty.

Custer turned, met the attorney's eyes. He smiled.

"Those were good patent attorneys you recommended, Al," Custer said. He lifted his briefcase to his lap, patted it. "No mincing around or mealy-mouthed excuses. Already got this thing on the way." Again he tapped the briefcase.

He brought that damn light gadget here with him? Wallace wondered. Why? He glanced at the briefcase. Didn't know it was that small . . . but maybe he's just talking about the plans for it.

"Let's keep our minds on this hearing," Wallace whispered. "This is the only thing that's important."

Into a sudden lull in the room's high noise level, the voice of someone in the press section carried across them: "greatest political show on earth."

"I brought this as an exhibit," Custer said. Again, he tapped the briefcase. It did bulge oddly.

Exhibit? Wallace asked himself.

It was the second time in ten minutes that Custer had shocked him. This was to be a hearing of a subcommittee of the Senate Interior and Insular Affairs Committee. The issue was Taylor grazing lands. What the devil could that . . . gadget have to do with the battle of words and laws to be fought here?

"You're supposed to talk over all strategy with your attorney," Wallace whispered. "What the devil do you . . ."

He broke off as the room fell suddenly silent.

Wallace looked up to see the subcommittee chairman, Senator Haycourt Tiborough, stride through the wide double doors followed by his coterie of investigators and attorneys. The Senator was a tall man who had once been fat. He had dieted with such savage abruptness that his skin had never recovered. His jowls and the flesh on the back of his hands sagged. The top of his head was shiny bald and ringed by a three-quarter tonsure that had purposely been allowed to grow long and straggly so that it fanned back over his ears.

The Senator was followed in close lock step by syndicated columnist Anthony Poxman, who was speaking fiercely into Tiborough's left ear. TV cameras tracked the pair.

If Poxman's covering this one himself instead of sending a flunky, it's going to be bad, Wallace told himself.

Tiborough took his chair at the center of the committee table facing them, glanced left and right to assure himself the other members were present.

Senator Spealance was absent, Wallace noted, but he had party organization difficulties at home and the Senior Senator from Oregon was, significantly, not present. Illness, it was reported.

A sudden attack of caution, that common Washington malady, no doubt. He knew where his campaign money came from . . . but he also knew where the votes were.

They had a quorum, though.

Tiborough cleared his throat, said: "The committee will please come to order."

The Senator's voice and manner gave Wallace a cold chill. We were nuts trying to fight this one in the open, he thought. Why'd I let Custer and his friends talk me into this? You can't butt heads with a United States Senator who's out to get you. The only way's to fight him on the inside.

And now Custer suddenly turning screwball.

Exhibit!

"Gentlemen," said Tiborough, "I think we can . . . that is, today we can dispense with preliminaries . . . unless my colleagues . . . if any of them have objections."

Again, he glanced at the other senators—five of them. Wallace swept his gaze down the line behind that table—Plowers of Nebraska (a horse trader), Johnstone of Ohio (a parliamentarian—devious), Lane of South Carolina (a Republican in Democrat disguise), Emery of Minnesota (new and eager—dangerous because he lacked the old inhibitions) and Meltzer of New York (poker player, fine old family with traditions).

None of them had objections.

They've had a private meeting—both sides of the aisle—and talked over a smooth steamroller procedure, Wallace thought.

It was another ominous sign.

"This is a subcommittee of the United States Senate Committee on Interior and Insular Affairs," Tiborough said, his tone formal. "We are charged with obtaining expert opinion on proposed amendments to the Taylor Grazing Act of 1934. Today's hearing will begin with testimony and . . . ah, questioning of a man whose family has been in the business of raising beef cattle in Oregon for three generations."

Tiborough smiled at the TV cameras.

The son-of-a-bitch is playing to the galleries, Wallace thought. He glanced at Custer. The cattleman sat relaxed against the back of his chair, eyes half lidded, staring at the Senator.

"We call as our first witness today Mr. William R. Custer of Bend, Oregon," Tiborough said. "Will the clerk please swear in Mr. Custer."

Custer moved forward to the "hot seat," placed his briefcase on the table. Wallace pulled a chair up beside his client, noted how the cameras turned as the clerk stepped forward, put the Bible on the table and administered the oath.

Tiborough ruffled through some papers in front of him, waiting for full attention to return to him, said: "This subcommittee . . . we have before us a bill, this is a United States Senate Bill entitled SB-1024 of the current session, an act amending the Taylor Grazing Act of 1934 and, the intent is, as many have noted, that we would broaden the base of the advisory committees to the Act and include a wider public representation."

Custer was fiddling with the clasp of his briefcase.

How the hell could that light gadget be an exhibit here? Wallace asked himself. He glanced at the set of Custer's jaw, noted the nervous working of a muscle. It was the first sign of unease he'd seen in Custer. The sight failed to settle Wallace's own nerves.

"Ah, Mr. Custer," Tiborough said. "Do you — did you bring a preliminary statement? Your counsel . . ."

"I have a statement," Custer said. His big voice rumbled through the room, requiring instant attention and the shift of cameras that had been holding tardily on Tiborough, expecting an addition to the question.

Tiborough smiled, waited, then: "Your attorney — is your statement the one your counsel supplied the committee?"

"With some slight additions of my own," Custer said.

Wallace felt a sudden qualm. They were too willing to accept Custer's statement. He leaned close to his client's ear, whispered: "They know what your stand is. Skip the preliminaries."

Custer ignored him, said: "I intend to speak plainly and simply. I oppose the amendment. Broaden the base and wider public representation are phases of the amendment. Broaden the base and wider public representation are phases of politician double talk. The intent is to pack the committees, to put control of them into the hands of people who don't know the first thing about the cattle business and whose private intent is to destroy the Taylor Grazing Act itself."

"Plain, simple talk," Tiborough said. "This committee . . . we welcome such directness. Strong words. A majority of this committee . . . we have taken the position that the public range lands have been too long subjected to the tender mercies of the stockmen advisors, that the lands . . . stockmen have exploited them to their own advantage."

The gloves are off, Wallace thought. I hope Custer knows what he's doing. He's sure as hell not accepting advice.

Custer pulled a sheaf of papers from his briefcase and Wallace glimpsed shiny metal in the case before the flap was closed.

Christ! That looked like a gun or something.

Then Wallace recognized the papers — the brief he and his staff had labored over — and the preliminary statement. He noted with alarm the penciled markings and marginal notations. How could Custer have done that much to it in just twenty-four hours?

Again, Wallace whispered in Custer's ear: "Take it easy, Bill. The bastard's out for blood."

Custer nodded to show he had heard, glanced at the papers, looked up directly at Tiborough.

A hush settled on the room, broken only by the scraping of a chair somewhere in the rear, and the whirr of cameras.

II

"First, the nature of these lands we're talking about," Custer said. "In my state . . ." He cleared his throat, a mannerism that would have indicated anger in the old man, his father. There was no break in Custer's expression, though, and his voice remained level. ". . . in my state, these were mostly Indian lands. This nation took them by brute force, right of conquest. That's about the oldest right in the world, I guess. I don't want to argue with it at this point."

"Mr. Custer."

It was Nebraska's Senator Plowers, his amiable farmer's face set in a tight grin. "Mr. Custer, I hope . . ."

"Is this a point of order?" Tiborough asked.

"Mr. Chairman," Plowers said, "I merely wished to make sure we weren't going to bring up that old suggestion about giving these lands back to the Indians."

Laughter shot across the hearing room. Tiborough chuckled as he pounded his gavel for order.

"You may continue, Mr. Custer," Tiborough said.

Custer looked at Plowers, said: "No, Senator, I don't want to give these lands back to the Indians. When they had these lands, they only got about three hundred pounds of meat a year off eighty acres. We get five hundred pounds of the highest grade protein — premium beef — from only ten acres."

"No one doubts the efficiency of your factory-like methods," Tiborough said. "You can . . . we know your methods wring the largest amount of meat from a minimum acreage."

Ugh! Wallace thought. That was a low blow — implying Bill's overgrazing and destroying the land value.

"My neighbors, the Warm Springs Indians, use the same methods I do," Custer said. "They are happy to adopt our methods because we use the land while maintaining it and increasing its value. We don't permit the land to fall prey to natural disasters such as fire and erosion. We don't . . ."

"No doubt your methods are meticulously correct," Tiborough said. "But I fail to see where . . ."

"Has Mr. Custer finished his preliminary statement yet?" Senator Plowers cut in.

Wallace shot a startled look at the Nebraskan. That was help from an unexpected quarter.

"Thank you, Senator," Custer said. "I'm quite willing to adapt to the Chairman's methods and explain the meticulous correctness of my operation. Our lowliest cowhands are college men, highly paid. We travel ten times as many jeep miles as we do horse miles. Every outlying division of the ranch — every holding pen and grazing supervisor's cabin is linked to the central ranch by radio. We use the . . ."

"I concede that your methods must be the most modern in the world," Tiborough said. "It's not your methods as much as the results of those methods that are at issue here. We . . ."

He broke off at a disturbance by the door. An Army colonel was talking to the guard there. He wore Special Services fourragere — Pentagon.

Wallace noted with an odd feeling of disquiet that the man was armed — a .45 at the hip. The weapon was out of place on him, as though he had added it suddenly on an overpowering need . . . emergency.

More guards were coming up outside the door now — Marines and Army. They carried rifles.

The colonel said something sharp to the guard, turned away from him and entered the committee room. All the cameras were tracking him now. He ignored them, crossed swiftly to Tiborough, and spoke to him.

The Senator shot a startled glance at Custer, accepted a sheaf of papers the colonel thrust at him. He forced his attention off Custer, studied the papers, leafing through them. Presently, he looked up, stared at Custer.

A hush fell over the room.

"I find myself at a loss, Mr. Custer," Tiborough said. "I have here a copy of a report . . . it's from the Special Services branch of the Army . . . through the Pentagon, you understand. It was just handed to me by, ah . . . the colonel here."

He looked up at the colonel, who was standing, one hand resting lightly on the holstered .45. Tiborough looked back at Custer and it was obvious the Senator was trying to marshal his thoughts.

"It is," Tiborough said, "that is . . . this report supposedly . . . and I have every confidence it is what it is represented to be . . . here in my hands . . . they say that . . . uh, within the last, uh, few days they have, uh, investigated a certain device . . . weapon they call it, that you are attempting to patent. They report . . ." He glanced at the papers, back to Custer, who was staring at him steadily. ". . . this, uh, weapon, is a thing that . . . it is extremely dangerous."

"It is," Custer said.

"I . . . ah, see." Tiborough cleared his throat, glanced up at the colonel, who was staring fixedly at Custer. The Senator brought his attention back to Custer.

"Do you in fact have such a weapon with you, Mr. Custer?" Tiborough asked.

"I have brought it as an exhibit, sir."

"Exhibit?"

"Yes, sir."

Wallace rubbed his lips, found them dry. He wet them with his tongue, wished for the water glass, but it was beyond Custer. Christ! That stupid cowpuncher! He wondered if he dared whisper to Custer. Would the senators and that Pentagon lackey interpret such an action as meaning he was part of Custer's crazy antics?

"Are you threatening this committee with your weapon, Mr. Custer?" Tiborough asked. "If you are, I may say special precautions have been taken . . . extra guards in this room and we . . . that is, we will not allow ourselves to worry too much about any action you may take, but ordinary precautions are in force."

Wallace could no longer sit quietly. He tugged Custer's sleeve, got an abrupt shake of the head. He leaned close, whispered: "We could ask for a recess, Bill. Maybe we . . ."

"Don't interrupt me," Custer said. He looked at Tiborough. "Senator, I would not threaten you or any other man. Threats in the way you mean them are a thing we no longer can indulge in."

"You . . . I believe you said this device is an exhibit," Tiborough said. He cast a worried frown at the report in his hands. "I fail . . . it does not appear germane."

Senator Plowers cleared his throat. "Mr. Chairman," he said.

"The chair recognizes the Senator from Nebraska," Tiborough said, and the relief in his voice was obvious. He wanted time to think.

"Mr. Custer," Plowers said, "I have not seen the report, the report my distinguished colleague alludes to; however, if I may . . . is it your wish to use this committee as some kind of publicity device?"

"By no means, Senator," Custer said. "I don't wish to profit by my presence here . . . not at all."

Tiborough had apparently come to a decision. He leaned back, whispered to the colonel, who nodded and returned to the outer hall.

"You strike me as an eminently reasonable man, Mr. Custer," Tiborough said. "If I may . . ."

"May I," Senator Plowers said. "May I, just permit me to conclude this one point. May we have the Special Services report in the record?"

"Certainly," Tiborough said. "But what I was about to suggest . . ."

"May I," Plowers said. "May I, would you permit me, please, Mr. Chairman, to make this point clear for the record?"

Tiborough scowled, but the heavy dignity of the Senate overcame his irritation. "Please continue, Senator. I had thought you were finished."

"I respect . . . there is no doubt in my mind of Mr. Custer's truthfulness," Plowers said. His face eased into a grin that made him look grandfatherly, a kindly elder statesman. "I would like, therefore, to have him explain how this . . . ah, weapon, can be an exhibit in the matter before our committee."

Wallace glanced at Custer, saw the hard set to the man's jaw, realized the cattleman had gotten to Plowers somehow. This was a set piece.

Tiborough was glancing at the other senators, weighing the advisability of high-handed dismissal . . . perhaps a star chamber session. No . . . they were all too curious about Custer's device, his purpose here.

The thoughts were plain on the Senator's face.

"Very well," Tiborough said. He nodded to Custer. "You may proceed, Mr. Custer."

"During last winter's slack season," Custer said, "two of my men and I worked on a project we've had in the works for three years — to develop a sustained-emission laser device."

Custer opened his briefcase, slid out a fat aluminum tube mounted on a pistol grip with a conventional appearing trigger.

"This is quite harmless," he said. "I didn't bring the power pack."

"That is . . . this is your weapon?" Tiborough asked.

"Calling this a weapon is misleading," Custer said. "The term limits and oversimplifies. This is also a brush-cutter, a substitute for a logger's saw and axe, a diamond cutter, a milling machine . . . and a weapon. It is also a turning point in history."

"Come now, isn't that a bit pretentious?" Tiborough asked.

"We tend to think of history as something old and slow," Custer said. "But history is, as a matter of fact, extremely rapid and immediate. A President is assassinated, a bomb explodes over a city, a dam breaks, a revolutionary device is announced."

"Lasers have been known for quite a few years," Tiborough said. He looked at the papers the Colonel had given him. "The principle dates from 1956 or thereabouts."

"I don't wish it to appear that I'm taking credit for inventing this device," Custer said. "Nor am I claiming sole credit for developing the sustained-emission laser. I was merely one of a team. But I do hold the device here in my hand, gentlemen."

"Exhibit, Mr. Custer," Plowers reminded him. "How is this an exhibit?"

"May I explain first how it works?" Custer asked. "That will make the rest of my statement much easier."

Tiborough looked at Plowers, back to Custer. "If you will tie this all together, Mr. Custer," Tiborough said. "I want to . . . the bearing of this device on our—we are hearing a particular bill in this room."

"Certainly, Senator," Custer said. He looked at his device. "A ninety-volt radio battery drives this particular model. We have some that require less voltage, some that use more. We aimed for a construction with simple parts. Our crystals are common quartz. We shattered them by bringing them to a boil in water and then plunging them into ice water . . . repeatedly. We chose twenty pieces of very close to the same size—about one gram, slightly more than fifteen grains each."

Custer unscrewed the back of the tube, slid out a round length of plastic trailing lengths of red, green, brown, blue and yellow wire.

Wallace noted how the cameras of the TV men centered on the object in Custer's hands. Even the senators were leaning forward, staring.

We're gadget crazy people, Wallace thought.

"The crystals were dipped in thinned household cement and then into iron filings," Custer said. "We made a little jig out of a fly-tying vise and opened a passage in the filings at opposite ends of the crystals. We then made some common celluloid—nitrocellulose, acetic acid, gelatin and alcohol—all very common products, and formed it in a length of garden hose just long enough to take the crystals end to end. The crystals were inserted in the hose, the celluloid poured over them and the whole thing was seated in a magnetic waveguide while the celluloid was cooling. This centered and aligned the crystals. The waveguide was constructed from wire salvaged from an old TV set and built following the directions in the Radio Amateur's Handbook."

Custer re-inserted the length of plastic into the tube, adjusted the wires. There was an unearthly silence in the room with only the cameras whirring. It was as though everyone were holding his breath.

"A laser requires a resonant cavity, but that's complicated," Custer said. "Instead, we wound two layers of fine copper wire around our tube, immersed it in the celluloid solution to coat it and then filed one end flat. This end took a piece of mirror cut to fit. We then pressed a number eight embroidery needle at right angles into the mirror end of the tube until it touched the side of the number one crystal."

Custer cleared his throat.

Two of the senators leaned back. Plowers coughed. Tiborough glanced at the banks of TV cameras and there was a questioning look in his eyes.

"We then determined the master frequency of our crystal series," Custer said. "We used a test signal and oscilloscope, but any radio amateur could do it without the oscilloscope. We constructed an oscillator of that master frequency, attached it at the needle and a bare spot scraped in the opposite edge of the waveguide."

"And this . . . ah . . . worked?" Tiborough asked.

"No." Custer shook his head. "When we fed power through a voltage multiplier into the system we produced an estimated four hundred joules emission and melted half the tube. So we started all over again."

"You are going to tie this in?" Tiborough asked. He frowned at the papers in his hands, glanced toward the door where the colonel had gone.

"I am, sir, believe me," Custer said.

"Very well, then," Tiborough said.

"So we started all over again," Custer said. "But for the second celluloid dip we added bismuth — a saturate solution, actually. It stayed gummy and we had to paint over it with a sealing coat of the straight celluloid. We then coupled this bismuth layer through a pulse circuit so that it was bathed in a counter wave — 180 degrees out of phase with the master frequency. We had, in effect, immersed the unit in a thermoelectric cooler that exactly countered the heat production. A thin beam issued from the unmirrored end when we powered it. We have yet to find something that thin beam cannot cut."

"Diamonds?" Tiborough asked.

"Powered by less than two hundred volts, this device could cut our planet in half like a ripe tomato," Custer said. "One man could destroy an aerial armada with it, knock down ICBMs before they touched atmosphere, sink a fleet, pulverize a city. I'm afraid, sir, that I haven't mentally catalogued all the violent implications of this device. The mind tends to boggle at the enormous power focused in . . ."

"Shut down those TV cameras!"

It was Tiborough shouting, leaping to his feet and making a sweeping gesture to include the banks of cameras. The abrupt violence of his voice and gesture fell on the room like an explosion. "Guards!" he called. "You there at the door. Cordon off that door and don't let anyone out who heard this fool!" He whirled back to face Custer. "You irresponsible idiot!"

"I'm afraid, Senator," Custer said, "that you're locking the barn door many weeks too late."

For a long minute of silence Tiborough glared at Custer. Then: "You did this deliberately, eh?"

III

"Senator, if I'd waited any longer, there might have been no hope for us at all."

Tiborough sat back into his chair, still keeping his attention fastened on Custer. Plowers and Johnstone on his right had their heads close together whispering fiercely. The other senators were dividing their attention between Custer and Tiborough, their eyes wide and with no attempt to conceal their astonishment.

Wallace, growing conscious of the implications in what Custer had said, tried to wet his lips with his tongue. Christ! he thought. This stupid cowpoke has sold us all down the river!

Tiborough signaled an aide, spoke briefly with him, beckoned the colonel from the door. There was a buzzing of excited conversation in the room. Several of the press and TV crew were huddled near the windows on Custer's left, arguing. One of their number—a florid-faced man with gray hair and horn-rimmed glasses—started across the room toward Tiborough, was stopped by a committee aide. They began a low-voiced argument with violent gestures.

A loud curse sounded from the door. Poxman, the syndicated columnist, was trying to push past the guards there.

"Poxman!" Tiborough called. The columnist turned. "My orders are that no one leaves," Tiborough said. "You are not an exception." He turned back to face Custer.

The room had fallen into a semblance of quiet, although there still were pockets of muttering and there was the sound of running feet and a hurrying about in the hall outside.

"Two channels went out of here live," Tiborough said. "Nothing much we can do about them, although we will trace down as many of their viewers as we can. Every bit of film in this room and every sound tape will be confiscated, however." His voice rose as protests sounded from the press section. "Our national security is at stake. The President has been notified. Such measures as are necessary will be taken."

The colonel came hurrying into the room, crossed to Tiborough, quietly said something.

"You should've warned me!" Tiborough snapped. "I had no idea that . . ."

The colonel interrupted with a whispered comment.

"These papers . . . your damned report is not clear!" Tiborough said. He looked around at Custer. "I see you're smiling, Mr. Custer. I don't think you'll find much to smile about before long."

"Senator, this is not a happy smile," Custer said. "But I told myself several days ago you'd fail to see the implications of this thing." He tapped the pistol-shaped device he had rested on the table. "I told myself you'd fall back into the old, useless pattern."

"Is that what you told yourself, really?" Tiborough said.

Wallace, hearing the venom in the Senator's voice, moved his chair a few inches farther away from Custer.

Tiborough looked at the laser projector. "Is that thing really disarmed?"

"Yes, sir."

"If I order one of my men to take it from you, you will not resist?"

"Which of your men will you trust with it, Senator?" Custer asked.

In the long silence that followed, someone in the press section emitted a nervous guffaw.

"Virtually every man on my ranch has one of these things," Custer said. "We fell trees with them, cut firewood, make fence posts. Every letter written to me as a result of my patent application has been answered candidly. More than a thousand sets of schematics and instructions on how to build this device have been sent out to varied places in the world."

"You vicious traitor!" Tiborough rasped.

"You're certainly entitled to your opinion, Senator," Custer said. "But I warn you I've had time for considerably more concentrated and considerably more painful thought than you've applied to this problem. In my estimation, I had no choice. Every week I waited to make this thing public, every day, every minute, merely raised the odds that humanity would be destroyed by . . ."

"You said this thing applied to the hearings on the grazing act," Plowers protested, and there was a plaintive note of complaint in his voice.

"Senator, I told you the truth," Custer said. "There's no real reason to change the act, now. We intend to go on operating under it — with the agreement of our neighbors and others concerned. People are still going to need food."

Tiborough glared at him. "You're saying we can't force you to . . ." He broke off at a disturbance in the doorway. A rope barrier had been stretched there and a line of Marines stood with their backs to it, facing the hall. A mob of people was trying to press through. Press cards were being waved.

"Colonel, I told you to clear that hall!" Tiborough barked.

The colonel ran to the barrier. "Use your bayonets if you have to!" he shouted.

The disturbance subsided at the sound of his voice. More uniformed men could be seen moving in along the barrier. Presently, the noise receded.

Tiborough turned back to Custer. "You make Benedict Arnold look like the greatest friend the United States ever had," he said.

"Cursing me isn't going to help you," Custer said. "You are going to have to live with this thing; so you'd better try understanding it."

"That appears to be simple," Tiborough said. "All I have to do is send twenty-five cents to the Patent office for the schematics and then write you a letter."

"The world already was headed toward suicide," Custer said. "Only fools failed to realize . . ."

"So you decided to give us a little push," Tiborough said.

"H. G. Wells warned us," Custer said. "That's how far back it goes, but nobody listened. 'Human history becomes more and more a race between education and catastrophe,' Wells said. But those were just words. Many scientists have remarked the growth curve on the amount of raw energy becoming available to humans—and the diminishing curve on the number of persons required to use that energy. For a long time now, more and more violent power was being made available to fewer and fewer people. It was only a matter of time until total destruction was put into the hands of single individuals."

"And you didn't think you could take your government into your confidence."

"The government already was committed to a political course diametrically opposite the one this device requires," Custer said. "Virtually every man in the government has a vested interest in not reversing that course."

"So you set yourself above the government?"

"I'm probably wasting my time," Custer said, "but I'll try to explain it. Virtually every government in the world is dedicated to manipulating something called the 'mass man.' That's how governments have stayed in power. But there is no such man. When you elevate the nonexistent 'mass man' you degrade the individual. And obviously it was only a matter of time until all of us were at the mercy of the individual holding power."

"You talk like a commie!"

"They'll say I'm a goddamn capitalist pawn," Custer said. "Let me ask you, Senator, to visualize a poor radio technician in a South American country. Brazil, for example. He lives a hand-to-mouth existence, ground down by an overbearing, unimaginative, essentially uncouth ruling oligarchy. What is he going to do when this device comes into his hands?"

"Murder, robbery and anarchy."

"You could be right," Custer said. "But we might reach an understanding out of ultimate necessity—that each of us must cooperate in maintaining the dignity of all."

Tiborough stared at him, began to speak musingly: "We'll have to control the essential materials for constructing this thing . . . and there may be trouble for a while, but . . ."

"You're a vicious fool."

In the cold silence that followed, Custer said: "It was too late to try that ten years ago. I'm telling you this thing can be patchworked out of a wide variety of materials that are already scattered over the earth. It can be made in basements and mud huts, in palaces and shacks. The key item is the crystals, but other crystals will work, too. That's obvious. A patient man can grow crystals . . . and this world is full of patient men."

"I'm going to place you under arrest," Tiborough said. "You have outraged every rule—"

"You're living in a dream world," Custer said. "I refuse to threaten you, but I'll defend myself from any attempt to oppress or degrade me. If I cannot defend myself, my friends will defend me. No man who understands what this device means will permit his dignity to be taken from him."

Custer allowed a moment for his words to sink in, then: "And don't twist those words to imply a threat. Refusal to threaten a fellow human is an absolute requirement in the day that has just dawned on us."

"You haven't changed a thing!" Tiborough raged. "If one man is powerful with that thing, a hundred are . . ."

"All previous insults aside," Custer said, "I think you are a highly intelligent man, Senator. I ask you to think long and hard about this device. Use of power is no longer the deciding factor because one man is as powerful as a million. Restraint—self-restraint is now the key to survival. Each of us is at the mercy of his neighbor's good will. Each of us, Senator—the man in the palace and the man in the shack. We'd better do all we can to increase that good will—not attempting to buy it, but simply recognizing that individual dignity is the one inalienable right of . . ."

"Don't you preach to me, you commie traitor!" Tiborough rasped. "You're a living example of . . ."

"Senator!"

It was one of the TV cameramen in the left rear of the room.

"Let's stop insulting Mr. Custer and hear him out," the cameraman said.

"Get that man's name," Tiborough told an aide. "If he . . ."

"I'm an expert electronic technician, Senator," the man said. "You can't threaten me now."

Custer smiled, turned to face Tiborough.

"The revolution begins," Custer said. He waved a hand as the Senator started to whirl away. "Sit down, Senator."

Wallace, watching the Senator obey, saw how the balance of control had changed in this room.

"Ideas are in the wind," Custer said. "There comes a time for a thing to develop. It comes into being. The spinning jenny came into being because that was its time. It was based on countless ideas that had preceded it."

"And this is the age of the laser?" Tiborough asked.

"It was bound to come," Custer said. "But the number of people in the world who're filled with hate and frustration and violence has been growing with terrible speed. You add to that the enormous danger that this might fall into the hands of just one group or nation or . . ." Custer shrugged. "This is too much power to be confined to one man or group with the hope they'll administer wisely. I didn't dare delay. That's why I spread this thing now and announced it as broadly as I could."

Tiborough leaned back in his chair, his hands in his lap. His face was pale and beads of perspiration stood out on his forehead.

"We won't make it."

"I hope you're wrong, Senator," Custer said. "But the only thing I know for sure is that we'd have had less chance of making it tomorrow than we have today."

Political Machine

JOHN JAKES

John Jakes (b. 1932) is the best-selling author of the Bicenten-
nial Series of novels about America's past and the equally successful and excellent *North and South* (1982). But before attaining
the best-seller lists and fame and fortune, he was an excellent pro-
ducer of science fiction, fantasy, and mystery novels and stories.
A solid collection of his science fiction can be found in *The Best
of John Jakes* (1977).

"Political Machine" dates from 1961, although it is as fresh
as if it were written yesterday. It concerns one of the nasty side-
effects of politics — the manipulation of people and ideas.

Five in the morning, EDT, with a spongy-wet tidewater wind pushing at the
limp draperies of the Illinois Suite. In the flaccid gloom a bell rang and a
lucite square turned pearl on one wall.

The Populist Custodian from Illinois, the Honorable Elwood Everett
Swigg sat up in bed like a mechanical man. His eyes flew open. Jagged streaks
flashed across the lucite screen. Custodian Swigg staggered to his feet. His
flannelette nightshirt clung sweatily to his body. Locks of silver-gray hair
fell across his impressive forehead. With groggy grandeur he raised a finger
in the air.

"Perils beset us on every hand," he said to the chest of drawers. "All
around, we are ringed by encircling enemies. Therefore, friends and neighbors, I say that this is no time to reward faith with a lack of faith, to repay
dutiful service with a kick in the hindquarters, as my uncle Elmer used to
say on the farm down in — "

"God damn it, operator," said a floating face on the lucite screen, "I said
no *bells.*"

The face focused: egg-like in its absence of hair, but deeply lined, as
though dipped in acid over a long period. Which, in a way, it had been.
From behind his glasses, Buster Poole, so-called hatchet man of the Illinois
Populists, peered into the Washington dawn from his atomic hideaway at

Starved Rock, hundreds of miles distant.

"Elwood, where are you? Come over here. God damn these operators any—"

"I am terribly sorree, sir, terribly sorree, and I promise—"

"—so when it's time to make your decision in November, folks, remember—"

In exasperation Buster Poole said: "The quick brown fox."

Elwood Everett Swigg blinked, lowered his finger. "You call me, Buster?"

"You bet your sweet cells I did. Get over here where I can see you."

"I was having a most peculiar dream."

"That operator's going to have a few when I report her."

Elwood fumbled with a humidor, lit an expensive cigar and rolled his shoulders back. He was a tall figure, slightly stooped, with a craggy, heroic face and a voice with molasses and thunder in it. "What seems to be the trouble, Buster?"

"Jay Milton Mossman's the trouble."

"That upstart? That Sociocratic slug?" Elwood's laugh was rich with the disdain of the veteran campaigner for the untried novice. "Why, he's only thirty-two."

"Be that as it may," Buster Poole snarled, "he's been awake for the last three nights, talking to people around the clock. Tuesday, Hereford Creek. Wednesday Brompton's Falls. Last night at Indian Dune. All I can say, Elwood, is that you'd better shag your carcass back here and get busy. We've got eight weeks to election. If this upstart, as you call him, wins your Custodial seat, you know where you'll wind up."

"Hold on a second, Buster." Elwood clasped his hands behind his nightshirt, smoke wreathing his head. He frowned as though deliberating. Wisdom personified.

"Don't 'hold on' me, you old fool."

"Buster, that's hardly the tone to take with one who has served—"

"Yeah, but unless you serve the party a little better than you've been serving it so far, Mr. Jay Milton Mossman's going to be state Custodian come January. And I repeat, if that happens to me, you know what happens to you."

A somewhat-undressed young woman peered imploringly into the scene behind Buster. "Not now, Dolly. Elwood, you shag yourself to the turboport. You've got a reservation on the noon Hustler direct to Indian Dune. You're going to debate with Mossman tonight."

"Debate?" Elwood's eyes popped in disbelief. "Tonight? Debate what?"

Buster opened a bag of peanuts and gobbled several with a bored sneer. " 'The Populist Stewardship And Why It Must Be Retained.' "

"I'm not prepared—"

"Shut up. Doc Radameyer's got the tapes ready."

A cadaverous, inward-turning sort of fellow floated into the screen, sucking on a pineapple drop. "That is correct," he said in a pale voice, and floated out again.

"Elwood, don't you have an inkling of the seriousness of the situation?" Buster asked.

With studied and theatrical elegance reminiscent of a Grander, Older Age, Elwood tapped an eighth-inch ash from the end of his glowing cigar. "You must be misinformed. Mossman could not possibly have remained awake three nights running. The public would smell a figurative rat, my boy, if it were true. Which is patently impossible, the laws being what they are."

"It's just a state commission decree, remember," Buster snarled. "Even if it is in all fifty-two."

"Are you certain about Mossman? Were you on the scene?"

"Elwood, don't sneer at me or I'll turn Radameyer loose on you."

From off-screen came a sepulchral voice: "Not just now, please." Plus the sucking of a pineapple drop and a shrill giggle.

Elwood frowned, then scowled—a perfect imitation of middlewestern moralism facing the decay of personal ethics. Buster Poole stood up. He began to pace in front of his lead-brick fireplace. The camera had trouble following him.

"Elwood, unless you're on that flight—"

"Three nights?" Elwood murmured. "Impossible."

"You've seen Mossman. He's young-looking. Vigorous."

"An appearance of boyish charm is no substitute for experience when it comes—"

"Oh, shut up, shut *up*. As I said, he's either a young man or—"

"An illegal model?" For the first time, Elwood sounded slightly alarmed. "That's—inconceivable. Have you checked? I mean, my boy, the commissioner—"

"I've talked enough, I'm sick of talking!" Buster shouted. "You be here today!"

"But I have my duty, Buster. This is the height of the Tourist Session, and—"

All at once Buster Poole's right hand seemed to leap out from his body, fisted, until it filled the screen. At the last second the camera pulled its zoom-ar. Buster's whole body shot into the background, miniaturizing to a spot. The screen blacked out.

For a long moment Elwood Everett Swigg did nothing but stare at the end of his cigar. Then he turned and pushed through the damp curtains to the tiny balcony overlooking the parking lot and Rock Creek Bridge. Against the dim hot dawn the traffic bullseyes stood out scarlet and green.

A sac in the corner of each of Elwood's eyes disgorged a glycerine tear. He picked up the hem of his nightshirt and dabbed at the gooey stuff. Then he turned and tottered back into his suite on spindly legs.

Much of what Buster Poole had told him had now begun to be absorbed into the cells of his sixty-year-old head. An expression of concern, even alarm, wrinkled his Olympian brow. This expression had not completely vanished when he bustled into the Shoreham lobby precisely at eight that morning, the solid silver head of his anachronistic walking stick winking richly.

Elwood wore his conventional costume—frock tunic, morning shorts and dickey with stickpin. All over the lobby young government clerks in various shades of gray shorts bustled to conferences with dispatch cases under their arms. Elwood tramped ahead briskly. He nodded to Murfree, the Sociocratic Custodian from Mississippi, who merely curled his fist more tightly about the bullwhip he always carried, and stalked on.

Near the lobby entrance a crowd of two dozen children in electric blue shorts, jumpers and beanies began to leap up and down and squeal. Two elderly women attempted to quiet them, uselessly. Several of the tots hoisted up a lopsided banner. It read:

> Illinois Powwow No 478
> Kiddee Kampers of America Says
> HELLO CUSTODIAN SWIGG!

Elwood stopped. He bowed formally, swept a palm over his mop of silver hair and flashed his famous smile.

"Good *morning,* Kiddee Kampers. Your Custodian welcomes you to Washington."

The two elderly ladies fumbled with lacy fichus at the collars of their sensible tunics. They nudged one another forward and introduced themselves as the leaders of the group, the Misses Teasdale and Hipp. Miss Hipp seemed unable to do much besides simper. But Miss Teasdale said it was simply thrilling for all the Kiddee Kampers to be able to view with their own tiny eyes the great legislative process taking place day and night on the floor of the Combined Congress.

"As your state Custodian," Elwood said, employing several theatrical gestures, "it is my pleasure to conduct you personally to the Illinois machine, which it is my privilege and duty, as your elected steward, to maintain and service in tiptop working order during my term as—"

"Pa says they ain't nothing but janitors," said a male Kiddee Kamper.

"Is your papa a Sociocrat, sonny?" Elwood said. Squeals of insane laughter convulsed the group, including Miss Hipp. Elwood's face instantly grew serious.

"Actually, sonny, one must not joke about the sacred responsibilities of the Custodians. Without their services the great and intelligent body which governs us would be unable to function effectively day and night, passing into the law of the land those rules which make this country a better place for one and all to live.

"(Step this way, kiddies. The chartered turbobus is waiting.) Of course, in our state—" (An indulgent glance at the Misses Teasdale and Hipp.) "—certain parties would have us believe that only youth can supply the knowledge and initiative to properly program our machine, whereas it is my deep and sincere conviction that only wisdom, garnered through four successful terms—"

The Kiddee Kampers continued to squeal and giggle as the group moiled out of the hotel and into the turbobus. Between the chilled temperature-control of the lobby and that of the bus Misses Teasdale and Hipp erupted into cascades of sweat. Elwood remained dry and cool, his silver-headed cane winking.

The turbobus shot up the causeway under the traffic bullseye. Elwood delivered his little lecture on the traditions of history which are the country's heritage, etc. etc., while gazing out the window at the busy scenes of early-morning Washington. A large Hustler travel poster shot by. It reminded him of Buster.

What should he do?

His head sorted the choices. Certainly he would not go back. He knew his duty. His duty had been taught to him most carefully, made a part of his very existence. He would not abandon it.

Thus, leonine and magnificent in the flashing sunlight, Elwood continued his lecture all the way to the Combined Congressional Building, grandly ignoring the few snide remarks and soft-drink envelopes thrown by Kiddee Kampers whose parents were obviously non-Populist.

It took two hours to conduct the group through just a fraction of the laboratories and control rooms buried beneath the Building, what with Elwood stopping every so often to pull open a wall panel and reveal miles of cable receding into the distance, or vast networks of pinpoint lights flashing on great boards behind thick glass walls. Since the Tourist Session was indeed at its peak, there were innumerable waits for lift tubes and floating stairways as other tourist delegations—Elks, Shriners, Girl Patriots, Non-Nuclearites, Birth Control Brigaders and the like—went through similar tours under the guidance of their own state Custodians. Shortly before eleven, however, the electric moment arrived.

With a finger to his lips and an expression of deep reverence on his face, Elwood turned his back on the Kiddee Kampers. He threw wide his arms and opened the double doors into the Chamber.

Dwarfed by the immense steel cases which towered three stories each, Elwood's group started down a long sloping walkway which, with the other walkways that were arranged like wheel-spokes, converged at the bottom of the bowl-like chamber before the dais where sat the Chairman-Printer.

"Ssssh!" Elwood breathed. "A bill has just been passed. See, it's coming out on the tape and going down the chute to the typesetter's. Let's see."

Elwood consulted one of the illuminated globes set at intervals along the walk. "P. L. Three-billion and nine, Retroactivity of Social Security Psycho-Happiness Credits During Odd Months. A most significant bill," he added, although the Kiddee Kampers were far too awestruck by the mammoth machines and the flickering lights to reply, facetiously or otherwise.

At last Elwood paused beside one of the larger machines. He placed his palm against its smoothly humming metallic side. Over his head a small engraved stainless steel plate read:

Illinois
(IBM)

"This is your computer, children. More perfect, more wise and fair than the most intelligent mortal representative could hope to be. It guarantees you perfect representation without emotion. Feel thankful, children, that you live in an America where the antiquated tradition of representation by human beings is recognized for what it is—disastrous, and impossible, I might add, in the light of the complexity of our world. However—" Elwood cleared his throat. "Under our democratic system we must, of course, guarantee representation to all. Therefore your parents have duly elected me State Custodian. I shall now give a brief demonstration of my duties."

The great chronometer at the north end of the chamber showed a few minutes past eleven. Elwood took out a silver key, unlocked a small panel in the computer's side and occupied himself for the next five minutes with the thoroughly spurious demonstration regularly given for tourists. He applied oil from an antique can to several false holes in the interior of a special non-functioning cavity in the computer's side. The oil can made little squirting sounds. These held the Kiddee Kampers, Misses Teasdale and Hipp spellbound, allowing Elwood to do a little electioneering:

"I have a message for you children before you leave. Next November, your parents will be asked to choose between Custodial experience and Custodial callowness, between—"

A pale figure stepped out from behind the Iowa computer, sucking a pineapple drop.

"I thought so," said Dr. Radameyer with a sigh. He was still rumpled from his quick Hustler trip from Starved Rock. Over the heads of the Kiddee Kampers Dr. Radameyer stared with highly magnified eyes at Elwood. "Oh Elwood."

"Yes? Who—Radameyer! Now Doctor, I made my position clear to Poole—"

"Phooey," said Radameyer tiredly. "I told him you wouldn't cooperate.

Oh, well." Another pineapple drop. "Don't sit under the apple tree with any-one else but me."

Elwood collapsed against the side of the computer, his face screwed up in pain.

"Custodian Swigg!" shrieked Miss Teasdale. "Why are you clutching your side?"

Radameyer floated forward. He made a cursory examination of Elwood, who was now stretched out on the walkway, groaning horribly. "I'm afraid some elements have fused." Radameyer knelt down and turned up Elwood's eyelid, disclosing a milky pupil. "The rest of the tour will have to be canceled. Please wait in the rotunda for further word of the Custodian's condition."

Little faces no longer smiling, the Kiddee Kampers milled out of the Chamber. When the mammoth doors had swung shut Radameyer poked Elwood in the rib cage.

"Quick brown fox, Elwood old boy. Get up. We've forty minutes to make the Hustler."

Elwood blinked and followed the doctor up the aisle, all trace of pain gone from his face.

"Was that necessary, Doctor?"

Radameyer shrugged. "Poole wants the election. You're paying too much attention to your duty program. We'll have to have a checkup after the debate tonight." He patted a bulging pocket. "All the debate tapes are in here. We can feed them on the flight. A lot of interesting stuff, actually."

Radameyer guided Elwood toward the underground monorail entrance, used only by Custodians. The Kiddee Kampers would just have to stand waiting and wondering.

"Written by one of the best boxes in the business," Radameyer went on. "Normally does women's novels. When that last box of yours blew up from resistor fatigue, we had to scratch. Luckily we hit it successful at the first auction. Come on, Elwood, pick up your feet. Do you want 'Don't sit — ?' " Radameyer paused deliberately, unwrapping some new pineapple drops.

"No, no, I'll come along. I see it's serious now. I'll be glad to debate. Glad to, my boy, glad to, *glad* to."

"That sounds more encouraging," said Radameyer as they descended through the cool caverns to the whistling monorail track. "Maybe we won't have to re-program after all."

The Hustler pierced the sky in a burst of silent white flame. Within an hour Custodian Elwood Swigg and Dr. Radameyer were inside a sun-heated tent erected for the rally on the steep bluffs over the Mississippi, just outside the little lead-mining community of Indian Dune.

The tent swarmed with members of the Populist state committee. Tickers chattered. Pitchers of lemonade were constantly emptied and refilled. A corps of the Ladies Auxiliary was busy preparing pitch-pine torches. ("Not my idea," Buster Poole scowled, sweaty and in shirtsleeves at a deal table behind a mound of memoranda. "Has something to do with one of the old Presidents that came from the state. Mossman thought of it. Or rather, that bastard Hawk. Pioneer spirit. Fresh blood. Etcetera. Makes me puke. Wait a sec, Elwood.")

Dr. Radameyer, holding firmly to Elwood's elbow, found himself overwhelmed at the collection of antique appurtenances freighted in for the rally—ancient telephones, for example. Buster Poole was talking into one, arranging for six turbobus-loads of rallyers. These would arrive, rally and demonstrate, one hundred a head, noisemakers and torches to be provided by the state committee.

Elwood picked up a handbill printed on a curious stuff. "Look at this."

Dr. Radameyer felt it. "My God. Real primitive paper."

Glancing down the list headed *Programme,* Elwood frowned.

"I wish I could talk to Buster a minute. This sounds like a program *I* should have arranged. Instead, I seem to have been forced to go along with what the opposition has set up." Immediately Elwood's tear sacs opened. He read the paper handbill aloud, large glycerine drops staining it like dark flowers: "Masson's Original Equestrian Troupe, Including Genuine Horses In Person. Lady Olivia on the Taut Wire. The Coal Valley Family Bell-Ringers."

"Bell-Ringers?" Radameyer grabbed the handbill. "Let me see that."

Buster Poole rushed up. "Know the speeches, Elwood?"

"Of course. Not precisely my style, but—"

"What a mess, what a miserable mess," Buster said vehemently. "Every act for miles is booked. We haven't got one lousy item on the program that says Courtesy State Populist Party. Oh, I tell you, Radameyer, this Mossman is a grand one. Youthful, healthy, vigorous."

"We'll have to do something about those bell-ringers, Buster," Radameyer said. "That's one trigger-error I've never been able to trace and correct."

"I know," Buster said. He shouted: "Charlie—remind me to memorize that Hawk crumb as soon as I get finished conferring with the Custodian."

He shoved Elwood, who was still dry and calm amidst the sweating crowds in the non-chilled tent, over to an entranceway. Buster lifted a corner of the moldy-smelling canvas. He pointed across to the edge of the bluff. Next to a pine-plank platform being hastily erected could be seen a small tent city, flag-festooned with the emblems of the Sociocrats. From the highest point of the biggest tent floated a huge dimensional styrene statue-balloon of the Sociocratic candidate, Jay Milton Mossman.

"You've got to turn on the charm, Elwood," Buster said. "You can get an idea of their organization. Out of nowhere, bang, they dig up this Mossman, and load him with gimmicks like this pioneer routine. Then they box us into accepting the debate, with only ten minutes' talk about ground rules. Next you waste half a day responding to your God damn duty program — " Poole waved aside Radameyer's mild protests that it wasn't really Elwood's fault. " — so now I'll lay it on the line to you, Custodian. You either get out there and win this crowd tonight, ooze them to death with your so-called charm, or you know what'll happen."

Elwood drew himself up to his full, rather regal height. "I know very well. You have taught me that most expressly."

"He can only do so much," Radameyer said.

"But he can do less than the most, if he wants," Buster snarled back.

"I revere and venerate my position as Custodian," Elwood said. "I shall give it full measure during the debate. However, I should like to ask one question. Have you ascertained anything about the nature of this Mossman? After all, it's quite a departure. Young. Handsome. Rather smart-alecky, if you wish my opinion."

"Times are changing," was all Buster would say. "In a minute, Charlie."

"Ah, yes, but when the computers replaced the representatives, and the non-humans subsequently replaced the human Custodians — experimentally at first, then on a permanent basis — it was thought psychologically correct to mold and model Custodial candidates in the fashion which would most perfectly appeal to the greatest number of voters."

As he spoke, Elwood did not respond emotionally to the fact that had been clearly taught him long ago: that non-humans were first employed in Custodian positions because the Custodial position was essentially a useless, harmless job. Except as it provided the voters with the satisfaction of electing somebody or something, once human beings became inadequate to fulfill legislative responsibilities. Further, the Custodial position kept the national party alive — perhaps the real reason non-humans had been tested and used first in this particular role. But Elwood's makeup didn't permit him to weep solely because he was useless. Though he knew, as a fact, that he was, he was so arranged as to act in the opposite fashion — for the benefit of the people, especially during the Tourist Session. This sense of purpose rang in Elwood's voice as he went on:

"Window dressing, you call it. Yet I have seen the sparkle in the eyes of a crowd when I pass among them." There was no smile on Elwood's face as he said this. Only a great solemnity. He brushed at his heroic silver locks and took a firmer grip on the head of his cane. "In fact, we discussed this morning the state commission decrees which require non-humans to be cast in human mold — sleeping, eating and so forth, so as not to effect too rapid a transition that would psychically upset the populace. This raises the question of Mossman's — "

"I don't know, I just don't know yet," Buster Poole interrupted, wiping sweat. "You just hang around, Elwood. I may want to talk to you some more."

Buster dashed off: "Ready to memorize, Charlie? Right. To Andy Hawk, Sociocratic Headquarters. Subject — bell-ringers. The one weak point in our candidate's programming is an uncontrolled circuit closure triggered by a bell stimulus." Poole paced, sneering at the invisible recipient of the memo as he talked. "Out of consideration for the way in which you have managed to prearrange this debate — and out of simple decency — " Poole grinned at his own cleverness. " — I would appreciate it if the Coal Valley Family Bell-Ringers could be struck from the program. I repeat, Andy, the bells represent the one point of disorganization peculiar to our model. Rest assured, that should a situation arise in which any action of ours should produce a disorderly reaction in your candidate — (That ought to trap him into telling us about Mossman, one way or another, eh, Charlie?) — I would take quick steps to remove that stimulus. You well know that, due to the complexity of our candidates, we must be careful not to upset the delicate balance of factors on which the population depends for its emotional release in the politico-patriotic area of our national life." And Poole spat: "Sign it 'Cordially.' "

Turning aside, Elwood walked to a campstool which a clerk had just vacated. He sat down and began to rehearse his debate material in a loud voice. A few minutes later he walked to the tent entrance and looked at the mammoth balloon-statue of Jay Milton Mossman floating above the Sociocratic tents. His sacs welled over with glycerine again. Still sucking pineapple drops, Dr. Radameyer guided him solicitously back to the camp stool, where the rehearsal continued through the remainder of the afternoon.

When the program began at eight in the evening five thousand pitch-pine torches had been lit, and the bluffs above the Mississippi flickered with the tufts of orange fire that cast immense shadows inside the Populist tent. The tent was empty except for Buster Poole, Dr. Radameyer and Elwood. In the litter of papers and cigars and cashier's check stubs made out in advance to the paid rallyers, the three sat silently while twenty-five thousand throats made a thunderous roar. Lady Olivia was performing a sensational trick on the taut wire.

No word had been received from the Sociocratic tents about the bell-ringers. They were the next turn on the program, the fifth before the debate was scheduled to begin. Buster Poole's bald head was adrip with orange sweat. He held his ear cocked, one eye closed. But it was difficult if not impossible, for him to hear the tiny shouts of six turbobus-loads of his rallyers among the thousands of voices that cheered when Lady Olivia unzipped part of her costume and dropped it down into the crowd — a fancy pink bustle embroidered *Mossman*.

Suddenly the tent flap lifted.

Three men walked in. One, rolling ponderously, was Andy Hawk, a sow-bellied five-foot fighter from the southern coal regions. Hawk walked straight up to Buster Poole, all confidence and stinking sweat.

Elwood rose from his campstool. Back in the shadows the other two visitors waited. Elwood made out the handsome young face of Jay Milton Mossman, deeply tanned above his crisply-white but inexpensive tunic.

The third figure was so deeply in shadows that even the reflected firelight from the rally grounds did not reveal him. Buster Poole backed off a step. He wiped fog from his glasses, staring down at the quivering, smiling little fat man.

"Well, Hawk?"

"I got your memo."

"About time you answered, I think."

"We'll strike the bell-ringers. That is, unless your candidate wishes to withdraw for an uncontested election."

"Are you out of your God-damned mind?" Buster screamed.

"*Sir—!*" Elwood brandished his cane, the head winking and flashing with bright lights in the shifting red shadows. "As a patriotic Custodian who has served the sovereign state of Illinois with dignity and faithfulness and courage, I *protest* your—"

"Can't you shut him off?" Hawk asked.

Buster snapped his fingers. Dr. Radameyer said, "Drink Pop-A-Cola."

Elwood's mouth fell open, his enunciation complex electronically frozen. But he retained the capacity to move, and the stimulus-code did not affect his tear sacs, which began to well with glycerine. It ran in two greasy trickles down his cheeks.

Buster Poole's voice had acquired the dangerous, raspish quality of the growl of the tiger jabbed once too often by the trainer's stick: "Speak your piece, Hawk. You know I won't pull Elwood."

"Oh?" Hawk's cheerful face beamed malice and triumph. "You mentioned in your memo, I think, that all non-humans, because of their complexity, inevitably wind up with some disordered relays or what-ever-you-call-them. That, Buster my friend, is due to the fact that they've been made, by law, to resemble humans. But I can guarantee you that our boy doesn't have such a weak point." Hawk lumbered around. "Do you, Jay?"

The face of Jay Milton Mossman broke wide in a white grin that shone like ivory in the dark. His electronic voice said warmly, "No, Andy, that's right, I do not."

"You know as well as I, you conniving bastard, that anything but a human-model non-human is illegal," Buster snarled.

"Don't call me names," said Hawk, lightly but dangerously. "Although I guess I can't blame you, seeing as how you've already lost November. For your information, Buster, the law here in Illinois was changed three weeks ago. The new executive decree will be made public at a press conference. Tomorrow. You don't have any legal recourse, either. We may have made

Jay contrary to what the law allowed — but he didn't start showing any of his little refinements publicly until *after* the new decree went into effect."

"Changed the law?" gasped Dr. Radameyer, surprised for perhaps the first time in his life. "*Changed?* Who changed it."

The third figure, tall, impeccably dressed, stirred out of the shadows. "I did."

Buster Poole's face collapsed into disbelief and rage. "Wing!"

"It was my pleasure to sign the executive order, with the governor's approval," said Willis Wing, who was Illinois State Commissioner of Robots. "Illinois has always led the fight for progressive technology. Soon the other states will follow our precedent, I'm sure. The population is quite ready, psychologically, to accept a non-human who neither sleeps, ingests or eliminates." A small, malicious smile curved the tonsured face. "And you might also be interested in knowing, Poole, that at noon tomorrow, following the press conference, I shall endorse the Custodial candidacy of Jay Milton Mossman."

"That is right," said Jay Milton Mossman with another jerk of the metallic musculature that pulled his artificial epidermis into a smile. "That's correct, he will."

Through it all the roar of voices from the rally-grounds had been growing to a thunder as Lady Olivia completed her act. Now searchlights wig-wagged back and forth wildly along the taut wire. Lady Olivia took her bows. Then a raucous voice on the public address system tried to announce the next act. Elwood stood balancing his weight from one artificial foot to another, hearing everything that was said but unable to speak out. His tear-sacs had overflowed, coating his face with a grease of glycerine. Their tiny orifices still pumped, but no more fluid came.

Buster Poole looked at Radameyer. "We'll build another Elwood."

"That," said Radameyer, around a pineapple drop, "will take time."

"And the model you've got," said Hawk, "has to sleep seven hours every night. I saw the circuitry depositions in the state vaults, just to check."

"Those vaults are *secret!*" Buster howled at Willis Wing. "You cheap crook, I thought you weren't for sale."

Willis Wing paused in the act of lighting a cigar. His eyes resembled hard bits of Illinois coal. "Why, Mr. Poole, you never tried to buy."

"Elwood can't possibly keep up with the kind of campaign Jay here will wage," Hawk said. "That's why I thought I'd at least give you the opportunity to withdraw your candidate tonight."

Poole seized Radameyer's shoulder. "Can we re-program him non-human?"

"Impossible. We'd have to begin all over again. The principles are different."

"I realize this puts you in a bad position, Buster," Hawk said, suddenly solicitous. "Elwood will lose, of course, because he can't keep up. Can't possibly duplicate Jay's coverage of the state. Besides, people are growing tired of silver-headed canes and silver hair and golden voices. They want a machine that *acts* like a machine—that thinks quickly, works tirelessly. In four years we'll be able to take off Jay's epidermis and let him show his real skin. One of these days people may even decide the whole business of a Custodian in Washington is stupid—which it is. But until they decide that way, and as long as we keep having elections, I want my party to win. This time, it will."

"That's very true," said Jay Milton Mossman. "I believe it will."

Hawk turned, ready to leave. "Sorry, Buster. I know how the National Committee may treat you if you lose. Believe me, I treasure your friendship, but—" Hawk lifted one shoulder in a porcine shrug. "Politics."

"—*and now ladies and gentlemen,*" a hoarse amplified voice thundered through the flame-shadowed tent, "*the next stellar act on this stellar bill, all brought to you through the courtesy of your Sociocratic candidate for Custodian, Jay Milton Mossman—a group of stellar artists who come from our own native state, and who—*"

"The bell-ringers," said Radameyer, in a warning whisper.

Hawk moved toward a field phone on one of the deal tables. "I'll strike them."

Buster Poole looked at Elwood Everett Swigg with hatred and loathing. "Forget it," he said. "Quick brown fox."

"My hands may not be clean," said Willis Wing, "but I will be very glad to see a man like you lose this election."

"Shut up," said Buster Poole, adding an obscenity. "Radameyer, we'll rebuild, and rebuild in time to beat—"

"Oh, we can't," Radameyer said listlessly. "We can't, we just can't."

"Don't say *can't,*" Buster screamed. "God damn you, don't *say* that."

Over the amplification system the Coal Valley Family began to ring their bells, playing *Humoresque.*

Elwood Everett Swigg raised one arm. He brandished his cane. His eyes were full of flame and shadow, and his hair gleamed like molten silver.

"When in the course of human events," he said, his voice booming out above Buster Poole's hysterical pleas to Radameyer, "a government of the people by the people for the people provides for the common defense and protects against the Illinois computer which you now see before you—"

Walking out of the tent, Elwood Everett Swigg turned into the darkness. He walked proudly, his head high, his shoulders thrown back, his eyes glinting for battle. He walked decisively, with no waver in his step. He walked away from the crowds and the torches and the clatter of the bell-ringers, straight toward the lip of the bluff.

"I pledge allegiance to the flag," he said to the night wind, flinging wide his arms, "and to the demonstration of my vital position as Custodian, friends and neighbors, which I shall now proceed to render unto Caesar that which—"

He walked into air over the bright ribbon of the Mississippi under the moon. He sang *The Battle Hymn of the Republic* all the way down.

The Children of Night

Frederik Pohl

Frederik Pohl (b. 1919) is a remarkable writer who has gotten better and better in a career that now spans some forty years. His early novels (several written in collaboration with the late C. M. Kornbluth) were characterized by biting social satire in which he attacked such institutions as the advertising industry (*The Space Merchants,* 1953) and the legal profession (*Gladiator-at-Law,* 1955). Although he continued to produce excellent work in the ensuing twenty years, he had another major burst of creative activity, beginning with the brilliant *Man Plus* in 1976, which was followed by such important novels as *Gateway* (1979), *Jem* (1979), *Beyond the Blue Event Horizon* (1980), and several others, and he gives no sign of slowing down.

He has had a lifelong interest in the political process, which he uses to good effect in this stunning story about an "advance man" in a political campaign of the future.

I

"We met before," I told Haber. "In 1988, when you were running the Des Moines office."

He beamed and held out his hand. "Why, darn it, so we did! I remember now, Odin."

"I don't like to be called Odin."

"No? All right. Mr. Gunnarsen—"

"Not 'Mr. Gunnarsen,' either. Just 'Gunner.' "

"That's right, Gunner; I'd almost forgotten."

I said, "No, you hadn't forgotten. You never knew my name in Des Moines. You didn't even know I was alive, because you were too busy losing the state for our client. I pulled you out of that one, just like I'm going to pull you out now."

The smile was a little cracked, but Haber had been with the company

70

a long time, and he wasn't going to let me throw him. "What do you want me to say, Gunner? I'm grateful. Believe me, boy, I know I need help—"

"And I'm not your boy. Haber, you were a fat cat then, and you're a fat cat now. All I want from you is, first, a quick look around the shop here and, second, a conference of all department heads, including you, in thirty minutes. So tell your secretary to round them up, and let's get started on the sight-seeing."

Coming in to Belport on the scatjet, I had made a list of things to do. The top item was:

1. Fire Haber.

Still, in my experience that isn't always the best way to put out a fire. Some warts you remove; some you just let wither away in obscurity. I am not paid by M & B to perform cosmetic surgery on their Habers, only to see that the work the Habers should have done gets accomplished.

As a public relations branch manager he was a wart, but as a tourist guide he was fine, although he was perspiring. He led me all around the shop. He had taken a storefront on one of the main shopping malls—air-curtain door, windows draped tastefully in gray silk. It looked like the best of four funeral parlors in a run-down neighborhood. In gilt letters on the window was the name of the game:

MOULTRIE & BIGELOW
Public Relations
Northern Lake State Division
T. Wilson Haber
Division Manager

"Public relations," he informed me, "starts at home. They know we're here, eh, Gunner?"

"Reminds me of the Iowa office," I said, and he stumbled where there wasn't even a sill. That was the Presidential campaign of '88, where Haber had been trying to carry the state for the candidate who had retained us, and those 12 electoral votes came over at the last minute only because we sent Haber to Nassau to rest and I took over from him. I believe Haber's wife had owned stock in the company.

His Belport layout was pretty good, at that, though. Four pry booths, each with a Simplex 9090 and an operator-receptionist in the donor's waiting room. You can't tell from appearances, but the donors who were waiting for their interrogation looked like a good representative sample—a good mixture of sexes, ages, conditions of affluence—and with proper attention to weighing he should at least be getting a fair survey of opinions. Integration of the pry scores was in a readout station in back—I recognized one of the programmers and nodded to him: good man—along with telefax equipment to the major research sources, the Britannica, Library of Congress, news-wire services, and so on. From the integration room the readout operator could construct a speech, a 3-V commercial, a space ad, or anything else, with the research lines to feed him any data he needed and test its appeal on his subjects. In the front of the building was a taping booth and studio. Everything was small and semiportable, but good stuff. You could put together a 3-V interview or edit one as well here as you could on the lot in the home office.

"An A-number-one setup, right, Gunner?" said Haber. "Set it up myself to do the job."

I said, "Then why aren't you doing it?" He tightened up. The eyes looked smaller and more intelligent, but he didn't say anything directly. He took my elbow and turned me to the data-processing room.

"Want you to meet someone," he said, opened the door, led me inside, and left me.

A tall, slim girl looked up from a typer. "Why, hello, Gunner," she said. "It's been a long time."

I said, "Hello, Candace."

Apparently Haber was not quite such a fat cat as he had seemed, for he had clearly found out a little something about my personal life before I showed up in his office. The rest of the list I had scribbled down in the scatjet was:

> 2. Need "big lie."
> 3. Investigate Children.
> 4. Investigate opponents' proposition.
> 5. Marry Candace Harmon?

This was a relatively small job for Moultrie & Bigelow, but it was for a very, very big account. It was important to win it. The client was the Arcturan Confederacy.

In the shop the word was that they had been turned down by three of four other PR agencies before we took them on. Nobody said why, exactly, but the reason was perfectly clear. It was just because they were the Arcturan Confederacy. There is nothing in any way illegal or immoral about a public relations firm representing a foreign account. That is a matter of statute—as most people don't take the trouble to know: the Smith-Macchioni Act of '71. And the courts held that it applied to extra-planetary "foreigners" as well as to terrestrials in 1985, back when the only "intelligent aliens" were the mummies on Mars. Not that the mummies had ever hired anybody on Earth to do anything for them. But it was Moultrie & Bigelow's law department that sued for the declaratory judgment, as a matter of fact. Just on the off chance. That's how M & B operates.

Any public relations man takes on the color of his clients in the eyes of some people. That's the nature of the beast. The same people wouldn't think of blaming a surgeon because he dissolved a malignancy out of Public Enemy No. 1, or even a lawyer for defending him. But when you are in charge of a client's emotional image and that image isn't liked, some of the dislike rubs off on you.

At M & B there is enough in the pay check at the end of every month so that we don't mind that. M & B has a reputation for taking on the tough ones — the only surviving American cigarette manufacturer is ours. So is the exiled Castroite government of Cuba, that still thinks it might one day get the State Department to back up its claim for paying off on the bonds it printed for itself. However, for two reasons — as a simple matter of making things easy for ourselves and because it's better doctrine — we don't flaunt our connection with the unpopular clients. Especially when the job is going badly. One of the surest ways to get a bad public response to PR is to let the public know that some hotshot PR outfit is working on it.

So every last thing Haber had done was wrong.

In this town it was too late for pry booths and M/R.

I had just five minutes left before the conference, and I spent it in the pry-booth section, anyhow. I noticed a tri-D display of our client's home planet in the reception room, where donors were sitting and waiting their turn. It was very attractive: the wide, calm seas with the vertical air-mount islets jutting out at intervals.

I turned around and walked out fast, boiling mad.

A layman might not have seen just how many ways Haber had found to go wrong. The whole pry-booth project was probably a mistake, anyway. To begin with, to get any good out of pry booths you need depth interviews, way deep-down M/R stuff. And for that you need paid donors, lots of them. And to get them you have to have a panel to pick from.

That means advertising in the papers and on the nets and interviewing 20 people for every one you hire. To get a satisfactory sample in a town the size of Belport you need to hire maybe 50 donors. And that means talking to a thousand people, every one of whom will go home and talk to his wife or her mother or their neighbors.

In a city like Chicago or Saskatoon you can get away with it. With good technique the donor never really knows what he's being interviewed *for*, although, of course, a good newspaperman or private eye can interview a couple of donors and work backward from the sense-impulse stimuli with pretty fair accuracy. But not in Belport, not when we never had a branch here before, not when every living soul in town knew what we were doing because the rezoning ordinance was Topic One over every coffee table. In short, we had tipped our hand completely.

As I say, an amateur might not have spotted that. But Haber was not supposed to be an amateur.

I had just seen the trend charts, too. The referendum on granting rezoning privileges to our client was going to a vote in less than two weeks. When Haber had opened the branch, sampling showed that it would fail by a four-to-three vote. Now, a month and a half later, he had worsened the percentage to three to two and going down-hill all the way.

Our client would be extremely unhappy—probably was unhappy already, if they had managed to puzzle out the queer terrestrial progress reports we had been sending them.

And this was the kind of client that a flackery didn't want to have unhappy. I mean, all the others were little-league stuff in comparison. The Arcturan Confederacy was a culture as wealthy and as powerful as all Earth governments combined, and as Arcturans don't bother with nonsense like national governments or private enterprise, at least not in any way that makes sense to us, this one client was—

As big as every other *possible* client combined.

They were the ones who decided they needed this base in Belport, and it was up to M & B—and specifically to me, Odin Gunnarsen—to see that they got it.

It was too bad that they had been fighting Earth six months earlier.

In fact, in a technical sense we were still at war. It was only armistice, not a peace, that had called off the H-bomb raids and the fleet engagements.

Like I say. M & B takes on the tough ones!

Besides Haber, four of the staff looked as though they knew which end was up. Candace Harmon, the pry-integration programmer, and two very junior T.A.'s. I took the head chair at the conference table without waiting to see where Haber would want to sit and said, "We'll make this fast, because we're in trouble here and we don't have time to be polite. You're Percy?" That was the programmer; he nodded. "And I didn't catch your name?" I said, turning to the next along the table. It was the copy chief, a lanky shave-headed oldster named Tracy Spockman. His assistant, one of the T.A.'s I had had my eye on, turned out to be named Manny Brock.

I had picked easy jobs for all the deadheads, reserving the smart ones for whatever might turn up, so I started with the copy chief. "Spockman, we're opening an Arcturan purchasing agency, and you're it. You should be able to handle this one; if I remember correctly, you ran the Duluth shop for a year."

He sucked on a cal pipe without expression. "Well, thanks, Mr. Gun—"

"Just Gunner."

"Well, thanks, but as copy chief—"

"Manny here should be able to take care of that. If I remember the way you ran the Duluth operation, you've probably got things set up so he can step right in." And so he probably did. At least, it surely would do no real harm to give somebody else a chance at lousing things up. I handed Spockman the "positions wanted" page from the paper I'd picked up at the scatport, and a scrawled list of notes I'd made up on the way in. "Hire these girls I've marked for your staff, rent an office, and get some letters out. You'll see what I want from the list. Letters to every real estate dealer in town, asking them if they can put together a five-thousand-acre parcel in the area covered by the zoning referendum. Letter to every general contractor, asking for bids on buildings. Make it separate bids on each—I think there'll be five buildings altogether. One exoclimatized—so get the air-conditioning, heating, and plumbing contractors to bid, too. Letter to every food wholesaler and major grocery outlet asking if they are interested in bidding on supplying Arcturans with food. Fax Chicago for what the Arcturans fancy; I don't remember—no meat, I think, but a lot of green vegetables—anyway, find out and include the data in the letters. Electronics manufacturers, office equipment dealers, car and truck agencies—well, the whole list is on that piece of paper. I want every businessman in Belport starting to figure out by tomorrow morning how much profit he might make on an Arcturan base. Got it?"

"I think so, Mr.—Gunner. I was thinking. How about stationery suppliers, attorneys, C.P.A's?"

"Don't ask—do it. Now, you down at the end there—"

"Henry Dane, Gunner."

"Henry, what about club outlets in Belport? I mean specialized groups. The Arcturans are hot for navigation, sailing, like that; see what you can do with the motorboat clubs and so on. I noticed in the paper that there's a flower show at the armory next Saturday. It's pretty late, but squeeze in a speaker on Arcturan fungi. We'll fly in a display. They tell me Arcturans are hot gardeners when they're home—love all the biological sciences—nice folks, like to dabble." I hesitated and looked at my notes. "I have something down here about veterans' groups, but I haven't got the handle for it. Still, if you can think of an angle, let me know—what's the matter?"

He was looking doubtful. "It's only that I don't want to conflict with Candy, Gunner."

And so, of course, I had to face up to things and turn to Candace Harmon. "What's that, honey?" I asked.

"I think Henry means my Arcturan-American Friendship League." It turned out that that had been one of Haber's proudest ideas. I wasn't surprised. After several weeks and about three thousand dollars it had worked up to a total of 41 members. How many of those were employees of the M & B branch? "Well, all but eight," Candace admitted at once. She wasn't smiling, but she was amused.

"Don't worry about it," I advised Henry Dane. "We're folding the Arcturan-American Friendship League, anyway. Candace won't have time for it. She'll be working with me."

"Why, fine, Gunner," she said. "Doing what?"

I almost did marry Candace one time, and every once in a while since I have wished I hadn't backed away. A very good thing was Candace Harmon.

"Doing," I said, "what Gunner says for you to do. Let's see. First thing, I've got five hundred Arcturan domestic animals coming in tomorrow. I haven't seen them, but they tell me they're cute, look like kittens, are pretty durable. Figure out some way of getting them distributed fast — maybe a pet shop will sell them for fifty cents each."

Haber protested, "My dear Gunner! The freight alone — "

"Sure, Haber, they cost about forty dollars apiece just to get them here. Any other questions like that? No? That's good. I want one in each of five hundred homes by the end of the week, and if I had to pay a hundred dollars to each customer to take them, I'd pay. Next: I want somebody to find me a veteran, preferably disabled, preferably who was actually involved in the bombing of the home planet — "

I laid out a dozen more working lines — an art show of the Arcturan bas-relief stuff that was partly to look at but mostly to feel, a 3-V panel show on Arcturus that we could plant . . . the whole routine. None of it would do the job, but all of it would help until I got my bearings. Then I got down to business. "What's the name of this fellow who's running for councilman — Connick?"

"That's right," said Haber.

"What've you got on him?" I asked.

I turned to Candace, who said promptly, "Forty-one years old, Methodist, married, three kids of his own plus one of the casualties, ran for State Senate last year and lost, but he carried Belport, running opposed to the referendum this year, very big in Junior Chamber of Commerce and V.F.W. — "

"No. What've you got *on* him?" I persisted.

Candace said slowly, "Gunner, look. This is a nice guy."

"Why, I know that, honey. I read his piece in the paper today. So now tell me the dirt that he can't afford to have come out."

"It wouldn't be fair to destroy him for nothing!"

I brushed aside the "fair" business. "What do you mean, 'for nothing'?"

"We're not going to win this referendum, you know."

"Honey, I've got news for you. This is the biggest account anybody ever had, and I want it. We *will* win. What've you got on Connick?"

"Nothing. Really nothing," she said quietly.

"But you can get it."

Candace said, visibly upset, "Of course, there's probably some—"

"Of course. Get it. Today."

II

But I wasn't relying totally on anyone, not even Candace. Since Connick was the central figure of the opposition I caught a cab and went to see him.

It was already dark, a cold, clear night, and over the mushroom towers of the business district a quarter moon was beginning to rise. I looked at it almost with affection; I had hated it so when I was there.

As I paid the cab, two kids in snowsuits came sidling out to inspect me. I said, "Hello. Is your Daddy home?"

One was about five, with freckles and bright blue eyes; the other was darker, brown-eyed, and he had a limp. The blue-eyed one said, "Daddy's down in the cellar. Mommy will let you in if you ring the doorbell. Just push that button."

"Oh, that's how those things work. Thanks." Connick's wife turned out to be a good-looking, skinny blonde in her thirties, and the kids must have raced around the back way and alerted the old man, because as she was taking my coat, he was already coming through the hall.

I shook his hand and said, "I can tell by the smells from your kitchen that it's dinnertime. I won't keep you. My name is Gunnarsen and—"

"And you're from Moultrie & Bigelow—here, sit down, Mr. Gunnarsen—and you want to know if I won't think it over and back the Arcturan base. No, Mr. Gunnarsen, I won't. But why don't you have a drink with me before dinner? And then why don't you have dinner?"

He was a genuine article, this Connick. I had to admit he had caught me off balance.

"Why, I don't mind if I do," I said after a moment. "I see you know why I'm here."

He was pouring drinks. "Well, not altogether, Mr. Gunnarsen. You don't really think you'll change my mind, do you?"

"I can't say that until I know why you oppose the base in the first place, Connick. That's what I want to find out."

He handed me a drink, sat down across from me, and took a thoughtful pull at his own. It was good Scotch. Then he looked to see if the kids were within earshot, and said: "The thing is this, Mr. Gunnarsen. If I could, I would kill every Arcturan alive, and if it meant I had to accept the death of a few million Earthmen to do it, that wouldn't be too high a price. I don't want the base here because I don't want anything to do with those murdering animals."

"Well, you're candid," I said, finished my drink, and added, "if you meant that invitation to dinner, I believe I will take you up on it."

I must say they were a nice family. I've worked elections before: Connick was a good candidate because he was a good man. The way his kids behaved around him proved it, and the way he behaved around me was the clincher. I didn't scare him a bit.

Of course, that was not altogether bad, from my point of view.

Connick kept the conversation off Topic A during dinner, which was all right with me, but as soon as it was over and we were alone, he said, "All right. You can make your pitch now, Mr. Gunnarsen. Although I don't know why you're here instead of with Tom Schlitz."

Schlitz was the man he was running against. I said, "You don't know this business, I guess. What do we need him for? He's already committed on our side."

"And I'm already committed against you, but I guess that's what you're hoping to change. Well, what's your offer?"

He was moving too fast for me. I pretended to misunderstand. "Really, Mr. Connick, I wouldn't insult you by offering a bribe—"

"No, I know you wouldn't. Because you're smart enough to know I wouldn't take money. So it isn't money. What is it, then? Moultrie & Bigelow working for me instead of Schlitz in the election? That's a pretty good offer, but the price is too high. I won't pay it."

"Well," I said, "as a matter of fact, we would be willing—"

"Yes, I thought so. No deal. Anyway, do you really think I need help to get elected?"

That was a good point, I was forced to admit. I conceded, "No, not if everything else were equal. You're way ahead right now, as your surveys and ours both show. But everything else isn't equal."

"By which you mean that you're going to help old Slits-and-fits. All right, that makes it a horse race."

I held up my glass, and he refilled it. I said, "Mr. Connick, I told you once you didn't know this business. You don't. It isn't a horse race because you can't win against us."

"I can sure give it a hell of a try, though. Anyway"—he finished his own drink thoughtfully—"you brainwashers are a little bit fat, I think. Everybody knows how powerful you are, and you haven't really had to show it much lately. I wonder if the emperor's really running around naked."

"Oh, no, Mr. Connick. Best-dressed emperor you ever saw, take my word for it."

He said, frowning a little bit, "I think I'll have to find out for myself. Anyway, frankly, I think people's minds are made up, and you can't change them."

"We don't have to," I said. "Don't you know why people vote the way they do, Connick? They don't vote their 'minds.' They vote attitudes and they vote impulses. Frankly, I'd rather work on your side than against you. Schlitz would be easy to beat. He's Jewish."

Connick said angrily, "There's none of that in Belport, man."

"Of anti-Semitism, you mean. Of course not. But if one candidate is Jewish and if it turns up that fifteen years ago he tried to square a parking ticket — and there's always something that turns up, Connick, believe me — then they'll vote against him for fixing parking tickets. That's what I mean by 'attitudes.' Your voter — oh, not all of them, but enough to swing any election — goes into the booth pulled this way and that. We don't have to change his mind. We just have to help him decide which part of it to operate on." I let him refill my glass and took a pull at it. I was aware that I was beginning to feel the effects. "Take you, Connick," I said. "Suppose you're a Democrat and you go in to cast your vote. We know how you're going to vote for President, right? You're going to vote for the Democratic candidate."

Connick said, not unbending much, "Not necessarily. But probably."

"Not necessarily, right. And why not necessarily? Because maybe you know this fellow who's running on the Democratic ticket — or maybe somebody you know has a grudge against him, couldn't get the postmaster's job he wanted, or ran against his delegates for the convention. Point is, you have something *against* him just because your first instinct is *for* him. So how do you vote? Whichever way happens to get dominance *at the moment of voting*. Not at any other moment. Not as a matter of principle. But right then. No, we don't have to change any minds . . . because most people don't have enough mind to change!"

He stood up and absentmindedly filled his own glass — I wasn't the only one who was beginning to feel the liquor. "I'd hate to be you," he said, half to himself.

"Oh, it's not bad."

He shook his head, then recollected himself and said, "Well, thanks for the lesson. I didn't know. But I'll tell you one thing you'll never do. You'll never get me to vote on the Arcturan side on *any* question."

I sneered, "There's an open mind for you! Leader of the people! Takes an objective look at every question!"

"All right, I'm not objective. They stink."

"Race prejudice, Connick?"

"Oh, don't be a fool."

"There is," I said, "an Arcturan aroma. They can't help it."

"I didn't say 'smell.' I said 'stink.' I don't want them in this town, and neither does anybody else. Not even Schlitz."

"You don't ever have to see them. They don't like Earth climate, you know. Too hot for them. Too much air. Why, Connick," I said, "I'll bet you a hundred bucks you won't set eyes on an Arcturan for at least a year, not until the base is built and staffed. And then I doubt they'll bother to — What's the matter?"

He was looking at me as though I were an idiot, and I almost began to think I was.

"Why," he said, again in that tone that was more to himself than to me, "I guess I've been overrating you. You think you're God, so I've been accepting your own valuation."

"What do you mean?"

"Inexcusably bad staff work, Mr. Gunnarsen," he said, nodding judgmatically. "It ought to make me feel good. But you know, it doesn't. It scares me. With the kind of power you throw around, you should always be right."

"Spit it out!"

"It's just that you lose your bet. Didn't you know there's an Arcturan in town right now?"

III

When I got back to the car, the phone was buzzing and the "Message Recorded" light blinked at me. The message was from Candace:

"Gunner, a Truce Team has checked into the Statler-Bills to supervise the election, and get this. One of them's an Arcturan!"

The staff work wasn't so bad, after all, just unpardonably slow. But there wasn't much comfort in that.

I called the hotel and was connected with one of the Truce Team staff — the best the hotel would do for me. The staff man was a colonel who said, "Yes, Mr. Knafti is aware of your work here and specifically does not wish to see you. This is a Truce Team, Mr. Gunnarsen. Do you know what that means, exactly?"

And he hung up on me. Well, I did know what it meant — strictly hands-off, all the way — I simply hadn't known that they would interpret it that rigidly.

It was a kick in the eye, any way I looked at it. Because it made me look like a fool in front of Connick, when I kind of wanted him scared of me. Because Arcturans do, after all, stink — not good public relations at all when your product smells like well-rotted garlic buds a few hundred feet away. I didn't want the voters smelling them.

And most of all because of the inference that I was sure any red-blooded, stubborn-minded, confused voter would draw: Jeez, Sam, you hear about that Arcturan coming to spy on us? Yeah, Charlie, the damn bugs are practically accusing us of rigging the election. Damn right, Sam, and you know what else? They stink, Sam.

Half an hour later I got a direct call from Haber. "Gunner boy! Good God! Oh, this is the reeking end!"

I said, "It sounds to me like you've found out about the Arcturan on the Truce Team."

"You know? And you didn't tell *me?*"

Well, I had been about to ream him for not telling *me,* but obviously that wasn't going to do any good. I tried, anyway, but he fell back on his fat ignorance. "They didn't clue me in from Chicago. Can I help that? Be fair now, Gunner boy!"

Gunner boy very fairly hung up.

I was beginning to feel very sleepy. For a moment I debated taking a brisk-up pill, but the mild buzz Connick's liquor had left with me was pleasant enough, and besides, it was getting late. I went to the hotel suite Candace had reserved for me and crawled into bed.

It only took me a few minutes to fall asleep, but I was faintly aware of an odor. It was the same hotel the Truce Team was staying at.

I couldn't really be smelling this Arcturan, Knafti. It was just my imagination. That's what I told myself as I dialed for sleep and drifted off.

The pillow-phone hummed, and Candace's voice said out of it, "Wake up and get decent, Gunner, I'm coming up."

I managed to sit up, shook my head, and took a few whiffs of amphetamine. As always, it woke me right up, but at the usual price of feeling that I hadn't had quite enough sleep. Still, I got into a robe and was in the bathroom fixing breakfast when she knocked on the door. "It's open," I called. "Want some coffee?"

"Sure, Gunner." She came and stood in the doorway, watching me turn the Hilsch squirt to full boil and fill two cups. I spooned dry coffee into them and turned the squirt to cold. "Orange juice?" She took the coffee and shook her head, so I just mixed one glassful, swallowed it, tossed the glass in the disposal hamper, and took the coffee into the other room. The bed had stripped itself already; it was now a couch, and I leaned back on it, drinking my coffee. "All right, honey," I said, "what's the dirt on Connick?"

She hesitated, then opened her bag and took out a photofax and handed it to me. It was a reproduction of an old steel engraving headed, in antique script, *The Army of the United States,* and it said:

Be it known to all men that
DANIEL T. CONNICK
ASIN Aj-32880515

has this date been separated from the service of the United States for the convenience of the government; and

Be it further known to all men that the conditions of his discharge are
DISHONORABLE

"Well, what do you know!" I said. "You see, honey? There's always something."

Candace finished her coffee, set the cup down neatly on a windowsill, and took out a cigarette. That was like her: She always did one thing at a time, an orderly sort of mind that I couldn't match—and couldn't stand, either. Undoubtedly she was thinking it, too, but there wasn't any nostalgia in her voice when she said: "You went and saw him last night, didn't you? . . . And you're still going to knife him?"

I said, "I'm going to see that he is defeated in the election, yes. That's what they pay me for. Me and some others."

"No, Gunner," she said, "that's not what M & B pay *me* for, if that's what you mean, because there isn't that much money."

I got up and went over beside her. "More coffee? No? Well, I guess I don't want any, either. Honey—"

Candace stood up, crossed the room, and sat down in a straight-backed chair. "You wake up all of a sudden, don't you? Don't change the subject. We were talking about—"

"We were talking," I told her, "about a job that we're paid to do. All right, you've done one part of it for me—you got me what I wanted on Connick."

I stopped, because she was shaking her head. "I'm not so sure I did."

"How's that?"

"Well, it's not on the fax, but I know why he got his DD. 'Desertion of hazardous duty.' On the Moon, in the U.N. Space Force. The year was 1998."

I nodded, because I understood what she was talking about. Connick wasn't the only one. Half the Space Force had cracked up that year. November. A heavy Leonid strike of meteorites and a solar flare at the same time. The Space Force top brass had decided they had to crack down and asked the U.S. Army to court-martial every soldier who cut and ran for an underground shelter, and the Army had felt obliged to comply. "But most of them got Presidential clemency," I said. "He didn't?"

Candace shook her head. "He didn't apply."

"Um. Well, it's still on record." I dismissed the subject. "Something else. What about these Children?"

Candace put out her cigarette and stood up. "Why I'm here, Gunner. It was on your list. So—get dressed."

"For what?"

She grinned. "For my peace of mind, for one thing. Also for investigating the Children, like you say. I've made you an appointment at the hospital in fifty-five minutes."

You have to remember that I didn't know anything about the Children except rumors. Bless Haber, he hadn't thought it necessary to explain. And Candace only said, "Wait till we get to the hospital. You'll see for yourself."

Donnegan General was seven stories of cream-colored ceramic brick, air-controlled, wall-lighted throughout, tiny asepsis lamps sparkling blue where the ventilation ducts opened. Candace parked the car in an underground garage and led me to an elevator, then to a waiting room. She seemed to know her way around very well. She glanced at her watch, told me we were a couple of minutes early, and pointed to a routing map that was a mural with colored lights showing visitors the way to whatever might be their destination. It also showed, quite impressively, the size and scope of Donnegan General. The hospital had 22 fully equipped operating rooms, a specimen and transplant bank, X-ray and radiochemical departments, a cryogenics room, the most complete prosthesis installation on Earth, a geriatrics section, O.T. rooms beyond number . . .

And, of all things, a fully equipped and crowded pediatric wing.

I said, "I thought this was a V.A. facility."

"Exactly. Here comes our boy."

A Navy officer was coming in, hand and smile outstretched to Candace. "Hi, good to see you. And you must be Gunnarsen."

Candace introduced us as we shook hands. The fellow's name was Commander Whitling; she called him Tom. He said, "We'll have to move. Since I talked to you, there's been an all-hands evolution scheduled for eleven — some high brass inspection. I don't want to hurry you, but I'd like it if we were out of the way . . . this is a little irregular."

"Nice of you to arrange it," I said. "Lead on."

We went up a high-rise elevator and came out on the top floor of the building, into a corridor covered with murals of Disney and Mother Goose. From a sun deck came the tinkle of a music box. Three children, chasing each other down the hall, dodged past us, yelling. They made pretty good time, considering that two of them were on crutches. "What the hell are you doing here?" asked Commander Whitling sharply.

I looked twice, but he wasn't talking to me or the kids. He was talking to a man with a young face but a heavy black beard, who was standing behind a Donald Duck mobile, looking inconspicuous and guilty.

"Oh, hi, Mr. Whitling," the man said. "Jeez, I must've got lost again looking for the PX."

"Carhart," said the commander dangerously, "if I catch you in this wing again, you won't have to worry about the PX for a year. Hear me?"

"Well, jeez! All right, Mr. Whitling." As the man saluted and turned, his face wearing an expression of injury, I noticed that the left sleeve of his bathrobe was tucked, empty, into a pocket.

"You can't keep them out," said Whitling and spread his hands. "Well, all right, Mr. Gunnarsen, here it is. You're seeing the whole thing."

I looked carefully around. It was all children — limping children, stumbling children, pale children, weary children. "But what am I seeing, exactly?" I asked.

"Why, the Children, Mr. Gunnarsen. The ones we liberated. The ones the Arcturans captured on Mars."

And then I connected. I remembered about the capture of the colony on Mars.

Interstellar war is waged at the pace of a snail's crawl, because it takes so long to go from star to star. The main battles of our war with Arcturus had been fought no farther from Earth than the surface of Mars, and the fleet engagement around Orbit Saturn. Still, it had taken 11 years, first to last, from the surprise attack on the Martian colony to the armistice signed in Washington.

I remembered seeing a reconstructed tape of that Martian surprise attack. It was a summer's day—hot—at full noon, ice melted into water. The place was the colony around the Southern Springs. Out of the small descending sun a ship appeared.

It was a rocket. It was brilliant gold metal, and it came down with a halo of gold radiation around its splayed front, like the fleshy protuberance of a star-nosed mole. It landed with an electrical crackle on the fine-grained orange sand, and out of it came the Arcturans.

Of course, no one had known they were Arcturans then. They had swung around the sun in a long anecliptic orbit, watching and studying, and they had selected the small Martian outpost as the place to strike. In Mars gravity they were bipeds—two of their ropy limbs were enough to lift them off the ground— man tall, in golden pressure suits. The colonists came running out to meet them—and were killed. All of them. All of the adults.

The children, however, had not been killed, not that quickly or that easily, at least. Some had not been killed at all, and some of those were here in Donnegan General Hospital.

But not all.

Comprehension beginning to emerge in my small mind, I said, "Then these are the survivors."

Candace, standing very close to me, said, "Most of them, Gunner. The ones that aren't well enough to be sent back into normal life."

"And the others?"

"Well, they mostly don't have families—having been killed, you see. So they've been adopted out into foster homes here in Belport. A hundred and eight of them—isn't that right, Tom? And now maybe you get some idea of what you're up against."

There were something like a hundred of the Children in that wing, and I didn't see all of them. Some of them were not to be seen.

Whitling just told me about but couldn't show me the blood-temperature room, where the very young and very bad cases lived. They had a gnotobiotic atmosphere, a little rich in oxygen, a little more humid than the ambient air, plus pressure to help their weak metabolism keep oxygen spread in their parts. On their right, a little farther along, were the small individual rooms belonging to the worst cases of all. The contagious. The incurables. The unfortunates whose very appearance was bad for the others. Whitling was good enough to open polarizing shutters and let me look in on some of those where they lay (or writhed or stood like sticks) in permanent solitary. One of the Arcturan efforts had been transplantation, and the project seemed to have been directed by a whimsical person. The youngest was about three; the oldest in the late teens.

They were a disturbing lot, and if I have glossed lightly over what I felt, it is because what I felt is all too obvious.

Kids in trouble! Of course, those who had been put back into population weren't put back shocking as these. But they would pull at the heartstrings — they even pulled at mine — and every time a foster parent or a foster parent's neighbor or a casual passer-by on the street felt that heartstring tug, he would feel, too, a single thought: *The Arcturans did this.*

For after killing the potentially dangerous adults, they had caged the tractable small ones as valuable research specimens.

And I had hoped to counteract this with 500 Arcturan pets!

Whitling had been all this time taking me around the wing, and I could hear in his voice the sound of what I was up against, because he loved and pitied those kids. "Hi, Terry," he said on the sun deck, bending over a bed and patting its occupant on his snow-white hair. Terry smiled up at him. "Can't hear us, of course," said Whitling. "We grafted in new auditory nerves four weeks ago — I did it myself — but they're not surviving. Third try, too. And, of course, each attempt is a worse risk than the one before: antibodies."

I said, "He doesn't look more than five years old." Whitling nodded. "But the attack on the colony was — "

"Oh, I see what you mean," said Whitling. "The Arcturans were, of course, interested in reproduction too. Ellen — she left us a couple of weeks ago — was only thirteen, but she'd had six children. Now this is Nancy."

Nancy was perhaps 12, but her gait and arm coordination were those of a toddler. She came stumbling in after a ball, stopped, and regarded me with dislike and suspicion. "Nancy's one of our cures," Whitling said proudly. He followed my eyes. "Oh, nothing wrong there," he said. "Mars-bred. She hasn't adjusted to Earth gravity, is all; she isn't slow — the ball's bouncing too fast. Here's Sam."

Sam was a near-teen-ager, giggling from his bed as he tried what was obviously the extremely wearing exercise of lifting his head off the mattress. A candy-striped practical nurse was counting time for him as he touched chin to chest, one and two, one and two. He did it five times, then slumped back, grinning. "Sam's central nervous system was almost gone," Whitling said fondly. "But we're making progress. Nervous tissue regeneration, though, is awfully — " I wasn't listening; I was looking at Sam's grin, which showed black and broken teeth. "Diet deficiency," said Whitling, following my look again.

"All right," I said, "I've seen enough, now I want to get out of here before they have me changing diapers. I thank you, Commander Whitling. I think I thank you. Which way is out?"

IV

I didn't want to go back to Haber's office. I was afraid of what the conversation might be like. But I had to get a fill-in on what had been happening with our work, and I had to eat.

So I took Candace back to my room and ordered lunch from room service.

I stood at the thermal window looking out at the city while Candace checked with the office. I didn't even listen, because Candace knew what I would want to know; I just watched Belport cycle through an average dull Monday at my feet. Belport was a radial town, with an urban center-cluster of the mushroom-shaped buildings that were popular 20 years ago. The hotel we were in was one, in fact, and from my window I could see three others looming above and below me, to right and left, and beyond them the cathedral spires of the apartment condominia of the residential districts. I could see a creeping serpent of gaily colored cars moving along one of the traffic-ways, pinpointed with sparks of our pro-referendum campaign parades. Or one of the opposition's. From 400 feet it didn't seem to matter.

"You know, honey," I said as she clicked off the 3-V, "there isn't any sense to this. I admit the kids are sad cases, and who can resist kids in trouble? But they don't have one solitary damned thing to do with whether or not the Arcturans should have a telemetry and tracking station out on the lake."

Candace said, "Weren't you the man who told me that logic didn't have anything to do with public relations?" She came to the window beside me, turned, and half-sat on the ledge and read from her notes: "Survey index off another half-point . . . . Haber says be sure to tell you that's a victory — would have been off two points at least without the Arcats. Supplier letters out. Chicago approves budget overdraft. And that's all that matters."

"Thanks." The door chimed, and she left me to let the waiter in with our lunch. I watched her without much appetite, except maybe for the one thing that I knew wasn't on the menu: Candace herself. But I tried to eat.

Candace did not seem to be trying to help me eat. In fact, she did something that was quite out of character for her. All the way through lunch she kept talking, and the one subject she kept talking about was the kids. I heard about Nina, who was 15 when she came to Donnegan General and had been through the occupation all the way — who wouldn't talk to anybody and weighed 51 pounds and screamed unless she was allowed to hide under the bed. "And after six months," said Candace, "They gave her a hand-puppet, and she finally talked through *that.*"

"How'd you find all this out?" I asked.

"From Tom. And then there were the germ-free kids . . ."

She told me about them, and about the series of injections and marrow transplants that they had needed to restore the body's immune reaction without killing the patient. And the ones with auditory and vocal nerves destroyed, apparently because the Arcturans were investigating the question of whether humans could think rationally in the absence of articulate words. The ones raised on chemically pure glucose for dietary studies. The induced bleeders. The kids with no sense of touch, and the kids with no developed musculature.

"Tom told you all this?"

"And lots more, Gunner. And remember, these are the survivors. Some of the kids who were deliberately—"

"How long have you known Tom?"

She put down her fork, sugared her coffee, and took a sip, looking at me over the cup. "Oh, since I've been here. Two years. Since before the kids came, of course."

"Pretty well, I judge."

"Oh, yes."

"He really likes those kids—I could see that. And so do you." I swallowed some more of my own coffee, which tasted like diluted pig swill, and reached for a cigarette and said, "I think maybe I waited too long about the situation here, wouldn't you say?"

"Why, yes, Gunner," she said carefully, "I think you maybe missed the boat."

"I tell you what else I think, honey. I think you're trying to tell me something, and it isn't all about Proposition Four on the ballot next week."

And she said, not irrelevantly, "As a matter of fact, Gunner, I'm going to marry Tom Whitling on Christmas Day."

I sent her back to the office and stretched out on my bed, smoking and watching the smoke being sucked into the wall vents. It was rather peaceful and quiet because I'd told the desk to hold all calls until further notice, and I wasn't feeling a thing.

Perfection is so rare that it is interesting to find a case in which one has been perfectly wrong all the way.

If I had taken out my little list, then I could have checked off all the points. One way or another. I hadn't fired Haber, and in fact, I really didn't want to anymore, because he wasn't much worse than I was at this particular job; the record showed it. I had investigated the Children, all right. A little late. I had investigated Connick, the number one opponent to the proposition, and what I had found would hurt Connick, all right, but I couldn't really see how it would help do our job. And I certainly wasn't going to marry Candace Harmon.

Come to think of it, I thought, lighting another cigarette from the stub of the old one, there had been a fifth item, and I had blown that one, too.

The classics of public relations clearly show how little reason has to do with M/R, and yet I had allowed myself to fall into that oldest and most imbecilic of traps set for flacks. Think of history's master strokes of flackery: "The Jews stabbed Germany in the back!" "Seventy-eight (or fifty-nine, or one hundred and three) card-carrying Communists in the State Department!" "I will go to Korea!" It is not enough for a theme to be rational; indeed it is *wrong* for a theme to be rational if you want to move men's glands, because, above all else, it must seem new and fresh and of such revolutionary simplicity that it illuminates an enormous, confused, and disagreeable problem in a fresh and hopeful light. Or so it must seem to the Average Man. And since he has spent any number of surly, worried hours groping for some personal salvation in the face of a bankrupt Germany or a threat of subversion or a war that is going nowhere, no *rational* solution can ever meet those strictures . . . since he has already considered all the rational solutions and found either that they are useless or that the cost is more than he wants to pay.

So what I should have concentrated on in Belport was the bright, irrational, distractive issue. The Big Lie, if you will. And I had hardly found even a Sly Insinuation.

It was interesting to consider in just how many ways I had done the wrong thing. Including maybe the wrongest of all: I had let Candace Harmon get away. And then in these thoughts, myself almost despising, haply the door chimed, and I opened it, and there was this fellow in Space Force olive-greens saying, "Come along, Mr. Gunnarsen, the Truce Team wants to talk to you."

For one frozen moment there, I was 19 years old again. I was a Rocketman 3/c on the Moon, guarding the Aristarchus base against invaders from outer space. (We thought that to be a big joke at the time. Shows how unfunny a joke can turn.) This fellow was a colonel, and his name was Peyroles, and he took me down the corridor, to a private elevator I had never known was there, up to the flat dome of the mushroom and into a suite that made my suite look like the cellar under a dog run in Old Levittown. The reek was overpowering. By then I had gotten over my quick response to the brass, and I took out a ker-pak and held it to my nose. The colonel did not even look at me.

"Sit down!" barked the colonel, and left me in front of an unlighted fireplace. Something was going on; I could hear voices from another room, a lot of them:

"— burned one in effigy, and by God we'll burn a real one —"

"— smells like a skunk —"

"— turns my stomach!" And that last fellow, whoever he was, was pretty near right at that — although actually in the few seconds since I'd entered the suite I had almost forgotten the smell. It was funny how you got used to it. Like a ripe cheese: The first whiff knocked you sick, but pretty soon the olfactory nerves got the hang of the thing and built up a defense.

"—all right, the war's over, and we have to get along with them, but a man's home town—"

Whatever it was that was going on in the other room, it was going on loudly. Tempers were always short when Arcturans were around, because the smell, of course, put everybody on edge. People don't like bad smells. They're not nice. They remind us of sweat and excrement, which we have buttressed our lives against admitting as real, personal facts. Then there was a loud military yell for order—I recognized the colonel, Peyroles—and then a voice that sounded queerly not-quite-human, although it spoke in English. An Arcturan? What was his name, Knafti? But I had understood they couldn't make human sounds.

Whoever it was, he put an end to the meeting. The door opened.

Through it I could see a couple of dozen hostile backs, leaving through another door, and coming toward me the Space Force colonel, a very young man with a pale angel's face and a dragging limp, in civilian clothes . . . and, yes, the Arcturan. It was the first one I had ever been with at so close range, in so small a group. He wobbled toward me on four or six of his coat-hanger limbs, breathing-thorax encased in a golden shell, his mantis face and bright black eyes staring at me.

Peyroles closed the door behind them.

He turned to me and said, "Mr. Gunnarsen . . . Knafti . . . Timmy Brown."

I hadn't the ghost of a clue whether to offer to shake, and if so, with what. Knafti, however, merely regarded me gravely. The boy nodded. I said: "I'm glad to meet you, gentlemen. As you perhaps know, I tried to set up an appointment before, but your people turned me down. I take it now the shoe is on the other foot."

Colonel Peyroles frowned toward the door he had just shut—there were still noises behind it—but said to me, "You're quite right. That was a meeting of a civic leaders' committee—"

The door interrupted him by opening, and a man leaned through and yelled: "Peyroles! Can that thing understand white man's talk? I hope so. I hope it hears me when I say that I'm going to make it my personal business to take it apart if it's still in Belport this time tomorrow. And if any human being, or so-called human being like you, gets in the way, I'll take him apart, too!" He slammed the door without waiting for an answer.

"You see?" said Peyroles gruffly, angrily. Things like that would never have happened with well-tempered troops. "That's what we want to talk to you about."

"I see," I said, and I did see, very clearly, because that fellow who had leaned through the door had been the Arcturan-property-sale standard bearer we had counted on, old—what had Connick called him?—old Slits-and-fits

Schlitz, the man we were attempting to elect to get our proposition through.

Judging by the amount of noise I'd heard from the citizens' delegation, there was lynching in the atmosphere. I could understand why they would reverse themselves and ask for me, before things got totally out of control and wound up in murder, if you call killing an Arcturan murder —

— although, it occurred to me, lynching Knafti might not be the worst thing that could happen; public sentiment might bounce back —

I shoved that thought out of my mind and got down to business. "What, exactly?" I asked. "I gather you want me to do something about your image."

Knafti sat himself down, if that's what Arcturans do, on a twining-rack. The pale boy whispered something to him, then came to me. "Mr. Gunnar-sen," he said, "I am Knafti." He spoke with a great precision of vowels and a stress at the end of each sentence, as though he had learned English out of a handbook. I had no trouble in understanding him. At least, not in understanding what it was he said. It did take me a moment to comprehend what he meant, and then Peyroles had to help.

"He means at this moment he's speaking for Knafti," said the colonel. "Interpreter. See?"

The boy moved his lips for a moment — shifting gears, it seemed — and said, "That is right, I am Timmy *Brown. Knafti's* translator and assis*tant!*"

"Then ask Knafti what he wants from me." I tried to say it the way he had — a sort of sneeze for the "K" and an indescribable whistle for the "f."

Timmy Brown moved his lips again and said, "I, Knafti, wish you to stop . . . to leave . . . to discontinue your operation in Bel*port.*"

From the twining-tree the Arcturan waved his ropy limbs and chittered like a squirrel. The boy chirped back and said: "I, Knafti, commend you on your effective work, but stop *it.*"

"By which," rumbled Colonel Peyroles, "he means knock it off."

"Go fight a space war, Peyroles. Timmy — I mean, Knafti, this is the job I'm paid to do. The Arcturan Confederacy itself hired us. I take my orders from Arthur S. Bigelow, Jr., and I carry them out whether Knafti likes it or not."

Chirp and chitter between Knafti and the pale, limping boy. The Arcturan left his twining-tree and moved to the window, looking out into the sky and the copter traffic. Timmy Brown said: "It does not matter what your orders may be. I, Knafti, tell you that your work is harm*ful.*" He hesitated, mumbling to himself. "We do not wish to obtain our base here at the cost of what is true, and —" he turned imploringly to the Arcturan — "it is apparent you are attempting to change the *truth.*"

He chirped at the Arcturan, who took his blind black eyes from the window and came toward us. Arcturans don't walk, exactly. They drag themselves on the lower part of the thorax. Their limbs are supple and thin, and what are not used for support are used for gestures. Knafti used a number of his now as he chirped one short series of sounds at the boy.

"Otherwise," Timmy Brown finished off, "I, Knafti, tell you we will have to fight this war over *again.*"

As soon as I was back in my room, I messaged Chicago for orders and clarification and got back the answer I expected:

Hold everything. Referring matter to ASB-jr. Await instructions.

So I awaited. The way I awaited was to call Candace at the office and get the latest sitrep. I told her about the near-riot in the Truce Team's suite and asked her what it was all about.

She shook her head. "We have their appointments schedule, Gunner. It just says, 'Meeting with civic leaders.' But one of the leaders has a secretary who goes to lunch with a girl from Records and Accounting here, and—"

"And you'll find out. All right, do that, and now what's the current picture?"

She began reading off briefing digests and field reports. They were mixed, but not altogether bad. Opinion sampling showed a small rise in favor of the Arcturans, in fact. It wasn't much, but it was the first plus change I had seen, and doubly puzzling because of Knafti's attitude and the brawl with the civic leaders.

I asked, "Why, honey?"

Candace's face in the screen was as puzzled as mine. "We're still digging."

"All right. Go on."

There were more pluses. The flower show had yielded surprisingly big profits in attitudes—among those who attended. Of course, they were only a tiny fraction of the population of Belport. The Arcats were showing a plus for us, too. Where we were down was in PTA meeting resolutions, in resignations from Candace's Arcturan-American Friendship League, in poor attendance at neighborhood *kaffeeklatsches.*

Now that I knew what to look for, I could see what the Children had done to us. In every family-situation sampling, the attitudes were measurably worse than when the subjects were interviewed in a nonfamily environment—at work, stopped on the street, in a theater.

The importance of that was just what I had told Connick. No man is a simple entity. He behaves one way when his self-image is as head of a family, another when he is at a cocktail party, another at work, another still when a pretty girl sits down beside him on a commutercopter. Elementary truths. But it had taken the M/R boys half a century to learn how to use them.

In this case the use was clear: Play down family elements, play up play. I ordered more floats, torchlight parades, and a teen-age beauty contest. I canceled the 14 picnic rallies we had planned and ordered a hold on the *kaffeeklatsches.*

I was not exactly obeying Chicago's orders. But it didn't matter. All this could be canceled with a single word, and, anyway, it was only nit-picking detail. The One Big Weeny still escaped me.

I lit a cigarette, thought for a minute, and said, "Honey, get me some of the synoptic extracts of opinion sampling from heads of families and particularly families containing some of the Children. I don't want the integration or analysis. Just the raw interviews, but with the scutwork left out."

And as soon as she was off the line, the Chicago circuit came in with a message they'd been holding:

> Query from ASB-jr. Provided top is taken off budget and your hand is freed, can you guarantee, repeat guarantee, win on referendum question?

It was not the response I had expected from them.

Still, it was a legitimate question. I took a moment to think it over.

Junior Bigelow had already given me a pretty free hand — as he always did; how else can a troubleshooter work? If he was now emphasizing that my hand was freed entirely, it would not be because he thought I hadn't understood him in the first place. Nor would it be because he suspected I might be cheese-paring secretarial salaries. He meant one thing: Win, no matter what.

Under those conditions, could I do it?

Well, of course I could win. Yes. Provided I found the One Big Weeny. You can always win an election, any election anywhere, provided you are willing to pay the right price.

It was finding the price to pay that was hard. Not just money. Sometimes the price you pay is a human being, in the role for which I had been lining up Connick. Throw a human sacrifice to the gods, and your prayer is granted. . . .

But was Connick the sacrifice the gods wanted? Would it help to defeat him, bearing in mind that his opponent was one of the men who had been screaming at Knafti in the Truce Team suite? And if so — had my knife enough edge to drain his blood?

Well, it always had had before. And if Connick wasn't the right man, I would find the man who was. I messaged back, short and sweet: Yes.

And in less than a minute, as though Junior had been standing by at the faxtape receiver, waiting for the word from me — and perhaps he had! — his reply came back:

> Gunner, we've lost the Arcturan Confederacy account. Arc Con liaison man says all bets off. They're giving notice of cancellation our contract, suggestion they will cancel entire armistice treaty, too. I don't have to tell you we need

them. Some possibility that showing strong results in Belport will get them back. That's what we have to play for. No holds barred, Gunner, win that election.

The office circuit chimed then. Probably it was Candace, but I didn't want to talk to her just then. I turned all the communication circuits to "hold," stripped down, climbed into the shower, set it for full needle spray, and let the water beat on me. It was not an aid to thought, it was a replacement for thought.

I didn't want to think anymore. I wanted time out.

I did not want to think about (a) whether the war would break out again, and, if so, in what degree I would have helped to bring that about; (b) what I was doing to Nice Guy Connick; (c) whether It Was All Worth It, or (d) how much I was going to dislike myself that coming Christmas Day. I only wanted to let the hot splash of scented foaming water anesthetize me. When my skin began to look pale and wrinkly, although I had not come to any conclusions or found any solutions, I came out, dressed, opened the communications circuits, and let them all begin blinking, ringing, and winking at once.

I took Candace first. She said, "Gunner! Dear Lord, have you heard about the Armistice Commission? They've just released a statement—"

"I heard. What else, honey?"

Good girl, she shifted gears without missing a beat. "Then there was that meeting of civic leaders in the Truce Team suite   "

"I saw. Feedback from the Armistice Commission's statement. What else?"

She glanced at the papers in her hand, hesitated, then said: "Nothing important. Uh—Gunner, that 3-V preempt for tonight—"

"Yeah, honey?"

"Do you want me to cancel it?"

I said, "No. You're right, we won't use the time for the Arcturan-American Friendship league or whatever we had scheduled, but you're wrong, we'll use the time some way. I don't know how right now."

"But Junior said—"

"Honey," I told her, "Junior says all sorts of things. Anybody looking to scalp me?"

"Well," she said, "there's Mr. Connick. I didn't think you'd want to see him."

"No, I'll see him. I'll see anybody."

"Anybody?" I had surprised her. She dove into her list again. "There's somebody from the Truce Team—"

"Make it everybody from the Truce Team."

"—and Commander Whitling from—"

"From the hospital. Sure, and tell him to bring some kids."

"— and . . ." She trailed off and looked at me. "Gunner, are you putting me on? You don't really want to see all these people."

I smiled and reached out and patted the viewphone. From her point of view it would look like an enormous cloudy hand closing in on her screen, but she would know what I meant. I said, "You could not be more wrong. I do. I want to see them all, the more the better, and the way I'd like to see them best is in my office all at once. So set it up, honey, because I'll be busy between now and then."

"Busy doing what, Gunner?"

"Busy trying to think of what I want to see them for." And I turned off the viewphone, got up, and walked out, leaving the others gobbling into emptiness behind me. What I needed was a long, long walk, and I took it.

When I was tired of walking, I went to the office and evicted Haber from his private quarters. I kept him standing by what had once been his own desk while I checked with Candace and found that she had made all my appointments for that evening; then I told him to get lost. "And thanks," I said.

He paused on his way to the door. "For what, Gunner?"

"For a very nice office to kill time in." I waved at the furnishings. "I wondered what you'd spent fifty grand on when I saw the invoices in the Chicago office, Haber, and I admit I thought there might have been a little padding. But I was wrong."

He said woundedly: "Gunner-boy! I wouldn't do anything like that."

"I believe you. Wait a minute." I thought for a second, then told him to send in some of the technical people and not to let anybody, repeat anybody, disturb me for any purpose whatever. I scared him good, too. He left, a shaken man, a little angry, a little admiring, a little excited inside, I think, at the prospect of seeing how the great man would get himself out of this one. Meanwhile the great man talked briefly to the technicians, took a ten-minute nap, drank the martinis out of his dinner tray, and pitched the rest of it in the dispos-all.

Then, as I had nearly an hour before the appointments Candace had set up for me, I scrounged around fat-cat Haber's office to see what entertainment it offered.

There were his files. I glanced at them and forgot them; there was nothing about the hoarded memoranda that interested me, not even for gossip. There were the books on his shelf. But I did not care to disturb the patina of dust that even the cleaning machines had not been able to touch. There was his private bar, and the collection of photographs in the end compartment of his desk drawer.

It looked like very dull times, waiting, until the studio men reported in that they had completed their arrangements at my request, and the 3-V tape-effects monitor could now be controlled by remote from my desk, and then I knew I had a pleasant way of killing any amount of time.

Have you ever played with the console of a 3-V monitor, backed by a library of tape-effects strips? It is very much like being God.

All that the machine does is take the stored videotapes that are in its files and play them back. But it also manipulates size and perspective or superimposes one over another . . . so that you can, as I, in fact, have done, put the living person of someone you don't like in a position embarrassing to him, and project it on a montage screen so that only a studio tech can find the dots on the pattern where the override betrays its presence.

Obviously, this is a way out of almost any propaganda difficulty, since it is child's play to make up any event you like and give it the seeming of reality.

Of course, everybody knows it can be done. So the evidence of one's own eyes is no longer quite enough, even for a voter. And the laws can cut you down. I had thought of whomping up some frightful frame around Connick, for example. But it wouldn't work; no matter when I did it, there would still be time for the other side to spread the word of an electoral fraud, and a hoax of this magnitude would make its own way onto the front pages. So I used the machine for something much more interesting to me. I used it as a toy.

I started by dialing the lunar base at Aristarchus for background, found a corps of Rocketmen marching off in the long lunar step, patched my own face onto one of the helmeted figures, and zoomed in and out with the imaginary camera, watching R3/c Odin Gunnarsen as a boy of 19, scared witless but doing his job. He was a pretty nice boy, I thought objectively, and wondered what had gone wrong with him later. I abandoned that and sought for other amusements. I found Candace's images on tape in the files and pleasured myself with her for a time. Her open, friendly face gave some dignity to the fantastic bodies of half a dozen 3-V strippers in the files, but I stopped that child's game.

I looked for a larger scope. I spread the whole panoply of the heavens across the screen of the tape machine. I sought out the crook of the Big Dipper's handle, traced its arc across half the heavens until I located orange Arcturus. Then I zoomed in on the star, as littler stars grew larger and hurtled out of range around it, sought its seven gray-green planets and located Number Five among them, the watery world that Knafti had spawned upon. I bade the computing mind inside the tape machine reconstruct the events of the orbit bombing for me and watched hell-bombs splash enormous mushrooms of poisonous foam into the Arcturan sky, whipping the island cities with tidal waves and drowning them in death.

Then I destroyed the whole planet. I turned Arcturan into a nova and watched the hot driven gases sphere out to embrace the planet, boil its seas, slag its cities . . . and found myself sweating. I ordered another drink from the dispenser and switched the machine off. And then I became aware that the pale blue light over the door to Haber's office was glowing insistently. It was time; my visitors had arrived.

Connick had brought his kids along, three of them; the lover from Donnegan General had brought two more; Knafti and Colonel Peyroles had Timmy Brown. "Welcome to Romper Room," I said. "They're making lynch mobs young this year."

They all yelled at me at once — or all but Knafti, whose tweeting chitter just didn't have the volume to compete. I listened, and when they showed signs of calming down, I reached into fat cat Haber's booze drawer and poured myself a stiff one and said, "All right, which of you creeps want first crack?" And they boiled up again while I drank my drink. All of them, except Candace Harmon, who only stood by the door and looked at me.

So I said, "All right, Connick, you first. Are you going to make me spread it all over the newscasts that you had a dishonorable discharge? . . . And by the way, maybe you'd like to meet my assistant blackmailer; Miss Harmon over there dug up the dirt on you."

Her boyfriend yelped, but Candace just went on looking. I didn't look back, but kept my eyes on Connick. He squinted his eyes, put his hands in his pockets, and said, with considerable self-restraint, "You know I was only seventeen years old when that happened."

"Oh, sure. I know more. You had a nervous breakdown the year after your discharge, space cafard, as they call it on the soapies. Yellow fever is what we called it on the Moon."

He glanced quickly at his kids, the two who were his own and the one who was not, and said rapidly: "You know I could have had that DD reversed —"

"But you didn't. The significant fact isn't that you deserted. The significant fact is that you were loopy. And, I'd say, still are."

Timmy Brown stuttered: "One mo*ment*. I, Knafti, have asked that you cease —"

But Connick brushed him aside. "Why, Gunnarsen?"

"Because I intend to win this election. I don't care what it costs — especially what it costs you."

"But, I, Knafti, have instructed —" That was Timmy Brown trying again.

"The Armistice Commission issued orders —" That was Peyroles.

"I don't know which is worse, you or the bugs!" And that was Candace's little friend from the hospital, and they all were talking at once again. Even Knafti came dragging toward me on his golden slug's belly, chirruping and hooting, and Timmy Brown was actually weeping as he tried to tell me I was wrong, I had to stop, the whole thing was against orders and why wouldn't I de*sist?*

I shouted: "Shut up, all of you!"

They didn't, but the volume level dropped minutely. I rode over it: "What the hell do I care what any of you want? I'm paid to do a job. My job is to make people act in a certain way. I do it. Maybe tomorrow I'll be paid to make them act the opposite way, and I'll do that, too. Anyway, who the hell are you to order me around? A stink-bug like you, Knafti? A GI quack like yourself, Whitling? Or you, Connick. A—"

"A candidate for public office," he said clearly. And I give him much mana—he didn't shout, but he talked right over me. "And as such I have an obligation—"

But I outyelled him, anyway. "Candidate! You're a candidate right up till the minute I tell the voters you're a nut, Connick. And then you're dead! And I will tell them, I promise, if—"

I didn't get a chance to finish that sentence, because all three of Connick's kids were diving at me, his own two and the other one. They sent papers flying off Haber's desk and smashed his sand-crystal decanter, but they didn't get to my throat, where they clearly were aimed, because Connick and Timmy Brown dragged them back. Not easily.

I allowed myself a sneer. "And what does that prove? Your kids like you, I admit—even the one from Mars. The one that Knafti's people used for vivisection—that Knafti himself worked over, likely as not. Nice picture, right? Your bug-buddy there, killing babies, destroying kids . . . or didn't you know that Knafti himself was one of the boss bugs on the baby-killing project?"

Timmy Brown shrieked wildly, "You don't know what you are do*ing.* It was not Knafti's fault at *all!*" His ashen face was haggard, his rotten teeth bared in a grimace. And he was weeping.

If you apply heat to a single molecule, it will take off like a tom with a spark under his tail, but you cannot say where it will go. If you heat a dozen molecules, they will fling out in all directions, but you still do not know which directions they will be. If, however, you heat a few billion, about as many as are in a thimble of dilute gas, you know where they will go: they will expand. Mass action. You can't tell what a single molecule may do— call it the molecule's free will if you like—but masses obey mass laws. Masses of anything, even so small a mass as the growling troop that confronted me in Haber's office. I let them yell, and all the yelling was at me. Even Candace was showing the frown and the darkening of the eyes and the working of the lips, although she watched me as silently and steadily as ever.

Connick brought it to a head. "All *right,* everybody," he yelled, "now listen to me! Let's get this thing straightened out!"

He stood up, a child gripped by each elbow, and the third, the youngest, trapped between him and the door. He looked at me with such loathing that I could feel it — and didn't like it, either, although it was no more than I had expected, and he said: "It's true. Sammy, here, was one of the kids from Mars. Maybe that has made me think things I shouldn't have thought — he's my kid now, and when I think of those stink bugs cutting — "

He stopped himself and turned to Knafti. "Well, I see something. A man who would do a thing like that would be a fiend. I'd cut his heart out with my bare hands. But you aren't a man."

Grimly he let go of the kids and strode toward Knafti. "I can't forgive you. God help me, it isn't possible. But I can't blame you — exactly — any more than I can blame lightning for striking my house. I think I was wrong. Maybe I'm wrong now. But — I don't know what you people do — I'd like to shake your hand. Or whatever the hell it is you've got there. I've been thinking of you as a perverted murderer and a filthy animal, but I'll tell you right now, I'd rather work together with you — for your base, for peace, for whatever we can get together on — than with some human beings in this room!"

I didn't stay to watch the tender scene that followed.

I didn't have to, since the cameras and tape recorders that the studio people had activated for me behind every one-way mirror in the room would be watching for me. I could only hope they had not missed a single word or scream, because I didn't think I could do that scene over again.

I opened the door quietly and left. And as I was going, I caught the littlest Connick kid sneaking past me, headed for the 3-V set in the waiting room, and snaked out an arm to stop him. "Stinker!" he hissed. "Rat fink!"

"You may be right," I told him, "but go back and keep your father company. You're in on living history today."

"Nuts! I always watch *Dr. Zhivago* on Monday nights, and it's on in five minutes, and — "

"Not tonight it isn't, son. You can hold that against me, too. We preempted the time for a different show entirely."

I escorted him back into the room, closed the door, picked up my coat, and left.

Candace was waiting for me with the car. She was driving it herself.

"Will I make the nine-thirty flight?" I asked.

"Sure, Gunner." She steered onto the autotraffic lane, put the car on servo, and dialed the scatport, then sat back and lit a cigarette for each of us. I took one and looked morosely out the window.

Down below us, on the slow-traffic level, we were passing a torchlight parade, with floats and glee clubs and free beer at the major pedestrian intersections. I opened the glove compartment and took out field glasses, looked through them —

"Oh, you don't have to check up, Gunner. I took care of it. They're all plugging the program."

"I see they are." Not only were the marchers carrying streamers that advertised our preempt show that was now already beginning to be on the air, but the floats carried projection screens and amplifiers. You couldn't look anywhere in the procession without seeing Knafti, huge and hideous in his gold carapace, clutching the children and protecting them against the attack of that monster from another planet, me. The studio people had done a splendid job of splicing in no time at all. The whole scene was there on camera, as real as I had just lived it.

"Want to listen?" Candace fished out and passed me a hyperboloid longhearer, but I didn't need it. I remembered what the voices would be saying. There would be Connick denouncing me. Timmy Brown denouncing me. The kids denouncing me, all of them. Colonel Peyroles denouncing me, Commander Whitling denouncing me, even Knafti denouncing me. All that hate and only one target.

Me.

"Of course, Junior'll fire you. He'll have to, Gunner."

I said, "I need a vacation, anyway." It wouldn't matter. Sooner or later, when the pressure was off, Junior would find a way to hire me back. Once the lawsuits had been settled. Once the Armistice Commission could finish its work. Once I could be put on the payroll inconspicuously, at an inconspicuous job in an inconspicuous outpost of the firm. With an inconspicuous future.

We slid over the top of a spiraling ramp and down into the parking bays of the scatport. "So long, honey," I said, "and Merry Christmas to you both."

"Oh, Gunner! I wish —"

But I knew what she really wished, and I wouldn't let her finish. I said, "He's a nice fellow, Whitling. And you know? I'm not."

I didn't kiss her good-bye.

The scatjet was ready for boarding. I fed my ticket into the check-in slot, got the green light as the turnstile clicked open, entered the plane, and took a seat on the far side, by the window.

You can win any cause if you care to pay the price. All it takes is one human sacrifice.

By the time the scatjet began to roar, to quiver, and to turn on its axis away from the terminal, I had faced the fact that the price once and for all was paid. I saw Candace standing there on the roof of the loading dock, her skirts whipped by the back-blast. She didn't wave to me, but she didn't go away as long as I could see her standing on the platform.

Then, of course, she would go back to her job and ultimately on Christmas morning to that nice guy at the hospital. Haber would stay in charge of his no-longer-important branch office. Connick would win his campaign. Knafti would transact his incomprehensible business with Earth, and if any of them ever thought of me again, it would be with loathing, anger, and contempt. But that is the way to win an election. You have to pay the price. It was just the breaks of the game that the price of this one was me.

2066: Election Day
Michael Shaara

Michael Shaara (b. 1929) is a distinguished American novelist and a winner of the Pulitzer Prize for fiction who published a small number of excellent science-fiction stories in the genre magazines early in his career, most of which were collected as *Soldier Boy* (1982). He has recently indicated an interest in returning to the field.

In "2066: Election Day," Shaara examines an idea first put forth thousands of years ago by Plato — a system in which leadership goes to the best qualified.

Early that afternoon Professor Larkin crossed the river into Washington, a thing he always did on Election Day, and sat for a long while in the Polls. It was still called the Polls, in this year 2066 A.D., although what went on inside bore no relation at all to the elections of primitive American history. The Polls was now a single enormous building which rose out of the green fields where the ancient Pentagon had once stood. There was only one of its kind in Washington, only one Polling Place in each of the forty-eight states, but since few visited the Polls nowadays, no more were needed.

In the lobby of the building, a great hall was reserved for visitors. Here you could sit and watch the many-colored lights dancing and flickering on the hung panels above, listen to the weird but strangely soothing hum and click of the vast central machine. Professor Larkin chose a deep soft chair near the long line of booths and sat down. He sat for a long while smoking his pipe, watching the people go in and out of the booths with strained, anxious looks on their faces.

Professor Larkin was a lean, boyish-faced man in his late forties. With the pipe in his hand he looked much more serious and sedate than he normally felt, and it often bothered him that people were able to guess his profession almost instantly. He had a vague idea that it was not becoming to look like a college professor, and he often tried to change his appearance — a loud tie here, a sport coat there—but it never seemed to make any difference. He remained what he was, easily identifiable, Professor Harry L. (Lloyd) Larkin, Ph.D., Dean of the Political Science Department at a small but competent college just outside of Washington.

It was his interest in Political Science which drew him regularly to the Polls at every election. Here he could sit and feel the flow of American history in the making, and recognize, as he did now, perennial candidates for the presidency. Smiling, he watched a little old lady dressed in pink, very tiny and very fussy, flit doggedly from booth to booth. Evidently her test marks had not been very good. She was clutching her papers tightly in a black-gloved hand, and there was a look of prim irritation on her face. But *she* knew how to run this country, by George, and one of these days *she* would be President. Harry Larkin chuckled.

But it did prove one thing. The great American dream was still intact. The tests were open to all. And anyone could still grow up to be President of the United States.

Sitting back in his chair, Harry Larkin remembered his own childhood, how the great battle had started. There were examinations for everything in those days—you could not get a job streetcleaning without taking a civil-service examination—but public office needed no qualifications at all. And first the psychologists, then the newspapers, had begun calling it a national disgrace. And, considering the caliber of some of the men who went into public office, it *was* a national disgrace. But then psychological testing came of age, really became an exact science, so that it was possible to test a man thoroughly—his knowledge, his potential, his personality. And from there it was a short but bitterly fought step to—SAM.

SAM. UNCLE SAM, as he had been called originally, the last and greatest of all electronic brains. Harry Larkin peered up in unabashed awe at the vast battery of lights which flickered above him. He knew that there was more to SAM than just this building, more than all the other forty-eight buildings put together, that SAM was actually an incredibly enormous network of electronic cells which had its heart in one place, but its arms in all. It was an unbelievably complex analytical computer which judged a candidate far more harshly and thoroughly than the American public could ever have judged him. And crammed in its miles of memory banks lay almost every bit of knowledge mankind had yet discovered. It was frightening, many thought of it as a monster, but Harry Larkin was unworried.

The thirty years since the introduction of SAM had been thirty of America's happiest years. In a world torn by continual war and unrest, by dictators, puppet governments, the entire world had come to know and respect the American President for what he was: the best possible man for the job. And there was no doubt that he was the best. He had competed for the job in fair examination against the cream of the country. He had to be a truly remarkable man to come out on top.

The day was long since past when just any man could handle the presidency. A full century before, men had begun dying in office, cut down in their prime by the enormous pressures of the job. And that was a hundred years ago. Now the job had become infinitely more complex, and even now President Creighton lay on his bed in the White House, recovering from a stroke, an old, old man after one term of office.

Harry Larkin shuddered to think what might have happened had America not adopted the system of "the best qualified man." All over the world this afternoon men waited for word from America, the calm and trustworthy words of the new President, for there had been no leader in America since President Creighton's stroke. His words would mean more to the people, embroiled as they were in another great crisis, than the words of their own leaders. The leaders of other countries fought for power, bought it, stole it, only rarely earned it. But the American President was known the world over for his honesty, his intelligence, his desire for peace. Had he not those qualities, "old UNCLE SAM" would never have elected him.

Eventually, the afternoon nearly over, Harry Larkin rose to leave. By this time the President was probably already elected. Tomorrow the world would return to peace. Harry Larkin paused in the door once before he left, listened to the reassuring hum from the great machine. Then he went quietly home, walking quickly and briskly toward the most enormous fate on Earth.

"My name is Reddington. You know me?"

Harry Larkin smiled uncertainly into the phone.

"Why . . . yes, I believe so. You are, if I'm not mistaken, general director of the Bureau of Elections."

"Correct," the voice went on quickly, crackling in the receiver, "and you are supposed to be an authority on Political Science, right?"

"Supposed to be?" Larkin bridled. "Well, it's distinctly possible that I —"

"All right, all right," Reddington blurted. "No time for politeness. Listen, Larkin, this is a matter of urgent national security. There will be a car at your door — probably be there when you put this phone down. I want you to get into it and hop on over here. I can't explain further. I know your devotion to the country, if it wasn't for that I would not have called you. But don't ask questions. Just come. No time. Good-by."

There was a click. Harry Larkin stood holding the phone for a long shocked moment, then he heard a pounding at the door. The housekeeper was out, but he waited automatically before going to answer it. He didn't like to be rushed, and he was confused. Urgent national security? Now what in blazes —

The man at the door was an Army major. He was accompanied by two young but very large sergeants. They identified Larkin, then escorted him politely but firmly down the steps into a staff car. Larkin could not help feeling abducted, and a completely characteristic rage began to rise in him. But he remembered what Reddington had said about national security and so sat back quietly with nothing more than an occasional grumble.

He was driven back into Washington. They took him downtown to a small but expensive apartment house he could neither identify nor remember, and escorted him briskly into an elevator. When they reached the suite upstairs they opened the door and let him in, but did not follow him. They turned and went quickly away.

Somewhat ruffled, Larkin stood for a long moment in the hall by the hat table, regarding a large rubber plant. There was a long sliding door before him, closed, but he could hear an argument going on behind it. He heard the word "SAM" mentioned many times, and once he heard a clear sentence: ". . . Government by machine. I will not tolerate it!" Before he had time to hear any more, the doors slid back. A small, square man with graying hair came out to meet him. He recognized the man instantly as Reddington.

"Larkin," the small man said, "glad you're here." The tension on his face showed also in his voice. "That makes all of us. Come in and sit down." He turned back into the large living room. Larkin followed.

"Sorry to be so abrupt," Reddington said, "but it was necessary. You will see. Here, let me introduce you around."

Larkin stopped in involuntary awe. He was used to the sight of important men, but not so many at one time, and never so close. There was Secretary Kell, of Agriculture, Wachsmuth, of Commerce, General Vines, Chief of Staff, and a battery of others so imposing that Larkin found his mouth hanging embarrassingly open. He closed it immediately.

Reddington introduced him. The men nodded one by one, but they were all deathly serious, their faces drawn, and there was now no conversation. Reddington waved him to a chair. Most of the others were standing, but Larkin sat.

Reddington sat directly facing him. There was a long moment of silence during which Larkin realized that he was being searchingly examined. He flushed, but sat calmly with his hands folded in his lap. After a while Reddington took a deep breath.

"Dr. Larkin," he said slowly, "what I am about to say to you will die with you. There must be no question of that. We cannot afford to have any word of this meeting, any word at all, reach anyone not in this room. This includes your immediate relatives, your friends, anyone—anyone at all. Before we continue, let me impress you with that fact. This is a matter of the gravest national security. Will you keep what is said here in confidence?"

"If the national interest—" Larkin began, then he said abruptly, "of course."

Reddington smiled slightly.

"Good. I believe you. I might add that just the fact of your being here, Doctor, means that you have already passed the point of no return . . . well, no matter. There is no time. I'll get to the point."

He stopped, looking around the room. Some of the other men were standing and now began to move in closer. Larkin felt increasingly nervous, but the magnitude of the event was too great for him to feel any worry. He gazed intently at Reddington.

"The Polls close tonight at eight o'clock." Reddington glanced at his watch. "It is now six-eighteen. I must be brief. Doctor, do you remember the prime directive that we gave to SAM when he was first built?"

"I think so," said Larkin slowly.

"Good. You remember then that there was one main order. SAM was directed to elect, quote, *the best qualified man.* Unquote. Regardless of any and all circumstances, religion, race, so on. The orders were clear — the best qualified man. The phrase has become world famous. But unfortunately" — he glanced up briefly at the men surrounding him — "the order was a mistake. Just whose mistake does not matter. I think perhaps the fault lies with all of us, but — it doesn't matter. What matters is this: SAM will not elect a president."

Larkin struggled to understand. Reddington leaned forward in his chair.

"Now follow me closely. We learned this only late this afternoon. We are always aware, as you no doubt know, of the relatively few people in this country who have a chance for the presidency. We know not only because they are studying for it, but because such men as these are marked from their childhood to be outstanding. We keep close watch on them, even to assigning the Secret Service to protect them from possible harm. There are only a very few. During this last election we could not find more than fifty. All of those people took the tests this morning. None of them passed."

He paused, waiting for Larkin's reaction. Larkin made no move.

"You begin to see what I'm getting at? *There is no qualified man.*"

Larkin's eyes widened. He sat bolt upright.

"Now it hits you. If none of those people this morning passed, there is no chance at all for any of the others tonight. What is left now is simply crackpots and malcontents. They are privileged to take the tests, but it means nothing. SAM is not going to select anybody. Because sometime during the last four years the presidency passed the final limit, the ultimate end of man's capabilities, and with scientific certainty we know that there is probably no man alive who is, according to SAM's directive, qualified."

"But," Larkin interrupted, "I'm not quite sure I follow. Doesn't the phrase 'elect the best qualified man' mean that we can at least take the best we've got?"

Reddington smiled wanly and shook his head.

"No. And that was our mistake. It was quite probably a psychological block, but none of us ever considered the possibility of the job surpassing human ability. Not then, thirty years ago. And we also never seemed to remember that SAM is, after all, only a machine. He takes the words to mean exactly what they say: Elect the best, comma, *qualified,* comma, man. But do you see, if there is *no* qualified man, SAM cannot possibly elect the best. So SAM will elect no one at all. Tomorrow this country will be without a president. And the result of that, more than likely, will mean a general war."

Larkin understood. He sat frozen in his chair.

"So you see our position," Reddington went on wearily. "There's nothing we can do. Re-electing President Creighton is out of the question. His stroke was permanent, he may not last the week. And there is no possibility of tampering with SAM, to change the directive. Because, as you know, SAM is foolproof, had to be. The circuits extend through all forty-eight states. To alter the machine at all requires clearing through all forty-eight entrances. We can't do that. For one thing, we haven't time. For another, we can't risk letting the world know there is no qualified man.

"For a while this afternoon, you can understand, we were stumped. What could we do? There was only one answer, we may come back to it yet. Give the presidency itself to SAM—"

A man from across the room, whom Larkin did not recognize, broke in angrily.

"Now, Reddington, I told you, that is government by machine! And I will not stand—"

"What else can you *do!*" Reddington whirled, his eyes flashing, his tension exploding now into rage. "Who else knows all the answers? Who else can compute in two seconds the tax rate for Mississippi, the parity levels for wheat, the probable odds on a military engagement? Who else but SAM! And why didn't we do it long ago, just feed the problems to *him,* SAM, and not go on killing man after man, great men, *decent* men like poor Jim Creighton, who's on his back now and dying because people like you—" He broke off suddenly and bowed his head. The room was still. No one looked at Reddington. After a moment he shook his head. His voice, when he spoke, was husky.

"Gentlemen, I'm sorry. This leads nowhere." He turned back to Larkin.

Larkin had begun to feel the pressure. But the presence of these men, of Reddington's obvious profound sincerity, reassured him. Creighton had been a great president, he had surrounded himself with some of the finest men in the country. Larkin felt a surge of hope that such men as these were available for one of the most critical hours in American history. For critical it was, and Larkin knew as clearly as anyone there what the absence of a president in the morning—no deep reassurance, no words of hope—would mean. He sat waiting for Reddington to continue.

"Well, we have a plan. It may work, it may not. We may all be shot. But this is where you come in. I hope for all our sakes you're up to it."

Larkin waited.

"The plan," Reddington went on, slowly, carefully, "is this, SAM has one defect. We can't tamper with it. But we *can* fool it. Because when the brain tests a man, it does not at the same time identify him. We do the identifying ourselves. So if a man named Joe Smith takes the personality tests and another man also named Joe Smith takes the Political Science tests, the machine has no way of telling them apart. Unless our guards supply the difference SAM will mark up the results of both tests to one Joe Smith. We can clear the guards, no problem there. The first problem was to find the eight men to take the eight tests."

Larkin understood. He nodded.

"Exactly. Eight specialists," Reddington said. "General Vines will take the Military; Burden, Psychology; Wachsmuth, Economics; and so on. You, of course, will take the Political Science. We can only hope that each man will come out with a high enough score in his own field so that the combined scores of our mythical 'candidate' will be enough to qualify him. Do you follow me?"

Larkin nodded dazedly. "I think so. But — "

"It should work. It has to work."

"Yes," Larkin murmured, "I can see that. But who, who will actually wind up — "

"As president?" Reddington smiled very slightly and stood up.

"That was the most difficult question of all. At first we thought there was no solution. Because a president must be so many things — consider. A president blossoms instantaneously, from nonentity, into the most important job on earth. Every magazine, every newspaper in the country immediately goes to work on his background, digs out his life story, anecdotes, sayings, and so on. Even a very strong fraud would never survive it. So the first problem was believability. The new president must be absolutely believable. He must be a man of obvious character, of obvious intelligence, but more than that, his former life must fit the facts: he must have had both the time and the personality to prepare himself for the office.

"And you see immediately what all that means. Most businessmen are out. Their lives have been too social, they wouldn't have had the time. For the same reason all government and military personnel are also out, and we need hardly say that anyone from the Bureau of Elections would be immediately suspect. No. You see the problem. For a while we thought that the time was too short, the risk too great. But then the only solution, the only possible chance, finally occurred to us.

"The only believable person would be — a professor. Someone whose life has been serious but unhurried, devoted to learning but at the same time isolated. The only really believable person. And not a scientist, you understand, for a man like that would be much too overbalanced in one direction for our purpose. No, simply a professor, preferably in a field like Political Science, a man whose sole job for many years has been teaching, who can claim to have studied in his spare time, his summers—never really expected to pass the tests and all that, a humble man, you see—"

"Political Science," Larkin said.

Reddington watched him. The other men began to close in on him.

"Yes," Reddington said gently. "Now do you see? It is our only hope. Your name was suggested by several sources, you are young enough, your reputation is well known. We think that you would be believable. And now that I've seen you"—he looked around slowly—"I for one am willing to risk it. Gentlemen, what do you say?"

Larkin, speechless, sat listening in mounting shock while the men agreed solemnly, one by one. In the enormity of the moment he could not think at all. Dimly, he heard Reddington.

"I know. But, Doctor, there is no time. The Polls close at eight. It is now almost seven."

Larkin closed his eyes and rested his head on his hands. Above him Reddington went on inevitably.

"All right. You are thinking of what happens after. Even if we pull this off and you are accepted without question, what then? Well, it will simply be the old system all over again. You will be at least no worse off than presidents before SAM. Better even, because if worst comes to worst there is always SAM. You can feed all the bad ones to him. You will have the advice of the cabinet, of the military staff. We will help you in every way we can, some of us will sit with you on all conferences. And you know more about this than most of us, you have studied government all your life.

"But all this, what comes later is not important. Not now. If we can get through tomorrow, the next few days, all the rest will work itself out. Eventually we can get around to altering SAM. But we must have a president in the morning. You are our only hope. You can do it. We all know you can do it. At any rate there is no other way, no time. Doctor," he reached out and laid his hand on Larkin's shoulder, "shall we go to the Polls?"

It passed, as most great moments in a man's life do, with Larkin not fully understanding what was happening to him. Later he would look back to this night and realize the enormity of the decision he had made, the doubts, the sleeplessness, the responsibility and agony toward which he moved. But in that moment he thought nothing at all. Except that it was Larkin's country, Larkin's America. And Reddington was right. There was nothing else to do. He stood up.

They went to the Polls.

At 9:30 that evening, sitting alone with Reddington back at the apartment, Larkin looked at the face of the announcer on the television screen, and heard himself pronounced President-elect of the United States.

Reddington wilted in front of the screen. For a while neither man moved. They had come home alone, just as they had gone into the Polls one by one in the hope of arousing no comment. Now they sat in silence until Reddington turned off the set. He stood up and straightened his shoulders before turning to Larkin. He stretched out his hand.

"Well, may God help us," he breathed, "we did it."

Larkin took his hand. He felt suddenly weak. He sat down again, but already he could hear the phone ringing in the outer hall. Reddington smiled.

"Only a few of my closest friends are supposed to know about that phone. But every time anything big comes up — " He shrugged. "Well," he said, still smiling, "let's see how it works."

He picked up the phone and with it an entirely different manner. He became amazingly light and cheerful, as if he was feeling nothing more than the normal political good will.

"Know him? Of course I know him. Had my eye on the guy for months. Really nice guy, wait'll you meet him . . . yup, college professor, Political Science, written a couple of books . . . must know a hell of a lot more than Polly Sci, though. Probably been knocking himself out in his spare time. But those teachers, you know how it is, they don't get any pay, but all the spare time in the world . . . Married? No, not that I know of — "

Larkin noticed with wry admiration how carefully Reddington had slipped in that bit about spare time, without seeming to be making an explanation. He thought wearily to himself I hope that I don't have to do any talking myself. I'll have to do a lot of listening before I can chance any talking.

In a few moments Reddington put down the phone and came back. He had on his hat and coat.

"Had to answer a few," he said briefly, "make it seem natural. But you better get dressed."

"Dressed? Why?"

"Have you forgotten?" Reddington smiled patiently. "You're due at the White House. The Secret Service is already tearing the town apart looking for you. We were supposed to alert them. Oh, by the saints, I hope that wasn't too bad a slip."

He pursed his mouth worriedly while Larkin, still dazed, got into his coat. It was beginning now. It had already begun. He was tired but it did not matter. That he was tired would probably never matter again. He took a deep breath. Like Reddington, he straightened his shoulders.

The Secret Service picked them up halfway across town. That they knew where he was, who he was, amazed him and worried Reddington. They went through the gates of the White House and drove up before the door. It was opened for him as he put out his hand, he stepped back in a reflex action, from the sudden blinding flares of the photographer's flashbulbs. Reddington behind him took him firmly by the arm. Larkin went with him gratefully, unable to see, unable to hear anything but the roar of crowd from behind the gates and the shouted questions of the reporters.

Inside the great front doors it was suddenly peaceful again, very quiet and pleasantly dark. He took off his hat instinctively. Luckily he had been here before, he recognized the lovely hall and felt not awed but at home. He was introduced quickly to several people whose names made no impression on him. A woman smiled. He made an effort to smile back. Reddington took him by the arm again and led him away. There were people all around him, but they were quiet and hung back. He saw the respect on their faces. It sobered him, quickened his mind.

"The president's in the Lincoln Room," Reddington whispered. "He wants to see you. How do you feel?"

"All right."

"Listen."

"Yes."

"You'll be fine. You're doing beautifully. Keep just that look on your face."

"I'm not trying to keep it there."

"You aren't?" Reddington looked at him. "Good. Very good." He paused and looked again at Larkin. Then he smiled.

"It's done it. I thought it would but I wasn't sure. But it does it every time. A man comes in here, no matter what he was before, no matter what he is when he goes out, but he feels it. Don't you feel it?"

"Yes. It's like—"

"What?"

"It's like . . . when you're in here you're *responsible.*"

Reddington said nothing. But Larkin felt a warm pressure on his arm.

They paused at the door of the Lincoln Room. Two Secret Service men, standing by the door, opened it respectfully. They went on in, leaving the others outside.

Larkin looked across the room to the great, immortal bed. He felt suddenly very small, very tender. He crossed the soft carpet and looked down at the old man.

"Hi," the old man said. Larkin was startled, but he looked down at the broad weakly smiling face, saw the famous white hair and the still-twinkling eyes, and found himself smiling in return.

"Mr. President," Larkin said.

"I hear your name is Larkin." The old man's voice was surprisingly strong, but as he spoke now Larkin could see that the left side of his face was paralyzed. "Good name for a president. Indicates a certain sense of humor. Need a sense of humor. Reddington, how'd it go?"

"Good as can be expected, sir." He glanced briefly at Larkin. "The president knows. Wouldn't have done it without his O.K. Now that I think of it, it was probably he who put the Secret Service on us."

"You're doggone right," the old man said. "They may bother the by-jingo out of you, but those boys are necessary. And also, if I hadn't let them know we knew Larkin was material —" He stopped abruptly and closed his eyes, took a deep breath. After a moment he said: "Mr. Larkin?"

"Yes, sir."

"I have one or two comments. You mind?"

"Of course not, sir."

"I couldn't solve it. I just . . . didn't have time. There were so many other things to do." He stopped and again closed his eyes. "But it will be up to you, son. The presidency . . . must be preserved. What they'll start telling you now is that there's only one way out, let SAM handle it. Reddington, too," the old man opened his eyes and gazed sadly at Reddington, "he'll tell you the same thing, but don't you believe it.

"Sure, SAM knows all the answers. Ask him a question on anything, on levels of parity tax rates, on anything. And right quick SAM will compute you out an answer. So that's what they'll try to do, they'll tell you to take it easy and let SAM do it.

"Well, all right, up to a certain point. But Mr. Larkin, understand this. SAM is like a book. Like a book, he knows the answers. *But only those answers we've already found out.* We gave SAM those answers. A machine is not creative, neither is a book. Both are only the product of creative minds. Sure, SAM could hold the country together. But growth, man, there'd be no more growth! No new ideas, new solutions, change, progress, development! And America *must* grow, must progress —"

He stopped, exhausted. Reddington bowed his head. Larkin remained idly calm. He felt a remarkable clarity in his head.

"But, Mr. President," he said slowly, "if the office is too much for one man, then all we can do is cut down on his powers —"

"Ah," the old man said faintly, "there's the rub. Cut down on what? If I sign a tax bill, I must know enough about taxes to be certain that the bill is the right one. If I endorse a police action, I must be certain that the strategy involved is militarily sound. If I consider farm prices . . . you see, you see, what will you cut? The office is responsible for its acts. It must remain responsible. You cannot take just someone else's word for things like that, you must make your own decisions. Already we sign things we know nothing about, bills for this, bills for that, on somebody's word."

"What do you suggest?"

The old man cocked an eye toward Larkin, smiled once more with half his mouth, anciently worn, only hours from death, an old, old man with his work not done, never to be done.

"Son, come here. Take my hand. Can't lift it myself."

Larkin came forward, knelt by the side of the bed. He took the cold hand, now gaunt and almost translucent, and held it gently.

"Mr. Larkin," the president said. "God be with you, boy. Do what you can. Delegate authority. Maybe cut the term in half. But keep us human, please, keep us growing, keep us alive." His voice faltered, his eyes closed. "I'm very tired. God be with you."

Larkin laid the hand gently on the bed cover. He stood for a long moment looking down. Then he turned with Reddington and left the room.

Outside he waited until they were past the Secret Service men and then turned to Reddington.

"Your plans for SAM. What do you think now?"

Reddington winced.

"I couldn't see any way out."

"But what about now? I have to know."

"I don't know. I really don't know. But . . . let me tell you something."

"Yes."

"Whatever I say to you from now on is only advice. You don't have to take it. Because understand this: however you came in here tonight you're going out the president. You were elected. Not by the people maybe, not even by SAM. But you're president by the grace of God and that's enough for me. From this moment on you'll be president to everybody in the world. We've all agreed. Never think that you're only a fraud, because you aren't. You heard what the president said. You take it from here."

Larkin looked at him for a long while. Then he nodded once briefly.

"All right," he said.

"One more thing."

"Yes?"

"I've got to say this. Tonight, this afternoon, I didn't really know what I was doing to you. I thought . . . well . . . the crisis came. But you had no time to think. That wasn't right. A man shouldn't be pushed into a thing like this without time to think. The old man just taught me something about making your own decisions. I should have let you make yours."

"It's all right."

"No, it isn't. You remember him in there. Well. That's you four years from tonight. If you live that long."

Now it was Larkin who reached out and patted Reddington on the shoulder.

"That's all right, too," he said.

Reddington said nothing. When he spoke again Larkin realized he was moved.

"We have the greatest luck, this country," he said tightly. "At all the worst times we always seem to find all the best people."

"Well," Larkin said hurriedly, "we'd better get to work. There's a speech due in the morning. And the problem of SAM. And . . . oh, I've got to be sworn in."

He turned and went off down the hall. Reddington paused a moment before following him. He was thinking that he could be watching the last human President the United States would ever have. But—once more he straightened his shoulders.

"Yes, sir," he said softly, "Mr. President."

On the Campaign Trail

BARRY N. MALZBERG

Barry N. Malzberg's novels and stories of passion, psychosis, and deep humor were highlights of the science fiction of the 1970s, a decade in which his work helped to center the field while at the same time expanding it. Particularly noteworthy are *Beyond Apollo* (1972), *Herovit's World* (1973), *Guernica Night* (1974), *The Destruction of the Temple* (1974), and *Chorale* (1978). After a few years of relative inactivity, he is returning to the field he helped to shape.

"On the Campaign Trail" is one of his best, most bitter, and least-known stories.

I

At Fargo another assassination attempt. Small, pockmarked man three or four feet from us in a huddle of autograph-seekers was seized by private guards (national security is worthless; I believe that they are merely functioning as spies), taken hurriedly into local shop, Happy Hosiery & Outerwear, where under rough frisking he gave up one thirty-eight-caliber Smith & Wesson, two hunting knives, and a small needle. Disclaimed any interest in hurting the candidate, said that he simply went around with such implements because of dangerous times, etc., but at our insistence he was booked by local police. Candidate shielded from this flurry of activity, although when he came to the door of Happy Hosiery & Outerwear he looked at me peculiarly for a moment or two. "Something wrong?" he said. "Nothing," I said. "Something seems to be wrong," he said, while shaking hands of three female customers (outerwear dept.). I believe that he suspects something amiss but will not bring this up again.

114

II

Good crowd in Hastings, brought to their feet three times by fighting speech which had been pre-tested in survey areas but never before used in exactly this frame. "New tomorrow, a new vision, a destruction of the forces of evil, the need for purgation and return to our older values," and so on. One woman became hysterical and had to be helped from auditorium, a dismaying moment, since we thought she might be a plant from the administration. Given first-aid in ladies' room she turned out to be harmless, having hundreds of photographs of the candidate in her purse, scraps of unfinished letters to him, etc. Later at reception raised several thousand dollars in new pledges. Candidate somewhat distracted and wearied from the pace of last few weeks; became inebriated after several cocktails and began to tell intimate sexual reminiscences to mayor, but we were able to get him out of there without further difficulty.

III

Fire in the motel this morning, choking vapors, sparks flying, three wagon companies called, etc. Candidate slept through all of this in rear wing, unaware, but four were overcome by smoke in the east palisade and a busy morning was spent checking them into hospitals, dealing with the press, shielding candidate from the seriousness of the incident, and so on. Some espionage is suspected, but it would be very difficult to prove, and since all in hospital are expected to recover with or without ill effects, state police have suggested that we treat it as an unfortunate accident, act of God, so on. Reports that assassin in Fargo has tested sane on preliminary investigation and thus we may be faced with a decision: do we proceed with formal charges or allow him to be released? Either way, it seems that we lose.

IV

Fire bomb in Huntsville went off during candidate's speech, enormous crowd packed solidly, some panic, the hall vacated as quickly as possible, so on. Local police continuing investigation. Candidate motioned me to come over to him while surrounded by press asking for his opinion; ordered me to see him in his room that night. Quite nervous about this (but how can I be held responsible?), but no way around it. Afterwards, while waiting for new arrangements to clear, had a few ecstatic moments with Mary in a vacated prefabricated classroom behind the senior high school. "I think that someone is trying to disrupt this campaign," she said. I asked her how she possibly could weave together a fire bomb, a fire, an assassination attempt into an intricate network of menace, but she had no reply. She is an attractive girl and one of the few solaces of the difficult swing, but she is rather paranoid.

V

"These incidents must stop," the candidate said to me, hitting his fist into palm (the other palm) in that abrupt forceful gesture which the media have already so exploited. "I don't know if these are unhappy coincidences or a genuine attempt on the part of the opposition or the administration to destroy me, but it is intolerable to continue in such circumstances. I want it stopped! I want better security," and he pounded that abused palm yet again, but in his eyes I saw a certain bleakness and uncertainty, a hint of genuine fear. Is it possible that he is concerned about his own safety? The thought had never occurred to me before. I would certainly think less of him if he was a physical coward, although he was right in adding that a person holding the office for which we are campaigning need not be an expert in self-defense.

VI

Alone with Mary in Wellington for a brief, dry coupling on the unchanged sheets of her motel room, then off to the amphitheater alone for a rally. Candidate at his best tonight but sweating heavily behind the makeup, and his voice cracked twice during last phrases of his speech. Later, at the reception, I found him leaning against a wall, a hand stroking a potted palm whispering, "I can't stand it any more, I can't stand it any more," but I put this down to a temporary neurasthenic episode and brought him back into the center of the room where several people shook his hand and pledged further new contributions bringing our total now into the hundreds of thousands of dollars.

VII

Back to Fargo, a decision made collectively. Unfortunate assassination attempt cannot prevent us from campaigning in all parts of the nation; we will not be frightened away, etc. Candidate strangely distracted on the plane, but then the decision was not his. At Fargo, debarking, was pulled aside by Mary, who said that she is going home. "I can't take the pressure any more," she said, and then, "besides, I feel that you're just using me." Tried to tell her that this was not the case, felt a genuine and sincere regard for her, etc., but she was adamant. Showed me plane ticket indicating that she was booked on the next eastern flight out of the airport. "What can I say?" I said. "You misunderstand the situation." She pulled me into some recess of the arrival building and kissed me desperately, her mouth uncoiling in a moistness which her cunt had never shown, at least for me, but even as I responded longingly, seeking her with my abused but hidden genitals, she was gone, running at high speed down the slick corridors and toward an exit gate. I stood looking after for a while thinking about the profound union of sexuality and politics, to no real conclusion.

VIII

Good crowd at Sea Girt, large enthusiastic audience which applauded everything candidate had to say and which remained quite cheerful despite the presence of police with drawn guns, security forces everywhere, etc. Campaign seems to have sparked and is now picking up momentum. Candidate rather distracted at reception, but this is to be expected; he has been under great strain recently, and rumors of assassins are everywhere. Four militants are in police custody, accused of having masterminded an assassination plot which might have succeeded except for the presence of two agents placed in the group.

Later called Mary to bring her up to date. Initially hostile, she became warmer as we talked, and when I replaced the receiver it was damp with little beads of sweat and saliva that clung to it like aphids.

IX

Candidate assassinated during rally, apparently by the same man detained by local police during our first visit. Hard to be sure; things, needless to say, are rather confused. Four shots, crossing from hip to temple, the last opening up his face disastrously in a resemblance to a pulped fruit. He fell very quietly behind the rostrum and lay there kicking. Local police, ambulance corps, medical personnel, and so on responded promptly, and the candidate was taken to hospital within five minutes of incident where he died at 12:17 a.m. of massive cerebral damage. The accused assailant is in the hands of police, and a further statement is expected shortly.

Hail to the Chief RANDALL GARRETT

Randall Garrett (b. 1927) worked as an industrial chemist before turning to full-time writing. Although he has produced only a dozen books in the science-fiction field, he was a tremendously prolific short-fiction writer who probably had more stories in *Astounding Science Fiction* in the late 1950s and early 1960s than any other writer. His work appeared so frequently that it required the use of at least seventeen pseudonyms. Particularly popular are his "Lord Darcy" stories about a future in which magic has become a science.

"Hail to the Chief" raises two of the most important questions about government — What constitutes "good" government? and Is this the result of having the right structure or the right people?

The tumult in Convention Hall was a hurricane of sound that lashed at a sea of human beings that surged and eddied around the broad floor. Men and women, delegates and spectators, aged party wheelhorses and youngsters who would vote for the first time that November, all lost their identities to merge with that swirling tide. Over their heads, like agitated bits of flotsam, pennants fluttered and placards rose and dipped. Beneath their feet, discarded metal buttons that bore the names of two or three "favorite sons" and those that had touted the only serious contender against the party's new candidate were trodden flat. None of them had ever really had a chance.

The buttons that were now pinned on every lapel said: "Blast 'em With Cannon!" or "Cannon Can Do!" The placards and the box-shaped signs, with a trifle more dignity, said: WIN WITH CANNON and CANNON FOR PRESIDENT and simply JAMES H. CANNON.

Occasionally, in the roar of noise, there were shouts of "Cannon! Cannon! Rah! Rah! Rah! Cannon! Cannon! Sis-boom-bah!" and snatches of old popular tunes hurriedly set with new words:

118

On with Cannon, on with Cannon!
   White House, here we come!
He's a winner, no beginner;
   He can get things done!
   (Rah! Rah! Rah!)
   And, over in one corner, a group of college girls were enthusiastically chanting:
   He is handsome! He is sexy!
   We want J.H.C. for Prexy!
   It was a demonstration that lasted nearly three times as long as the eighty-five minute demonstration that had occurred when Representative Matson had first proposed his name for the party's nomination.

   Spatially, Senator James Harrington Cannon was four blocks away from Convention Hall, in a suite at the Statler-Hilton, but electronically, he was no farther away than the television camera that watched the cheering multitude from above the floor of the hall.
   The hotel room was tastefully and expensively decorated, but neither the senator nor any of the other men in the room were looking at anything else except the big thirty-six-inch screen that glowed and danced with color. The network announcer's words were almost inaudible, since the volume had been turned way down, but his voice sounded almost as excited as those from the convention floor.
   Senator Cannon's broad, handsome face showed a smile that indicated pleasure, happiness, and a touch of triumph. His dark, slightly wavy hair, with the broad swathes of silver at the temples, was a little disarrayed, and there was a splash of cigarette ash on one trouser leg, but otherwise, even sitting there in his shirt sleeves, he looked well-dressed. His wide shoulders tapered down to a narrow waist and lean hips, and he looked a good ten years younger than his actual fifty-two.
   He lit another cigarette, but a careful scrutiny of his face would have revealed that, though his eyes were on the screen, his thoughts were not in Convention Hall.
   Representative Matson, looking like an amazed bulldog, managed to chew and puff on his cigar simultaneously and still speak understandable English. "Never saw anything like it. Never. First ballot and you had it, Jim. I know Texas was going to put up Perez as a favorite son on the first ballot, but they couldn't do anything except jump on the bandwagon by the time the vote reached them. Unanimous on the first ballot."
   Governor Spanding, lantern-jawed, lean man sitting on the other side of Senator Cannon, gave a short chuckle and said, "Came close not t' being unanimous. The delegate from Alabama looked as though he was going to stick to his 'One vote for Byron Beauregarde Cadwallader' until Cadwallader

himself went over to make him change his vote before the first ballot was complete."

The door opened, and a man came in from the other room. He bounced in on the balls of his feet, clapped his hands together, and dry-washed them briskly. "We're in!" he said, with businesslike glee. "Image, gentlemen! That's what does it: Image!" He was a tall, rather bony-faced man in his early forties, and his manner was that of the self-satisfied businessman who is quite certain that he knows all of the answers and all of the questions. "Create an image that the public goes for, and you're in!"

Senator Cannon turned his head around and grinned. "Thanks, Horvin, but let's remember that we still have an election to win."

"We'll win it," Horvin said confidently. "A properly projected image attracts the public—"

"Oh, crud," said Representative Matson in a growly voice. "The opposition has just as good a staff of PR men as we do. If we beat 'em, it'll be because we've got a better man, not because we've got better public relations."

"Of course," said Horvin, unabashed. "We can project a better image because we've got better material to work with. We—"

"Jim managed to get elected to the Senate without any of your help, and he went in with an avalanche. If there's any 'image projecting' done around here, Jim is the one who does it."

Horvin nodded his head as though he was in complete agreement with Matson. "Exactly. His natural ability plus the scientific application of mass psychology make an unbeatable team."

Matson started to say something, but Senator Cannon cut in first. "He's right, Ed. We've got to use every weapon we have to win this election. Another four years of the present policies, and the Sino-Russian Bloc will be able to start unilateral disarmament. They won't have to start a war to bury us."

Horvin looked nervous. "Uh . . . Senator—"

Cannon made a motion in the air. "I know, I know. Our policy during the campaign will be to run down the opposition, not the United States. We are still in a strong position, but *if this goes on*—Don't worry, Horvin; the whole thing will be handled properly."

Before any of them could say anything, Senator Cannon turned to Representative Matson and said: "Ed, will you get Matthew Fisher on the phone? And the Governor of Pennsylvania and . . . let's see . . . Senator Hidekai and Joe Vitelli."

"I didn't even know Fisher was here," Matson said. "What do you want him for?"

"I just want to talk to him, Ed. Get him up here, with the others, will you?"

"Sure, Jim, sure." He got up and walked over to the phone.

Horvin, the PR man, said: "Well, Senator, now that you're the party's candidate for the Presidency of the United States, who are you going to pick for your running mate? Vollinger was the only one who came even close to giving you a run for your money, and it would be good public relations if you chose him. He's got the kind of personality that would make a good image."

"Horvin," the senator said kindly, "I'll pick the men; you build the image from the raw material I give you. You're the only man I know who can convince the public that a sow's ear is really a silk purse, and you may have to do just that.

"You can start right now. Go down and get hold of those news boys and tell them that the announcement of my running mate will be made as soon as this demonstration is over.

"Tell them you can't give them any information other than that, but give them the impression that you already know. Since you *don't* know, don't try to guess; that way you won't let any cats out of the wrong bags. But you *do* know that he's a fine man, and you're pleased as all hell that I made such a good choice. Got that?"

Horvin grinned. "Got it. You pick the man; I'll build the image." He went out the door.

When the door had closed, Governor Spanding said: "So it's going to be Fisher, is it?"

"You know too much, Harry," said Senator Cannon, grinning. "Remind me to appoint you ambassador to Patagonia after Inauguration Day."

"If I lose the election at home, I may take you up on it. But why Matthew Fisher?"

"He's a good man, Harry."

"Hell yes, he is," the governor said. "Tops. I've seen his record as State Attorney General and as Lieutenant Governor. And when Governor Dinsmore died three years ago, Fisher did a fine job filling out his last year. But—"

"But he couldn't get re-elected two years ago," Senator Cannon said. "He couldn't keep the governor's office, in spite of the great job he'd done."

"That's right. He's just not a politician, Jim. He doesn't have the . . . the personality, the flash, whatever it is that it takes to get a man elected by the people. I've got it; you sure as hell have it; Fisher doesn't."

"That's why I've got Horvin working for us," said Senator Cannon. "Whether I need him or not may be a point of argument. Whether Matthew Fisher needs him or not is a rhetorical question."

Governor Spanding lit a cigarette in silence while he stared at the quasi-riot that was still coming to the screen from Convention Hall. Then he said: "You've been thinking of Matt Fisher all along, then."

"Not Patagonia," said the senator. "Tibet."

"I'll shut up if you want me to, Jim."

"No. Go ahead."

"All right. Jim, I trust your judgment. I've got no designs on the Vice Presidency myself, and you know it. I like to feel that, if I had, you'd give me a crack at it. No, don't answer that, Jim; just let me talk.

"What I'm trying to say is that there are a lot of good men in the party who'd make fine VP's; men who've given their all to get you the nomination, and who'll work even harder to see that you're elected. Why pass them up in favor of a virtual unknown like Matt Fisher?"

Senator Cannon didn't say anything. He knew that Spanding didn't want an answer yet.

"The trouble with Fisher," Spanding went on, "is that he . . . well, he's too autocratic. He pulls decisions out of midair. He—" Spanding paused, apparently searching for a way to express himself. Senator Cannon said nothing; he waited expectantly.

"Take a look at the Bossard Decision," Spanding said. "Fisher was Attorney General for his state at the time.

"Bossard was the Mayor of Waynesville—twelve thousand and something population, I forget now. Fisher didn't even know Bossard. But when the big graft scandal came up there in Waynesville, Fisher wouldn't prosecute. He didn't actually refuse, but he hemmed and hawed around for five months before he really started the State's machinery to moving. By that time, Bossard had managed to get enough influence behind him so that he could beat the rap.

"When the case came to trial in the State Supreme Court, Matt Fisher told the Court that it was apparent that Mayor Bossard was the victim of the local district attorney and chief of police of Waynesville. In spite of the evidence against him, Bossard was acquitted." Spanding took a breath to say something more, but Senator James Cannon interrupted him.

"Not 'acquitted,' Harry. 'Exonerated.' Bossard never even should have come to trial," the senator said. "He was a popular, buddy-buddy sort of guy who managed to get himself involved as an unwitting figurehead. Bossard simply wasn't—and isn't—very bright. But he was a friendly, outgoing, warm sort of man who was able to get elected through the auspices of the local city machine. Remember Jimmy Walker?"

Spanding nodded. "Yes, but—"

"Same thing," Cannon cut in. "Bossard was innocent, as far as any criminal intent was concerned, but he was too easy on his so-called friends. He—"

"Oh, *crud,* Jim!" the governor interrupted vehemently. "That's the same whitewash that Matthew Fisher gave him! The evidence would have convicted Bossard if Fisher hadn't given him time to cover up!"

Senator James Cannon suddenly became angry. He jammed his own cigarette butt into the ash tray, turned toward Spanding, and snapped: "Harry, just for the sake of argument, let's suppose that Bossard wasn't actually guilty. Let's suppose that the Constitution of the United States is really true — that a man isn't guilty until he's proven guilty.

"Just *suppose*" — his voice and expression became suddenly acid — "that Bossard was *not* guilty. Try that, huh? Pretend, somewhere in your own little mind, that a mere accusation — no matter what the evidence — doesn't prove anything! Let's just make a little game between the two of us that the ideal of equality under the law means what it says. Want to play?"

"Well, yes, but —"

"O.K.," Cannon went on angrily. "O.K. Then let's suppose that Bossard really *was* stupid. He could have been framed easily, couldn't he? He could have been set up as a patsy, couldn't he? *Couldn't he?*"

"Well, sure, but —"

"Sure! Then go on and suppose that the prosecuting attorney had sense enough to see that Bossard *had* been framed. Suppose further that the prosecutor was enough of a human being to know that Bossard either had to be convicted or completely exonerated. What would he do?"

Governor Spanding carefully put his cigarette into the nearest ash tray. "If that were the case, I'd *completely* exonerate him. I wouldn't leave it hanging. Matt Fisher didn't do anything but make sure that Bossard couldn't be legally convicted; he didn't prove that Bossard was innocent."

"And what was the result, as far as Bossard was concerned?" the senator asked.

Spanding looked around at the senator, staring Cannon straight in the face. "The result was that Bossard was left hanging, Jim. If I go along with you and assume that Bossard was innocent, then Fisher fouled up just as badly as he would have if he'd fluffed the prosecution of a guilty man. Either a man is guilty, or he's innocent. If, according to your theory, the prosecutor knows he's innocent, then he should exonerate the innocent man! If not, he should do his best to convict!"

"He should?" snapped Cannon. "He *should?* Harry, you're letting your idealism run away with you. If Bossard were guilty, he should have been convicted — sure! But if he were innocent, should he be exonerated? Should he be allowed to run again for office? Should the people be allowed to think that he was lily-white? Should they be allowed to re-elect a nitwit who'd do the same thing again because he was too stupid to see that he was being used?

"No!" He didn't give the governor time to speak; he went on: "Matthew Fisher set it up perfectly. He exonerated Bossard enough to allow the ex-mayor to continue in private life without any question. *But* — there remained just enough question to keep him out of public office for the rest of his life. Was that wrong, Harry? Was it?"

Spanding looked blankly at the senator for a moment, then his expression slowly changed to one of grudging admiration. "Well . . . if you put it that way . . . yeah. I mean, no; it wasn't wrong. It was the only way to play it." He dropped his cigarette into a nearby ash tray. "O.K., Jim; you win. I'll back Fisher all the way."

"Thanks, Harry," Cannon said. "Now, if we—"

Congressman Matson came back into the room, saying, "I got 'em, Jim. Five or ten minutes, they'll be here. Which one of 'em is it going to be?"

"Matt Fisher, if we can come to an agreement," Cannon said, watching Matson's face closely.

Matson chewed his cigar for a moment, then nodded. "He'll do. Not much political personality, but, hell, he's only running for Veep. We can get him through." He took the cigar out of his mouth. "How do you want to run it?"

"I'll talk to Fisher in my bedroom. You and Harry hold the others in here with the usual chitchat. Tell 'em I'm thinking over the choice of my running mate, but don't tell 'em I've made up my mind yet. If Matt Fisher doesn't want it, we can tell the others that Matt and I were simply talking over the possibilities. I don't want anyone to think he's second choice. Got it?"

Matson nodded. "Whatever you say, Jim."

That year, late August was a real blisterer along the eastern coast of the United States. The great megalopolis that sprawled from Boston to Baltimore in utter scorn of state boundaries sweltered in the kind of atmosphere that is usually only found in the pressing rooms of large tailor shops. Consolidated Edison, New York's Own Power Company, was churning out multimegawatts that served to air condition nearly every enclosed place on the island of Manhattan—which only served to make the open streets even hotter. The power plants in the Bronx, west Brooklyn, and east Queens were busily converting hydrogen into helium and energy, and the energy was being used to convert humid air at ninety-six Fahrenheit into dry air at seventy-one Fahrenheit. The subways were crowded with people who had no intention of going anywhere in particular; they just wanted to retreat from the hot streets to the air-conditioned bowels of the city.

But the heat that can be measured by thermometers was not the kind that was causing two groups of men in two hotels, only a few blocks apart on the East Side of New York's Midtown, to break out in sweat, both figurative and literal.

One group was ensconced in the Presidential Suite of the New Waldorf— the President and Vice President of the United States, both running for re-election, and other high members of the incumbent party.

The other group, consisting of Candidates Cannon and Fisher, and the high members of *their* party, were occupying the only slightly less pretentious Bridal Suite of a hotel within easy walking distance of the Waldorf.

Senator James Cannon read through the news release that Horvin had handed him, then looked up at the PR man. "This is right off the wire. How long before it's made public?"

Horvin glanced at his watch. "Less than half an hour. There's an NBC news program at five-thirty. Maybe before, if one of the radio stations think it's important enough for a bulletin break."

"That means that it will have been common knowledge for four hours by the time we go on the air for the debate," said Cannon.

Horvin nodded, still looking at his watch. "And even if some people miss the TV broadcast, they'll be able to read all about it. The deadline for the *Daily Register* is at six; the papers will hit the streets at seven-fifteen, or thereabouts."

Cannon stood up from his chair. "Get your men out on the streets. Get 'em into bars, where they can pick up reactions to this. I want as good a statistical sampling as you can get in so short a time. It'll have to be casual; I don't want your men asking questions as though they were regular pollsters; just find out what the general trend is."

"Right." Horvin got out fast.

The other men in the room were looking expectantly at the senator. He paused for a moment, glancing around at them, and then looked down at the paper and said: "This is a bulletin from Tass News Agency, Moscow." Then he began reading.

"Russian Luna Base One announced that at 1600 Greenwich Standard Time (12:00 N EDST) a presumed spacecraft of unknown design was damaged by Russian rockets and fell to the surface of Luna somewhere in the Mare Serenitas, some three hundred fifty miles from the Soviet base. The craft was hovering approximately four hundred miles above the surface when spotted by Soviet radar installations. Telescopic inspection showed that the craft was not — repeat: not — powered by rockets. Since it failed to respond to the standard United Nations recognition signals, rockets were fired to bring it down. In an attempt to avoid the rockets, the craft, according to observers, maneuvered in an entirely unorthodox manner, which cannot be attributed to a rocket dive. A nearby burst, however, visibly damaged the hull of the craft, and it dropped toward Mare Serenitas. Armed Soviet moon-cats are, at this moment, moving toward the downed craft.

"Base Commander Colonel A. V. Gryaznov is quoted as saying: 'There can be no doubt that we shall learn much from this craft, since it is apparently of extraterrestrial origin. We will certainly be able to overpower any resistance it may offer, since it has already proved vulnerable to our weapons. The missiles which were fired toward our base were easily destroyed by our own antimissile missiles, and the craft was unable to either destroy or avoid our own missiles.'

"Further progress will be released by the Soviet Government as it occurs."

Senator Cannon dropped the sheet of paper to his side. "That's it. Matt, come in the bedroom; I'd like to talk to you."

Matthew Fisher, candidate for Vice President of the United States, heaved his two-hundred-fifty-pound bulk out of the chair he had been sitting in and followed the senator into the other room. Behind them, the others suddenly broke out into a blather of conversation. Fisher's closing of the door cut off the sound abruptly.

Senator Cannon threw the newssheet on the nearest bed and swung around to face Matthew Fisher. He looked at the tall, thick, muscular man trying to detect the emotions behind the ugly-handsome face that had been battered up by football and boxing in college, trying to fathom the thoughts behind the broad forehead and the receding hairline.

"You got any idea what this *really* means, Matt?" he asked after a second.

Fisher's blue-gray eyes widened almost imperceptibly, and his gaze sharpened. "Not until just this moment," he said.

Cannon looked suddenly puzzled. "What do you mean?"

"Well," Fisher said thoughtfully, "you wouldn't ask me unless it meant something more than appears on the surface." He grinned rather apologetically. "I'm sorry, Jim; it takes a second or two to reconstruct exactly what *did* go through my mind." His grin faded into a thoughtful frown. "Anyway, you asked me, and since you're head of the Committee on SPACE Travel and Exploration —" He spread his hands in a gesture that managed to convey both futility and apology. "The mystery spacecraft is ours," he said decisively.

James Cannon wiped a palm over his forehead and sat down heavily on one of the beds. "Right. Sit down. Fine. Now, listen: We — the United States — have a space drive that compares to the rocket in the same way that the jet engine compares to the horse. We've been keeping it under wraps that are comparable to those the Manhattan Project was kept under 'way back during World War II. Maybe more so. But —" He stopped, watching Fisher's face. Then: "Can you see it from there?"

"I think so," Fisher said. "The Soviet Government knows that we have something . . . in fact, they've known it for a long time. They don't know what, though." He found a heavy briar in his pocket, pulled it out, and began absently stuffing it with tobacco from a pouch he'd pulled out with the pipe. "Our ship didn't shoot at their base. Couldn't, wouldn't have. Um. They shot it down to try to look it over. Purposely made a near-miss with an atomic warhead." He struck a match and puffed the pipe alight.

"Hm-m-m. The Soviet Government," he went on, "must have known that we had something 'way back when they signed the Greenston Agreement." Fisher blew out a cloud of smoke. "They wanted to change the wording of that, as I remember."

"That's right," Cannon said. "We wanted it to read that 'any advances in *rocket engineering* shall be shared equally among the Members of the United Nations', but the Soviet delegation wanted to change that to 'any advances in *space travel'*. We only beat them out by a verbal quibble; we insisted that the word 'space,' as used, could apply equally to the space between continents or cities or, for that matter, between any two points. By the time we got through arguing, the UN had given up on the Soviet amendment, and the agreement was passed as was."

"Yeah," said Fisher. "I remember. So now we have a space drive that doesn't depend on rockets, and the USSR wants it." He stared at the bowl of his briar for a moment, then looked up at Cannon. "The point is that they've brought down one of our ships, and we have to get it out of there before the Russians get to it. Even if we manage to keep them from finding out anything about the drive, they can raise a lot of fuss in the UN if they can prove that it's our ship."

"Right. They'll ring in the Greenston Agreement even if the ship technically isn't a rocket," Cannon said. "Typical Soviet tactics. They try to time these things to hit at the most embarrassing moments. Four years ago, our worthy opponent got into office because our administration was embarrassed by the Madagascar Crisis. They simply try to show the rest of the world that, no matter which party is in, the United States is run by a bunch of inept fools." He slapped his hand down on the newssheet that lay near him. "This may win us the election," he said angrily, "but it will do us more harm in the long run than if our worthy opponent stayed in the White House."

"Of what avail to win an election and lose the whole Solar System," Fisher paraphrased. "It looks as though the President has a hot potato."

" 'Hot' is the word. Pure californium-254." Cannon lit a cigarette and looked moodily at the glowing end. "But this puts us in a hole, too. Do we, or don't we, mention it on the TV debate this evening? If we don't, the public will wonder why; if we do, we'll put the country on the spot."

Matt Fisher thought for a few seconds. Then he said, "The ship must have already been having trouble. Otherwise it wouldn't have been hovering in plain sight of the Soviet radar. How many men does one of those ships hold?"

"Two," the senator told him.

"We do have more than one of those ships, don't we?" Fisher asked suddenly.

"Four on Moon Base; six more building," said Senator Cannon.

"The downed ship must have been in touch with—" He stopped abruptly, paused for a second, then said: "I have an idea, Senator, but you'll have to do the talking. We'll have to convince the President that what we're suggesting is for the good of the country and not just a political trick. And we don't have much time. Those moon-cats shouldn't take more than twelve or fifteen hours to reach the ship."

"What's your idea?"

"Well, it's pretty rough right now; we can't fill in the details until we get more information, but—" He knocked the dottle from his pipe and began outlining his scheme to the senator.

Major Valentin Udovichenko peered through the "windshield" of his moon-cat and slowed the vehicle down as he saw the glint of metal on the Earthlit plain ahead. "Captain!" he snapped. "What does that look like to you?" He pointed with a gloved hand.

The other officer looked. "I should say," he said after a moment, "that we have found what we have been looking for, major."

"So would I. It's a little closer to our base than the radar men calculated, but it certainly could have swerved after it dropped below the horizon. And we know there hasn't been another ship in this vicinity."

The captain was focusing a pair of powerful field glasses on the object. "That's it!" he said, bridling his excitement. "Egg-shaped, and no sign of rocket exhausts. Big dent in one side."

Major Udovichenko had his own binoculars out. "It's as plain as day in this Earthlight. No sign of life, either. We shouldn't have any trouble." He lowered the binoculars and picked up a microphone to give the other moon-cats their instructions.

Eight of the vehicles stayed well back, ready to launch rockets directly at the fallen spacecraft if there were any sign of hostility, while two more crept carefully up on her.

They were less than a hundred and fifty yards away when the object they were heading for caught fire. The major braked his vehicle to a sudden halt and stared at the bright blaze that was growing and spreading over the metallic shape ahead. Bursts of flame sprayed out in every direction, the hot gases meeting no resistance from the near-vacuum into which they spread.

Major Udovichenko shouted orders into his microphone and gunned his own motor into life again. The caterpillar treads crunched against the lunar surface as both moon-cats wheeled about and fled. Four hundred yards from the blaze, they stopped again and watched.

By this time, the blaze had eaten away more than half of the hulk, and it was surrounded by a haze of smoke and hot gas that was spreading rapidly away from it. The flare of light far outshone the light reflected from the sun by the Earth overhead.

"Get those cameras going!" the major snapped. He knew that the eight moon-cats that formed the distant perimeter had been recording steadily, but he wanted close-ups, if possible.

None of the cameras got much of anything. The blaze didn't last long, fierce as it was. When it finally died, and the smoke particles settled slowly to the lunar surface, there was only a blackened spot where the bulk of a spaceship had been.

"Well . . . I . . . will . . . be —," said Major Valentin Udovichenko.

The TV debate was over. The senator and the President had gone at each other hot and heavy, hammer and tongs, with the senator clearly emerging as the victor. But no mention whatever had been made of the Soviet announcement from Luna.

At four thirty-five the next morning, the telephone rang in the senator's suite. Cannon had been waiting for it, and he was quick to answer.

The face that appeared on the screen was that of the President of the United States. "Your scheme worked, senator," he said without preamble. There was an aloofness, a coolness in his voice. Which was only natural, considering the heat of the debate the previous evening.

"I'm glad to hear it, Mr. President," the senator said, with only a hair less coolness. "What happened?"

"Your surmise that the Soviet officials did not realize the potential of the new craft was apparently correct," the President said. "General Thayer had already sent another ship in to rescue the crew of the disabled vessel, staying low, below the horizon of the Russian radar. The disabled ship had had some trouble with its drive mechanism; it would never have deliberately exposed itself to Russian detection. General Thayer had already asked my permission to destroy the disabled vessel rather than let the Soviets get their hands on it, and, but for your suggestion, I would have given him a go-ahead.

"But making a replica of the ship in plastic was less than a two-hour job. The materials were at hand; a special foam plastic is used as insulation from the chill of the lunar substrata. The foam plastic was impregnated with ammonium nitrate and foamed up with pure oxygen; since it is catalyst-setting, that could be done at low temperatures. The outside of the form was covered with a metallized plastic, also impregnated with ammonium nitrate. I understand that the thing burned like unconfined gunpowder after it was planted in the path of the Soviet moon-cats and set off. The Soviet vehicles are on their way back to their base now."

After a moment's hesitation, he went on: "Senator, in spite of our political differences, I want to say that I appreciate a man who can put his country's welfare ahead of his political ambitions."

"Thank you, Mr. President. That is a compliment I appreciate and accept. But I want you to know that the notion of decoying them away with an inflammable plastic replica was not my idea; it was Matt Fisher's."

"Oh? My compliments to Mr. Fisher." He smiled thinly. It was obviously forced, but, just as obviously, there was sincerity behind it. "I hope the best team wins. But if it does not, I am secure in the knowledge that the second best team is quite competent."

Firmly repressing a desire to say, *I am sorry that I don't feel any such security myself,* Cannon merely said: "Thank you again, Mr. President."

When the connection was cut, Cannon grinned at Matthew Fisher. "That's it. We've saved a ship. It can be repaired where it is without a fleet of Soviet moon-cats prowling around and interfering. And we've scotched any attempts at propagandizing that the Soviets may have had in mind." He chuckled. "I'd like to have seen their faces when that thing started to burn in a vacuum. And I'd like to see the reports that are being flashed back and forth between Moscow and Soviet Moon Base One."

"I wasn't so much worried about the loss of the disabled ship as the *way* we'd lose it," Matthew Fisher said.

"The Soviets getting it?" Cannon asked. "We didn't have to worry about that. You heard him say that Thayer was going to destroy it."

"That's exactly what I meant," said Fisher. "*How* were we going to destroy it? TNT or dynamite or Radex-3 would have still left enough behind for a good Soviet team to make some kind of sense out of it — some kind of hint would be there, unless an awful lot of it were used. A fission or a thermonuclear bomb would have vaporized it, but that would have been a violation of the East-West Agreement. We'd be flatly in the wrong."

Senator Cannon walked over to the sideboard and poured Scotch into two glasses. "The way it stands now, the ship will at least be able to limp out of there before anyone in Moscow can figure out what happened and transmit orders back to Luna." He walked back with the glasses and handed one to Fisher. "Let's have a drink and go to bed. We have to be in Philadelphia tomorrow, and I'm dead tired."

"That's a pair of us," said Fisher, taking the glass.

Another month of campaigning, involving both televised and personal appearances, went by without unusual incidents. The prophets, seers, and pollsters were having themselves a grand time. Some of them — the predicting-by-past-performances men — were pointing out that only four Presidents had failed to succeed themselves when they ran for a second term: Martin Van Buren, Grover Cleveland, Benjamin Harrison, and Herbert Hoover. They argued that this presaged little chance of success for Senator James Cannon. The pollsters said that their samplings had shown a strong leaning toward the President at first, but that eight weeks of campaigning had started a switch toward Cannon, and that the movement seemed to be accelerating. The anti-pollsters, as usual, simply smiled smugly and said: "Remember Dewey in '48?"

Plays on Cannon's name had caught the popular fancy. The slogan "Blast 'em with Cannon" now appeared on every button worn by those who supported him — who called themselves "Cannoneers." Their opponents sneeringly referred to them as "Cannon fodder" and made jokes about "that big bore Cannon."

The latter joke was pure epithet, with no meaning behind it; when Senator James Cannon spoke, either in person or over the TV networks, even his opponents listened with grudging interest.

The less conservative newspapers couldn't resist the gag either, and printed headlines on the order of CANNON FIRES BLAST AT FOREIGN POLICY, CANNON HOT OVER CIA ORDER, BUDGET BUREAU SHAKEN BY CANNON REPORT, and TREASURY IS LATEST CANNON TARGET.

The various newspaper columnists, expanding on the theme, made even more atrocious puns. When the senator praised his running mate, a columnist said that Fisher had been "Cannonized" and proceeded to call him "Saint" Matthew. The senator's ability to remember names and faces of his constituents caused one pundit to remark that "it's a wise Cannon that knows its own fodder."

They whooped with joy when the senator's plane was delayed by bad weather, causing him to arrive several hours late to a bonfire rally in Texas. Only a strong headline writer could resist: CANNON MISSES FIRE!

As a result, the senator's name hit the headlines more frequently than his rival's did. And the laughter was *with* Cannon, not *at* him.

Nothing more was heard about the "mysterious craft" that the Soviets claimed to have shot down, except a terse report that said it had "probably been destroyed." It was impossible to know whether or not they had deduced what had happened, or whether they realized that the new craft was as maneuverable over the surface of the moon as a helicopter was over the surface of Earth.

Instead, the Sino-Soviet bloc had again shifted the world's attention to Africa. Like the Balkan States of nearly a century before, the small, independent nations that covered the still-dark continent were a continuing source of trouble. In spite of decades of "civilization," the thoughts and actions of the majority of Africans were still cast in the matrix of tribal taboos. The changes of government, the internal strife, and the petty brush wars between nations made Central and South America appear rigidly stable by comparison. It had been suggested that the revolutions in Africa occurred so often that only a tachometer could keep up with them.

If nothing else, the situation had succeeded in forcing the organization of a permanent UN police force; since back in 1960, there had not been a time when the UN Police were not needed somewhere in Africa.

In mid-October, a border dispute between North Uganda and South Uganda broke out, and within a week it looked as though the Commonwealth of Victorian Kenya, the Republic of Upper Tanganyika, and the Free and Independent Popular Monarchy of Ruanda-Urundi were all going to try to jump in and grab a piece of territory if possible.

The Soviet Representative to the United Nations charged that "this is a purely internal situation in Uganda, caused by imperialist *agents provocateur* financed by the Western Bloc." He insisted that UN intervention was unnecessary unless the "warmongering" neighbors of Uganda got into the scrap.

In a televised press interview, Vice Presidential Candidate Matthew Fisher was asked what he thought of the situation in East Africa.

"Both North and South Uganda," he said, "are communist controlled, but, like Yugoslavia, they have declared themselves independent of the masters at Moscow. If this conflict was stirred up by special agents — and I have no doubt that it was — those agents were Soviet, not Western agents. As far as the UN can be concerned, the Soviet Minister is correct, since the UN has recognized only the government of North Uganda as the government of all Uganda, and it is, therefore, a purely internal affair.

"The revolution — that is, *partial* revolution — which caused the division of Uganda a few years ago, was likewise due to Soviet intervention. They hoped to replace the independent communist government with one which would be, in effect, a puppet of the Kremlin. They failed. Now they are trying again.

"Legally, UN troops can only be sent there at the request of the Northern Uganda government. The Secretary General can send police troops there of his own accord only if another nation tries to invade Uganda.

"But — and here is the important point — if the Uganda government asks the aid of a friendly government to send troops, and if that friendly government complies with that request, *that cannot be considered an invasion!*"

Question from a reporter: "Do you believe that intervention from another country will be requested by Uganda?"

"I do. And I am equally certain that the Soviet Representative to the UN, and his superiors in Moscow, will try to make a case of invasion and aggression out of it."

Within twenty-four hours after that interview, the government of North Uganda requested aid from Victorian Kenya, and a huge contingent of Kenyan troops marched across the border to help the North Uganda army. And the Soviet representative insisted that the UN send in troops to stop the "imperialist aggression" of Victorian Kenya. The rigidly pro-Western VK government protested that the Sino-Soviet accusations were invalid, and then asked, on its own accord, that a UN contingent be sent in to act as observers and umpires.

"Win one, lose one," Matthew Fisher said privately to Senator Cannon. "Uganda will come out of this with a pro-Western government, but it might not be too stable. The whole African situation is unstable. Mathematically, it has to be."

"How's that?" Senator Cannon asked.

"Do you know the Richardson-Gordon Equations?" Fisher asked.

"No. I'm not much of a mathematician," Cannon admitted. "What do they have to do with this?"

"They were originally proposed by Lewis Richardson, the English mathematician, and later refined by G. R. Gordon. Basically, they deal with the causes of war, and they show that a conglomeration of small states is less stable than a few large ones. In an arms race, there is a kind of positive feedback that eventually destroys the system, and the more active small units there are, the sooner the system reaches the destruction point."

Senator Cannon chuckled. "Any practical politician could have told them that, but I'm glad to hear that a mathematical tool to work on the problem has been devised. Maybe one of these days we won't have to be rule-of-thumb empiricists."

"Let's hope so," said Matt Fisher.

By the end of October, nearly two weeks from Election Day, the decision had been made. There were still a few Americans who hadn't made up their minds yet, but not enough to change the election results, even if they had voted as a bloc for one side or the other. The change from the shouting and arguing of mid-summer was apparent to anyone who knew what he was looking for. In the bars and restaurants, in the subways and buses, aboard planes and ships and trains, most Americans apparently seemed to have forgotten that there was a national election coming up, much to the surprise of Europeans and Asians who were not familiar with the dynamics of American political thought. If a foreigner brought the subject up, the average American would give his views in a calm manner, as though the thing were already settled, but there was far more discussion of the relative merits of the horses running at Pimlico or the rise in Lunar Developments Preferred than there was of the election. There were still a few people wearing campaign buttons, but most people didn't bother pinning them on after the suit came back from the cleaners.

A more detailed analysis would have shown that this calmness was of two types. The first, by far in the majority, was the calmness of the complacent knowledge of victory. The second was the resignation to loss manifested by those who knew they were backing the wrong man, but who, because of party loyalty or intellectual conviction or just plain stubbornness, would back him.

When Senator Cannon's brother, Dr. Frank Hewlitt Cannon, took a short leave of absence from Mayo Clinic to fly to the senator's campaign headquarters, there was a flurry of speculation about the possibility of his being appointed Secretary of Health, Education, and Welfare, but the flurry didn't amount to much. If President Cannon wanted to appoint his brother, that was all right with the voters.

A tirade by the Soviet Premier, charging that the UN Police troops in Victorian Kenya were "tools of Yankee aggressionists," Americans smiled grimly and said, in effect: "Just wait 'til Cannon gets in—he'll show 'em."

Election Day came with the inevitability of death and taxes. The polling booths opened first on the East Coast, and people began filing in to take their turns at the machines. By the time the polls opened in Nome, Alaska, six hours later, the trend was obvious. All but two of the New England states went strongly for Cannon. New York, Pennsylvania, New Jersey, West Virginia, and Ohio dropped into his pocket like ripe apples. Virginia, North Carolina, South Carolina, Georgia, and Florida did the same. Alabama wavered at first, but tagged weakly along. Tennessee, Kentucky, Indiana, and Michigan trooped in like trained seals.

In Mississippi, things looked bad. Arkansas and Louisiana were uncertain. But the pro-Cannon vote in Missouri, Illinois, Iowa, Wisconsin, and Minnesota left no doubt about the outcome in those states. North Dakota, South Dakota, Nebraska, Kansas, Oklahoma, Texas — all Cannon by vast majorities.

And so the returns came in, following the sun across the continent. By the time California had reported three-fourths of its votes, it was all over but the jubilation. Nothing but an honest-to-God, genuine, Joshua-stopping-the-sun type of miracle could have saved the opposition. And such was not forthcoming.

At Cannon's campaign headquarters, a television screen was blaring to unhearing ears, merely adding to the din that was going on in the meeting hall. The party workhorses and the volunteers who had drummed for Cannon since the convention were repeating the scene that had taken place after Cannon's nomination in the summer, with an even greater note of triumph.

In Cannon's suite, six floors above, there was less noise, but only because there were fewer people.

"Hey!" Cannon yelled good-naturedly. "Lay off! Any more slaps on my back, and I'm going to be the first President since Franklin Roosevelt to go to my Inauguration in a wheelchair! Lay off, will you?"

"A drink, a drink, we got to have a drink," chanted Representative Edwin Matson, his bulldog face spread wide in a happy grin while he did things with bottles, ice, and glasses. "A drink, a drink — "

Governor Harold Spanding's lantern-jawed face looked as idiotically happy as Matson's, but he was quieter about it. Verbally, that is. It was he who had been pounding Cannon on the back, and now he was pounding Matthew Fisher almost as hard.

Matt Fisher finally managed to grab his hand, and he started pumping it. "What about you, Harry? I'm only a poor, simple Vice President. You got re-elected governor!"

Dr. Frank Cannon, looking like an older, balder edition of his brother, was smiling, too, but there was a troubled look in his eyes even as he congratulated the senator. Congressman Matson, passing out the drinks, handed the first one to the senator.

"Have a drink, Mr. President! You're going to have to make a speech pretty soon; you'll need a bracer!" He handed the second one to the physician. "Here you go, Doc! Congratulations! It isn't everyone who's got a President in the family!" Then his perceptive brain noticed something in the doctor's expression. "Hey," he said more softly, "what's the trouble? You look as though you expected sickness in the family."

The doctor grinned quickly. "Not unless it's my own. I'm used to worrying about a patient's health, not a Presidential election. I'm afraid my stomach's a little queasy. Wait just a second; I've got some pills in my little black bag. Got pills in there for all ailments. Find out if anyone else needs resuscitation, will you?" Drink in hand, he went toward the closet, where his little black bag was stashed.

"Excitement," said Senator Cannon. "Frank isn't used to politics."

Matson chuckled. "Do him good to see how the other half lives." He walked off, bearing drinks for the others. Governor Spanding grabbed one and came over to the senator. "Jim! Ready to tear up your capitulation speech now?"

Cannon glanced at his watch. "Almost. The polls closed in Nome just ten minutes ago. We'll wait for the President's acknowledgment of defeat before we go downstairs." He glanced at his brother, who was washing something down with water.

Behind him, he heard Matson's voice saying: "I'm sure glad Horvin isn't here! I can hear him now: 'Image! Image! That's what won the election! Image!' " Matson guffawed. "Jim Cannon was winning elections by landslides before he even heard of Horvin! Jim Cannon projects his own image."

"Sure he does," Matt Fisher said, "but what about me?"

"You? Hah! You're tops, Matt. Once a man gets to know you, he can see that, if he's got any brains."

Fisher chuckled gently. "Ed, you've got what it takes to be a politician, all right."

"So do you, Mr. Vice President! So do you! Hey!" He turned quickly. "We got to have a toast! Doc, you're his brother. I think the honor should be yours."

Dr. Frank Cannon, looking much more chipper since swallowing the pills, beamed and looked at his brother. "It will be a pleasure. Gentlemen, come to attention, if you will." They did, grinning at first, then forcing solemnity into their expressions.

"Gentlemen," said Dr. Cannon gravely, "I give you my brother, Senator James Harrington Cannon, the next President of the United States!"

"To the President!" said Governor Spanding.

"To the President!" chorused the others.

Glasses clinked and men drank solemnly.

Then, before anyone could say anything, Dr. Cannon said: "I further propose, gentlemen, that we drink to the man who will spend the next four years in the White House — God willing — in the hope that his ability to han-

dle that high office will be equal to the task before him, and that he will
prove worthy of the trust placed in him by those who had faith in that ability."

"Amen," said Congressman Matson softly.

And they all drank again.

Senator Cannon said: "I thank you, gentlemen. I—"

But, at that moment, the ubiquitous clatter of noise from the television
changed tenor. They all turned to look.

". . . And gentlemen," the announcer's voice was saying, "The President
of the United States!"

The Presidential Seal which had been pictured on the screen faded suddenly, to be replaced by the face of the President. He looked firmly resigned,
but neither haggard, tired, defeated, nor unhappy. To the five men who stood
watching him in that room, it was obvious that the speech to come was on
tape.

The President smiled wanly. "Fellow Americans," he began, "as your
President, I wish both to congratulate you and thank you. As free citizens
of a free country, exercising your franchise of the ballot to determine the
men and women who are to represent and lead you during their coming terms
of office, you have made your decision. You have considered well the qualifications of those men and women, and you have considered well the problems
that will face our country as a whole and each individual as a free citizen
desiring to remain free, and you have made your choice accordingly, as is
your right and duty. For that, I congratulate you."

He paused for a dramatic moment.

"The decision, I think, was not an easy one. The citizens of our great
democracy are not sheep, to be led first this way and then that; they are not
dead leaves to be carried by every vagrant breeze that blows; they are not
children, nor are they fools."

He looked searchingly from the screen, as though to see into the minds
of every person watching.

"Do not mistake my meaning," he said levelly, "I do not mean that there
are no fools among us. There are." Again he paused for effect. "Every man,
every woman, who, through laziness or neglect or complacency, failed to
make his desire known at the polls in this election—is a fool. Every citizen
who thinks that his vote doesn't count for much, and therefore fails to register
that vote—is a fool. Every person who accepts the *privileges* of American
citizenship and considers them as *rights,* and who neglects the *duties* of citizenship because they are tiresome—is a fool."

He waited for half a second.

"Fortunately for us all, the fools are in a minority in our country. This
election shows that. Most of you have done your duty and followed your
conscience as you saw fit. And I congratulate you for that."

The smile became less broad—by just the right amount.

"Four years ago, exercising that same privilege and duty, you, the citizens of the United States, honored me and those who were working with me by electing us to the highest offices in this nation. You elected us, I believe, because we made certain promises to you—solemn promises that were made in our platform four years ago."

He took a deep breath and folded his hands below his chin.

"I am certain that you all know we have endeavored to keep those promises. I am certain that you know that we have kept faith with the people of this nation."

He looked down for a moment, then looked up again.

"This year, in our platform, we made more promises. We outlined a program that we felt would be of the greatest benefit to this nation." He unclasped his hands and spread them with an open gesture.

"Senator James Cannon and his party have also made promises—promises which, I am sure, they, too, feel are best for our nation."

Another pause.

"You, the citizens of the United States, have, in the past few months, carefully weighed these promises against one another—weighing not only the promises themselves, but the integrity and the ability of the men who made them.

"And you have made your choice.

"I cannot, and do not, quarrel with that choice. It is the essence of democratic government that disagreements in the upper echelons of that government shall be resolved by the action and the will of the governed. You, the people of the United States, have done just that.

"And—for that, I thank you."

A final hesitation.

"Next January, Senator James Harrington Cannon will be inaugurated as President of the United States. Let us show him, and the men who are to work with him, that we, as citizens of this great nation, resolving our differences, will strive unceasingly under his administration to further the high resolves and great ideals of our country.

"I believe—I *know*—that you are all with me in this resolution, and, for that, too—

"—I thank you."

The face of the President of the United States faded from the screen.

After a few seconds, Matson sighed, "Not bad at all, really," he said, stepping over to shut off the set. "He's been taking lessons, from you, Jim. But he just hasn't quite got it."

Senator Cannon took another swallow of his drink and said nothing.

"Sincerity," said Governor Spanding. "That's what's lacking. He hasn't got it, and the voters can feel it."

"He managed to be elected President of the United States on it," Senator Cannon said dryly.

Spanding didn't turn to look at Cannon: he kept looking at the dead TV screen. "These things show up by comparison, Jim. In comparison with some of us—most of us, in fact—he looks pretty good. I've known him since he was a fresh junior senator, and I was just attorney for the House Committee for Legislative Oversight." He turned around. "You know what, Jim? When I first heard him talk, I actually thought about changing parties. Yeah. Really." He turned around again.

"But," he went on, "he's all hot air and no ability. Just like Matt, here, is all ability and no hot air. No offense meant, Matt, believe me," he added, glancing at Fisher.

"I know," Fisher said quietly.

Spanding turned around once more and looked Cannon squarely in the eyes. "You've got both, Jim. The blarney to put yourself over, and the ability to back it up. And you know I'm not trying to flatter you when I say that."

When Cannon nodded wordlessly, Spanding gave himself a short, embarrassed laugh. "Ah, Hell. I talk too much." And he took a hefty slug of his drink.

Matthew Fisher took the overcharge out of the sudden outburst of emotion by saying: "It's more than just ability and sincerity, Harry. There's determination and honesty, too."

Matson said, "Amen to that."

Dr. Frank Cannon was just standing there, looking at his brother. There was a definite look of respect on his face.

Senator Cannon said: "You're all great guys—thanks. But I've got to get downstairs and make a speech. Ed, get the recording tape out of that set; I want to make some notes on what he said. And hurry it up, we haven't got too long."

"No canned speech for you, eh, Jim?" Spanding said.

"Amen to that, too," said Representative Matson as he opened the panel in the side of the TV set.

From a hundred thousand loudspeakers all over the United States, from the rockbound coast of Maine to the equally rockbound coast of Alaska, from the sun-washed coast of Florida to the ditto coast of Hawaii, the immortal voice of Bing Crosby, preserved forever in an electronic pattern made from a decades-old recording, told of a desire for a White Christmas. It was a voice and a tune and a lyric that aroused nostalgia even in the hearts of Floridians and Californians and Hawaiians who had never seen snow in their lives.

The other carols rang out, too—"Silent Night," "Hark! The Herald Angels Sing," "God Rest Ye Merry Gentlemen," "O Little Town of Bethlehem," and all the others. All over the nation, in millions upon millions of Christian homes, the faithful prepared to celebrate the birth, the coming, of their Saviour, Who had come to bring peace on Earth to men.

And in millions of other American homes, the Children of Abraham celebrated the Festival of Lights — *Chanukah,* the Dedication — the giving of thanks for the Blessing of God upon the priestly family of the Maccabees, who, twenty-odd centuries before, had taken up arms against the tyranny of a dynasty which had banned the worship of Almighty God, and who, by winning, had made themselves a symbol forever of the moral struggle against the forces that oppress the free mind of Man.

The newspapers and television newscasts were full of the age-old "human interest stories" which, in spite of their predictability — the abandoned baby, the dying child, the wretchedly ill oldster — still brought a tear to the eye during the Holiday Season.

As President-elect Cannon slowly made his cabinet appointments, the announcements appeared, but there was hardly any discussion of them, much less any hue and cry.

One editorial writer did make a comment: "It is encouraging to see that President-elect Cannon consults with Vice-President-elect Matthew Fisher regularly and frequently as the appointments are made. For a good many years, ever since the Eisenhower Administration, back in the Fifties, it has been the policy of most of our Chief Executives to make sure that the Vice President is groomed to take over smoothly if anything should happen to the President. Senator Cannon, however, is, as far as we know, the first President-elect who has begun this grooming before the Inauguration. This, in our opinion, shows both wisdom and political astuteness."

By the second week of the New Year, the new Cabinet had been picked. Contrary to the rumors before the election, the senator's brother had not been selected for any post whatever, but the men who *were* picked for Cabinet posts were certainly of high caliber. The United States Senate had confirmed them all before Inauguration Day.

That day was clear and cold in Washington. After the seemingly endless ceremonies and ceremonials, after the Inaugural Ball, and the Inaugural Supper, and the Inaugural Et Cetera, President James Cannon went to bed, complaining of a "slight headache."

"Frankly," he told Vice President Matthew Fisher, "it is a real headsplitter." He took four aspirin and went to bed.

He said he felt "a little better" the next day.

The fifth of February.
Ten forty-eight in the evening.
The White House, Washington, D.C.

Dr. Frank Hewlitt Cannon stood in a darkened bedroom in Blair House, across the street from the Executive Mansion, nervously looking out the window at the big white house across the way. He was not nervous for himself, although he had plenty of reason to be. He was clad in pajamas, as his brother had ordered, and had even taken the extra precaution of rumpling up his hair.

He looked at his watch, and then looked back at the White House. *How long?* he thought. *How long?*

He looked at his wrist again. The sweep hand only moved when he looked at it, apparently. He dropped his hands and clasped them behind his back. How long before he would know?

My kid brother, he thought. *I could always outthink him and outfight him. But he's got something I haven't got. He's stuck to his guns and fought hard all these years. I couldn't do what he's doing tonight, and I know it. You're a better man than I am, kid.*

Across Pennsylvania Avenue, President James Cannon was doing some heavy consideration, too. He sat on the edge of his bed and looked at the small tubular device in his hand.

Will Frank be safe? That's the only weak point in the plan.

Frank was safe. He *had* to be. Frank hadn't been over from Blair House in three days. They hadn't even *seen* each other in three days. The Secret Service men—

He threw a glance toward the door that led from his bedroom to the hall.

The Secret Service agents would know that Frank couldn't possibly have had anything to do with it. The only possible connection would be the hypogun itself. He looked at the little gadget. *Hell,* he thought; *now or never.*

He got up and strode purposefully into the bathroom. He smiled crookedly at his own reflection in the mirror. It was damnably difficult for a President to outwit his own bodyguard.

Get on with it!

He swallowed the capsule Frank had given him. Then, placing the muzzle against the precise spots Frank had shown him, James Cannon pulled the trigger. Once . . . twice . . . thrice . . .

Against each nerve center in his left side. Fine.

Now that it was done, all fear—all trepidation—left President James Cannon. Now there was no way to go but ahead.

First, the hypogun that had blown the drug into his body. Two minutes to get rid of that, for that was the only thing that could tie Frank in to the plan.

They had already agreed that there was no way to get rid of it. It couldn't be destroyed or thrown away. There was only one way that it could be taken from the White House . . .

Cannon left his fingerprints on it, dropped it into the wastebasket, and covered it with tissue paper. Then he left the bathroom and walked toward

the hall door. Beyond it, he knew, were the guarding Secret Service men.
And already his left side was beginning to feel odd.

He walked to the door and opened it. He had a scowl on his face.

"Hello, Jenkins — Grossman," he said, as the two men turned. "I've got
a hell of a headache again. Aspirin doesn't seem to help, and I can't get any
sleep." He looked rather dazed, as though he wasn't sure of his surroundings. He smiled lopsidedly. "Call Frank, over at Blair House, will you? Hurry?" Then he swallowed, looked dazed, and fell to the floor in a heap.

The two Secret Service men didn't move, but they shouted loudly. Their
orders were to guard the body of the President — *literally!* Until it was declared
legally dead, that body was their responsibility.

The other Secret Service men in the White House came on the run. Within one minute after Cannon had fallen, a call had gone to Blair House, asking for the President's brother.

Inside of another two minutes, Dr. Frank Cannon was coming through
the front door of the Executive Mansion. In spite of the chill outside, he
was wearing only a topcoat over his pajamas.

"What happened?" he snapped, with the authority that only a physician
can muster. "Where is he?"

He heard the story on the way to the President's room. Jenkins and Grossman were still standing over the fallen Chief Executive. "We haven't moved
him, except to make him more comfortable," said Grossman. "He's still O.K.
. . . I mean, he's breathing, and his heart's still going. But we didn't want
to move him —"

"Fine!" snapped the doctor. "Best thing." He knelt over his brother and
picked up his wrist. "Have you called anyone else?" he asked sharply while
he felt the pulse.

"The Naval Hospital," said another agent. "They're coming fast!"

"Fine!" repeated Dr. Frank. By this time, most of the White House staff
was awake. Frank Cannon let go the wrist and stood up quickly. "Can't tell
for sure, but it looks like a slight stroke. Excuse me."

He went into the Executive bedroom, and on into the bathroom. He closed
the door. Quickly, he fished the hypogun out of the wastebasket and dropped
it into the little black bag which he had carried with him. He came out with
a glass of water. Everything was taken care of.

PRESIDENT SUFFERS STROKE!
JHC Taken To US Naval Hospital
In Washington After Stroke In
White House

All over the world, headlines and newscasts in a hundred tongues carried
the story. And from all over the world came messages of sympathy and con-

cern for the stricken Chief Executive. From England, simultaneous messages arrived from the Sovereign and the Prime Minister; from France, notes from both the President and the Premier of the Seventh Republic; from Ethiopia, condolences from His Imperial Majesty and from the Chief Executive. The United German Federation, the Constitutional Kingdom of Spain, the Republic of Italy, the United Austro-Yugoslavian Commonwealth, and the Polish Free State all sent rush radiograms. So did Argentina, Bolivia, Brazil, Chile, Colombia, Ecuador, Paraguay, Peru, Uruguay, and Venezuela. From Africa, Australia, Southern Asia, Oceania, and Central America came expressive words of sorrow. Special blessings were sent by His Holiness from Vatican City, by the Patriarch of Istanbul, and by the Archbishop of Canterbury. The Presidente of the Estados Unidos Mexicanos personally took a plane to Washington, as did the Governor General of Canada, carrying a personal message from the Prime Minister. Even the Soviet Union sent a radiogram, and the story of the tragedy was printed in *Pravda,* accompanied by an editorial that almost approached straight reporting.

President James Harrington Cannon knew none of this. He was unconscious and unable to receive visitors.

As far as actual news from the White House was concerned, news commentator Barton Wayne gave the best summary over a major American TV network on the morning of the sixth of February:

"Last night, at approximately eleven p.m., James Harrington Cannon, President of the United States, collapsed at the feet of the Secret Service men who were guarding him. Within a few minutes, Dr. Frank Cannon, the President's brother, called by the Secret Service in obedience to the President's last conscious words, had arrived from Blair House, where he had been staying.

"Dr. Frank Cannon diagnosed the President's illness as a — quote — slight stroke — unquote. Later, after the President had been taken to the Naval Hospital for further diagnosis, Dr. Cannon released a statement. Quote — further tests have enabled the medical staff of this hospital to make a more detailed analysis. Apparently, the President has suffered a slight cerebral hemorrhage which has, temporarily at least, partially paralyzed the muscles of his left side. The President, however, has regained consciousness, and his life is in no danger — unquote.

"After only sixteen days in the White House, the President has fallen ill. We can only wish him Godspeed and an early recovery."

Dr. Frank Cannon stood firmly by his brother's bedside, shaking his head firmly. "No, commander; I cannot permit that. I am in charge of this case, and I shall remain in charge of it until my patient tells me otherwise."

The graying Navy medical officer pursed his lips. "In cases of this sort, doctor," he said primly, "the Navy is in charge. The patient is, after all, the President of the United States."

Dr. Frank went right on shaking his head. "Cuts no ice, commander. I was specifically summoned by the patient. I agreed to take the case. I will be most happy to accept your cooperation; I welcome your advice and aid; but I will *not* allow my patient to be taken from my charge."

"It is hardly considered proper for the physician in charge of a serious case to be a relative of the patient."

"Possibly. But it is neither unethical nor illegal." He gave the commander a dry smile. "I know my brother, commander. Quite well. I also know that you have the authority and the means to expel me from this hospital." The smile became positively icy. "And, in view of the former, I should not advise you to exercise the latter."

The commander wet his lips. "I have no intention of doing so, doctor," he said rather huffily. "But, inasmuch as the X-rays show no—"

There came a mumble from the man on the bed, and, in that instant, both men forgot their differences and became physicians again, as they focused their attention on the patient.

President Cannon was blinking his eyes groggily. Or, rather, *eye*. The left one refused to do more than show a faint flicker of the lid.

"Hullo, Jamie," Dr. Frank said gently. "How d'you feel?" It took nerves of steel to show that tender composure. The drug should wear off quickly, but if Jim Cannon's mind was still fuzzy, and he said the wrong thing—

For a moment, the President said nothing as he tried to focus his right eye.

"Don't try to move, Mr. President," said the Navy doctor softly.

President Cannon smiled lopsidedly, the left side of his face refusing to make the effort. "Arright," he said, in a low, blurred voice. "Wha' happen', Frang?"

"Apparently," said Dr. Frank carefully, "you've had a little bit of a stroke, kid. Nothing to worry about. How do you feel?"

"Funny. Li'l dizzy. Don't hurt, though."

"Good. Fine. You'll be O.K. shortly."

The President's voice became stronger. "I'm glad you're here, Frank. Tell me—is it . . . bad?"

" 'Tain't good, kid," Dr. Frank said with a bedside grin. "You can't expect a stroke to put you in the best of health, now, can you?"

The lopsided smile came back. "Guess not." The smile went away, to be replaced by a puzzled frown. "My whole left side feels dead. What's the matter?"

Instead of answering, Dr. Frank Cannon turned to the Navy medic. "I'll let the commander explain that. What's your diagnosis, doctor?"

The commander ran his tongue nervously over his lips before speaking. "There's apparently a small blood clot in the brain, Mr. President, interfering with the functioning of the efferent nerves."

"Permanent?"

"We don't know yet, sir. We hope not."

President Cannon sighed. "Well. Thank you, commander. And now, if you don't mind, I'd like to speak to my brother — alone."

The commander glanced at Dr. Frank, then back at the President. "Certainly, sir." He turned to leave.

"Just a moment, commander," Dr. Frank said. "There'll be news reporters out there. Tell them — " He frowned a little. "Tell them that the President is conscious and quite rational, but that there is still some weakness. I don't think anything more than that will be necessary."

"I agree. Certainly, doctor." At the door, the commander paused and said: "I'll keep everyone out until you call."

"Thanks," said Dr. Frank as the door closed behind the Navy man.

As soon as it closed, President Cannon struggled to get up.

"Don't try it, kid," the doctor said, "those muscles are paralyzed, even if you aren't sick. Here, let me help you."

"How did it come off?" Cannon asked as his brother propped him up.

"Perfectly. No one doubts that it's a stroke. Now what?"

"Give me a cigarette."

"All right, but watch it. Use your right hand, and smoke with the right side of your mouth. Here." The doctor lit a cigarette and handed it to his brother. "Now, what's the next step?"

"The next step is to tell Matthew Fisher," said the President.

Dr. Frank Cannon scowled. "Why? Why not just go through with the thing and let him be fooled along with the rest? It seems to me he'd be . . . well, more secure in his own position if he didn't know."

"No." The President hunched himself up on his pillows. "Can't you raise the head of this bed?"

Dr. Frank touched a button on the bedside panel, and the upper portion of the bed rose smoothly at an angle. "Better?"

"Fine. Much better."

"You were saying — "

"Yeah. About Matt Fisher. He has to know. He'll guess eventually, in the next four years, anyway — unless I hide away somewhere. And I have no intention of doing that.

"Oh, I'm not trying to show Matt what a great guy I am, Frank. You know better than that, and so will he. But Matt will have to have all the facts at hand, if he's to do his job right, and it seems to me that this is a pretty important fact. What do you say, Frank?"

The doctor nodded slowly. "I think you know more about the situation than I do. And I trust your judgment, kid. And Matt's, too, I guess."

"No." President Cannon's voice was firm as he looked at his brother with one bright eye. "Don't trust Matt's judgment, because he doesn't have any."

Dr. Frank looked astonished. "Then *what*—?" He stopped.

"Matthew Fisher," said President Cannon authoritatively, "doesn't need judgment any more than *you* need instinct. No more so, and no less. I said he doesn't have any judgment, but that's not exactly true. He has it, but he only uses it for routine work, just as you or I use instinct. We can override our instinctive reactions when we have to. Matt can override his judgment when he has to.

"I don't pretend to know how Fisher's mind works. If I did, I wouldn't be doing this. But I *do* know that Matt Fisher—by some mental process I can't even fathom—almost invariably knows the *right* thing to do, and he knows it without using judgment."

"And you're still convinced that this is the only way out?" Dr. Frank asked. "Couldn't you stay in office and let him run things under cover?"

"We discussed all this months ago, Frank," Cannon said wearily. "My reasons remain the same. Matt couldn't possibly operate efficiently if he had to go through me every time. And I am human, too; I'd have a tendency to impose my judgment on his decisions.

"No, Frank; this is the only way it can work. This country needs Matthew Fisher as President, but he could never have been elected. Now I've done my job; now it's time for me to get out of the way and turn the Presidency over to a man who can handle the office far better than any other man I know."

"You make him sound like some sort of superman," said Dr. Frank with a wry grin.

"Hell," said President Cannon, "you don't think I'd turn this job over to anything less, do you?" He chuckled. "Call him in, will you?"

PRESIDENT CANNON RESIGNS!
Ill Health Given As Reason;
Doctors Say Recovery
Unlikely In Near Future.
VP Fisher To Take Oath Tomorrow.

A Rose by
Other Name . . .   CHRISTOPHER ANVIL

All that we know about "Christopher Anvil" is that his real name
is Harry C. Crosby and that he is the author of scores of interesting science-fiction stories that usually take social ideas and stand
them on their heads. He specializes in examining social trends and
carrying them out to their frequently illogical conclusions. He was
one of the steadiest contributors to *Analog* in the 1960s, but his
few novels do not compare with the best of his shorter work, a
good example of which is "A Rose by Other Name . . ." which
takes a wry look at the importance of language in international
politics.

A tall man in a tightly-belted trenchcoat carried a heavy brief case toward
the Pentagon building.

A man in a black overcoat strode with a bulky suitcase toward the
Kremlin.

A well-dressed man wearing a dark-blue suit stepped out of a taxi near
the United Nations building, and paid the driver. As he walked away, he
leaned slightly to the right, as if the attaché case under his left arm held lead
instead of paper.

On the sidewalk nearby, a discarded newspaper lifted in the wind, to lie
face up before the entrance to the United Nations building. Its big black headline read:

U.S. WILL FIGHT!

A set of diagrams in this newspaper showed United States and Soviet missiles, with comparison of ranges, payloads, and explosive powers, and with
the Washington Monument sketched into the background to give an idea
of their size.

146

The well-dressed man with the attaché case strode across the newspaper to the entrance, his heels ripping the tables of missile comparisons as he passed.

Inside the building, the Soviet delegate was at this moment saying:

"The Soviet Union is the most scientifically advanced nation on Earth. The Soviet Union is the most powerful nation on Earth. It is not up to you to say to the Soviet Union 'Yes' or 'No.' The Soviet Union has told you what it is going to do. All I can suggest for you is, you had better agree with us."

The United States delegate said, "That is the view of the Soviet government?"

"That is the view of the Soviet government."

"In that case, I will have to tell you the view of the United States government. If the Soviet Union carries out this latest piece of brutal aggression, the United States will consider it a direct attack upon its own security. I hope you know what this means."

There was an uneasy stir in the room.

The Soviet delegate said slowly, "I am sorry to hear you say that. I am authorized to state that the Soviet Union will not retreat on this issue."

The United States delegate said, "The position of the United States is already plain. If the Soviet Union carries this out, the United States will consider it as a direct attack. There is nothing more I can say."

In the momentary silence that followed, a guard with a rather stuporous look opened the door to let in a well-dressed man, who was just sliding something back into his attaché case. This man glanced thoughtfully around the room, where someone was just saying:

"Now what do we do?"

Someone else said hesitantly, "A conference, perhaps?"

The Soviet delegate said coolly, "A conference will not settle this. The United States must correct its provocative attitude."

The United States delegate looked off at a distant wall. "The provocation is this latest Soviet aggression. All that is needed is for the Soviet Union not to do it."

"The Soviet Union will not retreat in this issue."

The United States delegate said, "The United States will not retreat on this issue."

There was a dull silence that lasted for some time.

As the United States and the Soviet delegates sat unmoving, there came an urgent plea, "Gentlemen, doesn't anyone have an idea? However implausible?"

The silence continued long enough to make it plain that now no one could see any way out.

A well-dressed man in dark-blue, carrying an attaché case, stepped forward and set the case down on a table with a solid *clunk* that riveted attention.

"Now," he said, "we are in a real mess. Very few people on Earth want to get burned alive, poisoned, or smashed to bits. We don't want a ruinous war. But from the looks of things, we're likely to get one anyway, whether we want it or not.

"The position we are in is like that of a crowd of people locked in a room. Some of us have brought along for our protection large savage dogs. Our two chief members have trained tigers. This menagerie is now straining at the leash. Once the first blow lands, no one can say where it will end.

"What we seem to need right now is someone with skills of a lion tamer. The lion tamer controls the animals by understanding, timing, and *distraction.*"

The United States and Soviet delegates glanced curiously at each other. The other delegates shifted around with puzzled expressions. Several opened their mouths as if to interrupt, glanced at the United States and Soviet delegates, shut their mouths and looked at the attaché case.

"Now," the man went on, "a lion tamer's tools are a pistol, a whip, and a chair. They are used to distract. The pistol contains blank cartridges, the whip is snapped above the animal's head, and the chair is held with the points of the legs out, so that the animal's gaze is drawn first to one point, then another, as the chair is shifted. The sharp noise of gun and whip distract the animal's attention. So does the chair.

". . . And so long as the animal's attention is distracted, its terrific power isn't put into play. This is how the lion tamer keeps peace.

"The thought processes of a war machine are a little different from the thought processes of a lion or a tiger. But the principle is the same. What we need is something corresponding to the lion tamer's whip, chair, and gun."

He unsnapped the cover of the attaché case, and lifted out a dull gray slab with a handle on each end, several dials on its face, and beside the dials a red button and a blue button.

"It's generally known," he said, looking around at the scowling delegates, "that certain mental activities are associated with certain areas of the brain. Damage a given brain area, and you disrupt the corresponding mental action. Speech may be disrupted, while writing remains. A man who speaks French and German may lose his ability to speak French, but still be able to speak German. These things are well-known, but not generally used. Now, who knows if, perhaps, there is a special section of the brain which handles the vocabulary *related to military subjects?*"

He pushed in the blue button.

The Soviet delegate sat up straight. "What is that button you just pushed?"

"A demonstration button. It actuates when I release it."

The United States delegate said, "Actuates *what?*"

"I will show you, if you will be patient just a few minutes."

"What's this about brain areas? We can't open the brain of every general in the world."

"You won't have to. Of course, you have heard of resonant frequencies and related topics. Take two tuning forks that vibrate at the same rate. Set one in vibration, and the other across the room will vibrate. Soldiers marching across a bridge break step, lest they start the bridge in vibration and bring it down. The right note on a violin will shatter a glass. Who knows whether minute electrical currents in a particular area of the brain, associated with a certain characteristic mental activity, may not tend to induce a similar activity in the corresponding section of another brain? And, in that case, if it were possible to induce a sufficiently *strong* current, it might actually overload that particular—"

The United States delegate tensely measured with his eyes the distance to the gray slab on the table.

The Soviet delegate slid his hand toward his waistband.

The man who was speaking took his finger from the blue button.

The Soviet delegate jerked out a small black automatic. The United States delegate shot from his chair in a flying leap. Around the room, men sprang to their feet. There was an instant of violent activity.

Then the automatic fell to the floor. The United States delegate sprawled motionless across the table. Around the room, men crumpled to the floor in the nerveless fashion of the dead drunk.

Just one man remained on his feet, leaning forward with a faintly dazed expression as he reached for the red button. He said, "You have temporarily overloaded certain mental circuits, gentlemen. I have been protected by a . . . you might say, a jamming device. You will recover from the effects of *this* overload. The next one you experience will be a different matter. I am sorry, but there are certain conditions of mental resonance that the human race can't afford at the moment."

He pressed the red button.

The United States delegate, lying on the table, experienced a momentary surge of rage. In a flash, it was followed by an intensely clear vision of the map of Russia, the polar regions adjoining it, and the nations along its southern border. Then the map was more than a map, as he saw the economic complexes of the Soviet Union, and the racial and national groups forcibly submerged by the central government. The strong and weak points of the Soviet Union emerged, as in a transparent anatomical model of the human body laid out for an operation.

Not far away, the Soviet delegate could see the submarines off the coasts of the United States, the missiles arcing down on the vital industrial areas, the bombers on their long one-way missions, and the unexpected land attack to settle the problem once and for all. As he thought, he revised the plan continuously, noting an unexpected American strength here, and the possibility of a dangerous counterblow there.

In the mind of another delegate, Great Britain balanced off the United States against the Soviet Union, then by a series of carefully planned moves acquired the moral leadership of a bloc of uncommitted nations. Next, with this as a basis for maneuver —

Another delegate saw France leading a Europe small in area but immense in productive power. After first isolating Britain —

At nearly the same split fraction of an instant, all these plans became complete. Each delegate saw his nation's way to the top with a dazzling, more than human clarity.

And then there was an impression like the brief glow of an overloaded wire. There was a sensation similar to pain.

This experience repeated itself in a great number of places around the globe.

In the Kremlin, a powerfully-built marshal blinked at the members of his staff.

"Strange. For just a minute there, I seemed to see —" He shrugged and pointed at the map. "Now, along the North German Plain here, where we intend to . . . to —" He scowled, groping for a word. "Hm-m-m. Where we want to . . . ah . . . destabilize the . . . the ridiculous NATO protective counterproposals —" He stopped frowning.

The members of his staff straightened up and looked puzzled. A general said, "Marshal, I just had an idea. Now, one of the questions is: Will the Americans . . . ah — Will they . . . hm-m-m —" He scowled, glanced off across the room, bit his lip, and said, "Ah . . . what I'm trying to say is: Will they forcibly demolecularize Paris, Rome, and other Allied centers when we . . . ah . . . inundate them with the integrated hyperarticulated elements of our —" He cut himself off suddenly, a look of horror on his face.

The marshal said sharply, "What are you talking about — 'demolecularize?' You mean, will they . . . hm-m-m . . . disconstitute the existent structural pattern by application of intense energy of nuclear fusion?" He stopped and blinked several times as this last sentence played itself back in his mind.

Another member of the staff spoke up hesitantly, "Sir, I'm not exactly sure what you have in mind, but I had a thought back there that struck me as a good workable plan to deconstitutionalize the whole American government in five years by unstructing their political organization through intrasocietal political action simultaneously on all levels. Now —"

"Ah," said another general, his eyes shining with an inward vision, "I have a better plan. Banana embargo. Listen —"

A fine beading of perspiration appeared on the marshal's brow. It had occurred to him to wonder if the Americans had somehow just landed the ultimate of foul blows. He groped around mentally to try to get his mind back on the track.

At this moment, two men in various shades of blue were sitting by a big globe in the Pentagon building staring at a third man in an olive-colored uniform. There was an air of embarrassment in the room.

At length, one of the men in blue cleared his throat. "General, I hope your plans are based on something a little clearer than that. I don't see how you can expect us to co-operate with you in recommending *that* kind of a thing to the President. But now, I just had a remarkable idea. It's a little unusual; but if I do say so, it's the kind of thing that can clarify the situation instead of sinking it in hopeless confusion. Now, what I propose is that we immediately proceed to layerize the existent trade routes in *depth*. This will counteract the Soviet potential nullification of our sea-borne surface-level communications through their underwater superiority. Now, this involves a fairly unusual concept. But what I'm driving at — "

"Wait a minute," said the general, in a faintly hurt tone. "You didn't get my point. It may be that I didn't express it quite as I intended. But what I mean is, we've got to really bat those bricks all over the lot. Otherwise, there's bound to be trouble. Look — "

The man in Air Force blue cleared his throat. "Frankly, I've always suspected there was a certain amount of confusion in both your plans. But I never expected anything like this. Fortunately, *I* have an idea — "

At the United Nations, the American and Russian delegates were staring at the British delegate, who was saying methodically, "Agriculture, art, literature, science, engineering, medicine, sociology, botany, zoology, beekeeping, tinsmithing, speleology, wa . . . w . . . milita . . . mili . . . mil . . . hm-m-m . . . sewing, needlework, navigation, law, business, barrister, batt . . . bat . . . ba— Can't say it."

"In other words," said the United States delegate, "we're mentally hamstrung. Our vocabulary is gone as regards . . . ah— That is, we can talk about practically anything, except subjects having to do with . . . er . . . strong disagreements."

The Soviet delegate scowled. "This is bad. I just had a good idea, too. Maybe— " He reached for pencil and paper.

A guard came in scowling. "Sorry, sir. There's no sign of any such person in the building now. He must have gotten away."

The Soviet delegate was looking glumly at his piece of paper.

"Well," he said, "I do not think I would care to trust the safety of my country to this method of communication."

Staring up at him from the paper were the words:

"Instructions to head man of Forty-fourth Ground-Walking Club. Seek to interpose your club along the high ground between the not-friendly-to-us fellows and the railway station. Use repeated strong practical urging procedures to obtain results desired."

The United States delegate had gotten hold of a typewriter, slid in a piece of paper, typed rapidly, and was now scowling in frustration at the result.

The Soviet delegate shook his head. "What's the word for it? We've been bugged. The section of our vocabulary dealing with . . . with . . . you know what I mean . . . that section has been burned out."

The United States delegate scowled. "Well, we can still stick pins in maps and draw pictures. Eventually we can get across what we mean."

"Yes, but that is no way to run a wa . . . wa . . . a strong disagreement. We will have to build up a whole new vocabulary to deal with the subject."

The United States delegate thought it over, and nodded. "All right," he said. "Now, look. If we're each going to have to make new vocabularies, do we want to end up with . . . say . . . sixteen different words in sixteen different languages all for the same thing? Take a . . . er . . . 'strong disagreement.' Are you going to call it 'gosnick' and we call it 'gack' and the French call it 'gouk' and the Germans call it 'Gunck'? And then we have to have twenty dozen different sets of dictionaries and hundreds of interpreters so we can merely get some idea what each other is talking about?"

"No," said the Soviet delegate grimly. "Not that. We should have an international commission to settle that. Maybe there, at least, is something we can agree on. Obviously, it is to everyone's advantage not to have innumerable new words for the same thing. Meanwhile, perhaps . . . ah . . . perhaps for now we had better postpone a final settlement of the present difficulty."

Six months later, a man wearing a tightly-belted trenchcoat approached the Pentagon building.

A man carrying a heavy suitcase strode along some distance from the Kremlin.

A taxi carrying a well-dressed man with an attaché case cruised past the United Nations building.

Inside the United Nations building, the debate was getting hot. The Soviet delegate said angrily:

"The Soviet Union is the most scientifically advanced and unquestionably the most gacknik nation on Earth. The Soviet Union will not take dictation from anybody. We have given you an extra half-year to make up your minds, and now we are going to put it to you bluntly:

"If you want to cush a gack with us over this issue, we will mongel you. We will grock you into the middle of next week. No running dog of a capitalist imperialist will get out in one piece. You may hurt us in the process, but *we* will absolutely bocket *you*. The day of decadent capitalism is *over*."

A rush of marvelous dialectic burst into life in the Soviet delegate's mind. For a split instant he could see with unnatural clarity not only why, but how, his nation's philosophy was bound to emerge triumphant—if handled properly—and even without a ruinous gack, too.

Unknown to the Soviet delegate, the United States delegate was simultaneously experiencing a clear insight into the stunning possibilities of basic American beliefs, which up to now had hardly been tapped at all.

At the same time, other delegates were sitting straight, their eyes fixed on distant visions.

The instant of dazzling certainty burnt itself out.

"Yes," said the Soviet delegate, as if in a trance. "No need to even cush a gack. Inevitably, victory must go to communi . . . commu . . . comm . . . com—" He stared in horror.

The American delegate shut his eyes and groaned, "Capitalis . . . capita . . . capi . . . cap . . . rugged individu . . . rugged indi . . . rugge . . . rug . . . rug—" He looked up. "Now we've got to have *another* conference. And then, on top of that, we've got to somehow cram our new definitions down the throats of the thirty per cent of the people they *don't* reach with their device."

The Soviet delegate felt for his chair and sat down heavily. "Dialectic materia . . . dialecti . . . dial . . . dia—" He put his hand in both hands and drew in a deep shuddering breath.

The British delegate was saying, "Thin red li . . . thin re . . . thin . . . thin— This *hurts.*"

"Yes," said the United States delegate. "But if this goes on, we may end up with a complete, new, unified language. Maybe that's the idca."

The Soviet delegate drew in a deep breath and looked up gloomily. "Also, this answers one long-standing question."

"What's that?"

"One of your writers asked it long ago: 'What's in a name?' "

The delegates all nodded with sickly expressions.

"*Now* we know."

Beyond Doubt   ROBERT A. HEINLEIN

Robert A. Heinlein (b.1907) was a major figure in American science-fiction from almost his first appearance in the magazines in 1939. His contributions to the field include breaking SF out of the pulp magazines and into the "slicks" like the *Saturday Evening Post* and introducing the genre to an entire generation of readers through his excellent "Young Adult" series of novels in the late 1940s and 1950s. He has recently made a remarkable recovery from a serious illness and is again turning out books at the rate of one a year.

In "Beyond Doubt" (originally published as by "Lyle Monroe and Elma Wentz") he gives us a satirical look at one of the great weapons of modern political campaigns — the political cartoon.

Savant solves secret of Easter Island images According to Professor J. Howard Erlenmeyer, Sc.D., Ph.D., F.R.S., director of the Archaeological Society's Easter Island Expedition. Professor Erlenmeyer was quoted as saying, "There can no longer be any possible doubt as to the significance of the giant monolithic images which are found in Easter Island. When one considers the primary place held by religious matters in all primitive cultures, and compares the design of these images with artifacts used in the rites of present day Polynesian tribes, the conclusion is inescapable that these images have a deep esoteric religious significance. Beyond doubt, their large size, their grotesque exaggeration of human form, and the seemingly aimless, but actually systematic, distribution gives evidence of the use for which they were carved, to wit; the worship of . . ."

Warm and incredibly golden, the late afternoon sun flooded the white-and-green city of Nuria, gliding its maze of circular criss-crossed streets. The Towers of the Guardians, rising high above the lushly verdant hills, gleamed like translucent ivory. The hum from the domed buildings of the business district was muted while merchants rested in the cool shade of luxuriant, moistly green trees, drank refreshing okrada, and gazed out at the great hookprowed green-and-crimson ships riding at anchor in the harbor — ships from Hindos, from Cathay, and from the far-flung colonies of Atlantis.

In all the broad continent of Mu there was no city more richly beautiful than Muria, capitol of the province of Lac.

But despite the smiling radiance of sun, and sea, and sky, there was an undercurrent of atmospheric tenseness — as though the air itself were a tight coil about to be sprung, as though a small spark would set off a cosmic explosion.

Through the city moved the sibilant whispering of a name — the name was everywhere, uttered in loathing and fear, or in high hope, according to the affiliations of the utterer — but in any mouth the name had the potency of thunder.

The name was Talus.

Talus, apostle of the common herd; Talus, on whose throbbing words hung the hopes of a million eager citizens; Talus, candidate for governor of the province of Lac.

In the heart of the tenement district, near the smelly waterfront, between a narrow side street and a garbage alley was the editorial office of Mu Regenerate, campaign organ of the Talus-for-Governor organization. The office was as quiet as the rest of Nuria, but with the quiet of a spent cyclone. The floor was littered with twisted scraps of parchment, overturned furniture, and empty beer flagons. Three young men were seated about a great, round, battered table in attitudes that spoke their gloom. One of them was staring cynically at an enormous poster which dominated one wall of the room. It was a portrait of a tall, majestic man with a long, curling white beard. He wore a green toga. One hand was raised in a gesture of benediction. Over the poster, under the crimson-and-purple of crossed Murian banners, was the legend:

Talus for Governor!

The one who stared at the poster let go an unconscious sigh. One of his companions looked up from scratching at a sheet of parchment with a stubby stylus. "What's eating on you, Robar?"

The one addressed waved a hand at the wall. "I was just looking at our white hope. Ain't he beautiful? Tell me, Dolph, how can anyone look so noble, and be so dumb?"

"God knows. It beats me."

"That's not quite fair, fellows," put in the third, "the old boy ain't really dumb; he's just unworldly. You've got to admit that the Plan is the most constructive piece of statesmanship this country has seen in a generation."

Robar turned weary eyes on him. "Sure. Sure. And he'd make a good governor, too. I won't dispute that; if I didn't think the Plan would work, would I be here, living from hand to mouth and breaking my heart on this bloody campaign? Oh, he's noble all right. Sometimes he's so noble it gags me. What I mean is: Did you ever work for a candidate that was so bull-headed stupid about how to get votes and win an election?"

"Well . . . no."

"What gets me, Clevum," Robar went on, "is that he could be elected so easily. He's got everything; a good sound platform that you can stir people up with, the correct background, a grand way of speaking, and the most beautiful appearance that a candidate ever had. Compared with Old Bat Ears, he's a natural. It ought to be just one-two-three. But Bat Ears will be re-elected, sure as shootin'."

"I'm afraid you're right," mourned Clevum. "We're going to take such a shellacking as nobody ever saw. I thought for a while that we would make the grade, but now—Did you see what the *King's Men* said about him this morning?"

"That dirty little sheet—What was it?"

"Besides some nasty cracks about Atlantis gold, they accused him of planning to destroy the Murian home and defile the sanctity of Murian womanhood. They called upon every red-blooded one hundred per cent Murian to send this subversive monster back where he came from. Oh, it stank! But the yokels were eating it up."

"Sure they do. That's just what I mean. The governor's gang slings mud all the time, but if we sling any mud about governor Vortus, Talus throws a fit. His idea of a news story is a nifty little number about comparative statistics of farm taxes in the provinces of Mu . . . What are you drawing now, Dolph?"

"This." He held up a ghoulish caricature of Governor Vortus himself, with his long face, thin lips, and high brow, atop of which rested the tall crimson governor's cap. Enormous ears gave this sinister face the appearance of a vulture about to take flight. Beneath the cartoon was the simple caption:

BAT EARS FOR GOVERNOR

"There!" exclaimed Robar, "that's what this campaign needs. Humor! If we could plaster that cartoon on the front page of *Mu Regenerate* and stick one under the door of every voter in the province, it 'ud be a landslide. One look at that mug and they'd laugh themselves sick—and vote for our boy Talus!"

He held the sketch at arm's length and studied it, frowning: Presently he looked up. "Listen, dopes—Why not do it? Give me one last edition with some guts in it. Are you game?"

Clevum looked worried. "Well . . . I don't know . . . What are you going to use for money? Besides, even if Oric would crack loose from the dough, how would we get an edition of that size distributed that well? And even if we did get it done, it might boomerang on us—the opposition would have the time and money to answer it."

Robar looked disgusted. "That's what a guy gets for having ideas in this campaign—nothing but objections, objections!"

"Wait a minute, Robar," Dolph interposed. "Clevum's kicks have some sense to them, but maybe you got something. The idea is to make Joe Citizen laugh at Vortus, isn't it? Well, why not fix up some dodgers of my cartoon and hand 'em out at the polling places on election day?"

Robar drummed on the table as he considered this. "Umm, no, it wouldn't do. Vortus' goon squads would beat the hell out of our workers and highjack our literature."

"Well, then how about painting some big banners with old Bat Ears on them? We could stick them up near each polling place where the voters couldn't fail to see them."

"Same trouble. The goon squads would have them down before the polls open."

"Do you know what, fellows," put in Clevum, "what we need is something big enough to be seen and too solid for Governor's plug-uglies to wreck. Big stone statues about two stories high would be about right."

Robar looked more pained than ever. "Clevum, if you can't be helpful, why not keep quiet? Sure, statues would be fine—if we had forty years and ten million simoleons."

"Just think, Robar," Dolph jibed, with an irritating smile, "if your mother had entered you for the priesthood, you could integrate all the statues you want—no worry, no trouble, no expense."

"Yeah, wise guy, but in that case I wouldn't be in politics—Say!"

" 'S trouble?"

"Integration! Suppose we *could* integrate enough statues of old Picklepuss—"

"How?"

"Do you know Kondor?"

"The moth-eaten old duck that hangs around the Whirling Whale?"

"That's him. I'll bet he could do it!"

"That old stumblebum? Why, he's no adept; he's just a cheap unlicensed sorcerer. Reading palms in saloons and a little jackleg horoscopy is about all he's good for. He can't even mix a potent love philter. I know; I've tried him."

"Don't be too damn certain you know all about him. He got all tanked up one night and told me the story of his life. He used to be a priest back in Egypt."

"Then why isn't he now?"

"That's the point. He didn't get along with the high priest. One night he got drunk and integrated a statue of the high priest right where it would show up best and too big to be missed — only he stuck the head of the high priest on the body of an animal."

"Whew!"

"Naturally when he sobered up the next morning and saw what he had done all he could do was run for it. He shipped on a freighter in the Red Sea and that's how come he's here."

Clevum's face had been growing longer and longer all during the discussion. He finally managed to get in an objection. "I don't suppose you two red hots have stopped to think about the penalty for unlawful use of priestly secrets?"

"Oh, shut up, Clevum. If we win the election, Talus'll square it. If we lose the election — Well, if we lose, Mu won't be big enough to hold us whether we pull this stunt or not."

Oric was hard to convince. As a politician he was always affable; as campaign manager for Talus, and consequently employer of Robar, Dolph, and Clevum, the boys had sometimes found him elusive, even though chummy.

"Ummm, well, I don't know—" He had said, "I'm afraid Talus wouldn't like it."

"Would he need to know until it's all done?"

"Now, boys, really, ah, you wouldn't want me to keep him in ignorance . . ."

"But Oric, you know perfectly well that we are going to lose unless we do something, and do it quick."

"Now, Robar, you are too pessimistic." Oric's pop eyes radiated synthetic confidence.

"How about that straw poll? We didn't look so good; we were losing two to one in the back country."

"Well . . . perhaps you are right, my boy." Oric laid a hand on the younger man's shoulder. "But suppose we do lose this election; Mu wasn't built in a day. And I want you to know that we appreciate the hard, unsparing work that you boys have done, regardless of the outcome. Talus won't forget it, and neither shall, uh, I . . . It's young men like you three who give me confidence in the future of Mu—"

"We don't want appreciation; we want to win this election."

"Oh, to be sure! To be sure! So do we all — none more than myself. Uh — how much did you say this scheme of yours would cost?"

"The integration won't cost much. We can offer Kondor a contingent fee and cut him in on a spot of patronage. Mostly we'll need to keep him supplied with wine. The big item will be getting the statues to the polling places. We had planned on straight commercial apportation."

"Well, now, that will be expensive."

"Dolph called the temple and got a price—"

"Good heavens, you haven't told the priests what you plan to do?"

"No, sir. He just specified tonnage and distances."

"What was the bid?"

Robar told him. Oric looked as if his first born were being ravaged by wolves. "Out of the question, out of the question entirely," he protested.

But Robar pressed the matter. "Sure it's expensive — but it's not half as expensive as a campaign that is just good enough to lose. Besides — I know the priesthood isn't supposed to be political, but isn't it possible with your connections for you to find one who would do it on the side for a smaller price, or even on credit? It's a safe thing for him; if we go through with this we'll *win* — it's a cinch."

Oric looked really interested for the first time. "You might be right. Mmmm — yes." He fitted the tips of his fingers carefully together. "You boys go ahead with this. Get the statues made. Let me worry about the arrangements for apportation." He started to leave, a preoccupied look on his face.

"Just a minute," Robar called out, "we'll need some money to oil up old Kondor."

Oric paused. "Oh, yes, yes. How stupid of me." He pulled out three silver pieces and handed them to Robar. "Cash, and no records, eh?" He winked.

"While you're about it, sir," added Clevum, "how about my salary? My landlady's getting awful temperamental."

Oric seemed surprised. "Oh, haven't I paid you yet?" He fumbled at his robes. "You've been very patient; most patriotic. You know how it is — so many details on my mind, and some of our sponsors haven't been prompt about meeting their pledges." He handed Clevum one piece of silver. "See me the first of the week, my boy. Don't let me forget it." He hurried out.

The three picked their way down the narrow crowded street, teeming with vendors, sailors, children, animals, while expertly dodging refuse of one kind or another, which was unceremoniously tossed from balconies. The Whirling Whale tavern was apparent by its ripe, gamey odor some little distance before one came to it. They found Kondor draped over the bar, trying as usual to cadge a drink from the seafaring patrons.

He accepted their invitation to drink with them with alacrity. Robar allowed several measures of beer to mellow the old man before he brought the conversation around to the subject. Kondor drew himself up with drunken dignity in answer to a direct question.

"Can I integrate simulacra? My son you are looking at the man who created the Sphinx." He hiccoughed politely.

"But can you still do it, here and now?" Robar pressed him, and added, "For a fee, of course."

Kondor glanced cautiously around. "Careful, my son. Some one might be listening . . . Do you want original integration, or simply re-integration?"

"What's the difference?"

Kondor rolled his eyes up, and inquired of the ceiling. "What do they teach in these modern schools? Full integration requires much power, for one must disturb the very heart of the aether itself; re-integration is simply a rearrangement of the atoms in a predetermined pattern. If you want stone statues, any waste stone will do."

"Re-integration, I guess. Now here's the proposition—"

"That will be enough for the first run. Have the porters desist." Kondor turned away and buried his nose in a crumbling roll of parchment, his rheumy eyes scanning the faded hieroglyphs. They were assembled in an abandoned gravel pit on the rear of a plantation belonging to Dolph's uncle. They had obtained the use of the pit without argument, for, as Robar had reasonably pointed out, if the old gentleman did not know that his land was being used for illicit purposes, he could not possibly have any objection.

Their numbers had been augmented by six redskinned porters from the Land of the Inca—porters who were not only strong and untiring but possessed the desirable virtue of speaking no Murian. The porters had filled the curious ventless hopper with grey gravel and waited impassively for more toil to do. Kondor put the parchment away somewhere in the folds of his disreputable robe, and removed from the same mysterious recesses a tiny instrument of polished silver.

"Your pattern, son."

Dolph produced a small waxen image, modeled from his cartoon of Bat Ears. Kondor placed it in front of him, and stared through the silver instrument at it. He was apparently satisfied with what he saw, for he commenced humming to himself in a tuneless monotone, his bald head weaving back and forth in time.

Some fifty lengths away, on a stone pedestal, a wraith took shape. First was an image carved of smoke. The smoke solidified, became translucent. It thickened, curdled. Kondor ceased his humming and surveyed his work. Thrice as high as a man stood an image of Bat Ears—good honest stone throughout. "Clevum, my son," he said, as he examined the statue, "will you be so good as to hand me that jug?"

The gravel hopper was empty.

Oric called on them two days before the election. Robar was disconcerted to find that he had brought with him a stranger who was led around through the dozens of rows of giant statues. Robar drew Oric to one side before he left, and asked in a whisper, "Who is this chap?"

Oric smiled reassuringly. "Oh, he's all right. Just one of the boys—a friend of mine."

"But can he be trusted? I don't remember seeing him around campaign headquarters."

"Oh, sure! By the way, you boys are to be congratulated on the job of work you've done here. Well, I must be running on — I'll drop in on you again."

"Just a minute, Oric. Are you all set on the apportation?"

"Oh, yes. Yes indeed. They'll all be distributed around to the polling places in plenty of time — every statue."

"When are you going to do it?"

"Why don't you let me worry about those details, Robar?"

"Well . . . you are the boss, but I still think I ought to know when to be ready for the apportation."

"Oh, well, if you feel that way, shall we say, ah, midnight before election day?"

"That's fine. We'll be ready."

Robar watched the approach of the midnight before election with a feeling of relief. Kondor's work was all complete, the ludicrous statues were lined up, row on row, two for every polling place in the province of Lac, and Kondor himself was busy getting reacquainted with the wine jug. He had almost sobered up during the sustained effort of creating the statues.

Robar gazed with satisfaction at the images. "I wish I could see the Governor's face when he first catches sight of one of these babies. Nobody could possibly mistake who they were. Dolph, you're a genius; I never saw anything sillier looking in my life."

"That's high praise, pal," Dolph answered. "Isn't it about time the priest was getting here? I'll feel easier when we see our little dollies flying through the air on their way to the polling places."

"Oh, I wouldn't worry. Oric told me positively that the priest would be here in plenty of time. Besides, apportation is fast. Even the images intended for the back country and the far northern peninsula will get there in a few minutes — once he gets to work."

But as the night wore on it became increasingly evident that something was wrong. Robar returned from his thirteenth trip to the highway with a report of no one in sight on the road from the city.

"What'll we do?" Clevum asked.

"I don't know. Something's gone wrong; that's sure."

"Well, we've got to do something. Let's go back to the temple and try to locate him."

"We can't do that; we don't know what priest Oric hired. We'll have to find Oric."

They left Kondor to guard the statues and hurried back into town. They found Oric just leaving campaign headquarters. With him was the visitor he had brought with him two days before. He seemed surprised to see them. "Hello, boys. Finished with the job so soon?"

"He never showed up," Robar panted.

"Never showed up? Well, imagine that! Are you sure?"

"Of course we're sure; we were there!"

"Look," put in Dolph, "what is the name of the priest you hired to do this job? We want to go up to the temple and find him."

"His name? Oh, no, don't do that. You might cause all sorts of complications. I'll go to the temple myself."

"We'll go with you."

"That isn't necessary," he told them testily. "You go on back to the gravel pit, and be sure everything is ready."

"Good grief, Oric, everything has been ready for hours. Why not take Clevum along with you to show the priest the way?"

"I'll see to that. Now get along with you."

Reluctantly they did as they were ordered. They made the trip back in moody silence. As they approached their destination Clevum spoke up, "You know, fellows—"

"Well? Spill it."

"That fellow that was with Oric—wasn't he the guy he had out here, showing him around?"

"Yes; why?"

"I've been trying to place him. I remember now—I saw him two weeks ago, coming out of Governor Vortus' campaign office."

After a moment of stunned silence Robar said bitterly, "Sold out. There's no doubt about it; Oric has sold us out."

"Well, what do we do about it?"

"What can we do?"

"Blamed if I know."

"Wait a minute, fellows," came Clevum's pleading voice, "Kondor used to be a priest. Maybe he can do apportation."

"Say! There's a chance! Let's get going."

But Kondor was dead to the world.

They shook him. They poured water in his face. They walked him up and down. Finally they got him sober enough to answer questions.

Robar tackled him. "Listen, pop, this is important: Can you perform apportation?"

"Huh? Me? Why, of course. How else did we build the pyramids?"

"Never mind the pyramids. Can you move these statues here tonight?"

Kondor fixed his interrogator with a bloodshot eye. "My son, the great Arcane laws are the same for all time and space. What was done in Egypt in the Golden Age can be done in Mu tonight."

Dolph put in a word. "Good grief, pop, why didn't you tell us this before?" The reply was dignified and logical. "No one asked me."

Kondor set about his task at once, but with such slowness that the boys felt they would scream just to watch him. First, he drew a large circle in the dust. "This is the house of darkness," he announced solemnly, and added the crescent of Astarte. Then he drew another large circle tangent to the first. "And this is the house of light." He added the sign of the sun god.

When he was done, he walked widdershins about the whole three times the wrong way. His feet nearly betrayed him twice, but he recovered, and continued his progress. At the end of the third lap he hopped to the center of the house of darkness and stood facing the house of light.

The first statue on the left in the front row quivered on its base, then rose into the air and shot over the horizon to the east.

The three young men burst out with a single cheer, and tears streamed down Robar's face.

Another statue rose up. It was just poised for flight when old Kondor hiccoughed. It fell, a dead weight, back to its base, and broke into two pieces. Kondor turned his head.

"I am truly sorry," he announced; "I shall be more careful with the others."

And try he did — but the liquor was regaining its hold. He wove to and fro on his feet, his aim with the images growing more and more erratic. Stone figures flew in every direction, but none travelled any great distance. One group of six flew off together and landed with a great splash in the harbor. At last, with more than three fourths of the images still untouched he sank gently to his knees, keeled over, and remained motionless.

Dolph ran up to him, and shook him. There was no response. He peeled back one of Kondor's eyelids and examined the pupil. "It's no good," he admitted. "He won't come to for hours."

Robar gazed heartbrokenly at the shambles around him. There they are, he thought, worthless! Nobody will ever see them — just so much leftover campaign material, wasted! My biggest idea!

Clevum broke the uncomfortable silence. "Sometimes," he said, "I think what this country needs is a good earthquake."

Frank Merriwell
in the White House

WARD MOORE

The late Ward Moore (1903–1978) was a vastly underrated writer whose 1953 novel *Bring the Jubilee,* about a present in which the South has won the Civil War, is a classic among "alternative world" stories. Other notable novels include *Greener Than You Think* (1947), and *Joyleg* (1962; written with Avram Davidson). A largely self-educated man, Moore was a true working-class intellectual.

"Frank Merriwell in the White House" is a wonderful story about American political culture and the role of "progress" in our electoral tradition.

Once there was a political boss in love with the daughter of a mad scientist. Stevenson Woolsey had no paunch, did not chew cigars (didn't smoke at all, in fact), never wore striped suits or dark glasses, never slapped a back or kissed a baby. He had taken a degree, *cum laude,* from Western Reserve, had read *Finnegan's Wake* through twice and understood some of it. At thirty-two he was the sleeping partner in a number of businesses which consistently sold goods or services to the city or county—he was the unquestioned wheel of the Fifth Ward Horace Greeley Club. Four councilmen of the city's nine owed their election to his support—the mayor was his political ally. He had supplied the margin of victory to the sheriff and two of the county supervisors and the three local state legislators consulted Steve before they voted on important bills. He was handsome in a subdued sort of way but he never spoke in public because of a slight stammer.

If Steve Woolsey conformed more to the pattern of the modern political manipulator than the popular stereotype of the wardheeler, Aurelie van Ten Bosch was the quintessential ideal of a mad scientist's daughter. The Eurasian strain introduced into the Bosch family in the eighteenth century—which, suddenly reappearing in Willem van Ten Bosch, gave him a properly sinis-

164

ter expression—made of Aurelie a living doll. She was dainty, exquisite, flaw-less, charming, graceful. And if she did not inherit her father's genius—make no mistake, he was as brilliant as he was paranoid; mad as a milliner—she was probably smart enough to come in out of the rain before the downpour soaked her through enough to reveal her enticing curves.

"Steve, darling, I could never, just never go for a politician. Besides, I'm not old enough to vote. If you were an outfielder, or even a first baseman—you're tall enough and you've certainly got the reach—" here she firmly removed his hands—"I might be faintly . . . But all those figures and pre-cincts and percentages give me a headache."

"I don't know where b-baseball would b-be without percentages," said Woolsey, feinting a bunt, wistfully aware that you couldn't steal first base.

"Who cares? It's like a ballet—so precise, so cerebral, so fluent. When the batter judges the ball and it soars through that lovely curve and the cen-terfielder runs back, back, back, up against the fence and leaps into the air . . . Percentages!"

"Just the same it's the percentages that d-decide next year's contracts."

"See what I mean? You're so material. Like no ideals."

"My ideal is to get my boys elected and to hit the ball clear through the hole between first and second to s-score."

"And besides, you have no sense of humor and you're just an old tory at heart."

"I'm a liberal p-progressive," cried Steve, outraged. "I've always been for labor, the minorities, civil rights, m-medicare, honest laboring—the whole w-works."

"Just old tory window dressing, like Daddy says. Daddy is making a robot that will destroy all the tory fakery and phoniness—Daddy is a philosophi-cal nihilist—"

"Your Daddy is a philosophical n-nut."

"—because it will do everything perfectly. At bat it will hit only home runs on the first pitch because its vision and coordination will be superhuman—pitching, it will throw nothing but strikes."

"They'll never let him in the game."

"Just what Daddy says. A reactionary plot."

"So what's he wasting his time for?"

"You wouldn't understand. Daddy's an idealist."

Sore and frustrated, Steve pondered the problem of Aurelie. Fortunately he had other problems to act as counter-irritants. The ninth-ward council-man, who had been in office twenty years and firmly believed Earl Warren had been a dangerous radical, was retiring—if Steve could run a successful candidate he would have a majority of the city council in his pocket. How-ever, the ninth ward had been gerrymandered and regerrymandered until it had become a political enigma. Part of it was silk-stocking, with cooperative apartment houses guarded by doormen with stripes down their pants and galloons on their sleeves. Part was unredeemed slum inhabited by blacks, West Indian immigrants and a small but densely populated enclave of Hassidic Jews and shanty Irish. The retiring councilman had been elected and reelected by managing never to offend any of these groups. He had publicly denounced the Arabs (there was not one Mussulman in the county, much less the city) — his office sported a mezuzah from Israel and a crucifix blessed by the Pope. He was vociferously against all taxes, whether levied by county, state or federal government.

"We have to put up an all-around liberal," said Steve. "An FDR-Kennedy-Lindsay type. That's the only thing will go over in the ninth."

"Jose Garcia Alvaroes," suggested Appalachia Bethune Lee, who was not only Steve's secretary but a very shrewd member of the Fifth Ward Horace Greeley Club, a lovely girl the color of the finest milk chocolate. To Stevenson Woolsey she was a good right arm — the silly man had no eyes for any woman but Aurelie van Ten Bosch. He was a man of limited insights.

He shook his head. "Jose? No. The blacks won't buy him. The button-down collar set will think he's cute but they're liable to have cramps in the voting booth if they ever get that far. The Irish won't mind his going to mass but city hall is for keeps. And the Jews — " he shrugged. "Who understands Jews? They vote for Catholics. But Garcia? I wouldn't put money on it."

Appalachia patiently suggested a number of other names, but Steve wasn't fired by any of them. One was known to have split his ticket at the last election. A second had done time as a peeping tom ("if only it had been embezzlement or armed robbery, or even arson," groaned Stevenson Woolsey, "but a peeping tom! He's poison — "). A third had written a novel, a fourth loathed dogs, a fifth was not only a vegetarian but chewed raw wheat instead of gum.

"All right," summed up Appalachia, ticking off the points on her long, slender fingers, "a young man but mature, good-looking but not too energetic, loyal but able to stand on his own feet, good to his mother but one of the boys, god-fearing but nonsectarian, good speaker but no smoothie. Anything else?"

"Modern. Progressive. Moving with the times. No horse-and-buggy man."

"I pass," said Appalachia, running out of fingers. "Maybe you better get your girl friend's old daddy-o, van Frankenstein, to hurry up with his mechanical man."

"It's an idea," said Woolsey thoughtfully. "It's an idea."

"Oh, you're impossible," exclaimed Appalachia.

Willem van Ten Bosch stared through the thick-lensed glasses, which enlarged his madly glittering eyes into maniacal incandescence. "What?" he bellowed, "make my pilot model into a demagogue, a mere vote-getter, tool of an unscrupulous wardheeler, a prop of decadent democracy? Do you think for a moment I would consent to turn my homonechal, my ultrabot, my final solution to the human problem — "

"You m-mean it will b-blow up the world?"

The mad scientist sneered. "Blow up the world? Childish prattle. The human race is doomed, but not the world it disgraces. It is doomed — " here he gave a fiendish chuckle — "to be replaced by mechanical intelligence, the first truly aristocratic being in the solar system. And you want me to turn him into a mere guzzler in the hog trough, a rooter in the pork barrel?"

"Your metaphors are a little mixed," said Steve coldly. "I hope you realize that in dooming the human race you will be extinguishing your own descendants?"

"Bah!" retorted van Ten Bosch. "Progeny of my daughter, who lacks the intelligence of a first-generation computer, and some befuddled numbskull — you or another halfwit manipulated by blind biological urge, egged on by the use of cosmetics manufactured from the glands of dead goats and skunks? Do you think a dedicated scientist would be moved by such greeting-card sentimentality? Besides, what's in it for me?"

Steve, having already worked this one out, replied promptly, "Any salary he — it — may earn. Less taxes and upkeep, of course."

"Bah!" repeated the inventor with some lack of originality. "I'd be crazy to settle for such pigeon-feed. Salary! Anyone running for anything spends twice his salary to get elected. I want ninety percent of the gross."

They haggled for some time, Ten Bosch with the greedy cunning of a madman, Woolsey with the calm assurance of the pure in heart. At length they came to an agreement and the scientist, picking up a microphone, said, "Mr. Watson, come here."

"Is that its name, Mr. Watson?"

Ten Bosch looked at him contemptuously. "If you weren't such an ignoramus you'd know I was merely quoting an illustrious predecessor."

Steve's disappointment was overwhelming when the mechanical man obeyed the summons. He had not expected an android, a facsimile of a Shriner from Los Angeles or a Soroptimist from Osceola. Nor did the robot look like the Tin Woodman or Tik-Tok. His feet and hands were articulated with toes and fingers, though with many more than the normal number of joints. If he lacked hips he did so no more than L'il Abner or any other American ideal and his chest, which no doubt contained the nuclear power-plant, memory banks and the rest of the electronic fricassee, was Princetonian rather than Martian in its bulge. To where the collarbone would have been if robots had collarbones, as Ko-ko might have said, he could be draped in continental slacks and a sports jacket without loss to his masculine appeal. Shoes, of course, and gloves. Clemenceau has always worn gloves and they hadn't hindered his political career. But from the neck up . . .

To begin with, he had no neck. None whatever. No more than an octo-

pus, jellyfish, egg, or a whole salami. But whereas these have a certain organ-
ically fluid line which is not inconsonant with Hogarth's curve of beauty,
the robot's neckless head was no more than an undersized immovable drum
set directly on his shoulders, a drum with five convex bands running unin-
terruptedly around it, obviously for speech, smell, sight, hearing and some
vibrations imperceptible to coarse human senses. Efficient no doubt, but
quite incapable of getting more than three votes against, in one long-dead
politician's immortal words, a Chinaman running on a laundry ticket.

"Im-im-p-possible," stammered Woolsey.

The robot turned himself slightly toward the boss. "If I grasp your
thought — " the baritone voice was smooth, the enunciation clear, the projection effortless — "you are dismayed that the electorate will automatically
reject a candidate with whom they cannot literally see eye to eye. This is
something that can be remedied. At present, though not entirely functional,
I am constructed for efficiency. The usefulness of my upper works would
be reduced approximately nineteen and a half percent if mounted on a column
capable of revolving one hundred and eighty degrees and encased in a flexible plastic mask indistinguishable from animal flesh and able to simulate
movements of lips, jaw, nostrils and eyes so as to convey appropriate
expression."

"Never!" shouted Willem van Ten Bosch. "I would be insane to consent
to have my work — my lifework — debased."

"Your consent would be superfluous," said the robot rather pedantically.
"On legal grounds (I regret I have been so far unable to pick up much legal
knowledge except some oddments Mr. Woolsey seems to have acquired over
the years, but I believe Masters & Servants, 2 Edward IV and 5 Henry VII
might cover the ground) an agent is bound to regard as valid a contract made
on his behalf by his principal. And on pragmatic grounds I remind you of
the multiple-choice circuits that make it possible for me to select a
reasonable — that is a least inconvenient, most socially acceptable — course
of conduct."

The angry scientist gnashed his teeth. "I only installed them to please
my stupid daughter. So you could be a perfect ballplayer."

"Ah, well," said the robot philosophically, "to err is human."

"I will destroy you," threatened Ten Bosch furiously.

"How? I perceive you are running through possible means — "

"Can you read m-minds?" asked Woolsey.

"Not precisely. My perception is like that of humans reading the expression on another human's face, only far more penetrating. I receive images
that are vividly present in the conscious mind — the more emotionally
projected the clearer they are to me. Thus I perceive pictures of a pistol,
a bomb, a garbage truck with shredding machinery, a bessemer furnace, a

ship hovering over deep water, myself clamped to a workbench with hack-
saws, blowtorches, sledgehammers and pinch bars ripping me into scrap.
None of these is practicable."

"You'll see," predicted Ten Bosch darkly.

"I think we had better leave now," suggested the robot. "I am receiving
strong images of your being attacked on the evident theory that your demise
will void the contract. Perhaps you would be well advised to convey it to
an incorporated company."

"You may escape physically," said Ten Bosch, "but you can't get away
from your built-in programing. It is true that you have multiple choice, but
the ultimate outlook that will decide which choice you take is mine. You
will always be my creature."

"That remains to be seen," said the robot confidently.

The only refuge Steve could think of was the Fifth Ward Horace Greeley Club. But once locked in the inner office — the back room behind the
back room — guarded by a squad of cops and four trustworthy club members roused from their beds, he didn't know how to proceed beyond phon-
ing Appalachia Bethune Lee.

"You want me to come down there at this time of night? I mean morning? Oh, Steve, I'm simply thrilled, you lecherous man."

"This is no time for j-joking. I have a serious p-problem."

"Haven't we all? Take a cold shower and think pure thoughts. I'll be there
as soon as I can fix myself up to look ravishing."

"Will you be s-serious?"

"No. But I'll be there before you change your mind."

The security precautions being not yet perfected so as to admit the
unwanted and bar friends, Appalachia arrived quickly.

"I'm panting," she said as she came in. "Ooh! What's that?"

"P-possibly our candidate for ninth-ward councilman. Thanks to your
impulsive suggestion."

"Always blame the woman."

The robot turned toward her. "I hope, Miss Lee, that you are not
prejudiced against fellow beings who happen to be of a different color and
facial configuration?"

"We-ell — let's say I'm in favor of faces. Especially for prospective councilmen. Say, what's your name, anyway?"

"Shall I say Four-X?"

"You a Muslim? You won't get ten votes."

"I have at present no denominational affiliation. I gather it is advisable
for a candidate to have one. If necessary I could be a Unitarian, like William Howard Taft."

"Twelve votes," amended Appalachia. "Can't you come up with something real cool? Like Clark Gable Roosevelt Kennedy Elvis Dayan Castro?"

"Aurelie used to call me Frank Merriwell. Because I can pitch nothing but strikes, hit nothing but home runs. A literary allusion, I believe, to my prowess."

"Mac, if you're going to be a councilman, lay off the literary allusions — they're poison. Stick to straight pornography."

"N-now see here, Appalachia, this is serious. You put the f-finger on it yourself. If he—"

"Frank Merriwell. How about it? Can't think of anything better except maybe Lincoln Truman Eisenhower."

"Okay. M-Merriwell it is. This is the problem. He has to have a head, a face. Where are we going to get an electronics engineer and a p-plastic surgeon we can trust?"

"No need, " said Frank Merriwell. "I can do it all myself. I have acquired the technical knowledge from my manufacturer — isn't it good Americanism to confess that all wisdom comes from the creator? All I need is some trustworthy help at the critical moment."

Appalachia groaned. "I could see it coming. Just call me Aunt Tammy."

"I shall make a list of the tools and materials needed," Merriwell went on, "and construct a head and neck. Since my movements are not controlled by circuits in my upper works my fingers will remain capable of detaching my present head and reattaching it after I have fitted it into the plastic mask and connected the impulses which will serve in the place of muscles to move the neck, eyes, eyelids and all the rest—"

"Fix it so you can wiggle your ears," suggested Appalachia. "There's something irresistible about a man who can wiggle his ears."

"—but there will be an interval between disconnection and reconnection when I shall be blind, deaf, speechless and unable to pick up mental images. Miss Lee will therefore have to make a temporary connection in my visual circuit. After that I can do all the rest."

"Lordy, what a responsibility. Aren't you afraid I'll gum up the works?"

"I am programed for normal precaution but not abstract fear."

"All these technicalities are f-fascinating, but what I want to know is how you stand. Are you a liberal?"

"What is a liberal?" inquired Frank Merriwell.

"Let's not quibble. How do you stand on human rights versus property rights?"

"What is property?"

"P-Proudhon, for God's sake," muttered Steve disgustedly. "Look, let's keep it simple. How do you feel about tax rebates for new industries moving into the city?"

"What industries?" asked Frank Merriwell.

Woolsey, whose vocabulary was usually restrained, uttered a scatological word. "What about public housing?" he demanded roughly.

"On one hand everyone is entitled to a livable home. On the other hand—"

"He's a liberal, all right," said Appalachia.

The nervousness with which she and Steve looked forward to Merriwell's alteration—the robot himself, having nerves of stainless steel and silver wire, displayed no anxiety—was postponed while the question of his future complexion was decided. At last they settled on the black Irish type—dark blue eyes, ruddy cheeks and a black wig with just a faint waviness. Meanwhile Frank was busy with soldering guns, solenoids, servometers, flexible plastic, paper-thin steel plates and other paraphernalia. The mask he constructed was something of a cross between the young Spencer Tracy and an ageless Jimmy Walker. The actual operation went without a hitch, except for one agonizing moment when Frank's drum head lay inert on the desk being used as a workbench and his fingers fumbled with the wires protruding from where his trachea would have been if he'd had one.

The convex bands had not glowed or reflected, had not showed any variation—yet, lying on the desk where Frank Merriwell had placed the cylinder they circled, they looked extremely and finally dead. It was hard for Steve and Appalachia to remember that Merriwell's sentience was in his torso, that he was not acting reflexively, like a decapitated chicken. Suppose his confidence in the skill he had acquired from Ten Bosch were misplaced and he proved unable to put himself together—or would botch the job so as to be a defective, a metal moron, less a potential councilman than a radio announcer, a postal clerk or an advertising executive?

Appalachia moaned, "That damn diagram looked as simple as *Fun with Dick and Jane*. Blue wire with red spots . . . Oh, Steve—"

But at last she found it and its counterpart and put them in Frank Merriwell's left hand and the soldering gun in the right. In no time at all the cylinder had sight again and Merriwell fitted the plastic and metal mask around it. Then he connected the other senses. The eyelids blinked, the ears wiggled, the nostrils dilated, the lips smiled and opened.

"Everything under control," he said.

"But what's the m-matter with your voice? I can hardly hear you."

"Five-sixths of my vocal band is now covered," explained Frank. "I'll have to amplify it. And I'm afraid my extrasensory perception is practically useless."

"The question is, are you f-fit to run for councilman?"

"My friends have been kind enough to say so and while I am reluctant to thrust myself forward as one seeking office, the gross corruption and manifest incompetence of the majority of the present city council force me to overcome my natural preference. At the insistence of those who wish for a thorough housecleaning at city hall, I am willing to accept the burden of doing my humble part to bring good government to our great municipality. Civic duty must come before personal inclination."

"He's got the w-words and m-music, but can he put the tune across?"

The opposition (amid cries of "Carpetbagger—" "Whoever heard of Merriwell?" "A machine candidate, a Charlie McCarthy for Boss Woolsey—" "We must have a councilman with a warm human heart that beats for all, not a mere mechanical loudspeaker for a greedy manipulator—") nominated Adolphus Washington Hammer.

"How do you suppose they c-caught on?" asked Steve.

"Campaign oratory," said Appalachia. "They haven't the foggiest."

Jose Garcia Alvaroes announced that he would run as a progressive independent on the Peoples Freedom Nationalist Equal Rights and Cultural Commonwealth ticket.

Aurelie van Ten Bosch was sitting in the front row when Frank opened his campaign in Carpenters Hall. She looked so entrancing that Woolsey was hard put not to forget politics and scoop her up in his arms and run off with her.

"Pay attention to business," Appalachia hissed in his ear. "Moon on your own time. Our boy is about to sound off and God only knows what he'll say."

"That's more than I do."

A spattering of applause vigorously led by Aurelie greeted Frank Merriwell as he strode forward. His black shoes were brilliantly polished. His olive-green suit with natural shoulders fitted perfectly. His white shirt was dazzling. His fawn-and-green bow tie was tied just imperfectly enough to show it wasn't one of those snap-on vulgarities. He bowed, turning his head smoothly to the right and left. He blinked his long-lashed eyes, smiled to show white teeth and spoke in a voice that carried so perfectly that even the deaf old gentleman in the last row who had dropped in by mistake heard every word.

"Voters," said Frank Merriwell, "I am opposed to all progress. Thank you."

Gasps of outrage filled the hall as though the audience were composed of geese or muscovy ducks. Steve turned purple. Appalachia turned pale (a becoming café au lait). A. W. Hammer turned pink with pleasure. Jose Garcia Alvaroes turned red with repressed oratory. A dowager with the figure of a dress form rose to ask a question, then sat down again. Clearly the magnitude of Merriwell's statement was too enormous to grapple with.

Finally a young man who didn't look old enough to vote called out, "You mean you want everybody to run around naked, live in trees, eat grass?"

"Sir," replied Merriwell, "I am running for councilman, not for a position as regulator of dress and life styles. It is not within the power of the city to regulate dress—the ordinance against nudist camps has, I believe, been declared unconstitutional. Furthermore, it would be a foolish official indeed who attempted to dictate fashion. Besides, going without clothes is impractical, leading to frostbite in temperate zones and dangerous burns in the torrid. Disillusionment with progress is a rational conclusion, not a blanket denial of all history. Let us view things empirically. And please, let us stick to municipal issues."

Some of the tension went out of the listeners. Obviously Merriwell knew how to hedge as well as any other politician. They didn't have to take what he said seriously.

Someone spoke up. "How about living in trees like monkeys? Nobody's gonna make a monkey outa me."

"Nature cannot be improved upon," replied Merriwell. "Not all monkeys live in trees—if we broaden the term to include apes, some of whom live in caves quite as dark, dank, uncomfortable and verminous as a ninth-ward tenement."

There was some handclapping. Then: "If you tear them down like these urban renewers want and we got to sleep in the park—so why not in the trees? Because when they wreck the old places they either put up projects like penitentiaries where you can't spit without a housing cop giving you a summons or else they build classy coops for the fat cats."

Louder applause. "There seems to be a natural human predilection for arboreal habitations," said Merriwell. "Children build treehouses at every chance. However it seems to me it would be better and cheaper to make the tenements habitable."

"Ain't that progress?"

"Light, air, cleanness aren't progress—they've always been. Slums, overcrowding, profits for landlords are progress."

"You wanna do away with relief and welfare? Let people starve like in the old days?"

"Welfare and relief are hardly progress. They are palliatives that try to make progress endurable."

Appalachia passed Steve an aspirin.

"It could be worse," she whispered.

"You mean he could come out against s-sex?"

"Mr. Merriwell, aren't you just calling everything you're opposed to 'progress?'"

"If I am it's because progress is what I'm opposed to. I think humanity has confused motion with direction, so that any movement at all has become an end in itself, desirable simply because it is going somewhere—it doesn't matter where. Take sanitation. That's a municipal problem. It isn't for animals or primitive man. But civilized man poisoned the streams he drank from, polluted the air he breathed. So he paid the price in epidemics and plagues for living cozily in towns and cities. Then he paid the price for alleviating the plagues with sewage systems and garbage disposals, which dumped the wastes in the nearest lake, river, or ocean to sicken outlanders instead of home-folks, to kill the fish, birds and game — upsetting the whole ecological balance. Next step in the march of progress — by no means completed — was to treat the raw sewage and make it innocuous. Or so it is claimed. But the same ecological balance that was upset when farmers began plowing the subsoil and burning the weeds — instead of dibbling holes in which to drop seeds — called for manure to restore the fertility of the soil. Progress gave them artificial fertilizers, chemicals that made crops grow like mad but lacked the virtue of those grown with natural manure, the same natural manure that was being thrown uselessly away. So in a few — very few — communities the nutrient wastes are dehydrated, sacked up and sold to gardeners. Progress. The longest way around is the shortest way home."

"Back to Chic Sale, huh mister? It that what you want?"

"History is irreversible. No man bathes twice in the same stream. You can't go home. We cannot restore the past, nor would anyone want to, any more than he would want to have his memory erased and reconstructed to fit some idealized notion. Until — if ever — the over-saturated concentration of people can be dissolved and spread out in a more rational pattern, all we can do is make the least damaging compromises, avoiding such progressive solutions as total incineration. What is now an expensive operation to get rid of valuable products can be reorganized so some of the cost can be recovered."

"Well, now," whispered Appalachia, "you'll have to admit he's in the groove at last. What could be safer or duller? Conservation plus money-saving without cutting payrolls? And nothing warms the voter's heart more than defecation."

"If he hadn't s-started off with that manifesto about being against p-progress I'd say he'd had it made. If he were human I'd call him a screwball — unreliable, a wild-pitch artist. But he's a machine — rational, predictable, logical. Why drag in p-poison like that?"

"Catch their attention?" suggested Appalachia. "Set them up so they'll listen."

"You know b-better than that. I wrote him a good speech, tried to c-coach him — delivery, g-gestures, everything — tutored him carefully on not saying too much, committing himself, leaving himself wide open. I really thought I'd gotten across to him, but he's evidently a m-maverick. I wonder if we could deal with Garcia?"

"What would it get you? The Tin Woodman could come in, but Jose can never do better than place. Honey, you're all shook up for the moment but there's no irrevocable damage done. Chew him out till his transistors are jelly but don't throw him overboard. There are going to be other elections and some voters have memories. He hasn't really alienated anybody with his against-all-progress line—"

"Y-yet."

"—and his cracks about the slums didn't hurt him. Everyone's against slums."

The race for councilman wasn't important enough for anyone to take a straw vote, but Stevenson Woolsey's antennae told him that Merriwell and A. W. Hammer were running neck and neck with Jose Garcia Alvaroes far behind. Except for an editorial sneer or two at Merriwell's slogan, the press ignored him. As might have been expected, both Alvaroes and Hammer concentrated their fire on him, disregarding each other. But while Jose denounced Merriwell almost impersonally as an imperialist tool, the voice of the exploiters of oppressed colonial peoples, Hammer's attacks were in the fine old American tradition of personal vituperation—except that he lacked the vocabulary. "The machine can'idate," he roared, "is against progress. You know what this means, ladies? No more nylons, no more girdles, no more washing machines, no more telephones, radios, television. No more votes for women! How do you like that? Back to the scrubboards, woodstoves, flatirons, tallow candles, washboilers, high-button shoes—and you won't be allowed to say a thing about it. That'll be for your lords and masters, just like it was in the good old days before there was progress. The men'll do the voting and you'll do the drudgery. No vacuum cleaners, no frozen foods, no toasters, no percolators, no instant coffee, no beauty parlors—no lipsticks even . . . Ladies, I say to you, the can'idate who'd propose such things is a monster in human form, a dupe of the communists if not a card-carrying communist himself, a tearer-down of the American way of life, a man unfit to breathe the pure air of our country and our century . . ."

"That'll give our boy the epicure vote, the eggheads and maybe all those who'd rather fight than switch. If there just weren't any women in the ninth ward . . . I suppose we can live with Hammer—wasn't he mixed up in some pinball deal?"

Frank Merriwell's reply was short, direct and dignified. "I am not now nor have I ever been a communist. Communism represents the ultimate in progress—the deification of science, the absolute rule of bureaucracy, 'government by experts,' the final stultification of free will. The charge that I would repeal the Nineteenth Amendment is as absurd as the amendment itself was superfluous. All citizens are enfranchised and always have been. The word 'men' in the Declaration of Independence has common gender and applies equally to women, as the nineteenth-century feminists insisted. I do not feel that nylons or flatirons are an issue in this election. Whatever the aesthetic objection to girdles, I propose no restraint on their confinement. As for the pure air, I am in favor of it, free of carbon monoxide and strontium ninety as well as campaign speeches."

On election day Steve and Appalachia checked the registration lists against the reports of voting which were continuously phoned in. Late morning the volunteer baby-sitters and those who offered free transportation to the polls shifted from a haphazard basis of waiting to be called for to methodical visits to those who had not yet voted. Lesser members of the Horace Greeley Club advised poll watchers and precinct captains of what to do where routine instructions for dealing with challenges and other problems were inadequate.

In the eighteenth, nineteenth, twentieth and twenty-first precincts the voting was running ahead of normal expectation for an off-year, minor election. In the twenty-second it was average. In the twenty-third and twenty-fourth it was light. The first three were the slum districts, the twenty-first and twenty-second were the Hassidic neighborhood—the rest was silkstocking.

"Looks pretty good," commented Appalachia.

"Under ordinary circumstances," conceded Woolsey. "But who can figure this one? I p-particularly don't like the pattern of the Jewish vote. Are they sitting on their hands in the twenty-second? Or are they going to clobber us after work?"

" 'Morning votes are "no" votes.' " she reminded him.

"Sure, but who are they saying no to? T-take it for granted they're saying no to Hammer, but who are they negatively for? Garcia?"

"Not a chance," said Appalachia bravely.

The early-afternoon lull seemed ominously long. At any other time a pro like Steve would have known the results by now, even though not a vote had been counted and the polls would be open for another five hours. But there were too many unknown quantities on this occasion. The subtle projection of Merriwell's nonhuman personality—was it or wasn't it unconsciously perceived with or without hostility?—the size of Jose's protest vote, the depth of middle-class interest. Like the eminent amateur characterized by Harry Truman as knowing "no more about politics than a pig does of Sunday," he had to wait for the first returns.

Perhaps not quite. "They're piling up in the twenty-second precinct—looks like there'll be a line when the polls close. Twenty-third and twenty-fourth are normal."

Steve and Appalachia looked at each other, allowed themselves the faintest of cheerful smiles.

"If not the world, at least the ninth ward. Apparently,"she added, careful to avoid hubris.

The first returns were incomplete, in fact they were nothing more than the first bakers' dozen ballots counted in one of the two silkstocking precincts. "Merriwell five, Hammer five, Alvaroes three."

"Fluke," said Steve. "Some family of nuts all voted together." He also sidestepped hubris.

"Well, how's this from the eighteenth? Hammer six, Alvaroes seven. Merriwell fifteen . . ."

Steve sighed, "We're in."

Frank Merriwell not only carried the slum and Hassidic precincts by majorities — Jose Garcia Alvaroes ran ahead of Hammer where there was a threat of urban renewal — but was barely edged by Hammer in the wealthier neighborhoods. Steve didn't wait for Hammer's concession to have a serious talk with Frank Merriwell.

"Well, Councilman," he began.

Woolsey shared with Napoleon and Joseph Pulitzer the ability to simulate rage while remaining perfectly calm. "Listen, you refugee from Smith and T-Tinker," he snarled. "You collection of electronic junk. You think you're riding pretty high right now, d-don't you? You know what's lower than a councilman? Only the g-gastric growlings of an amoeba bucking for undersecretary to a minor worm, that's what. And do you know how you got to this unexalted position? By your own efforts? By the weight of your thinking, the length of your political foresight, the sharpness of your wit, the p-power of your oratory? Not a bit. We m-made you, the organization and I, with the sort of w-work that wins elections — and we can unmake you the second you stop being regular."

"Steve!" cried Aurelie van Ten Bosch, "how can you rave and rant this way at Frank? And all for nothing. I do believe you're jealous because he won the election."

"Oh, Aurelie," exclaimed Steve in anguish. "How can you think I'd be jealous of a m-machine?"

"Don't be gruesome," said Aurelie. "Besides, it's a low form of bigotry to belittle Frank for the way he was born — uh — manufactured."

"Name a high form of bigotry. Oh, Aurelie, do we have to quarrel?"

"Yes, we do, because we don't agree on anything. I keep telling you and telling you — we're not compatible."

By the end of his term as councilman Frank Merriwell had cut the heart out of the local urban renewal program. This was done not by one speech or vote but by his methodical chipping away at the figures during budget sessions. His lightning calculations exposed the inflated sums before the councilmen got through reading them and his cold logic impressed the other members. When Frank rapped his gloved steel hand for emphasis and insisted that this or that old building deserved better than the steel ball and bulldozer he was heard respectfully. When he charged them with acting mechanically out of a mindless fascination with the idea of a city full of indistinguishable boxes made to house indistinguishable tenants they nodded. In the end architectural renderings already paid for were scrapped and federal money already allocated was withheld.

At the Horace Greeley Club, Appalachia said, "Isn't it time you gave some thought to where it will all lead, Steve?"

"There are only two places it could lead to, Congress or the state senate. I haven't d-decided which."

Appalachia placed herself between her boss and the window so that his view of the airshaft and the inside window box where he grew African violets was complicated by her interesting silhouette. "Time's not standing still," she reminded him. "We're not — I mean Frank's not getting any younger."

"Thinking of obsolescence? What if the opposition comes out with a new model?" He looked at her thoughtfully. "No one but van Ten Bosch could make one, but suppose he decided to try — just for spite? I must see Aurelie about this."

Aurelie said, "You don't understand Daddy at all. He's mad you know."

"No k-kid?" muttered Steve.

"I mean he's mad on the subject of destroying the world. But he's fair — even you will have to admit he's fair."

"I'll admit anything when you look at m-me like that. Oh, Aurelie, we could be so h-happy together."

"Please, Steve, let's not get romantic. My ideal of a lover is one who is firm as steel, logical, precise, brainy, unwavering, unmoved by selfish considerations — "

"A d-damn robot, in fact. What will you do if your father builds one whose sole function is to charm women?"

"But that's exactly what I'm trying to explain to you. As long as Frank is doing exactly what Daddy designed him to do Daddy won't make another. You can stop worrying about that."

"And s-start worrying about being an accessory to the d-destruction of civilization."

"Are progress and civilization the same thing?" asked Aurelie prettily. "Daddy and Frank don't think so."

Steve said to Appalachia, "I'm going to ditch him. I can't have his career on my c-conscience."

"What can you do?" asked Appalachia. "Deny him the nomination? He'll run as an independent and win in a walk. Listen, he made a speech last night to a really advanced group — the Association of Stitchers, Hemmers and Embroiderers — and he had them gasping in the aisles, gasping for more, that is. And you know the line he fed them? He told them they were being exploited by the machines. That they had lost all pride in their craft, had become mere slaves to the machines. And they were demanding newer, better, more automatic machines to enslave themselves further instead of higher wages for the skill only they possessed. They were doing themselves out of their jobs and a higher standard of living by their shortsighted worship of progress. He painted a rosy picture of life with twice, three times as much money in their pay envelopes for half the time they now put in — and work spread around so they had no fear of scabs taking their jobs. And what would they come home to with their bigger pay? Why, a life without television commercials, overworked spouses, neurotic children, cars to keep payments up on and ride bumper to bumper on Sundays, the air poisoned by their fumes, people killed in fantastic numbers by them, instead of keeping a horse and buggy—that's what he said, right out—a horse and buggy to ride quietly to the grocery store instead of a madhouse supermarket. And they lapped it up. I know he's just a machine but he sounds so sincere they'll buy anything he says."

Frank Merriwell was nominated to run for the Fifteenth Congressional District seat the following summer. In his acceptance speech he said, "I am against schools."

His audience, conditioned by his rapidly burgeoning reputation to applaud whatever he said, paused with hands in midair.

"Now he's d-done it," Steve whispered to Appalachia. "He might as well have c-come right out flat against m-motherhood and be done with it."

"Hush. Wait and see what happens."

There were mutterings of: "Education's the most important thing there is—" but they were met by counter-mutterings of: "Never did anything for me—" "I got a real smart kid, see, and what does he bring home? Nothing but *F*s—" "I was beat out of this job by a guy with a string of degrees as long as your arm and he don't know the time of day—" "All these teachers are overpaid anyhow. I'd sure like a eight-to-three job with four months off a year—"

The applause came first in a liquid splatter, like the first drops of a hard storm, then in a forceful ovation.

Frank won the primary, but there competition was not serious and he coasted to his victory on the reputation he had made as councilman, plus the assurances of his supporters that being against schools implied no hostility to education—quite the contrary. Progress had locked pupils and teachers into a cage—he proposed to do away with this imprisonment and let them find each other again freely.

The general election was something else. Just as the ninth ward had been, the fifteenth district was an enigma. For as long as anyone could remember it had been sending to Congress Tyrconnel Costello, a Presbyterian minister who owed his continuing success to keeping his mouth shut. His constituency voted him into office without looking at its ballots—he ran for office without even making a speech, often without leaving Washington. But after a series of lucky investments, Reverend Tyr had announced his retirement. It remained for Frank to run against the incumbent's hand-picked successor, Lemuel Fox. Again dissident groups joined to back a third candidate, but running in front were Merriwell and Fox.

"No use to write him a speech," Steve declared. "When did I ever write him a speech he d-didn't ignore?"

"He doesn't ignore them—he stores them in his memory banks," said Appalachia Lee. "If you listen closely you can hear the pure accents of Western Reserve coming through now and then. That pest from the wire service is still waiting like a cat sitting down in front of a bird cage. What do you want me to tell him?"

Steve clutched his brow in a gesture he had developed since Frank Merriwell had come on the political scene. "T-tell him to d-drop dead. He's out to do a hatchet job."

"You're slipping, Steve—that robot is getting you down. Remember what happened to Nixon when he antagonized the working press. And Wilton Ogilvie can do you, if not your boy, a lot of harm."

"T-tell him anything. Make up a story, that's a sweetheart. I've got to wrestle with Frank's statement repudiating the support of the John Birch Society."

"What's so tough about that?"

"If I can't get him to tone it down—and when have I ever got him to t-tone anything d-down?—he's going to slap some of his most ardent s-supporters in the face. Listen. 'I want no help, nor will I accept any from the forward-looking John Birch Society. I am opposed to all progress, and the society represents the progress from McKinley to Harding.' How can I let that go?"

"Sleep on it," advised Miss Lee. "Meanwhile I advise you to sweet-talk Wilton Ogilvie. He's fairly sharp as newspapermen go and he won't take a runaround. He thinks he's got something on Frank and he wants a complete life story, beginning exactly with what little old log cabin Frank was born in and whose child he was."

Steve groaned. "I knew this was bound to happen. Okay, I'll t-talk to him out there. Let one of these fellows in your private office and something's b-bound to catch his eye that shouldn't."

Wilton Ogilvie, UPI, looked like a Pekingese with glasses. His air of baffled pugnacity didn't fool Steve Woolsey for a moment. "Ah, M-Mr. Ogilvie." Steve nervously offered his hand and got a relaxed bundle of icy fingers.

Ogilvie riffled a notebook. "Few little questions here, Mr. Woolsey. For a starter, how old's your candidate and when's his birthday?"

"March fifteenth," said Steve, picking the date he had led Frank away from Ten Bosch's laboratory. "And he's not m-my candidate. Frank Merriwell is the p-people's choice of a c-candidate. His m-meteoric rise—"

"Year," cut in Ogilvie, "of birth?"

"N-nineteen forty three," said Steve, rapidly counting backward. "If elected—and we have every re-reason to believe—"

"Where?"

"Where? Wisconsin," Stevenson said, naming a county seat where he knew the courthouse had burned to the ground in 1950. "But he's spent his entire life in this city. Frank was an orphan." Steve, momentarily encouraged by Ogilvie's slacklipped grin and warmed by the sound of his own voice, ran on recklessly. "An excellent s-scholar, good at sports, Frank was—"

"Where?"

"Where did he g-go to school? Oh, PS number—ah-ah—I've forgotten, but I'll check any details you want and l-let you know."

The newsman's lips changed into the rigid shape of a trap. "Who you trying to snow, Woolsey?" Steve blinked. Ogilvie flipped more pages in the notebook, began to read—or pretend to read. "Says here Frank Merriwell was born in Kearney, Nebraska, April first, nineteen forty-two, youngest of five. I went to see Merriwell before I came here."

"Ha-ha. A great kidder, Frank. A regular b-buffoon. April Fool's Day—catch on?"

Ogilvie flicked his wrist in a brushing motion. "Save it," he advised. "I've been working on this a long time. Also been out to see this guy—" he riffled more pages—"Vanderbosh."

The story—CONGRESSIONAL CANDIDATE EXPOSED AS ROBOT; ARTIFICIAL MAN SERVED ON CITY; COURTS DECIDE LEGALITY—was in all the evening papers and the next day the morning ones had UPI interpretives delving into all possible ramifications of letting a machine run for office. Suppose Soviet scientists invented a way of tuning in on his wavelength and making him a tool? A communist tool right in the United States Congress? Or suppose he ran amuck, as computers do from time to time, and attacked other Congressmen with his steel fists. There was no end to the possible dangers. There was also an interview with Lemuel Fox. "Let a machine take over from our beloved Reverend Costello? It would be un-American. Talk about dehumanizing the office-seeker! Open the door to this kind of corruption and pretty soon Boss Woolsey will have a hundred robots on Capitol Hill running his errands. Anarchy! Chaos! If this mess of nuts and bolts can run for Congress—even though he'll be swamped as all my polls predict—our next governor could be a Marchant calculator and our next Senator a Burroughs bookkeeping machine!"

The New York Times editorial said in part, ". . . disagreeing with his callow philosophy we would advise the voters of his district to repudiate him at the polls, it is not because of his origin. It is for the courts to decide whether he can legally represent the people in Congress. Without anticipating the decision we feel that an artificial man has many advantages to offer the electorate. A robot needs no sleep and can work at the public business twenty-four hours a day. Having no appetites he is incorruptible."

The *Daily News* said, "Merriwell may be a better American than many officials. At least he was MADE IN USA, which is more than can be said for many commie-coddlers."

Since the story was national, many columnists commented. A leading conservative wrote: "Merriwell is a subtle plant by the liberal establishment. On the surface he appeals to the normally conservative voter, but once in office he is likely to turn on the police force and shelter crooks from punishment for their peccadilloes, for not having a soul . . ."

A nationally syndicated rumor-monger chanted: "Surely an honest machine is better than a machine politician like 'Foxy' Fox, who has yet to explain a $10,000 fee from the Elves, Gnomes and Little Men Marching and Chowder Society. Why did they give you ten grand, Foxy?"

A liberal commentator spoke wistfully of the unenviable position of Steve Woolsey, exposed and lonely.

Time began its cover story, "Robot Merriwell made history and litigation as well as news. Worried was opponent Lemuel 'Foxy' Fox. . . ."

A nationwide poll produced the following answers to this question:

Do you believe a robot should be	Yes	No	Don't Know
elected to Congress?	30%	30%	40%
Do you regard a robot as a fellow being?	10%	50%	40%
Would you want a robot as a neighbor?	0%	99%	1%

The American Civil Liberties Union asked biblically, "What is man?" and answered Aristotelianly, "A political engine." The Americans for Democratic Action issued a statement that democracy was not only color blind but ignorant of biology, and students on campuses as far north as the University of Alaska and as far west as Hilo were aroused on Frank's behalf. Demonstrations were held, placards went up and Frank received altogether far more publicity than if his campaign had been run by Madison Avenue. An Association for the Preservation of the Rights of Machines was formed and the Elves, Gnomes and Little Men Marching and Chowder Society denied through its president that it had ever paid Foxy Fox ten thousand dollars, insisting that it had never had a dime in its treasury—that it had no treasury, in fact, that it subsisted solely on golden dew gathered on midsummer mornings. The President of the United States, speaking to a Congress of Inventors, asserted that he took no sides and when he said, as he did now, that a public servant must have a heart, he was speaking in the Pickwickian sense.

On election eve Steve was asked by the press—in the form of Wilton Ogilvie, to whom the Horace Greeley Club had evidently been assigned as a permanent beat—if he thought disclosure of Frank's origin had hurt his chances. And Steve, filled with intimations of Frank's ruin and his own, replied with a resounding, "N-no."

Frank Merriwell began to be mentioned for the Presidency while he was still a freshman Congressman. Stevenson Woolsey saw only three things that would stand in his way. Merriwell had no national organization. He was not married. And the court case was still pending over whether he was in fact qualified to be a Representative in Congress.

He had won an earlier case testing whether he was a citizen of the United States when the court construed the word "born" in the Constitution also to mean "manufactured."

"I am not worried," Frank said. (He no longer bothered to point out that he wasn't programed to worry—after having been exposed as a machine he had behaved as if he no longer believed he had ever been anything more or less than human.) "I have faith in our courts. I shall abide by whatever judgment is made."

"You're d-damn right you will," Steve said. "You will also keep your big mouth shut for once and let Harry do all the talking. This time."

"I am opposed to progress," Frank said simply. "The Common Law will deliver me."

The Harry referred to was Harry Shapiro, an attorney famous for having successfully argued on behalf of a number of unconventional clients, including a lady who had put her fist through a glass door (Shapiro won her substantial damages for cuts and abrasions as well as mental anguish), a bigamist being sued simultaneously by both wives (Harry proved both suits invalid because his client had not been convicted of bigamy), and a contractor who had run up a twenty-story building on the wrong site.

Steve, Aurelie and Appalachia occupied the front row during Frank's hearing. To begin with, counsel for the plaintiff, an "interested citizen," argued that no person who had been born—or manufactured—on the date it was stipulated Frank had been turned out in the van Ten Bosch laboratory, was old enough to hold office as a Representative and that Frank's election should be nullified.

Harry Shapiro rose to the occasion like a porpoise to sunshine. A small man, gray and squinting, with the voice of a cannon, he called a curious bevy of witnesses—a man with a metal hand, another with a prosthetic leg, a surgeon who testified to implanting an artificial kidney and the patient with said kidney. Of each Shapiro inquired the date of birth, the date of installation of the particular prosthesis, calling attention to the fact that the date of one had no connection with the other. His point was clear long before he had finished. The parade was closed with the most important witness of all.

Dr. van Ten Bosch looked much the same as he had the day Steve first laid eyes on him—the day Aurelie had said, *This is Daddy—he's so far out in left field he's playing in another league.* His bushy white hair was wild. His eyes were glowing embers. His mouth was set in a perpetual sneer.

He began by refusing to be sworn. "Hocus-pocus for superstitious minds. I will say my say and if you think it is untrue, convict me of perjury."

"I shall fine you for contempt of court instead," said the judge. "I will allow you to affirm, if you prefer."

"It's all humbug," snarled Ten Bosch. "This I will affirm with all my heart."

One of the jurymen looked so pleased at this that Steve suspected he had been planted by one or the other lawyer. Then, under Shapiro's sharp questioning, Ten Bosch affirmed that he had been at a loss for a particular part and in his haste had made use, in Frank's construction, of the handiest substitute, a transformer from a thirty-five-year-old radio that was lying around.

Opposing counsel called no witnesses. He addressed the jury.

"Ladies and gentlemen. It has seldom been my pleasure to look upon a jury so alert, so clearly unbiased, so eager to weigh the evidence and bring in a patriotic verdict—it is really superfluous for me to address you. My learned adversary has proved that the date of a mechanical appliance does not invalidate the date of birth or manufacture. Now the date of manufacture of this mechanical thing, known as Four-X alias Frank Merriwell, is less than twenty-five years old, consequently, even if he were a sentient human being—which he is not as I shall demonstrate to your satisfaction—he would not be old enough to serve in Congress. My learned friend would like to date his creation from the installation of a part from a thirty-five-year-old radio. Why not from the date his metal was mined? This is nonsense. Suppose a man uses his grandfather's false teeth—does this date his birth from that of his grandfather's dentistry? Let us assume, as my learned opponent might imply if he thought of it, that this transformer or transistor or transubstantiator is of such importance that this mechanical oddity could not exist without it. Does this lend weight? I think not. I think not. Consider the case of a baby born at midnight. The head, clearly the most important part of a congressman—ahem—(laughter from the jury)—clearly the most important part, emerges at eleven fifty-nine, the legs only at twelve-oh-one. The baby is credited to the later day, not the earlier. I'm sure this disposes of learned counsel's spare parts. Your honor, if the court please, I meant no disrespect to my colleague. I spoke only of what was brought forth in his direct examination. I withdraw spare parts and speak instead of the transformer by which my learned adversary would transform this machine into a human being. But with a jury such as I see before me he cannot do it. I repeat, he cannot do it. For what is the definition of a sentient human being, capable of bearing responsibility of election to a governing body? Why, he must be able to distinguish between right and wrong. Is this the function of a machine? Members of the jury, you know as well as I that no machine can distinguish between right and wrong. If it could, our whole judicial system would fall to the ground—we would install machines to return our verdicts and other machines to pass sentences." Here the jury began yawning. "A machine cannot weep, cannot laugh, and without tears or laughter how can one say, "This is good or this is evil?" A juryman dozed. "Ladies and gentlemen, I thank you."

Without leaving the box the jury brought in a verdict for Frank. The court recapitulated by saying that if a man had an artificial leg made in 1960 this didn't invalidate his having been born in 1930. On the other hand, his having parts dating from 1930 is prima facie evidence of his having existed at that time. As for learned counsel's argument that ability to distinguish between right and wrong defined the capability to serve in Congress — this was the first time he had heard of this doctrine. He, the court, wished it could be applied, and rigorously. To resume, right and wrong were absolutes — the court had no sympathy with the notions that they were relative matters. But to a savage from the wilds of New Guinea (he meant no disrespect to that distinguished member of the United Nations — this was only by way of example) it was necessary to instill a concept of what constituted social as opposed to antisocial behavior in Western culture. No testimony had been offered that Mr. Merriwell had not had such concepts inculcated. As for machines taking over the judicial functions, he for one would welcome such a relief. The court warmly agreed with the jury's eminently sensible verdict and gave judgment and costs to the defendant whom he congratulated on his recent political victory. (Cheers.)

"Somehow," said Appalachia, "I've begun to think of Frank as one who can't lose."

"Why, of course, dear," said Aurelie. "What else?"

While he was in Congress Frank helped curb highway building, tariff-raising, defense-spending. He voted *no* on practically everything, including funds for the un-American Activities Committee, except foreign aid — as long as it didn't include munitions ("Isolation is progress."), cultural exchanges ("I am opposed to schools, not to knowledge."), increased income taxes in the upper brackets ("Wealth is progress. Let us have primitive equality."), and programs calling for aid to artists and writers ("Art knows nothing of progress. Even James Joyce is not an improvement on Laurence Sterne."). He introduced a bill to tax all advertising and voted for higher taxes on cigarettes but to remove all excise on liquors. ("As well tax cheese," he said. "Fermentation is a natural process."). He voted to favor labor unions ("The most unprogressive force in the country."), and for civil rights ("Enslaving the black man is progress — he was free before the white man set foot in Dahomey.").

Despite his stand on civil rights, southern politicians were not unfavorably inclined toward the Merriwell-for-President boom. What better solutions to the bitter pill of integration than the abolition of schools altogether? Before the New Hampshire primary Frank had a hundred pledged delegates from Dixie. Steve Woolsey — noting one day in his office how the sun on Appalachia's skin made him think of a vacation in the tropics — said, "Frank's career has been too quick, too s-slick. He may even get the nomination. But he isn't ready for the P-Presidency."

"How's that?" asked Appalachia, tenderly scratching a pale brown arm with long brown fingers. "It seems to me he was born ready—and I use the word born in the broad legal sense. He goes straight to his objective." She sighed. "Sometimes I wish—"

Steve, all politics, ignored the sigh and the unfinished sentence. "The worst drawback and the one we c-can't do anything about is his n-not being married. No one except Buchanan and Cleveland has been elected who wasn't married. Jackson was a widower."

"So was Jefferson," she reminded him. "Not being married won't hurt him with the old maids. Besides—"

"Go on."

"He'll get married."

"How can he? I mean he's not—Who would marry him?"

"Aurelie van Ten Bosch, of course. He was made for her."

Stevenson waited for the impact of the shock to crush him. All the time he had known Aurelie would throw him over for another man. Another *man,* that is. He had always feared she would give the heart he could never quite command to a four-minute miler or a centerfielder batting .400 or a pitcher winning twenty-five games in a season—or even a catcher. But this was— this was . . . Words, even stuttered ones, failed him. A machine candidate, he remembered at last. He had groomed his own rival. And yet—somehow he wasn't shattered. If Aurelie really preferred the Tin Woodman to the Wizard of Oz, her mind was not functioning, poor girl. Perhaps—perhaps she would realize her mistake before it was too late. If only she were as sensible as—as, say, some one like Appalachia Lee. Feminine, yet with a grasp of reality . . .

Wilton Ogilvie broke the story of the engagement three days later. Four days after that Congressman Merriwell and his betrothed eloped to Mexico. No Presidential aspirant could have asked for a better press. Frank, every black-Irish hair of his wig smoothed not quite enough to hide the slight wave, was quoted as saying, "I am opposed to all progress," while astride a burro in Sonora with his wife riding pillion. Swimming at Puerto Vallarta—Frank's torso in sunburned makeup looked as good as any other on the beach—he challenged the usefulness of computers, praised the abacus and the quill pen, denounced submarines, elevators and miniskirts. In all the pictures, Aurelie was radiant.

"That's what the caption says," muttered Steve gloomily. "What's she got to be radiant about?"

"I asked her the same thing," admitted Appalachia. "You might call it feminine curiosity. All she did was give me a look and say, 'Science is wonderful, progress or no progress.' "

"N-nonsense. A girl like you—"

"Yes, go on," urged Appalachia. "What about a girl like me?"

"I was only going to say a g-girl like you wouldn't settle for s-science. Progress or no progress."

"Oh, Stevenson, you do have the neatest way of putting things. In a nutshell."

"I c-could have been on the debating team if it wasn't for m-my s-stutter."

"I think your stutter is adorable."

Frank continued his winning streak. He won the New Hampshire primary. He was nosed out in North Dakota but swept Wisconsin and Nebraska. He carried Oregon and got most of the California delegates. He went to the convention with four hundred votes and Steve Woolsey worked out a deal with the runner-up for the Vice Presidency. Frank was nominated on the first ballot.

His opponent was a maverick Kennedy who had as running mate an equally maverick Rockefeller. "Young" (fifty) Kennedy declared, "I am for progress. I don't intend to give up the steam locomotive or the steel plow for any renegade who has turned against the very force that created it. The only progress I'm dubious about is that which allows artificial men to run for office. When the steel plow was first invented they said it would poison the soil. When the first passengers traveled at a hair-raising fifteen miles an hour by locomotive they were warned they would hemorrhage to death. Those are the kind of people who are against progress and want to go back to the hoe and the handcart."

"My esteemed opponent," replied Frank smoothly, "is for the steel plow— the plow that broke the plains and gave us the dustbowl of the nineteen-thirties. He is for the steam locomotive—which is now to be found only in museums. If this is the kind of progress my opponents are for, let me say, Go to the museums and dustbowls, my friends, and give us pure air and pure food . . ." But it really didn't matter what Frank said. People asked themselves for the first time what progress had brought them. Installment buying? Planned obsolescence? Devitalized food? The AMA? Electric lights that burned out as fast as they could be replaced? Automobiles that broke down carrying people at eighty miles an hour to new billboards, new hot-dog stands? Jerry-built housing developments that became slums before the crumbling houses were paid for? H-bombs? Napalm? Starvation in Mississippi and New Mexico? The UN? Policemen, censors and the PTA? Cities with elephantiasis? Fashions? Caramel-colored grain neutral spirits? A morality based on The Pill? Enough people came up with an answer to elect Frank. He carried every state but Arizona, Alabama, Georgia, South Carolina and Vermont. He even squeaked through in Maine and Florida.

At his inauguration Frank wore a three-cornered hat with a red-white-and-blue cockade and rode down Pennsylvania Avenue in an open horse-drawn carriage. The music for the Inaugural Ball was provided by hurdy-gurdies. In doing over the White House Aurelie had the electric lights ripped out and candles ordered for the chandeliers. The Master Chandlers Association sent her a set of antique brass bedwarmers in token of gratitude. A golden age dawned.

Except for a few scattered diehards, Frank Merriwell's view had become the popular view. People discovered a new content, even a new prosperity in abandoning television, the all-electric kitchen and the princess telephone in every room. All open-air movie theaters were turned into archery ranges, and cracker barrels returned to the corner groceries. Advertising was so heavily taxed that Madison Avenue became a ghost street. Automobiles were not prohibited but they were considered to be a sign of drivers who hadn't yet made it into the horsey set. Smoke and soot gradually vanished from the shrinking cities as factory after factory for manufacturing useless gadgets closed down.

And there were charming fringe benefits. One week Aurelie appeared in public in a fascinator and the next every secretary from Boston to Los Angeles appeared in fascinators. Of course, the country had fewer secretaries (and bookkeepers and time-study experts) now that competition among businesses was slackening. Wimples became popular. Most girls stayed home to bake bread, be wed young and discover that large families sharing the burdens of the household could accomplish more with greater ease than all the silent, automatic mobil-maid, pop-up, drip-dry, and press-to-release items had in the dreary past.

Sociologists studied the phenomenon and announced it was a perfectly normal synthesis brought about by the pressure of the new feminism versus the new antifeminism and would have happened without Frank Merriwell, he being only the product of his age and not vice versa. It is doubtful if President Merriwell ever scanned it, he being busy with the erection and dedication of the grandest of Washington's memorials, that dedicated to Sir William Schwenck Gilbert, the only non-American ever to be so honored. As the President cut the ribbon before the mammoth replica of the Savoy Theater, he said tersely, "He was absolutely against all progress."

Receiving the account by special courier who had used up several relays of horses, Stevenson Woolsey absently laid the heavy parchment aside.

"Appalachia—what an appalling name for such a g-girl. May I call you P-Polly?"

"Oh, Steve—all my life I've wanted to be called Polly. Now I'll never let anyone call me anything else."

"Well, no use going overb-board about it. Appalachia's still your legal name, you know. Appalachia Lee. You think it might sound awkward if you changed it to Polly Woolsey?"

His political partner, removing his hands from just below her waist in the back, murmured, "What a turn you've given me! Just let me have a few days to think it over, will you? Or at least a few minutes?" And she allowed a becoming blush to creep up under her milk-chocolate complexion.

"Frank wants us to go along as p-part of his staff to Ulan Bator for his summit conference with the chairman and party secretary, and ninety days on a clipper ship can be pretty boresome to those who aren't married — while it would be just the thing for a honeymoon."

"Why, Stevenson, you romantic old darling, you. Three months on a sailing ship. Whatever will we do?"

It was something short of a year later, after the historic Merriwell summit talks had borne fruit and the world, stimulated by Frank's honest antagonism to any weapon more lethal than a rock, decided to scrap every gun, rifle, plane, tank, warship, pistol, bayonet and bomb, that the unheard-of happened. It came first as a laconic statement from White House Press Secretary Wilton Ogilvie, transmitted by heliograph and semaphore all over the country and around the world:

"After the most conscientious consideration, President Merriwell has decided to resign."

Pressed immediately for reasons, Ogilvie gave out his next communique: "The President is taking this step because he feels his objectives have been achieved and progress is at an end."

All over the world heads of state dropped whatever they were doing to call Frank Merriwell — they forgot or ignored the open secret of his origin — "A great human being . . ." "A man for the ages . . ." "A soul to admire . . ." and so on.

Some reporter even got to Frank's father-in-law, nested as befitted Frank's position in a hermit's cave high up in the Great Smokies, complete with bats and familiars. Madder than ever, too, he took full credit for everything. "I made Frank Merriwell," he said for publication by various town criers. "I made him what he is. I promised I would destroy civilization and I have done so. What little nests of progress remain in isolated spots will disappear in a few years as soon as the formulas for soft drinks and calculating the velocity of light have been forgotten. We have won, beaten all the false prophets, kept the human race from going to the stars in order to build a heaven on Earth."

Mrs. Merriwell, invited to comment on her father's pronouncement, said only, "Oh, Daddy's an old fuddy-duddy, still living back in the scientific age." First Ladyship had done well by Aurelie. Her charms were the delight of the wood-engravers who had succeeded the photographers.

The clincher came at the press conference when they asked Frank Merriwell what, as ex-President, he proposed to do. He said, "I've had an offer from — " in the pause a score of minds filled in: the Vatican, Oxford University, The Society for the Rights of Man, the ReUnited Nations. But Frank finished, "—the Mets, which I've decided to take."

So he did.

Hail to the Chief

SAM SACKETT

Americans love conspiracy theories, as a quick examination of books and articles about the assassination of John F. Kennedy will readily indicate. Many of us have toyed with the idea of a "captured" president, one who is secretly controlled by forces unknown to the public. "Hail to the Chief" by Sam Sackett (about whom we know nothing) is a powerful story on this always interesting theme.

Prologue

Henry Logan paused, panting. He could no longer hear the bootsteps of his pursuers. It was a good thing that he had reached so high a position in the Government; he knew the passages of the immense Administration Building better than anyone else except the Chief himself. Otherwise he would never have escaped the relentless guards. Logan wasn't young any more, and he had never been much of a runner.

He leaned against the wall and breathed deeply. This wall was not made from beautiful marble, like those the public saw; it was plain concrete, built as part of a honeycomb-defense against even a direct H-bomb hit on the Administration Building. He was getting into the outer perimeter of the Center—that region where the Chief stayed. Only a few dozen people besides himself, except for the Personal Guardians who surrounded the Chief, had ever gone into the Center; only a few hundred even knew it existed. The rest were content to accept the elaborate maze of marbled halls that surrounded it, and the impressive offices that lined them, as the whole of the Administration Building.

But Logan knew that, although he had got into the Center, his job was not yet over. The corridors in the Center were an ingeniously-constructed labyrinth, designed to lead astray even those who knew them well. They, and the lead-layered walls of the building, were dotted with booby-traps— some activated from controls in the Chief's quarters, others from triggers which an unwary invader might stumble against wholly accidentally. Even when he succeeded in penetrating deeper into the Center, to the Chief's quarters, there was the still tougher task of fighting past the Personal Guardians.

But the Chief had to be killed.

That was a job that only one man could do, and it was a job that could not be done by any one of the hundred younger men who were willing to do it. Only Logan had the knowledge — knowledge too intricate and detailed to be transferred to anyone else by any means short of an actual impression of his neural circuits upon the other's brain tissues. One little man — five feet three and weighing 120 pounds, with graying hair and tortoise-shell glasses — was called upon to challenge the greatest concentration of power in the history of the human race.

And Henry Logan had taken up that challenge.

He looked around him in the silence. Just plain gray walls stretching into the distance — that was all there was to be seen. He checked on his armament. He had a .38 pistol in a shoulder holster; he had practiced drawing it for months and had spent tedious hours in target practice with it. He carried extra clips for it in three coat pockets and on his hip. Daggers were strapped to his left forearm and right leg; he had been thoroughly trained in their use. Under his shirt he wore a light but sturdy bullet-proof vest, especially designed for him. He looked — and he smiled at the idea — surprisingly dangerous for a former political science professor who had joined the Government, ostensibly as a minor figure in the Office for Foreign Affairs.

Logan wanted a cigarette badly, but he was afraid that somewhere behind the concrete wall there was an apparatus analyzing the odors of the air — or perhaps breaking down its chemical content. Perhaps even now electronic computers were informing the Chief that in such-and-such a compartment of the Center the amount of water vapor and carbon dioxide in the air had risen slightly as a result of his breathing. Or perhaps the sound of his panting had already been amplified into thunder in the Chief's ears.

Well, it was the chance he had decided to take. And if his progress was reported on, the only thing to do was to keep moving.

Logan looked back at the heavy door he had come through. On the outside, it was a section of a marble corridor; inside it was heavily insulated with lead and steel. As a safety-measure, he bolted it from the inside.

Logan moved slowly, keeping his eyes roving around him. Ahead of him, a surprising distance ahead, he could see the gloomy dead end of the hallway. He could not see any passages, either to the right or the left; but he knew that they were there, ready to open responsively to the sure and subtle pressures of those who were familiar with them. Logan did not have a thorough acquaintance with this particular corridor — although they all looked

so much alike that it was hard to tell them apart. But he was close enough
to the inner workings of the Center to be able to spot the signs of secret
passages. To a casual observer a crack between two slabs of concrete might
not look any deeper than any other crack. But Logan was no casual observer; he was one of the few real intimates of the Chief, and he had trained
himself to sense these slight differences.

There was danger, though; at any point Logan might meet with a trap.
He had to be constantly on his guard.

He continued forward cautiously, scanning the ground for a sign of anything dangerous, scanning the walls for any sign of a way farther into the
building. He knew that he had to go into the interior, and also down until
he was below the surface of the ground. It was hard to tell which way led
into the interior, considering the intricate plan of the building, and the un-
even floors in the Center also made it difficult to tell just how far down
he was getting. Logan's wrist-compass and his thorough knowledge of the
dimensions of the building helped him with the first problem; he had to rely
on his sense of balance and a pocket-level for the second. He was, he knew,
going on a tangent to the perimeter of the Center; and he was also, he believed, on a slightly downward incline.

Suddenly he paused. The concrete block immediately in front of him
looked suspicious. Was it a trap? Were those just deeper shadows? Or were
they really cracks, showing that this block was independent of its fellows
and capable of responding to human weight? He could not be sure. He might
be wrong; he might be afraid of nothing—but he couldn't take the chance.
Logan walked backward a few steps, ran, and jumped over the suspicious
block. The exertion made him pant harder.

Again he pressed forward, slowly and cautiously. At the rate he was going, it would take a long time for him to reach the Chief. Another man,
on another errand, might have become discouraged at the thought of the
patient hours of caution and vigilance that would be required of him—a long,
grueling mental and physical strain and then, at the end, exertion of the most
strenuous kind. But what Henry Logan was going to do would have to be
done. The Chief must be destroyed; government must be returned into the
hands of the people.

I

Logan had been a professor of political science at one of the nation's large
universities. He had a reputation as one of the most brilliant scholars in his
field, but the small enrollment in his classes showed that he was not popular
with his students.

The most recent contribution to his reputation was his book on the political theories of John Stuart Mill, which ended with an impassioned avowal of Mill's idea that in any election the votes of educated people should be weighted more heavily than those of the masses.

Logan had written in that final chapter, *"For democracy, in the last analysis, is the best form of government only by default. So many of the world's great thinkers—Plato, Mill, Czardas—have agreed that the best government is rule by an enlightened oligarchy, that it would be presumptuous to argue that any other system is better in theory.*

"In practice, however, it has always been found that power corrupts even the most high-minded of men, and that the most benevolent of despots loses his benevolence when placed in a position of political dominance. From tyranny, therefore, the political scientist must turn to democracy. The masses are, in theory, incapable of self-government. They are willful, ignorant, and capricious; they do not know what they want. But no man or group of men knows what they want better. Weak and ineffectual as democratic government has always been, it must remain the mature selection of political thinkers until some new genius in the science of government invents some new form, uniting the theoretical attractions of Plato's Republic with practicability."

The paragraph was buried in a work of interest only to teachers. But Logan knew that the influence of his ideas would not be confined to teachers alone; once you have convinced the teachers of a nation, it is only a little while before you have convinced their students. And Logan hoped that that paragraph would have the effect of leading teachers to discuss in their classes the desirability of replacing democracy with some more efficient system, one that would give more influence to educated men—like Logan.

Its effect was different. About a week after the book appeared, a man came to see Logan. Logan never learned his name, and never saw him again. But he came into Logan's office at the university and said, "Professor Logan, the President has empowered me to offer you a position in the Office for Foreign Affairs."

Logan looked up from the papers he was grading, surprised. "Why me?"

"Because of your book on John Stuart Mill."

The professor leaned back in his chair. "I hardly expected the book would appeal to President Morrison."

The man remained standing by his desk, looking down at him.

Finally Logan, to break the silence, said, "What kind of position is it?"

"Its confidential nature prevents me from telling you at this time; ostensibly, you would be named Assistant Under-Secretary for Latin American Affairs."

"I don't know anything about Latin America," Logan snapped, picking up his red pencil again.

"The title is only ostensible; it will give you an excuse for being seen in the Administration Building."

"See here," Logan said. "What the devil is all this? I don't know you. I don't understand what you're talking about. I'm busy. If you can't say what you mean, get out of my office."

The man reached into his coat pocket and drew out some tickets. "A compartment has been reserved for you on the 10:53 train tonight. You will be met at the Capital and taken to see the President; he will explain in greater detail what your duties will be."

"I'm not interested."

The man put the tickets on Logan's desk and left the office. Logan threw them in the wastebasket, marked an F on the test paper he had been grading without bothering to read the rest of it, and picked up the next one. He glanced over the first answer and wrote a sarcastic comment at the end of it.

Then he got up and paced the room. Service with the Government, he mused, would certainly be attractive. There would be an assured salary — and probably a higher salary than he would ever receive in the academic profession. He fished the tickets out of the wastebasket and looked at them carefully.

"Poo," he said, and threw them back into the wastebasket. "Assistant Under-Secretary for Hogwash." He re-seated himself at the desk and glanced over the second answer. His left hand clenched as he read. "Stupid idiot!" he muttered.

He steeled himself for the third answer, but somehow he could not face it. Every day — for how many years? — he had poured the fruits of his intellect on the classroom floor for a set of fools. He had examined the strengths and weaknesses of the various systems by which man had attempted to regulate himself, for boys interested only in football and hot rods, and for girls interested only in boys. He was giving them the finest part of himself.

Logan got up, took the tickets out of the wastebasket, and went out of the office. He left the papers scattered on his desk, just as they were. He did not drop into the chancellor's office to explain his departure; he went straight home, bathed, shaved, dressed, packed, ate at a near-by restaurant, and read in Czardas until it was about ten o'clock. Then he took a taxi to the station, waited until the train came in, took his place in his compartment, and went to sleep.

When he woke up, he was in the Capital.

He got off the train and was met by another man whose name he never learned. This one was much taller than the first, and his height made Logan feel at a disadvantage. "Follow me," the man ordered and set off at a brisk pace through the crowd.

Logan set his bag down and stood looking after the man's retreating back. A woman following him bumped into him. "Excuse me," she said; Logan said nothing.

After a while he saw the man turn to look for him. When the man found Logan he came striding back for him. "Come on," he said. "What are you waiting for?"

Logan took his time lighting a cigarette.

"Come on," the man said.

"Who are you?" Logan asked.

"That's of no importance. I've been assigned to pick up Professor Logan at the depot and take charge of him; you're Professor Logan, aren't you?"

"Yes," Logan admitted.

"Well, come on, then. Here; I'll carry your bag." The man picked up the suitcase and stood, waiting. "Let's go."

"What's the hurry?"

"After you've worked for the Government a little while you'll find out what the hurry is. Come on, let's get moving."

Logan followed the man out to a waiting automobile, chauffeur-driven, which bore the insignia of the Office for Foreign Affairs. The man climbed in after Logan and closed the door.

Logan said, "See here, I don't like these high-handed tactics of yours."

"What you like and what you don't like are of no importance yet."

"You're as insolent as a college freshman."

"What I'm like is of no importance; the important thing is that you have been chosen."

"Yes, but chosen for what?"

"I'm not at liberty to tell you."

Logan flounced back in the seat and sulked. After a while, he said, "What did you mean by saying that what I liked and didn't like were of no importance *yet?*"

"I'm not at liberty to say."

Logan was silent for a while. Then, as the car drove on and on through the streets of the Capital, he asked, "Are you at liberty to tell me where we're going?"

"No."

Finally they left the Capital and roared along a highway North. Logan squirmed. "I thought I was being taken to the President."

"You will see the President later."

"Where are we going now?"

"I'm not at lib—"

"Oh, hush up. See here, you can't kidnap me like this. I demand to know where I'm being taken; otherwise stop the car and let me out."

The other man said nothing. The chauffeur drove on silently. For a wild moment Logan thought of leaping at the men, but the foolishness of the idea deterred him, and he merely sat sulking in his corner of the back seat.

At length they pulled up before a three-story white frame building that looked somehow, from the road, like a military academy.

The man said, "All right, get out."

Logan looked at him and was about to speak, but thought better of it and followed orders, clutching his suitcase tightly. "Is the President here?" he asked.

"No."

The man led him to the front door. It was opened by another man, whose face was vaguely familiar to Logan from newspaper pictures. The second man said, "Come in, Professor Logan."

Logan entered. The man who had brought him from the station did not come in; he got back in the car and drove off again. Logan saw him once more, in a corridor of the Administration Building, but the man either did not see him or chose not to recognize him.

The second man said, "Professor Logan, I'm Arthur Friedlander."

Of course! This was the Director of the Division for Economic Aid in the Office for Foreign Affairs.

Logan said, "I'm glad to meet you, Mr. Friedlander, in spite of the circumstances in which I have been brought out here."

"Those conditions were necessary," Friedlander said, "as I hope you will be permitted to see later. First you will have to take certain tests which will determine your fitness for Government service. I am requesting that you take all of them voluntarily. I am afraid that I shall have to warn you that you will be forced to complete them once you have started them. I hope you will not object, because it has been determined that you are peculiarly fitted for the responsible position for which you have been selected."

Logan listened to this carefully. There was something wrong. Tests? He had never heard of anyone taking tests to determine his fitness for government service. He had himself often advocated standards for the election of government officials, to be enforced also on candidates for public office, but no one — he thought — had ever paid attention to him. He was curious about these tests; they bothered him. The other thing that bothered him was the curious official language that Friedlander used — very carefully chosen so as not to say anything. "It has been determined." Who determined it? Why the passive voice? "The responsible position for which you have been selected." What was it? Why all the vagueness? Friedlander was trying hard to keep something hidden.

Logan asked, "What is this position?"

"I'm not at liberty to tell you yet."

The same answer. He might as well give up. "All right," he said; "I'll take your tests."

"Fine," Friedlander said. "Have you had breakfast yet?"

"No," Logan admitted.

"We'll start them after you've eaten. They're rigorous, and you'll do better if you take them on a full stomach."

And the breakfast was good, Logan admitted. Country sausage—his favorite dish—and eggs fried just the way he liked them—how did they know even these intimate details about him?

But he put the question out of his mind as Friedlander rose and said, "Are you ready, Professor Logan?"

Logan rose and crushed out his cigarette. Friedlander led him into a large room, furnished only with a plain, heavy wooden armchair, fitted with arm clamps and a head clamp; a microphone; a motion-picture camera; and half a dozen flood lights. Logan frowned and turned to Friedlander, but the Economic Aid chief had disappeared.

"Professor Logan?" The voice made him whirl around. It belonged to a young, good-looking man in a turtle-neck sweater. Logan found out later that his name was Fred Hansen.

Hansen came over and shook Logan's hand. "Let me explain the procedure to you, Professor. You will be seated in that chair. Instruments will record your blood-pressure, pulse, body temperature, and involuntary muscle-twitches while you are being asked a series of questions. In addition, an electroencephalograph will record your brain-pulsations. The whole questioning procedure will be filmed in sound, including both my questions and your answers. The camera will be trained on you for the entire time. When the questioning is over, the film and records will be carefully studied—your expressions will be analyzed from still pictures made from the film as well as watched in action, and the records will be compared with the questions and answers to determine your exact reactions."

"It seems remarkably complete," Logan observed.

"It is; won't you sit down?"

"What if I don't?"

"That decision is not mine to make, and so I cannot tell you what will be determined. Possibly, nothing will happen to you. But if the decision *were* mine, I'll tell you frankly that I certainly would take some steps to prevent your telling anyone what you have seen so far."

"Will you tell me what this is all about?"

"Not until after the questioning."

Logan looked the younger man hard in the face. "Very well," he said; "I'd rather die in any other way you could think up than from curiosity." And he sat down in the big chair.

Hansen busied himself strapping the professor into the chair and adjusting the arm and head clamps. When he had finished, he stepped back without a word and turned on the flood lights. Logan was soon perspiring and wished he had thought to take off his coat; it was impossible to do so now, strapped in as he was. Hansen then pressed a button, and another young man came in from an adjoining room. Silently he took his place behind the camera and started it. Hansen walked back and forth out of camera range and began firing questions.

"What is your name?"

"Henry Logan."

"How long have you been a citizen of this country?"

"I was born here."

"How old are you?"

"Fifty-one."

They started innocuously enough, those questions. But then they began getting tricky.

"Who was the greater man, Hamilton or Jefferson?"

"Why — I suppose really Hamilton, because — "

"Do you attach any credence to Czardas' theory of dynamic social structure?"

"Why, of course, that's basic to the whole — "

"Why have you never run for political office?"

"Well — "

"Faster! Why have you never run for political office?"

"Damn it, I never thought about it!"

The sweat was streaming down his face now, and he was stiff from having sat in one position so long. It was as if he had died and gone to the particular hell of people who give examinations. And Hansen kept on without relenting.

"Why have you never married?"

"I don't know; I suppose I never found anyone — "

"Of what political party are you a member?"

"I don't belong to one. I think they're — "

"For whom did you vote in the last election?"

"Morrison."

Logan sat looking at the hands crawling around the face of his watch. It was amazing how slowly time could pass when your body ached and you were soaking in your own perspiration and somebody was hammering questions at you one after another. Finally he asked, "Can't we take a rest?"

"No. Come on; answer the question."

"I can't remember what it was."

"You're just stalling for time. Can Mill's idea of weighted voting be reconciled with the theories in his essay 'On Liberty'?"

"Of course."

"Do you feel that John Adams has been over- or under-estimated by historians?"

"Underestimated."

"Would you bear arms for the Government if requested to?"

"If they wanted me to."

Logan had shut his eyes against the glare of the lights now, and the whole experience was sinking into a monotonous pattern. It had been years since he had first entered the room, and Hansen had been firing questions at him continually, without a letup. He began answering them automatically, without thinking.

"What is your favorite color?"

"Blue."

"If you were asked to denounce your best friend as a traitor, would you do it?"

"I don't know."

"Come on, answer the question: Would you do it?"

"I guess not."

"Do you consider patriotism a virtue?"

"Rightly directed, yes."

And still the questions kept steadily on — until suddenly there was a silence. The questions had stopped. Logan raised his head and opened his eyes. Hansen was loosening the clamps. Logan struggled to get up, but his stiff body refused to function. He fell sprawling on the floor at the foot of the chair.

Hansen and the other young man helped Logan to a couch. They gave him a glass of water, which made his dry throat feel better. The questioning, all told, had taken four hours.

When Logan felt strong enough, he sat up. Before he could say anything, Hansen told him that Friedlander was awaiting him for lunch.

Logan joined the Economic Aid director in the dining room. Friedlander rose from the table and greeted him with a smile. "You seem to have come through the ordeal all right."

"I don't know," Logan said, "would you mind telling me now what all this is about?"

They sat down. Friedlander talked as they ate: "You were told that you were wanted for Government service, and that is quite correct. But it will surprise you to know that the Government I speak of isn't the Government you have in mind. Among ourselves we always call the Government *you* are thinking of 'the Administration,' to differentiate it."

"What in heaven's name —"

"You see, Professor Logan, such a genius in political science as you called for in your book exists, and has existed, for several years. Remember? *'Weak and ineffectual as democratic government has always been, it must remain the mature selection of political thinkers until some new genius in the science of government invents some new form, uniting the theoretical attractions of Plato's Republic with practicability.'* Well, although of course you didn't know it at the time you wrote that passage, that new form exists and is now under operation."

"I simply don't understand."

"I don't expect you to, yet. I'll try to explain it as rapidly as I can. The Government is not a democracy, nor yet a dictatorship. Nor is it a compromise; it is a tyranny so complete, a despotism so comprehensive, as to give the illusion of absolute and unlimited freedom."

"I can't even visualize anything like that."

"Perhaps not, now. But I'll give you a brief outline, and then, after you have started in your service, you will perhaps get a clearer picture. Let me start getting at it this way. For whom did you vote in the last election?"

"Morrison."

"Of course; so did nearly every citizen. He won by the most crushing landslide that any presidential candidate has ever had. It was imperative that he do so, because the policies he represents are the policies that must be carried out to preserve the peace of the world at this time. It is equally imperative that he be re-elected this fall."

"I'm not sure I see—"

"I'm sorry; I was getting ahead of my story. So you voted for Morrison. Have you ever seen Morrison, talked with him?"

"Why, no."

"How many people ever have?"

"I don't know. He's spoken to large gatherings throughout the country, and he's undoubtedly held conferences with all sorts of people."

"Yes, but you voted for him without having talked to him? And so did millions of other citizens?"

"Certainly."

"Of course. Because Benjamin Morrison does not exist."

"What?" Logan jumped to his feet. "But I've seen pictures; I've read speeches; I've—"

"You have seen pictures of a man whom we have chosen to call Benjamin Morrison, because the name has certain desirably euphonious characteristics. That was why his most recent opponent was named Silas Karp, by the way. Certain policies needed to be carried out, so we gave the people a choice between them and their opposites, as personified in two men; and we deliberately rigged the entire election so that every advantage would be on Morrison's side. Morrison was a man we had been grooming for our purposes for several years, as we had advanced him slowly to major and responsible positions where he would be well known throughout the nation. Karp, on the other hand, was a man we had been deliberately suppressing so that he would be an unknown with no attractions. He, by the way, is also one of us; he does not believe a word of the assertions he made during the last campaign."

"You don't mean that the people don't actually govern this country."

"But I do. That is just what I do mean. The people respond to the pressures we put on them to run the country the way we want them to."

Logan stared for a moment. "Well, I'll be damned. That *is* genius. Who's is charge?"

"The Chief; if you pass your test, you'll meet him."

"I certainly would like to."

"He wants to meet you, too," Friedlander said. "He's a great admirer of yours — especially of the book on Mill."

"Then it was he, and not the President —"

"Oh, President Morrison admired it, too. So did I; it fits in so well with our actual practice, that we all admired a man who could come, in theory, so close to what the Chief has been doing. The Chief said that if you only had his organizational abilities, you might have been able to form the Government yourself."

"This is really remarkable. But what sort of a group is the Government? What kind of people really *do* run this country?"

"We are an organization of the intellectually elite. Generally, the examination includes intelligence-tests as well as the sort of probing you underwent; and all of us are college graduates at least — most of us have the Ph.D. degree. The Chief felt that he should waive the intelligence-test in deference to you."

"Well! I'm flattered, of course. But this is all so new and strange to me that I can't get over it. The audacity of it! The sheer — oh, this is marvelous. What will I be doing in this Government of yours?"

Friedlander paused to eat some salad before replying. "If you pass your examination — we should know before you go to bed tonight — you will be made Special Assistant to the Chief. Your first duties will be to help arrange for President Morrison's re-election."

"What if I don't pass the examination?"

"We will have to kill you."

The very calmness and affability with which Friedlander spoke the words jolted Logan more than if there had been menace in the man's voice. Finally the professor made an effort to pass it off: "I hope not. I never *would* finish grading those examinations."

The news of the examination results came at about eight o'clock that evening, and with it the Chief. Logan was lying on a couch, reading a detective novel that Friedlander had lent him, when the Economic Aid director entered smiling, his hand extended toward the professor.

"Congratulations!" Friedlander said. "You've passed the examination; I knew you would."

Logan sat up and let his hand be shaken vigorously.

"And you have a visitor," Friedlander continued.

Logan's heart gave a bound. "Good Heavens! Is it the Chief?"

Friedlander nodded, smiling affectionately at the professor.

Logan stood up. "Well! This *is* exciting. Where is he?"

"Right in here," said a voice in the next room. It was an old man's voice, made graceful by the accents of culture.

Logan bounded into the next room to see the Chief, who was standing there grinning at him. He was a short man, about the same size as Logan, with a square face and a frame that was still wiry and powerfully shouldered. He gripped Logan's hand in a firm, warm clasp and said, "I'm glad to meet you, Professor Logan." Logan guessed he must be about seventy. "Shall we sit down and talk this over?"

They took chairs. Logan looked around and noticed that Friedlander had silently left them alone.

"I'm sorry," the Chief was saying, "that we had to subject you to the testing; but it is absolutely essential that we made certain that you really do believe in a rulership by the intellectually elite. We cannot afford any spies or turncoats; I think you can understand that."

Logan nodded.

"Like most of our members," the Chief continued, "you showed signs of independence of thought, and very little real patriotic loyalty. That was only to be expected; the kind of blind obedience that a man like Hitler demanded from his subordinates is not possible in an intelligent man — and very likely Hitler failed because the men with whom he surrounded himself were not intelligent and therefore were not fitting media through whom he could extend himself. So it is necessary that I surround myself with fitting media; and, since that is the case, I cannot expect unquestioning loyalty.

"Since that *is* the case, my organization of geniuses — we all score higher than 150 regularly on the standard I. Q. tests — is perhaps the least cohesive oligarchy in history. And I must rely on other things to keep it together. Would you like me to tell you the pressures that we feel, for instance, would keep Professor Henry Logan in our organization?"

"Yes, I would."

"Well, then, in the first place, you have loyalty to your theory of government. You know, yourself, that you're more capable of governing the members of certain intellectual strata of society than they are of governing themselves. I imagine the incapability of most people is brought in upon you daily as you read the papers written by unthinking college students — who, after all, don't come from the lowest strata intellectually. You will learn, as you progress farther into our organization, that it is possible for highly-intelligent people to disagree on what is best for the nation. But you will also discover that it is more important that the structure of the Government be retained than that this or that individual minor policy be adopted."

"I think I understand that."

"I hope so," the Chief grinned; "it's important that you do."

"Well, that was the first place. Is there a second?"

"Yes. After all, it would seem surprising to the average citizen, if he learned of the Government, that we would bother to do this at all. All we have done is taken over the responsibility of government. Why? Largely, I think, out of altruism. You, for instance, Professor Logan — you want to govern people better than they already are governed. Isn't that true? That altruism is a part of everyone who believes in a government by the intellectually elite. It makes no difference to you, in any personal, selfish way, how some garage-mechanic governs himself; you get nothing out of it. But, knowing better than he does, seeing more clearly than he can, you want to do these things for him. Isn't that right?"

He paused, and Logan, realizing that the question was not purely rhetorical, assented.

"Very well, then. The Government offers you the opportunity to perform this altruistic act. But the altruism is not enough. The satisfactions in government are not very great. There is a certain kind of satisfaction in self-immolation to help other people, of course; but one can grow tired of martyrdom. There is an appeal in power, especially such unlimited power as the Government exercises, but that soon palls when one weighs against it the heavy burdens — the mental strain that makes the job actually and physically what the man in the street calls it figuratively, 'a headache.' Some other system of rewards must be thought out to repay these geniuses for devoting their lives to taking on their own shoulders the responsibilities of government. And I have worked out the simplest and, in practice, the most satisfactory method. Would you like to know what it is?"

"Of course."

"Professor Logan, in asking you to join the Government in its service to the people of this nation, I shall be giving you a position of consequence second only to my own. But I can give you only the same reward that the other members of the Government have received. Which is merely this: you may have whatever you want."

"Whatever I want?"

"Certainly. You will be in our service until your death. During that time, you may have whatever you want. Money is not important to us, because we get what we want in other ways, but if you want money you can have that. With some men it's women — not, I imagine, with you. For those men, we keep them supplied with all the most beautiful women they want. You are a scholar. If you want unlimited access to the National Library, you may have that; if you want any books for your own private use, you may have them. So long as the existence of the Government is not revealed — and that is a matter of method rather than of an actual limitation to the promise — you may have whatever you want. That is the reward we offer our members. And that is the second reason why nobody ever leaves Government service; there is never anything that he can gain by it."

"It is certainly overwhelming."

"Of course. And now, I welcome you to the Government." The Chief rose, shook Logan's hand, and left the room.

III

The first official meeting of the Government that Logan attended was a preconvention conference in a smoke-filled room — but a very different kind of thing than he and the other citizens of the country were accustomed to regard as typical.

The scene was the Chief's private headquarters, deep in the Center of the Administration Building, protected from even a direct hydrogen-bombing by an ingenious construction of concrete-walled passageways, layer upon layer of them, between the Chief's hidden office and the splendid veneer of the Administration Building itself.

Logan did not know all the men present. One of them, of course, was the Chief himself. Another was the man whom he had known as President Morrison. Friedlander was there, too.

The Chief was saying, "We'll have to choose a bachelor to oppose Morrison. Morrison's family is a heavy asset, and we'll give them all the television play they need."

Friedlander said, "How about having a divorced man run? That would make a good contrast."

The Chief nodded vigorously. Logan was surprised to see how freely he accepted suggestions from his subordinates.

One of the other men remarked, "Pity we can't use Karp again; he was almost perfect for us."

"How about names?" Friedlander asked. "You can do a lot with names if you use them well."

The Chief said, "You might be interested in a Western governor named Hilary Velute. His name would make him unpopular with most of the people."

"Is he married?" Friedlander asked.

"No, I don't think his marital status has ever been an issue. We can supply him with a divorced wife, I think, and people will nod and say they'd forgotten."

Morrison said, "That's pretty risky."

The Chief said, "You're probably right; we'd have to leave him a bachelor. But maybe we could give him an ex-mistress."

Friedlander said, "That's always good stuff."

Morrison said, "He's on record with some pretty pro-Morrison statements. I think we're agreed after last time that the best policy is to have Morrison's opponents believe as much opposite to him as possible." Hearing the man he thought of as Morrison refer to himself in the third person made Logan suddenly very conscious of the enormity of the hoax the Chief had put over.

Friedlander said, "Issues aren't that important in a campaign." The Chief nodded but did not say anything.

A man Logan did not know said, "I'd like to get somebody from a border area. Velute may turn out to be the fairhaired boy of the West for some purely local reason and pull down enough of a regional vote to make him dangerous. Why can't we use Green? He couldn't win if he paid people ten dollars a vote."

The Chief said, "Green is out." And there was a quality in his voice that made Logan know he would never have questioned that statement.

Morrison said, "I don't think Velute could carry the West. I don't know of any reason why he'd be a local hero. But if you're worried about that, let's cast doubt on his patriotism. He must have belonged to an organization we can label traitorous, or maybe he knew someone." He turned to the Chief. "Remember those pictures you took of Morrison and Warner? We did it all very secretly, and there never was any real connection between them, but they're the most incriminating-looking photos I've ever seen. Do you have anything like that on Velute?"

The Chief grinned. "Oh, I have some material we can use. But maybe we'd better get hold of Velute and have him pose for some pictures. We'll work on the morals angle with his ex-mistress, and also on the subversive angle. We'll play on his relationships with Murray."

"Has he had any?" Friedlander asked.

"Not yet," the Chief said.

"Well, we can fix that up easily enough," Friedlander said. "But how about Morrison? We've torn Velute down pretty well, but we ought to build up Morrison."

One of the men spoke up. "I've got a peach of an idea; been saving it for something really big. Maybe this isn't big enough yet and I ought to save it, but it's still a good idea."

"Let's have it," the Chief said.

The man went on: "Get this picture. The campaign is going along nicely. Morrison seems to be comfortably ahead in all the polls, but not too much, so that it looks as if it may be a good hard fight. Morrison has an important speech scheduled in one of the big cities; everybody's looking forward to it because it seems as if the balance of the campaign hangs on it."

The man paused. Everyone was watching him tensely. His face was glowing, and he was gesturing expressively, a lighted cigarette between two of his fingers.

"Then," he continued, "just then, there is a nationalist rebellion in one of the protectorates. It's a national crisis — an emergency. You know, those things can have all kinds of implications and overtones in the international situation."

Friedlander put in, "It may even have been stirred up by foreign agents."

The man nodded. "That would be good. So Morrison cancels his speech. Everybody feels sorry for him because he has to stop campaigning, and in the suspense of the moment everybody is watching him. He returns to the Administration Building; he studies the situation. It looks grim. He's convinced that only his personal presence will put down the rebellion, so he flies down there. Maybe he's shot at by one of the rebels."

Morrison laughed. "Don't get carried away."

The man continued, "But his presence *does* do it. He takes command of the situation, saves lives, and does all kinds of heroic things. He shows that his interest is really in the people, not the kind of fake interest the nationalist leaders have been putting on to grab power. And then he comes back, right at the end of the campaign, to make one last speech. The polls go crazy!"

The Chief clapped the man on the back. "By George, Ted, that's a wonderful idea. I don't see how we can go wrong!"

And, as Logan saw in the next six months, that was the way it happened.

Interlude

Logan had come a long way, and now he was getting tired and short of breath. He was, he was confident, getting close to his goal. He had been going constantly downward for over three hours, and, although he was not fully certain that he had always been going in the right direction, he was not entirely discouraged either.

What he wanted to do more than anything else at the moment was sit down and have a cigarette and a can of beer. But he had no beer, and he was afraid to sit down and have a cigarette.

It was, he knew, getting to be late. Outside, it must already have been dark for a long while. But here, as everywhere in these corridors, some hidden lighting arrangement made every concrete surface a flat, dead gray.

Logan had had no dinner, and there was an empty feeling in his stomach; he wondered whether he would ever eat again.

His eyes were smarting now. He had scarcely allowed himself to blink, so alert had he kept himself to the slightest hint of a passageway—or of a trap. And the unrelieved grayness was bothering him.

It was strain all the way—strain of every sense, of every mental faculty, of every muscle. He felt taut, now, but he knew that he must go on. How much farther? He didn't know. At any step he might reach his goal; or, on the other hand, at any step he might be destroyed. One moment there would be the flicker of life that he was, a pencil-point in the gigantic labyrinth of the Chief's bastion, and the next moment there would be only the six gray concrete surfaces.

He stopped and looked closely at a crack in the wall; that might be a doorway. He flattened himself against the wall, to one side of the crack, and cautiously touched the area on the other side in the various patterns that he knew the Chief had installed in these doorways to respond to touch. He was right on this one; it swung open for him.

He waited for a few moments before venturing away from the wall against which he was pressing. Cautiously he brought out his pistol and got down on the floor. He inched himself forward on his stomach and peered, gun ready, around the corner.

It was another corridor just like the one he was in. Its floor was a little lower than the present one, and the dimensions were different—it was a little shorter, but a little wider and a little higher. He looked at the floor carefully. There did not seem to be any traps.

He scrambled to his feet and stepped into the other corridor. He looked up and down. There was nothing to tell him which way to go. Generally he went downward, as he was pretty sure that the Chief had not had any of these hallways built under his quarters. But this floor seemed even. He laid his pocket-level on it and—

Was that a doorknob?

Carefully, but impatiently, he walked about twenty feet down the corridor.

Yes, it was a doorknob. There was a wooden door, about three feet high and three feet wide, set in the wall of the corridor. He could crawl through it, but that was about all.

He lay down flat to one side of the door, on the handle side. Gingerly he reached up and took hold of the knob. Nothing happened. He turned it; still nothing happened. He began to open the door.

Suddenly there was a spurt of machine-gun fire, cutting through the wooden panel in a shower of splinters and ricocheting bullets. Although they came within inches, the bullets missed him.

He drew his hand back rapidly, and gravity pulled the door closed. The gun stopped.

He inspected the damage from a safe distance. Seven bullets had torn through the door and bounced off the opposite wall. Logan suspected, from the way the gun had started up when the door opened and shut off when it closed, that the action of the gun was automatic. After all, the Chief could hardly be expected to have machine-gunners stationed all over the building in spots like this, on the chance that someone might penetrate to them.

Or was it chance? Maybe the Chief was aware of his presence and had sent a gunner to this door. He looked at the holes in the wood more carefully. They were in a straight line, beginning at the side nearest the handle. Cautiously Logan opened the door again from the side, shutting it as soon as the next spurt started.

There were now eleven holes in the door. The four new holes were in the same place as the old ones, starting where the others had left off. Logan was pretty sure now that the gun was fixed, and its action was automatic.

He opened the door again enough to start the gun going and wedged it open with his pocket-level. Then he cautiously went down to the other end of the hallway, as far as he could get from the rebounding bullets. The chatter of the gun sounded thunderous in his ears after the silence in which he had come thus far. The bullets sprayed through the door back and forth, back and forth, for what seemed an interminable period.

Finally the gun stopped. It had, Logan surmised, run out of bullets. But he would still have to be cautious in going through that doorway. So tremendous a noise might have aroused the defenses of the Chief.

He went back over to the little portal. The gun had nearly ripped it in half. He got down on his hands and knees and pushed the door open wide.

Nothing happened.

Gun in hand, he peered around the corner.

It was only a little closet. There was the machine-gun and the exhausted clip that had fed it bullets; there wasn't space in the room for anything else.

Logan sighed.

He began to make his way down to the other end of the corridor, looking for another passageway. There might be none; that had happened before.

But suddenly he froze. A section of the wall swung back. And, as he watched in utter fascination, the black barrel of a rifle poked into the corridor.

IV

There came the day when the Chief called Logan into his private quarters for a conference. Clad in slacks and a gray turtle-neck sweater and sipping from a tall, cool glass, he was lounging in a comfortable armchair. "Sit down, Logan," he said brusquely.

Logan sat down, wondering what had gone wrong. This wasn't the tone of voice that the Chief generally used with him. He lit a cigarette to occupy his mind, while waiting for the Chief to speak again.

"You've had a pretty thorough look at the Government, Logan; what do you think of it?"

"I still can't get over it."

"Of course you can't."

Logan was annoyed but tried not to show it. He still respected the Chief, despite the intimate association he had had with him over the past six months. And he had considerable respect for the Chief's Government.

After all, he thought, it isn't a bad Government. The Chief is very good about taking suggestions so that his subordinates have nothing to fear from offering ideas or even, occasionally, criticism. He does shut you up pretty well, though, when it's an area that he's decided about beyond any shadow of disagreement. But he doesn't hold it against you if you mention one of these areas.

Logan shifted a little in his chair.

"Well?" the Chief said.

Logan frowned. "Well what?"

"You still haven't answered my question; I was serious. What do you think of the Government?"

"I like it."

"Good." The Chief smiled, bounded out of his chair, and gripped Logan's shoulder affectionately. "I was hoping you'd say that."

Logan was surprised at how suddenly the Chief's coldness had melted. This was the old friendly Chief who had so charmed him at their first meeting.

The Chief went over to the fireplace and stood by it a moment, playing with an hourglass on the mantel. "I'm very glad you said that," he said again, turning his face away so that Logan could not see it.

Logan fidgeted nervously. This was strange action on the Chief's part. He seemed to be breaking down from emotion. Could Logan's good opinion of him mean that much?

The Chief turned his face back again. Tears glistened in his eyes, and he was obviously struggling to keep his lower lip still. Logan squirmed in the chair, wishing he had been spared this.

Finally the Chief said, "Excuse me," and dashed into the next room, Logan supposed in order to cry.

Good Lord, Logan thought. *He's worse than a freshman girl.* He got up and walked around, feeling distinctly uncomfortable.

Finally the Chief reappeared. "I'm sorry for my outburst," he said, "but it meant so much to me. So few people are even aware of what the Government is — only a thousand or so throughout the entire country — and I think so highly of your opinion—" the Chief broke off and waved his hand. "However," he continued, "that's neither here nor there."

He sat down again in his armchair and gestured Logan back into his seat.

The Chief cleared his throat. "Professor Logan, I'm not going to live forever. I have the best medical care, of course; but I'm getting old, and I'm carrying the heaviest responsibility a human being has ever borne."

Logan was getting impatient again. This was a harrowing experience. He was interested in forms of government, not in seeing the soul of an individual laid bare—even if the individual was as remarkable as the Chief.

"In your opinion, Professor Logan, what will be the future of the Government if I should die?"

Logan was silent a moment, deciding how he could be both frank and tactful. "That is a weakness of absolute governments. They depend on the ability and personality of one man. When the one man is gone, his place cannot be supplied. In the first place, very often the dictator has removed anyone with the proper qualifications because of possible competition. In the second place, not all men of ability have the personality to carry on a powerful government—and, of course, vice versa."

"I know all that, I know all that." The Chief was impatient. "But answer the question: What will happen?"

"I can't be positive. But I imagine the Government will simply cease to be. The people will go on electing their representatives, only without your control; and, unless one of the members of the Government sells his experiences to a newspaper for money, very likely no one will ever have been aware of your existence."

The Chief was silent a long while. Logan's cigarette burned down and he lit a new one from it.

Finally the Chief spoke. "I knew that, too." He sounded incredibly old and broken. Logan was angry with the Chief for having brought on the whole unpleasant situation, but he tried not to show it. He could not sit still any longer, so he got up and began to pace the room.

"Morrison has the personality but not the ability," the Chief said suddenly, breaking the silence.

Logan nodded but did not speak.

"You—" The Chief sat up straight and looked Logan in the eye. The professor arrested his pacing; he shivered, though it was not cold. "You have the ability but not the personality."

Damn the man, Logan thought. He was so furious that he could not do anything for fear of showing his emotion. This was embarrassing beyond measure.

"Tell me the truth, Logan!" The Chief was in an agony of pleading now. "Tell me the truth! Would a committee—" He couldn't go on.

"No!" Logan howled at the top of his lungs and ran from the room. "No!"

he screamed again in the concrete corridor outside the Chief's quarters, although there was no one there to hear.

V

Logan was on the verge of declining the next meeting to which the Chief summoned him, but thought better of it when Friedlander came to his apartment to drive him to the Administration Building.

"Good of you to think of me," Logan said, climbing into the car.

"Don't mention it," the Economic Aid director said. They drove in silence for a while before Friedlander remarked, "You know, you've changed since you first came to the Capital."

"Have I?"

"You seemed rather sour and sharp to me when I first met you, but you've become much more relaxed and friendly."

"You met me under singularly inauspicious circumstances."

Friedlander laughed. "Yes, but it was more than that, I think; I don't imagine you liked teaching very much."

"No, I didn't," Logan confessed. "I hated it. This is much more to my taste; I feel as if I'm really a part of great things."

"That's the way I feel about it, too. You know, I was a teacher, too, before the Chief picked me up."

"I didn't know that," Logan said.

"I taught economics. It seemed to me that I couldn't stand another day of it; I got so that I hated everybody. But everybody in the Government is so—so congenial to my own personality that I've been very happy since I joined it."

"The Chief is a remarkable leader," Logan said. "He really doesn't seem to tyrannize anybody, and the people are happy, because they think they're governing themselves. I don't feel so much like a bride on the honeymoon now, however."

"Why?"

Logan told the story of his interview with the Chief.

At the conclusion, Friedlander whistled. "I've heard about some peculiar actions, but never anything that peculiar."

"I hadn't expected the Chief to show emotions like that; he seemed so capable and self-contained the first time I talked with him."

"He's like that usually," Friedlander agreed, "but I have heard some strange stories from people who are close to him. He has a large record-library, you know. Morrison walked in on him one evening about half an hour early for an appointment, wanted to ask him about something before the rest of us got there, and found him lying on the floor, crying like a baby, while the record player was going through one Tchaikowsky record after another. Morrison didn't know what to do, but the Chief didn't seem to mind."

"Remarkable."

"Yes, isn't it? He's thrown some pretty remarkable rages, too. You'll find out about those soon enough, I imagine."

"You don't suppose he'll be angry with me about what happened, do you?"

Friedlander shrugged. "You can't tell. There are whole areas of the Chief's personality that I'm thoroughly at sea about. The thing that really bothers me is the new business about Personal Guardians for himself."

"Is that new?"

"Yes, about four months before you came. Frankly, that alarmed me. I thought he might be a little off-balance—persecution, you know. I haven't really seen any of that in him, but I naturally thought of it at the time. Because if he gets that way, then that's the end of it all."

"Yes, I can see that."

They were drawing near the Administration Building now. It was an immense edifice, as big as a small city and towering high into the air. Friedlander turned down the employee's parking-ramp into the basement garages. He and Logan rode the elevator up to the fifth floor, which housed the Office for Foreign Affairs, where both men had their offices.

They followed the corridor down to Friedlander's office and went in. Closing and locking the door behind them, they touched the bookcase in a pattern of places. It swung outward and admitted them to a concrete corridor. They were accustomed to getting to the Chief's quarters by this route, so their penetration into the depths of the building went quickly. They knew just where to jump over traps, and where to find the doors that would let them into the next passageway.

Logan had, by now, entered into the secret recesses which the Chief had in the heart of the Administration Building by some half-a-dozen ways. He knew that there were others. The Chief had once gone over with him a chart of the paths through the labyrinth, so that Logan was probably as familiar with the arrangements as anyone. In fact, Logan had found out later that only a very few members of the Government ever received that particular kind of instruction. He had been mildly puzzled until the Chief had sprung the business about the succession on him, and then the reason for it became clear.

The audacity of having used the heart of the great Administration Building was something that Logan admired. It was a safe hiding place, for the building was so huge and complex that even the oldest employees knew their way around only one, or at the most two, floors. The complicated arrangement of the building discouraged the effort of the will necessary to master its intricacies, so that most Administration workers gave it up with a cheerful curse.

The building was about thirty years old. That gave Logan some idea of the age of the Government, as the erection of the Administration Building was likely one of the Chief's first projects after he came to power—but the peculiar adaptability of the building to the Chief's purposes showed that it could not have been planned before the beginning of the Chief's rule. Well, say that the Chief had governed the country for about thirty years—since he was, roughly, forty. That was a young age for a man to have acceded to so much power.

Logan wondered what the story behind it was, but he wondered in silence. It was a common rumor that various spots in the corridors were sensitized to carry sounds to the Chief's quarters. Neither Logan nor anyone else knew whether the rumors were true, but most people either were silent while going through the corridors, or spoke only on unexceptionable topics. He and Friedlander had adopted the policy of keeping quiet.

Then they entered the conference room and sat down. The others were there before them, and the Chief was at the head of the table.

The Chief called the meeting to order. His face, Logan saw, was flushed and puffy from lack of sleep. He looked more tired and harassed than Logan remembered ever having seen him. "Gentlemen," he began drily, "there is a crisis."

Logan squirmed a little on his seat. The Chief's voice held a note of portent, a note of grave decisions, that Logan didn't like. He glanced around the circle. Morrison was studying the wood on the table in front of him. Friedlander was resting his crossed arms on the table. Another man whom he did not know was industriously filing his nails. All avoided looking at the Chief.

The Chief talked on. The details of what he said were hard to grasp, dealing as they did with intricacies of secret diplomacy with which Logan was unfamiliar. But the broad outlines were frightening.

The defection of an ally had weakened the nation's position internationally to an alarming extent. Oriental scientists had perfected a remarkable new weapon, details of which were still unknown; roughly, its effect was to interfere with the electrical system—the ignitions of aircraft and ground-vehicles, for example—of anything upon which it was trained. The Orient threatened a new major war—a war that the nation would enter with every conceivable disadvantage—within a week unless the nation's foreign policy underwent certain radical changes, changes to which Morrison and his Administration were irrevocably opposed. Concessions were demanded, yet Morrison had made commitments from which he could not retreat.

At the end of the Chief's talk, Logan was leaning forward, his eyes on the old man. Everybody else was raptly attentive, except Morrison, who seemed not to have moved.

Friedlander asked, "What if we make the concessions, just to gain time?" His usually pleasant face was serious now.

"We'll have to," Morrison murmured.

The Chief replied to Friedlander as if the President had not spoken. "In the first place, we'll lose face throughout the world. And that's important; other countries have confidence in us and have taken certain positions in the past because of their faith in us. We can't just say, 'Okay, we're licked.' "

"Well, we *are* licked," a man said. Logan did not remember having seen him before.

The Chief flashed the last speaker a withering glance. He did not say anything more all during the conference.

A man whom Logan knew only as Ted said, "What are these commitments again?"

The Chief listed them over.

Ted said, "Do any of them depend on legislative action?"

The Chief shook his head.

"Too bad," Ted commented. "I thought maybe we could get a floor-fight started; a month or so of debating might give us enough time that we could think this out."

"That worked well enough during Young's Administration, when the Orientals claimed they'd shot down the *Thunderer* by mistake. But then all we had to do was stave off the pugnacity of our own angry population; now we have to placate a very dangerous foreign power."

There was silence. Logan found himself thinking about the Chief instead of the Oriental problem. The Chief implied that he had been in control of Young's Administration; and Young had taken office—Logan computed hurriedly—thirty-eight years ago. That was remarkable. The Chief must have come to power in his early thirties. Or maybe he was older than he looked.

Logan regarded him carefully. He seemed to be in the low seventies— the same estimate Logan made when he first met him. And well preserved at that, Logan thought, remembering some of his university colleagues, who were senile at seventy, and comparing them.

But then the Chief had access to unlimited medical facilities. Nothing that could be done to keep him healthy had been overlooked. Even so, medical science could go only so far, and—

But Friedlander was speaking, and Logan brought his attention back to the present.

"The public," he said, "is unaware of the Oriental ultimatum. Suppose that Morrison suddenly announces that he feels that certain problems have arisen that can be solved by a personal conference with the Oriental leader. So they meet on neutral ground and confer. Morrison can make the concessions they want; that will gain us time until we can repudiate them later, when we're in a stronger position. We'll tell them frankly that we'll do anything they want, if they'll only make one or two minor concessions themselves to save our face; then we can emphasize the concessions we've won, and minimize theirs."

The Chief brightened at that. "That would help give us time, at least. And I'm convinced that they'd rather get what they want without war than with. After all, a war is expensive even if you win it."

The man Logan knew as Ted said, "They'll never give us any concessions now that they have the whip hand, and they'd never trust us any more than we'd trust them. They'd know that we'd repudiate the agreements as soon as we could."

The brightness faded from the Chief's face. "Yes, you're probably right."

Logan glanced over at Friedlander. The Economic Aid director was sitting with his chin on his chest, staring at the floor. Logan felt his dejection very plainly.

"Does anyone else have any ideas?" the Chief asked. Everyone was silent. "Then," he said, rising, "I suppose that the meeting had better be adjourned. We have until next Thursday to make up our minds. If anyone gets an idea between now and then, please get in touch with me."

Everyone nodded. You got in touch with the Chief through Morrison, who was in almost daily communication with him. And everyone stood, looking serious and determined. Logan, too, was alarmed; the prospect of a war with a formidable adversary, when the odds are against you, is not cheering.

They left the Chief's quarters and went back out into the externals of the Administration Building, and Friedlander offered to drive Logan home.

When they were comfortably seated in Friedlander's car, Logan asked, "Just what is the Chief's history?"

"History?"

"Yes. How long has he been in power, and how did he come there?"

"I don't know; I've worked for him only about fifteen years myself. But I understand from the older men that he's lasted forty years or so."

"That's remarkable. How old is he now?"

"He's over eighty."

"He looks and seems ten years younger."

"Someone told me that he has a kind of glandular imbalance that makes him age more slowly. It's probably the same kind of arrangement that people have who live to be a hundred or so."

Logan nodded. "And I expect he's had the very best medical treatment."

"Oh, he certainly has."

"How did he come to power?"

"The Chief has a theory that a popular presidential candidate can swing his party into office after him. That's happened, you know. It's happened the other way, too—the Republicans couldn't elect Fremont, who was tremendously popular, but they could elect Lincoln, who was virtually unknown outside of Illinois, because Republicans had captured so many congressional seats.

"But that's beside the point. The Chief worked it from the other way. He and Young worked hard for Young's election through the usual methods. What people didn't realize was that Young, who was a tremendously popular candidate, was running really for the Government, not for the party that nominated him. When Young got in, everything was easy. The Chief was in a position to manipulate events the way he wanted them, and Young had the support of his party and could use them in the customary way. The Chief's power wasn't great then, of course, and he had some setbacks, but he was able to keep control and gradually build up his authority. In fact, Urquhart was president and followed orders religiously—yet he died never knowing that the Government existed. He was just the sort of man the Chief could use by putting pressures on him, and without making him a member of the Government at all."

"That's fabulous."

"It is. And that's the way the Chief gets power. He pressures people to do what he wants. With that kind of organization, he doesn't need large numbers of men to follow him actively. He can be highly selective in getting just the kind of man he wants—which is, as I believe I told you the first time I met you, an intelligent man who realizes his own superiority to the clods around him."

"It's still amazing."

"Oh, I agree," Friedlander laughed. "There are times when I've felt, as you said, that the honeymoon is over. But the advantages, both to myself and to the nation, are so great that I'm glad enough of the chance to stick it out."

"Oh," Logan said, "I don't have any thoughts of resigning."

"It's just as well," Friedlander said.

After Friedlander dropped him off, Logan went up to his apartment. As the Chief had promised him, the reward of membership in the Government was an adequate supply of everything he wanted. This, in Logan's case, had meant books. He switched on the lights when he entered, for it was growing dark, and took off his coat, throwing it on the davenport.

He took up a novel that he had been reading, intending to pick up where he had left off, but his mind refused to concentrate. Instead, he kept thinking of what he had seen and learned about the Chief.

When Logan had first found out about the Government, he had been eagerly enthusiastic. Now he was not so sure. He had no determined antipathy, but, as he had said to Friedlander, the honeymoon was over. He accepted his strange, new existence without much strong emotion at all. A year before, he had had no idea that there was such a thing as the Government. Now, today, he was a member of its inner council, a party to secrets of the most surprising and unexpected nature, a man whose influence (had he chosen to exercise it) would be great over millions of his fellow countrymen but of whom not more than a few hundred had ever heard. He had become, in the past year, a strange and romantic figure, despite his stature and myopia. And yet he felt not so much excitement as numbness.

The book could not hold his attention, so he put it down. He went to a window and looked for a while at the busy city, thronged with homebound Administration employees. Here and there might be one of them who had some realization of the actual structure of the Government. It was a hoax, a shell-game of unprecedented dimensions. The Cardiff Giant was a pigmy to the Chief.

What of that? It was a good Government. The Chief and his associates ran it as well as they could. All the members of the Government were highly intelligent and well educated. Undoubtedly they knew what was best for the people better than the people themselves did. That was what Logan had spent the first fifty years of his life preaching.

But, damn it! He clenched his fist and turned away from the window. It just didn't appeal to him somehow any more. He was — yes, he was tired of it. It had become a job, a drudgery. And the Chief could be as weak, could be as much a fool, as anybody else.

The street-lights were going on in the Capital. From his window it was a striking sight, but his back was to it, and he was thinking. He'd been handled with a velvet glove in the past year. But he recalled his first introduction to the Government. He had been threatened with death, and he had had no doubt that the threats would be made good. There was an iron fist in that velvet glove. He had cast in his lot with the Government, and there was no way out except by death.

Disturbed, he turned on his radio to a symphony orchestra and sat, trying to let the music calm him.

Suddenly the program was broken into: "We interrupt this concert to bring you an important news bulletin. President Benjamin Morrison was shot by an assassin at 5 p.m. today while he was leaving the Administration Building after an important conference concerning Oriental affairs. The murderer was slain by a presidential guard while attempting to escape. The President died within minutes after he had received the fatal wound. Vice President Clinton Allbright has called an emergency cabinet meeting to discuss the steps which should be taken to keep the government running smoothly."

The music continued. But Logan was not paying it much attention.

VI

The next morning Logan did not even make the pretence of going to his office in the Administration Building and overseeing the duties that pertained to his sinecure. He bought a newspaper and read all the accounts of Morrison's death thoroughly.

The hand of the Chief was behind it, he decided, when he had finished the newspaper stories. Even before that conference the day previous, the Chief had decided that Morrison had to die. The reason was not far to seek.

Allbright, the new Vice President, was known to agree with Morrison on domestic issues, but to hold a more conservative view of foreign affairs. With Morrison out of the way, the Orientals would feel that Allbright might accede to their demands; but, realizing that the transfer of administrative power would mean a delay, they would withdraw their ultimatum temporarily. That might give the Chief the time he needed to prepare for a war; if it did not, it would at least provide the Administration with a legitimate motive for changing its policy with regard to the Orient. The people would not be surprised if Allbright, acting apparently on his own initiative, made certain concessions to the Orient. The worst that could happen would be that he would become unpopular enough to be impossible for re-election.

Logan realized suddenly that the Chief must have selected Allbright for Vice President with just such an idea in mind. He recalled that the Chief had advanced him as the South's favorite-son candidate, and no discussion of his views had been made. But the Chief, looking ahead, must have seen that it might be necessary to reverse foreign policy—and had chosen just the man who could do it.

The shocking expendability which Morrison had proved to have alarmed Logan. The Chief had held Morrison in the highest esteem, had considered him as his successor equally with Logan himself.

Logan himself. What about Logan and his relations to the government? Was he to be chopped off as Morrison had been, with little or no compunction, sometime?

Profoundly disturbed, Logan lit a cigarette and looked over the newspaper stories again. There was a picture of Allbright. So far as Logan knew, he was not a member of the Government. This was, as the Chief had said, a time of crisis; and Logan was not sure whether, in a time of crisis, it was wise to depend on indirect pressures to achieve results. What would be Allbright's reaction to his discovery that Morrison had been engaged in secret communications and agreements with other powers? There might be a public reaction against anything that Morrison stood for—even to the extent that it would be difficult for the Government to control the nation.

And his mind kept coming back to himself and his own chances for survival. He was not in an important position; his removal would not advance the policies of the Government by very much. But if it could do so in any way, he realized now that the Chief would not even hesitate in giving the order. He might be struck by an automobile, or perhaps shot as Morrison was. He might be given some form of food poisoning.

There was another picture in the newspaper, that of the young guardian who had shot down the attacker. His name was Fred Hansen, and the face seemed familiar to Logan. Wasn't there a—

Of course. Fred Hansen was the young man who had put him through the examination when he first joined the Government. He had not seen him for almost the year that he had been a member, and he had not known that Hansen belonged to the Presidential guard.

On the impulse, Logan rose, determined to visit the younger man and talk with him about what was in his mind.

As he reached for his coat, he stopped. Hansen's loyalty to the Chief was under no question, or he would not have been in charge of the examination; he might reveal his doubts to the younger man and hasten his own death.

Maybe Friedlander—

He felt that he had to talk with someone, and Friedlander had been so genial toward him that he thought maybe the Economic Aid director would help him. He picked up the phone and dialed his office. After identifying himself to Friedlander's secretary, Logan heard his friend's voice.

"Hello, Arthur," Logan said.

"Oh, yes," Friedlander said. "Why aren't you down here, Henry?"

"I just didn't feel like coming today," Logan replied. "Morrison's death shocked me deeply."

"Oh, yes," Friedlander said. "But one must carry on. After all, we have a fine new leader now, and I'm sure President Allbright will be a particularly brilliant guide in foreign affairs."

Was Friedlander serious? Logan looked at the telephone in amazement.

"Are you there, Henry?"

"Why, yes," Logan said falteringly.

"I'm sure, after you think it over," Friedlander said, "you'll agree that it was all for the best."

"Well—"

"Was there anything else you wanted, Henry? I'm very busy."

"No, thanks, Arthur." Logan hung up the phone as if in a dream. Friedlander sounded like another man; he could scarcely believe his ears.

No, he could not talk with Friedlander. He could see that now.

Suddenly he threw the newspaper to the floor, shrugged on his coat, and left the apartment. He was determined to see Fred Hansen.

Hansen greeted him with a heart-warming smile. "Come on in, Professor! What can I do for you?"

Logan took a deep breath and began, "I'd like to learn more about President Morrison's death."

"I'd rather not talk about it."

Logan did not know what to say to that. He stood in the doorway, hat in hand, silently.

Hansen seemed as nervous as he. Finally he said, "Come in anyway."

He took Logan's hat and coat and led the older man over to a chair, where he sat. Hansen remained standing and offered the professor a cigarette.

Logan asked, just to make sure, "You're a member of the Government?"

"Yes," Hansen replied.

Good Lord, Logan thought. He didn't know how far to trust Hansen, and Hansen didn't know how far to trust him. Nobody would make any headway in this conversation unless he decided to be frank, and be damned to the consequences.

"Hansen," the professor said. "I'm not satisfied with things." And he began talking. He talked about the Chief's emotional outburst of a few days before, about his suspicions as to the reason behind Morrison's assassination. He put his cards on the table frankly.

Hansen listened with intense interest. When Logan had finished, he asked, "Are you telling me the truth, Professor?"

"Of course," Logan snapped, annoyed by the question.

"Good," Hansen said. "Then I'll level with you. You've got half of the key that puts the Chief behind Morrison's death—the motivation. But I've got the other half."

"You don't mean the Chief ordered you to shoot—"

"Nothing so crude as that. But we did have orders to shoot anyone who made any attempt on Morrison's life."

"Who gave them?"

Hansen licked his lips. "Morrison himself."

Logan almost rose out of his chair. "You mean—"

"A perfect circle. The assassin can't put the finger on the Chief because he's dead at Morrison's orders. The President can't do it either, because he's dead too. The two men in the whole plot who were in on the Chief's secret instructions killed themselves off. With me in the middle, because I did the dirty work."

The young man paced the floor angrily, Logan watching him absorbed. Hansen continued, "Have you ever been just a pawn, Professor? Have you ever known that people were using you for their own purposes and didn't care a damn about you? That's the way I feel now, and it isn't pleasant, believe me."

"I know," Logan replied. "Morrison's murder was so casual that it made me realize I'm not safe myself. Morrison himself was only a pawn."

Hansen sat down and began to talk again. "I'm one of the youngest men in the Government. I was a political science major in college, and all my profs said I was the most brilliant student they'd ever had. I had straight A's in everything, and I was a football-player, too. Anyhow, I got elected student-body president. And I ran things pretty well to suit myself. I knew what was best for everybody. I guess the Chief heard about me somehow, because he picked me up as soon as I graduated and I joined the Government. That was five years ago. When I first got into it, I loved every minute of it. And there was the hope that some day I might lead it myself. The Chief told me that I had the right combination of qualities to run something like this, and that if I were only older he'd make me his successor."

Logan squirmed uncomfortably in his chair.

The younger man continued, "But I'm mad now. It isn't just the Morrison thing, though right now I'm so sore about that, that I'm talking to you — which is very foolish. I've been cooling off for a couple of years now. I wasn't quite so sure that I could run things better than anybody else; I wasn't quite so sure that I knew what was best for everybody. I got a little more tolerant of people who weren't quite as bright as I was. I guess what happened was that I grew up."

Logan wondered with a shock if that was what had happened to him — suddenly, at the age of fifty, he had grown up. Good Lord! He shook his head dolefully and was about to speak, but Hansen was talking again.

"Here's where I really stick my neck out," he said. "I've got something to tell you. And I hope nothing goes wrong, because if it does, a lot of damage will be done." He leaned forward and his voice became confidential. "I'm fed up, and I'm not the only one; there are about a hundred of us. We've been holding secret meetings for about a year now. We're very careful, of course, and generally we hold a series of meetings of ten or twenty people each rather than one big meeting with us all together. Most of us are young men. I suppose we'd have revolted before now, only we don't know how to do it. I'm the only one who's ever been in the Center, where the Chief's quarters are, and that was only once, a long time ago. Most of the rest didn't even know it existed until we told them. And, too, we've been thinking that the Chief can't last forever, and maybe things will go to pieces when he dies."

"The Chief may live to be a hundred," Logan said. "It's something about his glands. And he's making plans to keep things going after his death. I agree with you; I think things will go to pieces when he dies. But not for a long time, and then only after a terrible upset, if he has time to groom a successor."

"It would be better to break it off clean," Hansen said.

The two men looked into each others' eyes, and both knew that the other had the same thought. The Chief must die and die now. Twenty years later would be too late. The Government had outlived its usefulness — had, in fact, become dangerous — and it had to be ended now. There was only one way to end it.

Hansen said, "Would you like to meet with some of my fellow malcontents?"

"Yes, I would."

The young man stood up. "Come along, then. And God help you if you're a spy."

VII

Henry Logan felt strange, now that he was actually going on his mission. The secret meetings, the hours of target practice, all the other activities of the past six months that had been so real and hopeful — they seemed dream-like, now that he was walking up the steps of the Administration Building, his revolver under his armpit, and knives strapped to his arm and leg.

He was recognizing how pitifully optimistic and childish their plan had seemed. He was to go to Friedlander's office, because it was the passageway from there that was most familiar to him. He was to disarm Friedlander by engaging in conversation about some appointment with the Chief. Then he was to go down the corridors, past the Personal Guardians, and insinuate himself into the Chief's presence. There, at the best opportunity, he would kill him. What would happen then? He wasn't to be concerned about that.

The plan might work; it just might — but Logan was feeling no optimism. The weight of the .38 under his armpit, the tension of the straps on his arm and leg made him self-conscious. He was sure that the people who glanced at him in passing could see some, at least, of the arsenal he carried on him. The gun, particularly, made a noticeable bulge at his shoulder; he was certain that he would be stopped by the Administration Building police for carrying concealed weapons.

But nothing happened as he walked up to Friedlander's office and opened the door. Friedlander's secretary smiled in recognition and said, "Go right in, Professor Logan."

Logan entered the office and said, "Hello, Arthur."

Friedlander looked up at him, smiling affably. "Hello, Henry; sit down."

"How are things going in the Economic Aid department?"

"Oh, well enough. You haven't been around much for the past few months; I hardly ever see you."

"I've been working on a book." It was the excuse that he and Fred Hansen had agreed on.

"Oh? What about?"

"The history of the decline of monarchy."

"Sounds interesting. You didn't just drop in for a chat, though, did you?"

"No, I didn't." Logan crossed his legs. This was the hard part. "The Chief wanted me to come down and see him."

"Oh, he did?"

Logan didn't like Friedlander's tone. He tried to think of what he might have said to betray himself, but he couldn't. After a pause—too long a pause, he was afraid—he replied, "Why, yes."

"That's interesting, Henry. For two months we've all had orders not to admit you unescorted into the Center. The Chief has had his doubts about you. I thought he was wrong. But *what's that under your coat?*"

Friedlander was standing, now, leaning forward on the desk. The affability of his countenance was gone, and in its place there was an intense hatred that shocked Logan perhaps more than Friedlander's words.

"You fool!" Friedlander was saying. "It's our bread and butter; do you want to grade freshman papers the rest of your life?"

He came around the desk and charged toward Logan, who now half rose and pulled out his gun.

It went off.

The sound was a thunderclap in the little office. Silence followed it. Logan stood, stupefied, the smoking gun in his hand, watching Friedlander, shot through the head, fall sprawling on the carpet.

And then he turned and ran, out through the office, past the startled secretary, and into the hallway. Her scream followed him. He bolted past throngs of people. Soon he heard, behind him, the noises of pursuit. He could hear the heavy treads of booted Administration Building police beating toward him.

He looked around him for a place to hide. Suddenly he realized he still had the gun in his hand and put it back in the holster; he felt lighter and freer.

There was no place to go, and so he ran on. He came to a flight of stairs and scrambled up them, panting heavily. At the top he dashed down the left-hand corridor, hoping that the police would choose the right. He saw a men's room and paused, his hand on the doorknob. Should he hide here? No, they would search it and there would be no escape. He ran on. There was what seemed to be a cross-corridor up ahead, and he made for it, dodging into it as he heard the boots thumping up the stairs behind him. He was perspiring now.

If he'd only kept his head, he could have ducked right into the pathway to the Center from Friedlander's office. But he'd panicked and run. So now—

There was another cross-corridor; he could hear the sounds of pursuit getting louder behind him, and he dodged down this side path. He was getting a pain in his side; he was not used to exercise. He looked wildly around him, hoping that he would recognize one of the myriad entrances to the Center. He was lost, in an area of the building unfamiliar to him, and he had made so many turnings he was not sure of his directions. But if he could find a section of the marble wall that showed the faintest depth in the cracks that set if off, he might be able to—

And there it was, like the answer to a prayer.

He touched it in the proper pattern, and it swung open. Quickly he ducked in, shut the panel, and bolted it from the inside.

Epilogue

Logan's eyes burned as he stared at that rifle-barrel, gleaming darkly at the other end of the corridor, thrust out from behind the protection of the thick concrete walls.

A voice said, "Throw your gun down here; put it on the floor and slide it."

Logan stooped down and put the gun on the floor. He pushed it a few inches as he tried to think, then gave it a shove and watched it skitter down the corridor and come to a thumping stop at the other end.

"All right. Come on down here. And keep your hands up."

Logan raised his hands as he had seen people do in the movies and went down to the aperture in the corridor wall. There were five of the Chief's Personal Guardians there with guns trained on him. One of them laid his gun down and searched Logan thoroughly. He took off Logan's empty shoulder-holster and quickly found and removed the knives strapped to the professor's arm and leg.

Well, this was it. All the high hopes of Fred Hansen and his friends trickled out in this. Logan's shoulders sagged. He was tired.

"You can put your hands down," the man who had searched him said, "but don't make any sudden moves."

Logan put his hands down. His dejection was thorough.

"Come on," he was ordered.

The men fell into place around him and conducted him through the next passageway to the quarters of the Chief's Personal Guardians.

"May I have a cigarette?" he asked.

"No," he was told.

They bound his arms, sat him down in a plain wooden chair, and fixed up a light so that it shone in his face. They kept him covered from behind the light, and one of them began to question him.

"Whose idea was this?"

"Mine."

"You're lying. Whose idea was it?"

"Mine."

The man struck him. "Come on. You weren't in this alone."

"Yes, I was."

The man hit him so hard that Logan fell down and had to be picked up and put back in the chair.

"Was this your own idea?"

Logan nodded, weakly.

"All right, then; it was your own idea. That means you were the ring-leader. That means you are fully responsible for what you did. That means you have to take all the punishment yourself. If you were somebody's tool, if somebody was just using you, was filling you full of lies, that would be a different story. We'd feel sorry for you; we'd punish him and go easy on you. See what I mean?"

Logan nodded again.

"All right, then. Come on. Whose idea was this?"

"Mine."

The man hit him. "You're lying," he said.

Logan didn't reply.

The man stood, looking down at him. "Who was in it with you?"

"Nobody."

The man hit him again. "That's a lie."

Logan sucked on his lower lip. It was cut.

The man lit a cigarette and blew smoke in Logan's face. "Who was in it with you?"

"Nobody."

"Why cover up for them? They'd tell on you if they got a chance."

Logan didn't say anything.

The man said, "Come on."

Logan was silent.

The man hit him. Logan toppled over and his glasses fell off. One of the lenses broke in the fall.

They picked him up and set him back on the chair. Logan felt like crying.

"Who was in it with you?"

"Nobody." Logan's lips formed the words, but he didn't say it loud enough for anyone to hear it.

The man drove his fist hard into Logan's stomach. The chair collapsed with a clatter and the professor fell, sprawling and gasping for breath. The tears came to his eyes. He was afraid that he would be sick, but he wasn't.

The man kicked him in the face, just hard enough to bruise his cheek. "Come on," he said. "Who was in it with you?"

Logan shook his head.

The man crouched down and blew smoke into Logan's face. "Come on."

Logan shook his head.

The man half-straightened. "Want a cigarette?"

Logan nodded.

"I'll give you one if you'll tell me who was in it with you."

"No." Logan breathed the word faintly.

The man stood up and nudged the side of Logan's nose with his boot. "I could smear that all over your face as easy as this," snapping his fingers.

Logan said nothing.

Suddenly there was a new voice. "Any luck, gentlemen?" It was the Chief. Logan tried to sit up, but the man kicked him back down.

The Chief came over where Logan could see him; in the strong light and deep shadows of the room the Chief's face looked like a frog's.

"Such a distinguished guest," the Chief said sadly. "We mustn't be inhospitable. After all, he wanted to see me so much that he killed a man to get to me. We should be honored." He turned to the man who had been questioning Logan. "I'd like to talk with him myself; you can have him later."

"Do you think it's safe?"

"Oh, of course. But you can come along if you like. Two of you carry him into my quarters." Logan was picked up like a sack of potatoes. "Come along, Professor," the Chief said gaily.

"Now then, Professor," he said, standing over him without gloating, after the Guardians had deposited him in a chair and left. "How did you come to get mixed up in all this?" Logan did not feel like replying, but fortunately the Chief went on without waiting for an answer. "I can't understand it. Unless you wanted to assassinate me so that you could become Chief in my place. But after that scene you put on down here one day I can hardly think that."

Logan shook his head.

The Chief smiled. "What's the matter, then? Haven't we treated you well enough?"

"Why—"

"We brought you out of the dead little college existence you were in and made you one of the most powerful men in the nation. We gave you everything you wanted. You had all the books you wanted for yourself; you had access to the National Library at all times, and even special privileges there. That was all you ever asked for, but if you'd wanted more you could have had it. What more could you have wanted? Freedom to disagree? You had even that; I have been most careful about that."

Logan was stung into answering. "I guess what I wanted was freedom from fear."

"Fear?" The Chief's eyes were shocked.

"Yes. I was afraid that you might have me removed the same way you removed Morrison."

"Why, I had nothing to do—"

Logan interrupted him and told him why he thought the Chief was in back of Morrison's assassination.

When he had finished, the Chief looked a little shaken. Logan was surprised that what he had said would disturb the older man.

The Chief stood silent for a moment, thinking. Then he said, "So you *did* have accomplices." He did not say it very heartily, however.

Logan asked, "Why do you say that?"

"You couldn't have found out these details about what the presidential guardians were instructed, unless you had a friend in the guardians. And that means, I think, Fred Hansen."

Logan sat quietly, trying not to let emotion show on his face.

The Chief was watching him narrowly. "Hansen is another strange case. If he had been older, I would have taken him to be my successor; I gave him every benefit he could desire. And yet he turned against me, just as you did. Have you no patriotism?"

Logan blinked. The question had thrown him off-balance. "Patriotism? I don't see how—"

"Oh, you fool!" The Chief's face flushed. "You knew that the affairs of the nation were in a perilous state; you knew that at any moment we might be plunged into a disastrous war with the Orient. You knew that it was my hand that was guiding us through this dreadful situation. And you would kill me and plunge the country into chaos."

Logan blinked again. The sudden revelation of the egotism of the man was amazing. He said, "I don't think it would have plunged the country into chaos."

"You don't think that poor fish Allbright could keep us out of war all by himself, do you?"

"I don't know, but he ought to have the chance."

It was the Chief's turn to blink. "Why?"

"Because he ought to have a free hand; you can't tell whether he can do something or not until he tries."

"That's a very risky philosophy. And I'm surprised at hearing it from you, Professor. What if we find out too late that he can't?"

"Then we find out. The point is, if Allbright's so poor as all that, who's responsible for making him President in the first place? You are. You got us into the whole mess; now you think you're the only one to get us out of it. But that's the way you've run the country for forty years—getting us into a hole and then making us be grateful to you for getting us back out of it and then into a deeper one."

Logan's voice was rising. "Maybe the people can't run their own government, but I'm not so sure now. Maybe if they'd been let alone they'd have made a better man than Allbright president."

"Maybe, maybe, maybe!" the Chief shouted back. "They're clay for me to mold! Look how I've had them eating out of my hand for forty years! If they had so much sense as that, would they have stood for it? Look how I can make them do what I want! They vote for a family man! That's how they pick their leaders!"

Logan struggled with his bound hands and swayed to his feet. "That's not fair! That's not true!"

"Yes, it is! It is!" The Chief's face was getting redder and redder as he could scarcely control his rage.

Logan screamed back at him, "Tyrant! Tyrant! How do you know so much? Why are you indispensable? Why are you any better?"

In an uncontrollable fury, the Chief leaped at Logan and grappled with him, trying to strangle him. He buried his hands in Logan's neck. Logan fell back into the chair, straining to free his bound hands. Both men were kicking out freely with their feet, trying to hurt the other.

After a violent kick, Logan slid off the chair and fell heavily to the floor. The Chief relaxed his grip for a moment, and Logan rolled away from him. "Coward!" the professor yelled. "Let me get my hands loose!" He tried to scramble to his feet, but the Chief, panting heavily, was up before him and kicked him back down again. The Chief began to kick him in the stomach, so Logan rolled over, trying to get away. Then the Chief kicked him in the back, in the ribs, anyplace he could.

Straining at the ropes was all that Logan could do. He was straining with all his might and then relaxing his hands, trying to make the rope loose enough that he could slip his hands through it. Finally he managed to slip one hand loose, and the rope fell loose on the other one.

He charged for the Chief, knocking him off-balance and to the floor. The Chief fell with a heavy thud. Logan jumped to his feet, breathing heavily. He was so tired that he could hardly stand. He caught a couple of deep breaths, so exhausted that he needed them more than he needed to follow up his advantage. His wrists were burning and the skin was rubbed raw.

Just then one of the Guardians rushed in, covering Logan with his gun.

Tiredly, resignedly, Logan raised his hands to shoulder-height. He looked at the Guardian negligently, expecting to be shot and not much caring. But then he noticed that the Guardian was not looking at him so much as at the Chief. Logan followed his gaze. The Chief was still lying on the floor, quietly, making no effort to get up. Logan's heart seemed to stop. Was he— No, he was breathing heavily and peacefully, as if he were asleep. He was just knocked out.

There were heavy bootsteps, and another Guardian poked his head into the room. "Good Lord!" he said. "You keep him covered; I'll get Dr. Franz."

A few hours before, the discovery that there was a physician to the Chief, perhaps permanently-resident in the Center, would have excited Logan. Now it didn't make any difference. He was tired and it was all over with him, and he wished somebody would shoot him and put an end to it. He had failed. He was not even particularly interested in the cause of his failure; he just wanted desperately to sit down, but he was afraid to ask the Guardian, who kept the gun pointed at him.

The Guardian who had kicked Logan came in and stood in a corner of the room, strangely subdued. He, too, kept his eyes fixed on the body of the Chief, which lay motionless except for the deep and regular breathing. He shot a glance at Logan but said nothing.

The second Guardian returned with a short, heavily moustached man; clad in dirty old brown trousers and a well-worn T-shirt. "All right," he snapped at Logan, "what happened?"

Logan tried to tell as little as he could, but the doctor kept snapping questions at him and forcing him to go into as many details of the fight as he could remember. Finally, feeling that he had stood about enough, Logan asked, "May I sit down?"

"All right," the doctor nodded.

The Professor sat gratefully.

"After you got the rope off your wrists, what happened?"

"I knocked him down."

"How?"

"I jumped at his legs. He wasn't expecting me, so I knocked his legs out from under him, and he went down."

"Then what?"

"That's all."

"What do you mean?"

"I suppose I'd have tried to figure out some way of killing him. But just then he"—pointing at the Guardian with the gun—"came in and stopped me."

"You didn't do anything to him after he fell?"

"No." Logan shook his head.

"Didn't kick him or hit him or anything?"

"No."

The doctor knelt and looked closely at the Chief, running his fingers over his head and raising one of his eyelids to look at his eye. "Here," he said, looking at the two Guardians who were standing by, watching. "Help me get him in on the bed." The third Guardian kept the rifle pointed unwaveringly at Logan as the doctor and the other two Guardians picked up the Chief's body, gently and tenderly, and carried him gingerly into the next room. The door was closed behind them. Logan was left outside, staring at the gun pointed at him.

"May I have a cigarette?" he asked. "They're in my shirt pocket. I don't have any weapons."

The Guardian threw him a cigarette and a package of matches. Logan got the cigarette going and gave the matches back to the Guardian. The minutes dragged on. Logan found an ashtray and sat, puffing smoke and flicking ashes into it. Finally he finished the cigarette down to the last inch and stubbed it out. By now he was thirsty, but he thought a drink would be refused him so he did not bother to ask. From the next room came mutterings and scufflings. Logan sat and waited, trying to make himself as comfortable as he could.

Then Dr. Franz came out of the room and stood looking at Logan. He ran his fingers through his untidy hair. "Well," he said, "damn you, you've done it; you're getting what you wanted."

"Is he dead?" Logan asked, blinking stupidly.

"No, but I'll bet he will be this time tomorrow. He's an old man; he couldn't take that kind of roughhouse. And now everything'll go to hell," he added morosely, scuffing his foot absently against a chair leg.

"This wasn't a bad deal," the doctor said. "Now I'll have to go back to treating Junior's mumps and Mama's imagination. That's the trouble with guys like you," he snapped, suddenly fixing Logan in an angry glare. "You don't think about other people. You've got your own little private grievance, and you don't realize that you mess up the lives of a lot of other people. Me, for instance, and everybody else in the Government. What'll they do?

"Some of 'em have government jobs, and they'll keep 'em until the new Administration runs 'em out of office. And then they'll go back to the sticks and rot there, doing anything they can do to scrape a living together. And thinking about what might have been. But a lot of 'em didn't have any government jobs. They just kind of disappeared. Now, suddenly, they're going to have to reappear. What explanation'll they give? And what'll they do? A lot of 'em gave up the chance for further training to join the Government."

He waved a hand at the Guardian with the gun. "What'll this guy do? You name it. Bank-teller, grocery-clerk, anything. One of the fine minds in the country, snapped up by the Government before he had a chance to finish his education. And now what? Right back into the crowd, worse off than before. Two years in his past he can't explain. No money; no training for anything. That's the trouble with you loonies, you never think of anybody else." He turned away, moodily.

Logan sat, staring. He could not believe that he had been so grossly and completely misunderstood. He was on the point of trying to defend himself, but gave it up. A man so massively, so monumentally prejudiced— It was more than a human being could do to convert him. At best he should crush him with a sharp retort, of the kind he had had on his lips constantly as a teacher. But he couldn't think of anything. He started to fish for his cigarettes in his shirt pocket, then suddenly realized that the Guardian —

And the last sound Henry Logan heard in this world was the report of the Guardian's rifle.

Polity and Custom of
the Camiroi
R. A. LAFFERTY

Raphael Aloysius Lafferty (b. 1914) is an Oklahoman who turned
to the writing of science fiction and fantasy in his forties. One
of the field's premier humorists, his is also a truly unique voice;
not one of his many short stories is like any of the others. Although he has published some fourteen novels, he is best known
for his shorter works, which can be found in collections like *Nine
Hundred Grandmothers* (1970) and *Does Anyone Else Have
Something Further to Add?* (1974).

In "Polity and Custom of the Camiroi" he speculates on the
important question of what kind of society would exist if any
three people could form a government!

From Report of Field Group for Examination of Off-Earth Customs and
Codexes to the Council for Governmental Renovation and Legal Rethink-
ing. Taken from the day-book of Paul Piggott, political analyst.

Making appointments with the Camiroi is proverbally like building with
quicksilver. We discovered this early. But they do have the most advanced
civilization of any of the four human worlds. And we did have a firm invitation to visit the planet Camiroi and to investigate customs. And we had
the promise that we would be taken in hand immediately on our arrival by
a group parallel to our own.

But there was no group to meet us at the Sky-Port.

"Where is the Group for the Examination of Customs and Codexes?"
we asked the girl who was on duty as Information Factor at the Sky-Port.

"Ask that post over there," she said. She was a young lady of mischie-
vous and almost rakish mien.

"I hope we are not reduced to talking to posts," said our leader Charles
Chosky, "but I see that it is some sort of communicating device. Does the
post talk English, young lady?"

"The post understands the fifty languages that all Camiroi know," the young lady said. "On Camiroi, even the dogs speak fifty languages. Speak to it."

"I'll try it," said Mr. Chosky. "Ah, post, we were to be taken in hand by a group parallel to our own. Where can we find the Group for the Examination of Customs and Codexes?"

"Duty! Duty!" cried the post in a girlish voice that was somehow familiar. "Three for a group! Come, come, be constituted!"

"I'll be one," said a pleasant-looking Camiroi, striding over.

"I'll be another," said a sprouting teenage boy of the same species.

"One more, one more!" cried the post. "Oh, here comes my relief. I'll be the other one to form the group. Come, come, let's get started. What do you want to see first, good people?"

"How can a post be a member of an ambulatory group?" Charles Chosky asked.

"Oh, don't be quaint," said the girl who had been the information factor and also the voice of the post. She had come up behind us and joined us. "Sideki and Nautes, we become a group for cozening Earthlings," she said. "I am sure you heard the rather humorous name they gave it."

"Are you as a group qualified to give us the information we seek?" I asked.

"Every citizen of Camiroi is qualified, in theory, to give sound information on every subject," said the teen-age sproutling.

"But in practice it may not be so," I said, my legal mind fastening onto his phrase.

"The only difficulty is our overliberal admission to citizenship," said Miss Diayggeia, who had been the voice of the post and the information factor. "Any person may become a citizen of Camiroi if he has resided here for one oodle. Once it was so that only natural leaders traveled space, and they qualified. Now, however, there are subsidized persons of no ability who come. They do not always conform to our high standard of reason and information."

"Thanks," said our Miss Holly Holm, "and how long is an oodle?"

"About fifteen minutes," said Miss Dia. "The post will register you now if you wish."

The post registered us, and we became citizens of Camiroi.

"Well, come, come, fellow citizens, what can we do for you?" asked Sideki, the pleasant-looking Camiroi who was the first member of our host group.

"Our reports of the laws of Camiroi seem to be a mixture of travelers' tales and nonsense," I said. "We want to find how a Camiroi law is made and how it works."

"So, make one, citizens, and see how it works," said Sideki. "You are now citizens like any other citizens, and any three of you can band together and make a law. Let us go down to Archives and enact it. And you be think-ing what sort of law it will be as we go there."

We strode through the contrived and beautiful parklands and groves which were roofs of Camiroi City. The extent was full of fountains and water-falls, and streams with bizarre bridges over them. Some were better than others. Some were better than anything we had ever seen anywhere.

"But I believe that I myself could design a pond and weir as good as this one," said Charles Chosky, our leader. "And I'd have some of those bushes that look like Earth sumac in place of that cluster there; and I'd break up that pattern of rocks and tilt the layered massif behind it, and bring in a little of that blue moss—"

"You see your duty quickly, Citizen," said Sideki: "You should do all this before this very day is done. Make it the way you think best, and re-move the plaque that is there. Then you can dictate your own plaque to any of the symbouleutik posts, and it will be made and set in. 'My composition is better than your composition,' is the way most plaques read, and some-times a scenery composer will add something humorous like 'and my dog can whip your dog.' You can order all necessary materials from that same post there, and most citizens prefer to do the work with their own hands. This system works for gradual improvement. There are many Consensus Masterpieces that remain year after year, and the ordinary work is subject to constant turnover. There, for instance, is a tree which was not there this morning and which should not be there tonight. I'm sure that one of you can design a better tree."

"I can," said Miss Holly, "and I will do so today."

We descended from the roof parklands into the lower streets of Camiroi City, and went to Archives.

"Have you thought of a new law yet?" Miss Dia asked when we were at Archives. "We don't expect brilliance from such new citizens, but we ask you not to be ridiculous."

Our leader Charles Chosky drew himself up to full height and spoke:

"We promulgate a law that a permanent group be set up on Camiroi to oversee and devise regulations for all random and hasty citizen's groups with the aim of making them more responsible, and that a full-scale review of such groups be held yearly."

"Got it?" Miss Dia called to an apparatus there in Archives.

"Got it," said the device. It ground its entrails, and coughed up the law inscribed on bronze, and set it in a law niche.

"The echo is deafening," said our Miss Holly, pretending to listen.

"Yes. What is the effect of what we have done?" I asked.

"Oh, the law is in effect," said young Nautes. "It has been weighed and integrated into the corpus of laws. It is already considered in the instructions that the magistrate coming on duty in a short time (usually a citizen will serve as magistrate for one hour a month) must scan before he takes his seat. Possibly in this session he will assess somebody guilty of a misdemeanor to think about this problem for ten minutes and then to attach an enabling act to your law."

"But what if some citizens' group passes a silly law?" our Miss Holly asked.

"They do it often. One of them has just done so. But it will be repealed quickly enough," said Miss Dia of the Camiroi. "Any citizen who has his name on three laws deemed silly by general consensus shall lose his citizenship for one year. A citizen who so loses his citizenship twice shall be mutilated, and the third time he shall be killed. This isn't an extreme ruling. By that time he would have participated in nine silly laws. Surely that's enough."

"But, in the meantime, the silly laws remain in effect?" our Mr. Chosky asked.

"Not likely," said Sideki. "A law is repealed thus: any citizen may go to Archives and remove any law, leaving the statement that he has abolished the law for his own reasons. He is then required to keep the voided law in his own home for three days. Sometimes the citizen or citizens who first passed the law will go to the house of the abolitionist. Occasionally they will fight to the death with ritual swords, but most often they will parley. They may agree to have the law abolished. They may agree to restore the law. Or they may together work out a new law that takes into account the objections to the old."

"Then every Camiroi law is subject to random challenge?" Chosky asked.

"Not exactly," said Miss Dia. "A law which has stood unchallenged and unappealed for nine years becomes privileged. A citizen wishing to abolish such a law by removal must leave in its place not only his declaration of removal but also three fingers of his right hand as earnest of his seriousness in the matter. But a magistrate or a citizen going to reconstitute the law has to contribute only one of his fingers to the parley."

"This seems to me to favor the establishment," I said.

"We have none," said Sideki. "I know that is hard for Earthlings to understand."

"But is there no senate or legislative body on Camiroi, or even a president?" Miss Holly asked.

"Yes, there's a president," said Miss Dia, "and he is actually a dictator or tyrant. He is chosen by lot for a term of one week. Any of you could be chosen for the term starting tomorrow, but the odds are against it. We do not have a permanent senate, but often there are hasty senates constituted, and they have full powers."

"Such bodies having full powers is what we want to study," I said. "When will the next one be constituted, and how will it act?"

"So, constitute yourselves one now and see how you act," said young Nautes. "You simply say, 'We constitute ourselves a Hasty Senate of Camiroi with full powers.' Register yourselves at the nearest symbouleutic post, and study your senate introspectively."

"Could we fire the president-dictator?" Miss Holly asked.

"Certainly," said Sideki, "but a new president would immediately be chosen by lot, and your senate would not carry over to the new term, nor could any of you three partake of a new senate until a full presidential term had passed. But I wouldn't, if I were you, form a senate to fire the present president. He is very good with a ritual sword."

"Then citizens do actually fight with them yet?" Mr. Chosky asked.

"Yes, any private citizen may at any time challenge any other private citizen for any reason, or for none. Sometimes, but not often, they fight to the death, and they may not be interfered with. We call these decisions the Court of Last Resort."

Reason says that the legal system on Camiroi cannot be as simple as this, and yet it seems to be. Starting with the thesis that every citizen of Camiroi should be able to handle every assignment or job on Camiroi, these people have cut organization to the minimum. These things we consider fluid or liberal about the legal system of Camiroi. Hereafter, whenever I am tempted to think of some law or custom of Earth as liberal, I will pause. I will hear Camiroi laughing.

On the other hand, there are these things which I consider adamant or conservative about the laws of Camiroi:

No assembly on Camiroi for purposes of entertainment may exceed thirty-nine persons. No more than this number may witness any spectacle or drama, or hear a musical presentation, or watch a sporting event. This is to prevent the citizens from becoming mere spectators rather than originators or partakers. Similarly, no writing—other than certain rare official promulgations—may be issued in more than thirty-nine copies in one month. This, it seems to us, is a conservative ruling to prevent popular enthusiasms.

A father of a family who twice in five years appeals to specialists for such things as simple surgery for members of his household, or legal or financial or medical advice, or any such things as he himself should be capable of doing, shall lose his citizenship. It seems to us that this ruling obstructs the Camiroi from the full fruits of progress and research. They say, however, that it compels every citizen to become an expert in everything.

Any citizen who pleads incapacity when chosen by lot to head a military operation or a scientific project or a trade combine shall lose his citizenship and suffer mutilation. But one who assumes such responsibility and then fails in the accomplishment of the task, shall suffer the loss and the mutilation only for two such failures.

Both cases seem to us to constitute cruel and unusual punishment.

Any citizen chosen by lot to provide a basic invention or display a certain ingenuity when there is corporate need for it, and who fails to provide such invention, shall be placed in such a position that he will lose his life unless he displays even greater ingenuity and invention than was originally called for.

This seems to us to be unspeakably cruel.

There is an absolute death penalty for impiety. But to the question of what constitutes impiety, we received a startling answer.

"If you have to ask what it is, then you are guilty of it. For piety is comprehension of the basic norms. Lack of awareness of the special Camiroi context is the greatest impiety of all. Beware, new citizens! Should a person more upright and less indulgent than myself have heard your question, you might be executed before night-rise."

The Camiroi, however, are straight-faced kidders. We do not believe that we were in any danger of execution, but we had been told bluntly not to ask questions of a certain sort.

Conclusion — Inconclusive. We are not yet able to understand the true legal system of Camiroi, but we have begun to acquire the viewpoint from which it may be studied. We recommend continuing study by a permanent resident team in this field. — PAUL PIGGOTT, Political Analyst.

From the journey-book of Charles Chosky, chief of field group.

The basis of Camiroi polity and procedure is that any Camiroi citizen should be capable of filling any job on or pertaining to the planet. If it is ever the case that even one citizen should prove incapable of this, they say, then their system has already failed.

"Of course, it fails many times every day," one of their men explained to me, but it does not fail completely. It is like a man in motion. He is falling off-balance at every step, but he saves himself, and so he strides. Our polity is always in motion. Should it come to rest, it would die."

"Have the Camiroi a religion?" I asked citizen after citizen of them.

"I think so," one of them said finally. "I believe that we do have that, and nothing else. The difficulty is in the word. Your Earth English word may come from *religionem* or from *relegionem;* it may mean a legality, or it may mean a revelation. I believe it is a mixture of the two concepts; with us it is. Of course we have a religion. What else is there to have?"

"Could you draw a parallel between Camiroi and Earth religion?" I asked him.

"No, I couldn't," he said bluntly. "I'm not being rude. I just don't know how."

But another intelligent Camiroi gave me some ideas on it.

"The closest I could come to explaining the difference," he said, "is by a legend that is told (as our Camiroi phrase has it) with the tongue so far in the cheek that it comes out the vulgar body aperture."

"What is the legend?" I asked him.

"The legend is that men (or whatever local creatures) were tested on all the worlds. On some of the worlds, men persevered in grace. These have become the transcendent worlds, asserting themselves as stars rather than planets and swallowing their own suns, becoming fully incandescent in their merged persons living in grace and light. The more developed of them are those closed bodies which we know only by inference, so powerful and contained that they let no light or gravity or other emission escape them. They become of themselves closed and total universes, of their own space and outside of what we call space, perfect in their merged mentality and spirit.

"Then there are the worlds like Earth where men did fall from grace. On these worlds, each person contains an interior abyss and is capable, both of great heights and depths. By our legend, the persons of these worlds, after their fall were condemned to live for thirty thousand generations in the bodies of animals and were then permitted to begin their slow and frustrating ascent back to remembered personhood.

"But the case of Camiroi was otherwise. We do not know whether there are further worlds of our like case. The primordial test-people of Camiroi did not fall. And they did not persevere. They hesitated. They could not make up their minds. They thought the matter over, and then they thought it over some more. Camiroi was therefore doomed to think matters over forever.

"So we are the equivocal people, capable of curious and continuing thought. But we have a hunger both for the depths and the heights which we have missed. To be sure, our Golden Mediocrity, our serene plateau, is higher than the heights of most worlds, higher than those of Earth, I believe. But it has not the exhilaration of height."

"But you do not believe in legends," I said.

"A legend is the highest scientific statement when it is the only statement available," the Camiroi said. "We are the people who live according to reason. It makes a good life, but it lacks salt. You people have a literature of Utopias. You value their ideals highly, and they do have some effect on you. Yet you must feel that they all have this quality of the insipid. And according to Earth standards, we are a Utopia. We are a world of the third case.

"We miss a lot. The enjoyment of poverty is generally denied to us. We have a certain hunger for incompetence, which is why some Earth things find a welcome here—bad Earth music, bad Earth painting and sculpture and drama, for instance. The good we can produce ourselves. The bad we are incapable of and must import. Some of us believe that we need it in our diet."

"If this is true, your position seems enviable to me," I said.

"Yours isn't," he said, "and yet you are the most complete. You have both halves, and you have your numbers. We know, of course, that the Giver has never given a life anywhere until there was real need for it, and that everything born or created has its individual part to play. But we wish the Giver would be more generous to us in this, and it is in this particularly that we envy Earth.

"A difficulty with us is that we do our great deeds at too young an age and on distant worlds. We are all of us more or less retired by the age of twenty-five, and we have all had careers such as you would not believe. We come home then to live maturely on our mature world. It's perfect, of course, but of a perfection too small. We have everything — except the one thing that matters, for which we cannot even find a name."

I talked to many of the intelligent Camiroi on our short stay there. It was often difficult to tell whether they were talking seriously or whether they were mocking me. We do not as yet understand the Camiroi at all. Further study is recommended. — CHARLES CHOSKY, Chief of Field Group.

From the ephemeris of Holly Holm, anthropologist and schedonahthropologist.

Camiroi, the word is plural in form, is used for the people in both the single and plural and for the planet itself.

The civilization of Camiroi is more mechanical and more scientific than that of Earth, but it is more disguised. Their ideal machine shall have no moving parts at all, shall be noiseless and shall not look like a machine. For this reason, there is something pastoral about even the most thickly populated districts of Camiroi City.

The Camiroi are fortunate in the natural furnishings of their planet. The scenery of Camiroi conforms to the dictate that all repetition is tedious, for there is only one of each thing on that world. There is one major continent and one minor continent of quite different character; one fine cluster of islands of which the individual isles are of very different style; one great continental river with its seven branches flowing out of seven sorts of land; one complex of volcanoes; one great range of mountains; one titanic waterfall with her three so different daughters nearby; one inland sea, one gulf, one beach which is a three hundred and fifty mile crescent passing through seven phases named for the colors of iris; one great rain forest, one palm grove, one leaf-fall grove, one of evergreens and one of eodendrons; one grain bowl, one fruit bowl, one pampas, one parkland; one desert, one great oasis; and Camiroi City is the one great city. And all these places are unexcelled of their kind.

There are no ordinary places on Camiroi!

Travel being rapid, a comparatively poor young couple may go from anywhere on the planet to Green Beach, for instance, to take their evening meal, in less time than the consumption of the meal will take them, and for less money than that reasonable meal will cost. This easy and frequent travel makes the whole world one community.

The Camiroi believe in the necessity of the frontier. They control many primitive worlds, and I gather hints that they are sometimes cruel in their management. The tyrants and proconsuls of these worlds are young, usually still in their teens. The young people are to have their careers and make their mistakes while in the foreign service. When they return to Camiroi they are supposed to be settled and of tested intelligence.

The earning scale of the Camiroi is curious. A job of mechanical drudgery pays higher than one of intellectual interest and involvement. This often means that the least intelligent and least able of the Camiroi will have more wealth than those of more ability. "This is fair," the Camiroi tell us. "Those not able to receive the higher recompense are certainly entitled to the lower." They regard the Earth system as grossly inequal, that a man should have both a superior job and superior pay, and that another man should have the inferior of both.

Though official offices and jobs are usually filled by lot, persons can apply for them for their own reasons. In special conditions there might even be competition for an assignment, such as directorship of trade posts where persons (for private reasons) might wish to acquire great fortunes rapidly. We witnessed confrontations between candidates in several of these campaigns, and they were curious.

"My opponent is a three and seven," said one candidate, and then he sat down.

"My opponent is a five and nine," said the other candidate. The small crowd clapped, and that was the confrontation or debate.

We attended another such rally.

"My opponent is an eight and ten," one candidate said briskly.

"My opponent is a two and six," said the other, and they went off together.

We did not understand this, and we attended a third confrontation. There seemed to be a little wave of excitement about to break here.

"My opponent is an old number four," said one candidate with a voice charged with emotion, and there was a gasp from the small crowd.

"I will not answer the charge," said the other candidate shaking with anger. "The blow is too foul, and we had been friends."

We found the key then. The Camiroi are experts at defamation, but they have developed a shorthand system to save time. They have their decalog of slander, and the numbers refer to this. In its accepted version it runs as follows:

My opponent (1) is personally moronic. (2) is sexually incompetent. (3) flubs third points in Chuki game. (4) eats Mu seeds before the time of the summer solstice. (5) is ideologically silly. (6) is physically pathetic. (7) is financially stupid. (8) is ethically weird. (9) is intellectually contemptible. (10) is morally dishonest.

Try it yourself, on your friends or your enemies! It works wonderfully. We recommend the listing and use to Earth politicians, except for numbers three and four which seem to have no meaning in Earth context.

The Camiroi have a corpus of proverbs. We came on them in Archives, along with an attached machine with a hundred levers on it. We depressed the lever marked Earth English and had a sampling of these proverbs put into Earth context.

A man will not become rich by raising goats, the machine issued. Yes, that could almost pass for an Earth proverb. It almost seems to mean something.

Even buzzards sometimes gag. That has an Earth sound also.

It's that or pluck chickens.

"I don't believe I understand that one," I said.

"You think it's easy to put these in Earth context, you try it sometime," the translation machine issued. "The proverb applies to distasteful but necessary tasks."

"Ah, well, let's try some more," said Paul Piggott. "That one."

A bird in the hand is worth two in the bush, the machine issued abruptly.

"But that is an Earth proverb word for word," I said.

"You wait I finish it, lady," the translation machine growled. "To this proverb in its classical form is always appended a cartoon showing a bird fluttering away and a man angrily wiping his hand with some disposable material while he says, 'A bird in the hand is *not* worth two in the bush.' "

"Are we being had by a machine?" our leader Charles Chosky asked softly.

"Give us that proverb there," I pointed one out to the machine.

There'll be many a dry eye here when you leave, the machine issued. We left.

"I may be in serious trouble," I said to a Camiroi lady of my acquaintance. "Well, aren't you going to ask me what it is?"

"No, I don't particularly care," she said. "But tell me if you feel an absolute compulsion to it."

"I never heard of such a thing," I said. "I have been chosen by lot to head a military expedition for the relief of a trapped force on a world I never heard of. I am supposed to raise and supply this force (out of my private funds, it says here) and have it in flight within eight oodles. That's only two hours. What will I do?"

"Do it, of course, Miss Holly," the lady said. "You are a citizen of Camiroi now, and you should be proud to take charge of such an operation."

"But I don't know how! What will happen if I just tell them that I don't know how?"

"Oh, you'll lose your citizenship and suffer mutilation. That's the law, you know."

"How will they mutilate me?"

"Probably cut off your nose. I wouldn't worry about it. It doesn't do much for you anyhow."

"But we have to go back to Earth! We were going to go tomorrow, but now we want to go today. I do anyhow."

"Earth kid, if I were you, I'd get out to Sky-Port awful fast."

By a coincidence (I hope it was no more than that) our political analyst Paul Piggott had been chosen by lot to make a survey (personally, minutely and interiorly, the directive said) of the sewer system of Camiroi City. And our leader Charles Chosky had been selected by lot to put down a rebellion of Groll's Trolls on one of the worlds, and to leave his right hand and his right eye as surety for the accomplishment of the mission.

We were rather nervous as we waited for Earth Flight at Sky-Port, particularly so when a group of Camiroi acquaintances approached us. But they did not stop us. They said good-by to us without too much enthusiasm.

"Our visit has been all too short," I said hopefully.

"Oh, I wouldn't say that," one of them rejoined. "There is a Camiroi proverb—"

"We've heard it," said our leader Charles Chosky. "We also are dry-eyed about leaving."

Final Recommendation. That another and broader Field Group be sent to study the Camiroi in greater detail. That a special study might fruitfully be made of the humor of the Camiroi. That no members of the first Field Group should serve on the second Field Group.

May the Best
Man Win

STANLEY SCHMIDT

Stanley Schmidt (b. 1944) received his doctorate in physics from
Case Western Reserve University and taught at Heidelberg College in Ohio from 1969 to 1978 before becoming the editor of
Analog Science Fiction/Science Fact, a position he currently
holds. And while he is an excellent editor, these duties have cut
deeply into his writing time, which is a loss to us all. Dr. Schmidt's
three science-fiction novels, *Newton and the Quasi-apple* (1975),
The Sins of the Fathers (1976), and *Lifeboat Earth* (1978) are
all excellent examples of "hard-core" SF.

In "May the Best Man Win" he addresses an issue that on the
surface seems simple—the age requirement for public office.

Matthew Kilroy's name was just a lucky coincidence, but the crowd down
on the floor of the convention hall remembered the ancient phrase and was
taking full advantage of it. Pete Haldrickson watched them on the monitor
in Kilroy's suite upstairs and wondered desperately how to make Matt see
that they were right. They carried huge placards of Matt's tanned, deeply
lined face with the slogan "Kilroy is here!," and though the monitor's sound
was turned low Pete could hear them chanting it over and over. There was
something down there that he had not seen at a party convention in the last
four Presidentials—an ebullience, a genuine sense of impending victory—
and Pete didn't want to lose it. Not when they were this close.

He turned to Matt's real face, even more engraved by experience than
the one on the placards and surrounded by thick shocks of graying hair.
"Matt," he said earnestly, "listen to them. They want you. You can't let them
down."

Matt shook his head. "I'm sorry, Pete. I'd like to do it, very much, but
I can't. I've said that ever since I got back, but they won't listen. I've been
out of touch far, far too long . . ."

"You can catch up fast. You're a bright boy, Matt."

". . . And I'm too young."

Pete let his breath out in an exasperated *whoosh*. "Come on, Matt, don't start *that* again!" He opened his attaché case, withdrew a document and waved it in front of Matt's face. "A photostat of your birth certificate," he reminded. "Denver, May 9, 2026. You're fifty plus, and the Constitution only requires thirty-five. What more could you ask?"

"We can't think that way any more, Pete," Matt said quietly. "Not with relativistic starflights here for real. I want them to continue as much as you do, and I agree that my election might help. But we have to face the new realities that come with them, even if it means legal complications. Time dilation is real, Pete. I'm only thirty-four, and I'll still be thirty-four at inauguration time. I can't run for President."

"You don't look thirty-four," Pete snapped. He walked across the room and poured himself a drink.

"I *could* look a young fifty," Matt granted. "Or an old thirty-four. Believe me, it's an old thirty-four. It wasn't an easy trip, Pete. It took a lot out of me." He waited for Pete to say something, but Pete didn't. He just toyed with his drink, waiting for Matt to get this out of his system. Matt finished, "You've heard the saying that a man is only as old as he feels. Well, that's going to have a new meaning from now on, and it can't be ignored."

Pete sipped nervously at his drink, trying to think of a new approach. Here was a man who was the party's great hope for revival—a man so idolized by the public that, if nominated, he would virtually guarantee victory at the polls. And a man with clear-cut legal qualifications so well documented that they couldn't possibly be challenged.

And yet, maddeningly, a man who was himself challenging those qualifications on the basis of some academic silliness. A man who had the Presidency within his grasp—within Pete's party's grasp—and was quite prepared to throw it away.

Pete finished his drink and looked at Matt. He didn't really have anything new to say, but he had been silent too long and time was short. "Look, Matt," he began, "you're being stubborn. Look at it this way. What difference does it make whether you *call* it thirty-four or fifty? By *our* records you're fifty, no buts about it, and that's what—"

He broke off, distracted by a thunder of applause from the TV monitor. He glanced at the screen and saw a familiar figure mounting the podium. "*Sh-h-h,*" he whispered, his own speech temporarily forgotten. "Ralston's starting your nomination speech."

"But I don't want—" Matt began. Then Pete glanced sharply at him and he stopped and watched the monitor.

The crowd had quieted. ". . . A man who needs no introduction," Ralston was chanting. "A man just back from the stars, with word of man's first successful colony beyond this Solar System. A man who personally led the founding of that colony, in the face of great hardships he never expected to be his. A man who joined the Epsilon Eridani expedition as third mate at the tender age of twenty-five — and who led it single-handedly to its destination after the tragic death of his commanding officers in an accident in space. A man who lost his own dear wife to the perils of an alien wilderness — but then stayed on to see the colony through its first precarious months. And a man who has made the long voyage home with a skeleton crew to bring us the good news — that the wide open spaces are there and mankind's baby is alive and kicking. I give you . . . *Matt Kilroy!*"

His voice rose shrilly on the last words, just in time to be heard over the tumult of cheers and stomping of feet from the floor. Pete caught the contagious excitement and succumbed to a wave of deep emotion. Out of the corner of his eye he saw Matt squirming uncomfortably in his chair, but paid that little heed. He settled back to listen with ever-growing excitement as the chairman began the roll-call vote and state after state announced, "Kilroy!" At this rate he would get it on the first ballot . . .

They don't understand, Matt Kilroy thought, still half incredulous. *They just don't understand. They actually think time dilation is something that only exists in physics books. They can't grasp that it's the real world the physicists are talking about.*

His appearance didn't help, he realized. The harshness of the trip and the frontier, and the work he had put into them, made it at least as easy to believe he was fifty as thirty-four — made it easy for Pete to ask, "What difference does it make?" And he was the only example they had ever seen.

But he knew. And they were going to have to learn.

He listened to the states' delegates flamboyantly casting their votes, mostly for him. He had to struggle to fully realize *this* was happening. The possibility of hero worship being carried to such a pitch on his return had never entered his mind — until he landed.

Now they were voting. And he was winning, and Pete Haldrickson wouldn't listen to reason. There wasn't much time left to put an end to it.

"Louisiana . . ."

He had to make them *realize* it wasn't purely academic.

"Maine . . ."

There was a way, he knew. He didn't like it, but maybe it was the only thing that would work.

Cindy.

The public had forgotten her, it seemed, or assumed that she had died with Marta. That was O.K. with Matt — he had been content to keep her out of the public eye. He hated to think what publicity — by journalists who thought they were cute — could do to her.

But maybe he could keep it private. Pete was an old friend from before the expedition. Maybe if Matt made just *him* realize, *he* could take it from there and keep Cindy out of it.

Matt hoped so, anyway.

"Maryland . . ."

"Pete," Matt said suddenly, "I don't believe you've met my daughter, have you?"

Pete glanced at him with a frown, mildly annoyed at the distraction, then back at the monitor where things were going so well. "Eh?" he said absently. "I don't think so. What's that got to do with the price of eggs?" A moment later what Matt had said sank in and Pete thought, confused, *Daughter? What daughter?*

Matt went to a closed door across the room, opened it slightly, and called, "Cindy, will you come here a minute?"

Light footsteps came from beyond the door and Pete glanced that way just in time to see a small girl of about nine, with pigtails and freckles, come in and look up at Matt. "Yes, Daddy?" she said.

"I want you to meet Mr. Haldrickson," Matt said. "Pete, this is my daughter Cindy."

"Hi," Pete grunted, trying to concentrate on the voting. "Can't this wait, Matt? Don't you even care what's going on downstairs?"

"I thought," Matt said offhandedly, "that, if I'm going to run for President, I'd let Cindy be my campaign manager."

Something started to sink in. Pete spun away from the monitor and snapped, "Don't be ridiculous, Matt. She's just a—"

"She's twenty-five," Matt said stoutly, "and as much a citizen as you because she was born in Texas shortly before we left." Cindy looked questioningly up at Matt and he patted her on the head. "Mr. Haldrickson's a little confused about ages," he explained.

The initial shock hit hard and passed quickly. Pete nodded dazedly, staring at the twenty-five-year-old little girl. He remembered, now, that the Kilroys had taken a baby girl with them to Epsilon Eridani. Quite abruptly, and quite forcefully, he realized what Matt had been driving at. A birth certificate wasn't good enough any more. What would it have to be, he wondered—a recording clock built into everyone's body at birth? No. Or—

The legal complications were staggering. Pete's head swam as he tried to visualize them.

And then, abruptly, it cleared and he was filled with a new determination. He would win this thing yet.

"Ohio," said the chairman.

"Matt," Pete asked quietly, more serious than he had ever been in his life, "do you really believe that, even if we measure your age your way, those few months should keep you from being President?"

Matt sensed that Pete was going to be difficult. "You'd better go, Cindy," he said. He closed the door after her and turned back to Pete. "You saw her," he said. "You consider her a qualified voter?"

"I don't know," Pete said evenly. "I asked you a question."

"Oregon . . ."

"What I think doesn't matter," Matt said. "The law's written with an age requirement—for the Presidency and a thousand other things."

"The law doesn't say a thing about Einsteinian formulas, Matt. I'm going to say it again, and I want you to listen close. The way the law's written now, your birth certificate proves your age beyond a shadow of a doubt. There's nothing to stop you from being President."

"And there's nothing to stop Cindy from voting for me! Pete, I'm trying to make you realize—the law will have to be changed. It'll have to recognize that when people ride starships, ship's time is what counts."

"Pennsylvania . . ."

"I won't argue with that," Pete said stubbornly. "But the old laws are the ones we have now. O.K., they'll have to change. But are you sure that's the way to change them? Just keep the old age requirements and write in some big ugly formula to figure out what a man's age is?"

Matt frowned. "What are you getting at, Pete?"

"Do you honestly believe a man's age—by *any* clock—is that good a measure of his competence? What we need in a President is not chronology and years—it's leadership. Do you honestly believe that you—with your thirty-four self-measured years of leading people through crisis after crisis and coming out on top—do you believe you're less fit to be President than those other guys with their fifty years of fund-raising dinners and smoke-filled rooms? You *can't* believe that, Matt! And you can't expect me to believe it.

"Look—the law's going to have to get more complicated on this age business, right? So why not take the chance to recognize that maybe the way to complicate it is to scrap the age criterion altogether—anyway for something as important as the Presidency. Give them an incentive to find another yardstick that means more—*after* the election. Because you, Matt, are without a doubt the best Presidential material this country's seen in twenty years. We need you—and under the *present* law your excuse won't hold up."

"West Virginia . . ."

"In principle," Matt admitted, "I agree with you. But—"

"No buts!" Pete interrupted sharply. "May the best man win—no matter how old he thinks he is. And then *after* the election let them find out about Cindy. She can make them then see the law needs changing; you can make them think twice about how they change it. You can help shape the change. Please, Matt—"

The last delegate's voice was drowned in a tremendous roar from the crowd. Pete and Matt turned toward the screen, toward the sea of cheering people and waving placards. Holding his breath, Pete watched Matt's face as the roar resolved itself into rhythmic applause and a swelling chant of *"We want Kilroy!"*

Then, slowly, the expression on Matt's face changed, and in a minute all hesitation had drained from it. He stood up.

And Pete watched with enormous relief as the next President started downstairs to answer them.

The Delegate
from Guapanga

WYMAN GUIN

Wyman Guin (b. 1915) has published only one novel, the very
interesting *Standing Joy* (1969) and one short-story collection, the
unfortunately hard-to-find *Living Way Out* (1967), which contains nearly all of his published short science-fiction. This is too
bad, because he is one of the most interesting writers in the history of the field.

"The Delegate from Guapanga" is about a political convention of a most unusual sort.

I

My eldest son, who looks so much like his mother, my chief wife, shrugged
his shoulders and glanced at the branch above his head.

He said sullenly, "Yes, I will swing into the tree when it's time."

I turned again to be sure the bearers were safely up on the bluff. I selected
an arrow and fitted it to my bow and cautiously walked out across the hot
glade of teree grass. In the far thicket the charl boar grubbed and snorted
unconcernedly.

Back at the lodge, a day's walk from here, all my elite people had paused
and were concentrating telepathically on our minds here. Through my eyes,
through my son's eyes, through the eyes of the nontelepathic bearers on the
bluff, they watched this scene, alerted by our tension.

My third wife, the dainty little one from Kewananga, stopped her romp-
ing with the children and hushed them. Innocently, she censured me.

"You should not have taken your son on this dirty killing."

My chief wife, the boy's mother, was not speaking to me.

My father, aging beside the small fire in his room of memories, whispered
to me in excitement. "Careful, son. He's a big brute. Hear the weight of him
when he moves."

Red Giant boiled hugely in the afternoon sky as if he trembled to engulf his tiny companion sun, White Dwarf. In this glade the pink teree grass reflected the red sunlight and shimmered ominously.

I glanced back one last time at my son. In that instant, I saw that he was not yet the "young man" I had thought to bring on his first hunt. He was just a slim boy confused by his noodle-headed mother. Well, it was too late now to leave him home as he and his mother wished.

The charl boar would have scented us long ago except for the pungent odor of the giant fungus he was grubbing. Now, I penetrated too far into the bittersweet aroma that drifted from the thicket. I felt the old thrill race along my back, and I glanced reassuringly across to my son.

His sudden thought shook me — far more than the sonic boom that came at that moment from some Matterist rocket beyond the Guapanga mountains. The boar, monstrous and unstoppable, charged from the thicket.

My son's task was to put an arrow into his driving rear flank. He was to yell and divert him toward the tree. He did neither. He threw down his bow and swung into the tree.

There was no place for me to run. The bearers were yelling from the rock . . . with no effect on the boar. Flashing toward me across the teree grass, the boar held the gleaming tusks high. A greasy chill clutched my belly while I cursed my chief wife with my mouth and with my mind.

The boar's head went down and I drew the bow. I watched the heaving spot at the base of his massive shoulder hump where the gray bristles make a swirl. There is an opening there. A spear will not enter it, but a man may somctimes put an arrow through it and sever the spinal cord.

I did. His front legs buckled. The great rump with its shoddy flag of a tail vaulted at me. I was knocked flat and the carcass crashed painfully across my legs.

At his shoulder this boar had stood almost as high as a man. I lay waiting for the bearers to get him off me. I looked up at the churning surface of Red Giant and marveled that I was still alive.

After I was standing, the head bearer grasped my arms in the traditional gesture but he avoided my eyes. He said, "Tawe tawa," which scholars say once meant, "Hunter of hunters," in the primitive vocal language.

The other bearers were blank-faced and they did not dance on the carcass or pass wine. I looked down on the charl boar . . . certainly the greatest I had ever killed.

I yelled with my mind and did not care that elite Guapanga might hear: "Woman! Because of your nuts-and-fruit thinking, I cannot mount this shameful head in our lodge!"

The chief bearer, knowing only the silence in the glade, took out his steel knife and began expertly to dress the animal. The other bearers got in his way helping. They were anxious to avoid my eyes. Their atelepathic minds cringed from the probing they hoped I was gentlemanly enough not to make.

I felt my face burn. I looked over to where my eldest son stood. Because of this boy's mother and the radical Mentalist thinking she had recently subscribed to, none of my three wives now admitted me to their rooms. Because of this boy and his goose of a mother, I was almost dead with a tusk from groin to throat.

I walked over to where his mind seethed with sanctimonious pride in his absurd Mentalist extremes, and with horror at the sight of the great boar bearing down on me.

The words in this confusion were, "I did what I knew at the last moment I had to do. I tried to explain my Mentalist principles to you and you wouldn't listen. My mother has condoned my decision."

Abruptly, my chief wife was in my mind, horrified at what had almost happened to me, protective of the boy and still stubborn with righteousness. "Our son will devote his life to building our beautiful Mentalist heritage. He cannot taint himself with killing."

I heard a groan from my lips. "Leave us, woman."

Now she wept. From the bench where she sat in the courtyard of the lodge the paving stones blurred as though in rain, and her mouth cried out, "My husband, we have almost killed you. Forgive us. The boy had never seen a live boar. He did not know. Forgive me, and I will give up my thinking."

"Leave us."

"You were dying and you cursed me before the elite world."

"Leave us."

I stood hot-eyed before the boy. I am a conservative Mentalist — which is the conservative party in the first place. I know exactly what the Matterists are after — and I am dead against it. I do not allow the use of any machines anywhere on my lands. My grandfather fought against the vote for women until the radical Mentalists finally beat him fifty years ago. To this day no elite woman from Guapanga casts a vote.

Among conservative Mentalists, I am rockbound conservative. To the radicals, I am "The Mountain Ogre." Now I faced a cowardly son because radical women's thinking had entered my own household. I was about as dead politically as a man can get and still cast a vote.

Even as I stood there I could hear the first repercussions of this shameful incident snickering off into the Mentalist world. "Oh, didn't he turn out to be an ogre at home?" "Well, you must admit, he's great with boars."

Another Matterist passenger rocket screamed overhead. Its parting thunder boomed back from the gorges of Guapanga. This irritating sound was, as they say, the gem that sank the boat. I slapped the boy.

Yet, even as my helpless rage propelled the hand, I felt my own guilt slow it.

Afterward, it was not a time to admit that feeling of guilt. It was time —
and far too late a time — to start contradicting his mother's thinking.

With my mind I said to him, "Very well. All is mind. Matter is an illusion. But a mental charl boar can kill a mental man as surely as if he were
material. And a mental son has a duty to his mental father."

Now his shame dominated his confusion and he bawled. I went on, "The
Mentalist culture of which you are so proud will not protect your feet from
stones, while this boar will make shoes for the whole lodge. You must eat
meat and meat must be killed."

Stubbornly, through his shame, he echoed his mother. "The killing should
be done by common men, not by a Mentalist."

These Mentalist fads and cults, such as the one my chief wife was dab-
bling in, had grown only in the last five years since the Chupa Uprisings.
They were unhealthy signs of the shock and fear left in us by the unexpected
revolt of the chupas.

I shook my head. "Arm your tenants and train them to hunt? One day
you will find them hunting you." I reached out and gripped his arm. "Your
grandfather built this Mentalist empire here in the Guapangas, sprang between two Matterist republics. Geographically and spiritually it *must* be the
most Mentalist of empires. It must be the conservative stronghold. And that
means, among many other things, killing your own meat."

Now I was through with him. I was not quite in a mood to start making
a chum of him. "You will return with the bearers. I am going back alone."

I walked over to the bearers. "The boy will return with you."

The head bearer looked me in the eye and nodded respectfully. "Yes, Excellency."

II

From that high valley at the feet of the Guapangas, I followed a great coni-
fered ridge that borders my lands. I walked in telepathic solitude, angry and
ashamed.

In the late afternoon I arrived at a craggy mountain that stands apart
from its parent Guapangas. There the ridge begins to drop toward my lodge.
At the base of this mountain there is a little lake and I stopped and bathed.
Afterward, I lay on the grassy bank and watched a herd of greathorns high
on the mountain as they made their dainty way from one perilous coign of
vantage to another.

I became aware of the approach of a Matterist. We both ceremonially
closed our minds.

"I pass your mind in peace. May Mr. Executive shield us both."

"I withdraw my mind with respect. I commend you to Old Man."

The present political divisions, Matterists and Mentalists, were left after all of the ancient telepathic cultures had fused or been annihilated. In the meantime there had evolved the institution of the Old Man. (The priggish Matterists call him Mr. Executive, but he is still just Old Man.)

The Old Man is one mind which stands between the two planet-wide political parties and acts as final law for both. Our greatest political crisis comes when an Old Man dies. Then hurriedly come the two planet-wide telepathic conventions—the building of the two new platforms—the election of two opposing candidates (one of which will become the new Old Man)—and finally, the moment of "war."

In the truce after the "war" the candidate of the victors cautiously contacts the minds of the defeated. With utmost care he synthesizes a pragmatic position for himself embracing, if he is a Mentalist, one after another of the Matterist points of faith, as "beliefs necessary to the well-being of my Matterist subjects." At the same time he rarefies his former Mentalist beliefs into pragmatic notions necessary to "guide my actions and obtain my end as Old Man."

Now his one mind handles the two conflicting faiths in a logical manner, and for his lifetime he keeps the peace.

He keeps the peace absolutely because none may plot against him for a moment. Awake or asleep, and without any bother on his part, his mind would automatically shunt contradictory beliefs into the mind of the plotter and thus confuse him completely.

I rose from the grass and dressed to meet the Matterist.

It was some time before he appeared around a wooded knoll. He had with him two bearers who carried the carcass of a greathorn. The beautiful curving horns were the color of nut meats.

His machine-made clothing was drab and unpretentious compared to the elegance of my cap and tunic, the silk of my breeches and the handsomely tooled leather of my boots. He wore the usual unadorned clothes and his machine-made boots were plain.

He was a neighbor of mine. As I looked to the south down his valley, I could see the ugly smudge from his pulp mills and paper factories. (The Matterists have a type of daily reading they are addicted to instead of enjoying books. Everything that has happened that day in their society, endless minutiae you would never pause over in telepathic scanning, they read about in the evening. They require enormous amounts of cheap paper to keep up this "papernews.")

The Matterist apologized unnecessarily. "I hope you don't mind that I pass through this part of your land. It is the only way I can get to the greathorns of this mountain."

I spread my hands. "You are welcome at any time."

Naturally we did not touch, and of course we spoke only with our mouths. Our minds were closed to each other. He was carrying a high-powered rifle with a telescopic sight. The telescope excited me. We may build telescopes to study Lalone and the other planets and moons. But to build or use a sight with which to kill would be a Matterist heresy.

I glanced up at the face of the mountain and found the herd of greathorns. "May I use your sight?"

Knowing I should not touch the rifle, he graciously dismounted the sight and handed it to me.

It was a wonderful thrill to me to have the herd of greathorns leap into close perspective. I watched their frightful, surefooted progress until retention of the sight became impolite. I returned it to him and he remounted it. Then he stood for a moment looking at the rusty sky where Red Giant hovered over the Guapangas.

He said, "Well, this time tomorrow we will each probably be casting our vote for the next Mr. Executive."

I stared at him in a stupid pause. He saw the ignorance on my face.

He said, "You must have spent the day absorbed in some very disturbing personal problem."

I focused in panic on the mind of Old Man.

He was dying. He had had a stroke and he was dying. The mountain beneath me rocked.

We looked at each other, the Matterist and I, and each saw the other's determination.

"Why are you so stubborn about this one thing? We only want to try it on one of them, and it is so far away."

I shook my head. "It is not just 'one thing.' I do not want to be told how many wives I may have, when I should work, or what I may read."

He flushed. "The last three Executives have been Mentalist candidates. Yet with the cooperation of your radical Mentalists these Executives have been able to afford us much of the change we needed. Why not this? We only want to try it on one of them."

He referred to a distant, yellow sun where the Matterists want to invade and colonize one of the planets. They have a theory that life is at its best under yellow suns. Three times now this ambition of theirs to colonize planets of yellow suns had been delayed because we had won the "war" and placed a Mentalist as Old Man.

This is the reason we Mentalists will not allow improvements in technology until we have improved our own souls. We see in the Matterists how the destructiveness of their engines has outstripped their ability to control themselves. They rationalize the crime they wish to carry out with the wide-eyed innocence of animals. It is to be only "one" experiment . . . at least until it has proved successful. That little insignificant yellow sun is so far away. Those distant semi-rationals who call their planet "Erth" do not even telepath. It is all so innocent and "progressive."

I said coldly, "I think your soul has plenty of room to improve right here under Red Giant and White Dwarf."

His face went rigid with anger. He saluted me stiffly and he and his bearers moved on.

I contacted my father-in-law in Basahn at once. "Councillor, I have had some personal problems. I did not realize . . ."

He is my chief wife's father. He said, "Yes, I have had tearful news of those problems. I reminded your wife that I would not tolerate her behavior myself and do not expect you to. In the name of my family, I apologize."

He proceeded bluntly to the plans for the Mentalist convention where he would certainly be the outstanding nominee for Old Man. He is a vigorous old lecher who keeps three wives and three concubines happy and still drinks a full gourd of wesah spirits a day. "I am sorry to say that your 'charl boar incident' has made you a laughing stock. There is now no chance to get you on the Council of Pragmatists until next fall."

"Yes, sir. I understand."

"Nevertheless, your voters are among the best trained in the Mentalist Party, and your pragmatic stand is very important to us."

"Yes, sir. I am aware."

"Begin contacting your elite people at once. Old Man has rallied momentarily, but the end might come suddenly."

"I will do so."

III

I had no desire to be in this part of my lands with elections coming up. The moment Old Man was dead, the Matterists would be able to send out groups of atelepathic non-voters carrying rifles and explosives to pick off our elite people.

For this they cannot of course spare elite people from the voting and the "war." Also they cannot use highly destructive, nuclear weapons, because the geography of the two parties is so interlaced. They can only be picky with such killing, but I did not intend to be "picked."

While I walked and trotted, I contacted my party lieutenants and instructed them in the grouping of our voters along their convictions in pragmatism. My voters would, of course, be voting for the things I believe in. Any man that didn't would find himself off my lands next day, packing his wife and kids for the polar mines.

Until this morning, when my chief wife had made a planet-wide ass of me, I had been a powerful force in our Mentalist party. I had campaigned several years now for her father who owns much of Basahn beyond the Guapangas.

I invented his campaign slogan, "A man who believes in nothing makes a great Old Man."

Night before last, while my son and I were at camp on our inglorious charl boar hunt, I had made a scheduled speech that was listened to across the planet by all Mentalists. My pragmatism was naturally cheered by conservative Mentalists and hissed by radical Mentalists. But the most heartening response had been from the chupas. These children from the union of an elite person with a common, atelepathic person (usually a concubine), lack nothing in intelligence and they telepath as well as elite people. Like the common people, however, they have minds of their own. Each chupa is a little culture to himself, completely independent.

They are realists, first and last, and seem always pragmatic. They like me. Now, since the Uprisings, they had become important politically.

Below the ridge the streaking lights of Matterist cars began to glow along their highway.

Only a few years ago Old Man had granted them this highway which crossed part of my land. It was not the least part of my disgust with the radical Mentalists that, to spite me, they had provided Old Man the necessary balance of opinion in this matter and allowed the desecration of a virgin Mentalist forest.

The moon nearest our planet, the little yellow one we call Falon the Messenger, came rocketing up in the east. By its waxy light I was able to descend at the proper point to the highway and cross under it through one of the wide tunnels which had been provided for moving wildlife. Above me the cars whistled on their pavement. The Matterist minds they carried were still closed to us, but they, too, were hurrying to be ready for Old Man's death.

As I came out of the tunnel, I became aware that the young chupa overseer of my lands was on his way to meet me with a lantern. I was pleased that he had not delegated this to an atelepathic on this dangerous night.

He called to me with his strong, cheerful mind. "Excellency, I have just crossed the creek above Serapon Marsh. On Skull Hill I will swing a lantern until you sight me."

"I am climbing toward Skull Hill now. We will meet there."

I envied him, the chupa. He is now a lieutenant in my political organization and a good one. In this election he would work hard for me, though he had fought skillfully *against* me in the Chupa Uprisings. He was not the least ashamed of the uprisings and, unlike many in the Mentalist elite, I do not hold those days against the chupas. The improvements in their station which they then gained had been due. After all, we in the elite worlds have only our own moral laxity to blame for the fact that there are chupas.

From the chupa lieutenant's mind came a solemn remark. "I, too, do not know for sure. But I would be honored if it were so."

The open minds which he and I kept with each other were occasionally embarrassing. It had passed through my mind that this chupa's mother had died without telling, but many have claimed that my own father was her elite lover.

One thing was sure, my father kept a stingy grip on that part of his memories.

I mounted the pass below the great rock skull that was bathed in the tallow light of Falon. His lantern came swinging toward me and he laughed with his mouth. "I saw your thatch before you saw my lantern."

I had taken off my cap, leaving my red hair loose.

The subtle mixture of lantern light and moonglow showed his firm features grinning at me. We grasped thumbs affectionately and started back the way he had come.

I noticed that when he was not speaking directly with his mind it closed rhythmically against me. I understood he would protect me against his thoughts about my son and chief wife.

I focused at once on my son's mind and spoke firmly but cheerfully. "How is your camp?"

"It is good, father. We are about half way back to the lodge from the high valleys."

"Have you seen to the comfort of your bearers?"

"Yes, we . . ." He paused and continued meekly. "We are broiling part of the boar and will eat soon."

"You realize that the Mentalist convention could start at any minute. Since you are not of voting age, close your mind at once and remain that way until contacted."

"Yes, father. I will do so."

The chupa shifted his lantern to his other hand and put his free arm on my shoulder. "I knew you would not continue to be harsh with the boy. It was not his fault, and he would never do it again."

Momentarily, the picture of thrashing a naked woman with a stick was embarrassingly sharp in his mind. He hastened his thinking to the words, "Of course, I have no rightful thoughts on whose fault it might have been."

As we started down the slopes above Serapon Marsh, he pointed east where Garrison Bluff was drenched in moonlight.

I nodded. The garrison was dark and deserted. My monks had already left their cells and each had departed alone for some impromptu retreat in the forest. There they would hold their convictions against Matterism and vote steadily for Mentalism. When the brief moment of "war" came, their full telepathic force would be against the Matterist platform. So now, if a Matterist non-voter chose to blow up the garrison, little would be lost.

As the chupa and I came up the stone walk to the lodge, my father-in-law contacted me again. "Old Man has weakened so that Intelligence is able to study the possible Matterist platform. I am confident that when the "war" comes we will win. If I am placed as Old Man I will ask immediately for you to be voted into the Council. You will lose due to that ridiculous charl boar business of this morning. However, I will keep asking and I am sure you will be voted in next fall."

My father-in-law withdrew his busy focus as the chupa and I passed beneath the autumn-spangled leera trees and entered the great stone-paved court of my lodge. I caught a glimpse of my chief wife hurrying along a portico in the waning light of Falon. Her robe blew about her fine figure in tallow folds that were mystically related to the wax-hard withdrawal of her proud mind.

The chupa grasped thumbs with me. "May the Mentalists win again." He saluted me ironically and left.

The lodge was dark and silent. The children were all asleep. The adults were awake and anxious about the convention. In his rooms off one of the upper porticos my aged father hummed to himself and dreamed of a convention and "war" in his youth. My second wife stirred uncomfortably in bed with the big baby she was carrying and resented its father profoundly. She would not speak with me when I focused comfortingly on her mind. She knew that I never cared to speak with her except to persuade her to have big heavy babies with heads like red melons.

A breeze moved through the trees and shrubs of the court. The splashing of the fountain was a great noise. The crackling of coals in the open cooking pit beyond the fountain was another noise. I found that I was desperately hungry.

Over the bed of coals the carcass of a black horn sizzled. There was a loaf of bread and a skin of wine on the stone table.

There were no servants to help me, of course. All the men were stationed about the grounds, guarding with bow and spear against the possible rifles and explosives of Matterist common people. Their women were huddled about their own cooking fire where they whispered the age-old superstitions about politics.

I cut a huge piece of the meat and ate it with the bread, sitting at the stone serving table. I drank the wine directly from the skin, chewed ravenously and stared into the coals.

My third wife, the little one from Kewananga, was no longer speaking with me, even to scold. She now sided completely with the chief wife whom I had cursed.

I decided to bathe again when I had finished eating. I threw off my harness of arrows and my clothes and left them in a heap on the stones of the court. I vaulted into the fountain, frightened the decorative fish into a shimmering explosion. Afterward I walked in angry nakedness across the court and along the great portico to my rooms.

The Matterists marry only one woman. I have often assumed from this basic stupidity springs the meanness of their culture. This night I had learned that three women are no certainty of affection.

Alone in my rooms, I shouted to all three of them with my mind, "Don't worry that I will not return from this convention with a firm mind! I will come back here with a stick and beat two of you all the way to the Basahn Hills. I will save the stick and when the other has whelped I will stand in one spot and beat affection into her. Her heart will melt for man and child."

I threw on a cap and left my rooms and let my boots crash theatrically on the stones. I went up the stairs and along the upper portico to my father's rooms.

He said with his mind, "Come in, son. After the convention I will come out on the portico to see you return with a stick. Then we will have peace and love about here once more."

I entered and stood before him. To me his face will always be the most beautiful of my life. There is written in those deep seams a long life of building and adventure and care. It was he who had fought in three elections to win and place a Mentalist Old Man and prevent the Matterists from invading the planets of other suns. It was he, too, who had counseled me during the Chupa Uprisings. The memory of his understanding in those days stirred in me a sudden question.

"Are you the father of my chupa?"

He was angry with me. "You think of trivia in the presence of this ceremony!"

I was ashamed. I had caught from his mind a hard ache of remembered love and a sweet face, and this I had tricked from him. But this thought left one certainty. It is a fine thing to love a woman who can't read your mind.

I gestured placatingly for the ceremony.

All over our planet, where it was now light and where it was now dark, these ancient Mentalist words were being spoken. The hands of an old man trembled on the kneeling young one and the primitive, almost meaningless words of mouth were said by the ancient. After these magical words of mouth one could go into the forest and lie on the ground and fight the telepathic war. For, in ancient times, before the institution of Old Man, *the election was the war.*

I walked out of the lodge along the great portico which is supported by thirteen caryatids carved as the demons spawned in "The Beginning" by White Dwarf. There my chief wife knelt on the stones and grasped my thighs.

I did not put my hand on her dark and lovely head. She drew herself up my body and sought my lips. I did not refuse her this, but I could not return the kiss. Too clearly, gleaming tusks flashed in the teree grass. It was cruel and insulting. Salty with tears, her lips moaned away from me. She turned and clung to a caryatid and it was the female demon, Paline. I left her sobbing face uncomforted between wooden breasts.

IV

Our autumn dawns start softly, a subtle, pink glowing without direction that grows and grows until suddenly day crashes in. Deep in a secret part of the forest I stood on a little eminence and leaned against a cold face of basalt.

I have always attended the political conventions from this secret place in my forests. Through the enormous rusty glowing a great black chahar winged his heavy way. Even as I watched his flight he gave his screaming cry, and it was day. The first ray from Red Giant lanced the black belly of a cloud, splashing blood across the high cliffs of Guapanga.

At that moment Old Man died.

His hand, held by that of his chief wife, relaxed. Over his fading telepathic fans, he muttered a name that was heard by waiting millions of us across the planet. Then he was dead.

The Mentalist convention began immediately. I walked over to a grassy knoll and lay down and closed my eyes.

Throughout the morning of voting on issues and principles that would make up our platform, there whispered outside our minds the ominous workings of the Matterist convention where an opposing platform was taking shape. These foreign arguments and all this communication we kept firmly from our minds. The moment would come soon enough when we would face them with our platform and they would face us with theirs. And in less time than it takes to melt a scoop of butter over a fire, the logic of the stronger side would begin to confuse and dissolve the logic of the weaker side. This would be the moment of "war." When it was finished one logic would stand intact across the planet and the victors would install the next Old Man.

While we were busy building the Mentalist platform our chupa minds stood respectfully aside. For a chupa thinks independently of the party platforms, just as a common man thinks pretty much as he pleases in his lonely world. But an elite man necessarily takes part in his telepathic culture (or, as we call it today, "platform"). It is the thing which forms his mental boundaries. Every elite person, upon the death of an Old Man, is deeply concerned with the changes that will occur in his allowable philosophy.

During the morning my chupa half-brother contacted me. "Excellency, can you spare a moment? It is important."

"Of course, but you know not to keep me too long."

"I have been increasingly aware that you intend to enter again your plea for dishonest government."

"Yes, I do. I suppose it will make as little impression this time as it has in the past. But it is an essential part of my conservatism and I can't neglect it."

"Pardon me, Excellency. I think it will make a very definite impression this time. We chupas, loyal to the Mentalists, have held a conference about it just now. We can promise you a solid vote for dishonesty in government."

I was stunned with pleasure. All morning, in the face of the general amusement over my first wife's disloyalty, I had availed myself only of my routine vote. Now I saw that my political fortune had turned in a moment.

"You see, Excellency, what this could mean when the two platforms are face to face."

Lying in the cool forest, I opened my eyes and looked across the rusty sky, and closed them. With a thrilling start I understood him. The chupas on the Matterist side would like this part of our platform as much as our chupas. They would *vote for* this aspect of *our platform.*

Shortly, the convention was at that point where the provincial law in Guapanga which forbids voting to woman was causing its usual trouble. A radical Mentalist from the east had the attention and was being particularly abusive.

This maneuver was not intended to do anything practical about the law itself. It was meant simply to discredit me, the law's chief defender, before I could propose any of my pragmatic aspects for our new platform.

The radical shouted, "Out there in those hills the women will try anything to get free."

This was the inevitable reference to "the charl boar incident." Everyone laughed, even the conservatives.

I held my peace. I would just have to wait my turn for attention which I could now see would not come again until afternoon. But when my turn did come, I was going to rock them.

I had been the first politician to see that pragmatism could be used within a party platform as well as by Old Man and the Council of Pragmatists. For example, I innovated having our common people vote against work. They continue to vote against work cheerfully and with great energy, knowing that they will be plowing their fields tomorrow. In our Mentalist platform a request for this vote is without difficulty, but in the final facing of the two platforms this strong vote cannot be absorbed by the Matterists to whom "work" must be the most important of virtues if they are to keep their factories going.

The parts of the platform coming up did not require unusual action. I decided to leave and have lunch. I contacted one of my elite lieutenants and left my vote for him to proxy with instructions for standard, conservative responses. If anything came up he had only to contact me.

When I opened my eyes to the red forest, I found a young woman sitting on a rock near me. She rose and came toward me gracefully. She carried a freshly cut hasam gourd and in the other hand one of the huge hasam leaves folded as a pouch.

She knelt before me and handed me the gourd. "It is water from the creek." She indicated the nearby sound of the stream.

The water had, only a short time ago, splashed from the high snows of Guapanga. It made my teeth ache.

She spread the huge hasam leaf before me and I found that she had provided for my lunch exactly as I had planned to do. She had gathered the autumn nuts and berries and several kinds of fruit. She had cracked and cleaned the nuts into a separate smaller leaf.

She was not telepathic, but she was an unusual beauty. Her features were sensual without being soft. I watched with pleasure the grace of her walk.

I asked with my mouth, "Who sent you here?"

"No one sent me."

"Did you know I would be here?"

She smiled mysteriously. "I knew."

She picked up some of the fruit for herself, a bunch of ice-blue wesah. Then she indicated the meal with her head.

"Eat, Excellency. You will have to get back to the convention."

I did not wish to think about the speech I would give in the afternoon. Instinct told me I would destroy essential spontaneity. I welcomed this woman as a diversion.

She sat and munched the wesah while I ate the meal and drank from the gourd. We watched each other in appreciative silence and grinned occasionally.

The little ginkas, both the red and the blue-furred ones, were gathering nuts beneath the red trees. In the forest there was only their chatter and the occasional belling of a black jay.

When she was satisfied that I was through eating, she asked, "Excellency, why doesn't your chief wife come to you?"

I saw that the common people, as well as the elite, knew of my problems. "You know it is unlawful for a delegate to be with his women during a convention."

She pretended to be naive. "Why is that, Excellency?"

"It used to be thought they might influence one's vote. Now they just vote contrary to one."

"And yet, Excellency, you may ask me to your arms."

I did not like her brazen calm. "That is not proper at any time."

Her strange smile angered me. I was about to order her away when she raised her arms and undid the knot of her honey-colored hair so that it fell to her shoulders as girls wear their hair before marriageable age.

"Do you recognize me, Excellency? Wasn't there a time during the telepathic fighting of the chupas when you felt less harshly against my company."

Then I recognized her. She was the daughter of one of my tenants. While I had rested from fighting the chupas five years ago, she had happened by here.

She smiled. It was entirely a forgiving smile. "I was only a girl then, Excellency. I am a woman now. I have heard that your wives do not come to you, election day or not."

She declared this as bluntly as she might say, "I see that your red thatch needs trimming."

We sat there for some time, looking at each other through knowing lids while I remembered her sweet youth and felt a ravenous need for her. I beckoned her to me, and as I did so I realized that the air-tide of our planet was rising.

Red Giant and White Dwarf were overhead. Together they draw an angry tide of storm through all our noons.

Even as the woman knelt to me the first confused gusts of the tide whirled crimson leaves about us. Presently the tide raced through the forest. It sang through bare autumn branches and half buried us in a drift of leaves. The woman's warm mouth whispered over my face. Then, far away I heard the mighty wave of wind bellow into the gorges of Guapanga, shrilling in the wild crags.

I lay dreaming. One day I would be Old Man. If I became a councillor next fall my way would be easy. This would be inevitable, because my grandfather and my father had built an empire and left it to me. With such an empire and my own good talent as a logician I could, as I lay there in the forest, decide that I wanted one day to be Old Man.

The woman lay still in my arms. Her eyes had been fixed on the depths of trees where Red Giant cast vermillion spears. Now they turned to me in a dream. I stroked her shoulder where coils of honey-colored hair buried my hand. The last gusts of the tide lifted lazy dervishes from the leaves about us and cooled the flame of her cheeks.

She said, "I have loved you since you came to me, like a god here in your forest."

I saw in her gentle mind that this was so, and also that she had hardly realized her capacity to love.

Suddenly I remembered the name that Old Man had muttered as he died. His elite wives had been gathered at his bed. His dearest friends had been there. But the last name he had uttered had been that of a common woman, a concubine who was not even allowed in the house.

I marveled that he had taken this atelepathic woman to himself and outraged elite people even before he became Old Man. And I saw that what this might have lost him in political support from elite women had been more than offset by his later popularity among the chupas.

I focused again on the mind of this gentle, passionate woman beside me, and I found that her adoration was tempered by a strong determination of her own. The strength of her will astonished me until she said in her mind, "He has hair like yours. It is red like the flame of Red Giant."

Then this woman's mind opened to me. I was happy with understanding. I kissed her face till she wept, and she said haltingly, "He is like Red Giant in another way. He takes a storm with him everywhere."

And suddenly, of all my children, I loved best the wild little chupa.

V

It is wrong by the old standards, but I lay beside the woman throughout the afternoon of the convention. She neither stirred nor spoke with her mouth in all that time. My awareness left the forest and centered entirely in the convention.

I had returned barely in time. The voting had reached subjects critical to me. My turn for attention before the delegates came quickly.

I began my speech gravely.

"Mr. Chairman, ladies and gentlemen, and delegates. I am going to return to my plea for dishonesty in government."

There was a massive, telepathed groan from the ranks of radical Mentalists and even some heavy sighs from conservatives. The radicals began hooting. It took the chair several seconds to quiet the disorder.

Afterward I spoke dramatically, directly to the chair. "Mr. Chairman, to protect this assembly against further outbursts of childishness, I am going to make an announcement. After I have made it, I think you may wish to grant a 15-second recess to allow the delegates to confirm the announcement.

"Mr. Chairman, ladies and gentlemen, and delegates. What I am going to ask as an integral part of our platform . . . what I am going to put into that platform concerning dishonesty in government . . . will in the terrible moment of "war" this afternoon . . . will in that crucial moment . . ."

I paused for a second while they sweated in anticipation of the moment that our logic would face the Matterist logic.

". . . will in that decisive moment, receive a solid vote of 'yes' from every . . . chupa . . . on . . . this . . . planet."

It was a stunning moment. They were getting the thrill that had come to me when my half-brother had told me the news and it had crashed into my mind that chupas on the Matterist side could join chupas on our side to vote for us.

In one moment our politics had been revolutionized.

After the recess which the Chairman eagerly called, I did not have to ask if chupa friends of the delegates had confirmed me. The attention on me had deepened to the absolute. I had indeed rocked them, and for the first time they would hear me.

"Mr. Chairman, ladies and gentlemen, and delegates. It remains for me to state a form suitable for our platform, the logic of our attitude toward dishonesty in government.

"Politicians who want your money want, at worst, the least part of you. Even then they usually take only a little of the least part. They take what will not cause much excitement, so that the source will remain fruitful. Such men are almost never dangerous.

"Give me the dishonest government. I know where they stand. We need only structure our laws so that their activities have the dignity of commercial defense. Then these clever foxes, while fleecing us lightly, will defend our freedom and our principles like lions. In such a strong government we need only one occasional politician who is a fanatic about 'honesty' to keep the rest in reasonable line."

I paused a few seconds and felt only profound attention focused on me. I had begun nicely, a logic that would fit our platform.

"No, it is among honest politicians that danger may lie! Show me the politician that has never gained money or made it possible for his friends to do so, or has never partaken of the other licenses that power provide, *and I will show you a fanatic.*

"The best that an honest politician can be is a fanatic about honesty. But he can be much worse. It behooves you first to ask why he is honest. If he can answer that satisfactorily it behooves you to ask why he is in government.

"How much of your freedom does the honest politician want in exchange for not taking your money? Does he want your right to vote? Your right to your land? Your right to your women, your right to drink spirits, or eat meat, or read books?

"Such questions become critical when many honest men congregate in one government. Why have they foregathered in this ominous way? Why this unnatural climate of sobriety and thrift? What is it these honest men are seeking to change? The foxes have flown and your society is sick.

"Let the next Old Man reduce the penalties against governmental dishonesty and embezzlement — just as I proposed at the last convention. Let the next Old Man make our political position attractive to clever and intelligent men who happen to be a little dishonest. Only in this way can we have a government strong enough to resist honest fanatics and radical encroachment."

I paused again, and I found a surprised approval falling toward me . . . a murmured phrase that was repeated over and over from all directions like a shower of autumn leaves. "Their money-economy. Their money-economy."

For the first time this assembly had caught a glimpse of my political pragmatism and the dimensions in which it could work for us. With the Matterists everything is organized . . . into management teams, labor unions and clubs. They have only black-and-white language for their supposed virtues such as "industry," "honesty" and "frugality." Yet there is less virtue in their higher circles than in my meanest tenant.

So now I shouted to the assembly. "Yes, their money-economy! The Matterists have an almost complete money-economy in which dishonesty and embezzlement are, at one and the same time, essentially prevalent and highly abhorred.

"But what of *our* semi-feudal economy? Need we be fearful of political dishonesty where power and position are the right of birth? Will not the chupas be pleased that we lower the penalties on dishonesty to give them greater opportunity to succeed in our world?

"So, if we have logical reasons, as I have given them, to accept dishonesty as a fundamental in our political platform, what will happen to the Matterists when we face them in the moment of 'war'?

"In that moment when our minds are open to them, won't their logic be confounded? For they cannot deny the prevalence of dishonesty. And they cannot deny that the most dangerous politicians are honest fanatics from whom we are protected by strong, dishonest government. Yet acceptance of these things implies destruction of their economy.

"Ladies and gentlemen, we will win the 'war' and lose nothing in the peace!"

This conclusion was greeted with a storm of approval.

My father-in-law focused tightly on me. "You will not have to wait till next fall. You will be voted to the Council of Pragmatists later in the afternoon. Why don't you tactfully leave the convention now, at the height of your approval? You need not return until the voting starts."

VI

I lay in quiet triumph beside the woman, and she knew I had returned. She did not say anything, but she thought about me unashamedly, and I knew her thoughts.

She offered me a drink from the hasam gourd and I took it. Then I asked with my mind, "How far is it to your father's house?"

In her mind there was not an answer to my question. Rather, her mind filled with the realization that I would buy her for a concubine.

So I had to repeat my question, and still there was in her mind only this realization.

Then I laughed and said loudly with my mouth, so that it startled her in the silent, afternoon forest. "How far is it to your father's house?"

Now I saw in her mind that the house would not be far beyond the creek. A place with a well in the yard and an arbor for wesah. The little chupa would be teasing the hopani fowl in cackling flurries around the house.

That was the way it was as we walked down from the forest except that the little chupa was not about. We crossed a field of freshly mown teree grass and walked up to the house. The woman straightened her hair self-consciously. I adjusted my tunic and my cap and found some leaves on my breeches. Red Giant hung in a cloudy blaze, waiting to start his plunge at the horizon.

The father and his workmen had finished in the fields for the day. They had just returned to the barns and the animals as the woman called him.

He came out, a tall, weathered man, straight and kindly faced. Yet I saw the face harden with resentment when he recognized me. This was a proud man who would never have asked me to right a wrong.

Nevertheless, he bowed with respect.

I spoke the proper idiom with warmth, for I respected the father of such a woman. "I withdraw respectfully from the door to your mind."

Now, as was proper, he straightened from his bow. I saw that in the interim he had understood what this was about. He was happy for his daughter, and that the wrong would now be righted.

Now the ceremony would have to come at once. In small talk there might occur exchanges which are thought to be bad omens. So I declared, "Man, I would buy your daughter for a concubine."

The woman at once turned her back to us and lowering her head, sighed.

The father's eyes were suddenly misted. Ceremonially, he looked up at the sky. "Red Giant witnesses what a fraud has come here."

He went to the barn and called his three workmen out as witnesses to the "fraud." He had had no wife for many years and so these would be the only witnesses. The workmen stood with their caps in their hands. Two of them who were married were smiling over the young woman's fortune, but the unsmiling bachelor had had a secret hope of his own.

Doing my best to remember this ceremony, I took the traditional coin of small worth from my purse and grasped the father's hand and placed the coin in it. I repeated, "I would buy your daughter, man."

The father cast the coin on the ground. I was grateful that he used the ancient, simpler form of the ceremony. He stamped on the coin and said,

"I count not your money but your honor. Thus I see that you will mistreat her."

"I will treat her with respect."

"And then you will bring her unhappiness."

"I will bring her love and tenderness."

"And finally, you will abandon her to wretchedness."

"I will keep her with me always."

The father turned to his witnesses and demanded, "You hear this fraud?"

And the workmen used the ancient form, retorting in ragged unison, "No, we deem it honorable."

The father then asked me, "You swear by Theda to do these things?"

"I swear by Theda I will do all these things."

The ceremony was over, and the father and I clasped thumbs while the woman remained as she was with bowed head.

He said, "I will take these witnesses to the village tomorrow and sign papers. They will be delivered to you for signing, will they not?"

"I think so. I have never done this."

He smiled and it was kind of him to say, "Though you think not, White Dwarf will reappear." This common figure, referring to the regular eclipse and return of White Dwarf, meant it had been beyond human power that I was five years late in purchasing his daughter.

I drew him aside at this point and this perturbed him. "No, Excellency, do not make a suggestion. There is no need for a purchase."

"I know there is no need, but I honor you and I insist."

"Please, no. I would not feel right."

I knew that he spoke the truth. I smiled and forced him to grasp thumbs again. "But you can do nothing if I sign to you whatever land you now cultivate."

With him this made a purchase possible because he need not physically accept something. It was an extravagant price that would outrage elite people.

He saw that this measured my respect for his inability to accept the usual money. He shook his head and stared at the ground, unable to hide his smile of pride.

The woman, who should have been standing in ceremonial silence some distance behind us, suddenly ran past calling, "Oh, my son, drop the thing. Throw it away. Father, you were supposed to look after him. Oh, my son, drop the thing."

It was the little chupa. He strode from the brush grimed and sweaty, holding in his hand a thin, lavender-striped nolegs as long as a man's arm. The woman would not approach her son when she reached him because he gleefully waved the coiling nolegs at her.

Her father left me and took the nolegs from the child and let it glide away in the grass. Only then did she kneel and scold the chupa, while she brushed the dust from his tunic and the grime from his face and picked leaves and twigs from his red hair.

He stared over her shoulder at me. Even when she used the hem of her gown to wipe the dirt from his face, pushing his face this way and that, he kept his wide eyes on me. I could feel his mind searching, and I opened my mind to him.

The workmen had laughed lightly about the nolegs. But when one of them saw the red-polled chupa being presented to me with my red hair falling from under my cap, he guffawed. The farmer ordered all three back to the barns.

I lifted the child so that he sat on my arm and his mind seemed to be coming from his eyes. Presently he put his hands on me and he loved me.

After a time the woman took him from me and he rested his head at her throat. She took her eyes from me and looked up at Red Giant. Then she said the simple thing that was true.

"If all were chupa there would be no need for this 'war.' "

What she said was even truer than she meant it. For, as I glanced with her at the sky, I saw the pale glow of our sister planet, Lalone, where the Matterists invaded and enslaved the semi-rationals during the reign of the last Matterist Old Man. If all were chupa we would not have to fight over and over against the Matterist ambitions.

I turned to her father. "Have her pack only what she may need for tonight. I will send servants tomorrow for whatever she wishes."

He started to agree but an expression of intense concentration came over his face. I spun to the woman and found the same look on her face.

One of my lieutenants was instructing them to begin voting.

I took just a moment to scan all of Guapanga, found the people voting hard against the Matterists' "organized labor," and the monks voting their subtle denials of Matterism, and the chupas voting like crazy for dishonest government. It was a fine panorama for the dead-serious Matterists to have to face when they opened their minds to us.

I promptly returned my awareness to the convention. I learned in an incidental flash that I had won my place on the Council, and I found the delegates in a hasty vote for our candidate for Old Man.

My father-in-law won, as had been foregone, and only just in time. The Matterists were already probing for our collective awareness. It was the moment of "war."

This probing of foreign logic acts as a catalyst. All elite Mentalists, including now even the women of Guapanga, opened their minds to the logic of our platform. Collectively and intensely we believed our platform in all its logical beauty; an algebra of faith, cemented at every possible point to reality. Every Mentalist on the planet partook of one mind and one logic.

Only three times in my life have I been part of this almost unendurable moment of total, social awareness. It is like a moment of being a god.

Our logic neatly encompassed and projected, on my pragmatic basis, the massive, uniform vote of the common people and the telepathing of the chupas. We saw, even as the collective mind of the Matterists became discernible, how impossible it would be for their logic to digest or deny these comically true assertions about life with which we could live so easily.

Now the two collective minds were completely interpenetrated. Age-old confusions were stirred in us by the Matterists' foreign logic. But we were stirring more than confusion in them. In only a few minutes they were in defeat, their collective logic fragmented by our stronger logic. Abruptly, they were asking individually for the placing of Old Man to begin.

While we still held our collective mind in order that the placing of Old Man could get safely under way, it was fascinating to listen to snatches of conversation back and forth between individual Matterists. They were contacting friends and family members now that their collective mind had been broken, and they spoke not as a stationary god, the way we continued to speak, but as mystified people.

"What in the name of Paline was that business about dishonest government being the best government?"

Then a woman to her prominent husband, "I tell you, you have to do something. How horrible to be ruled by an Executive with three wives and a raft of messy concubines!"

Then one industrialist to another: "There they were again with all their people voting against work. If our workers get that way we're doomed."

A young schoolman cursed angrily. "How can they go on disbelieving in progress and beat us every time?"

And still we millions of Mentalists held our collective mind, our god-like awareness of each other and the total, victorious platform of belief and logic we had put together that day. While we held this collective mind, our new Old Man, my father-in-law, made his delicate, pragmatic way into the Matterists' shattered faiths.

This process of becoming Old Man requires a consummate logician and the ardent assistance, throughout the truce, of his former enemies as well as his friends. Frequently, the first pretender to this position has had more ambition than talent for pragmatic logic and has gone out of his mind.

But my father-in-law would make it.

There was no doubt about the old lecher's ability. He would make a fine Old Man . . . and one who would not live too long for my ambitions.

VII

When at last we Mentalists were released from the collective mind by an order from the new Old Man, I found myself in the farmer's yard. Of course I had fallen to the ground during the great concentration.

The woman was kneeling near me without touching me. She explained, "Father has fed the boy and is putting him to bed."

Red Giant boiled on the crest of the black Guapangas and darkness streaked across the foothills. The larger moon, the electric blue Theda, Goddess of Love, had risen behind us.

So I said, "Our way home will be lighted by Theda and warmed by Red Giant."

My elite women consider me crude, and I saw that this woman and I would get along fine. For, in the common language, my remark had a double meaning and her quiet laugh had a hoydenish ring.

But we did not leave in time to be warmed by Red Giant. The father came out and announced, "You have had a victory."

I corroborated that and he added, "Then we have two things to drink to."

We went into the kitchen and he poured liberal glasses of cool wesah wine. We drank them slowly sitting before a wood fire and talking about how the father should have another wife. Then he poured us another glass, except for the woman who said she would have no more. So her father and I had two more.

After that I said, "No, thank you. I am sufficiently drunk to withstand a walk through the woods."

I carried the sleeping child and the woman carried her bundle. Sometimes we touched each other, but it was a little late for woodland love — especially since I was burdened with the past offense that slept on my shoulder.

When we reached the lodge we found servants out in the entrance with lanterns.

My chupa half-brother stated, "Excellency, you have kept a closed mind and we have been worried about you."

"Thank you. I have been well."

He stared at the honey-haired woman. The thought that crossed his mind was immediately picked up inside the lodge, and I felt the minds of all three elite wives tense. Well, they would stay tense all night, I could tell them.

I was weary of my role as strong father. I said to my half-brother, "Here, please carry this dumpling."

To a servant I said, "And you please take the woman's bundle."

Now, my half-brother was staring at the child's red poll, and he laughed aloud with his mouth. At that there was a flurry of telepathic gabbling from within the lodge. They left the bathing of the children and the roasting of a flank of the charl boar, and the overseeing of the setting of the table for the dining, and they were coming to meet us.

I put my arm about the woman's shoulder. We walked into the great lodge with its hundred rooms and many courts to meet my elite women. I felt her tremble and I pressed her shoulder to me reassuringly.

My eldest son came running pellmell and stopped before us. He stared in stunned silence at the honey-haired woman. She smiled at him and he smiled with widening eyes. Then he dashed forward and threw himself in my arms.

"Father, I'm so glad you're back."

I held the youth with one arm and stroked his dark head. "I'm glad to be back, son."

"Father, you know we have had big gray karks in the grain bins."

"Yes, they have been eating and spoiling too much grain."

"I killed three of them today with a club."

I looked him in the eye steadily. Then I removed my arm from the woman and took his head in my hands and kissed his cheek. "Thank you, son. That had to be done."

I pushed him away playfully. "Get along now. We have to meet your mother."

At the entrance to the central court my three elite wives stopped and stared at us. We stopped and the servants stopped.

With my mouth I announced to my elite wives, "I have brought home a concubine," and realized with embarrassment that I had made it sound like I had brought home some grand present for *them*.

Graciously, my chief wife said with her mouth, "Isn't she lovely." And she extended her hands and came forward to greet the woman.

To me she telepathed, "I had rather you came home with a stick, My Husband."

My father was suddenly in my mind, irritable and resentful. "I want to see her. I want to see the honey-haired woman and her red-haired child. I want to see the big club you have brought home."

"Forgive me, father. Please! Tomorrow. This is so short a night."

His mouth chuckled. "Tomorrow, son. This has been a fine convention all around."

This day had made it clear to me that the old worlds of the elite were very nearly over. As a politician first and an arch-conservative later, I had reached a radical conclusion. This admirable child with the red poll was the future.

As Old Man, I would help that chupa's future along by changing a few marriage laws. In that future, all will be chupa. That will end the Matterist plans to colonize yellow suns.

I stroked the child's red head and knew his dreaming mind. He was fascinated with the booming flight of the rockets. As surely as he lay there he would build more engines and fly into space.

Very well. He can go to that distant yellow sun and tell those semi-rationals on Erth how they have been saved by the conservative party of Guapanga. When he is old enough, I will be Old Man, and I will arrange the trip. It will give those Erth people something to think about besides that mechanical telepathing by Ed Sulvan and Joni Karson. How that stuff can jam the galaxy.

I envy him, the little chupa. There on Erth, they have a *blue* jay. It is one thing to telepath from the mind of a semi-rational who is there. It would be quite another thing to see, with your own eyes, one of those blue jays flash in the trees of Erth like a splinter struck from that *blue* sky.

The Chameleon
LARRY EISENBERG

Larry Eisenberg (b. 1919) is co-director of the Electronics Laboratory at Rockefeller University in New York City. In spite of his
engineering and scientific background, his stories frequently fea-
ture good humor and a concern for social issues. He has published only one collection to date, the wonderful *Best Laid
Schemes* (1971), but many more are uncollected and a second volume is long overdue.

"The Chameleon" focuses on the role of the media in political life, a subject growing in importance by the day.

I was indulging my hobby and tracking marine iguana in the Galapagos,
when the news flash came through. Senator Maynard had been shot down
right on the Senate floor by a lunatic bystander in the gallery. It ruined my
vacation. Once again the nation was stunned and took to its television sets
for the catharsis of a prolonged and somber funeral.

The reaction of Congress, for once, was swift. Gun control was, of
course, out of the question. But after a brief and highly emotional debate,
it was decided to close Congress to visitors. In addition, a rider was added
stipulating that henceforth all candidates for Federal office were to conduct
their campaigns on television. Under no circumstances were they to address
live audiences in excess of two hundred and fifty people.

It was this rider that almost ruined me. As the head of the leading publicity and advertising firm in the country, and the acknowledged master of
the multimedia, I had landed Clint Speare as my client. Clint was an Oklahoman, owner of uncounted oil wells, and reputed to be worth several hundred millions. He ran perennially for the Presidential nomination and had
never gotten it, although in each case he'd spent a small fortune trying.

I liked Clint. He was no intellectual and had a limited grasp of the sub-
tleties of domestic and international politics, but he knew how to multiply
dollars. And there was a huge bonus in the pot if I could get him the
Presidency.

As soon as I returned to New York, I called Clint and told him it was important for us to get together that evening. He sensed the urgency in my voice and agreed. I arrived with Al Dix, my confidant and general business major-domo.

Clint Speare was a hospitable host, short, round, somewhat paunchy, but with a firm handclasp and a booming laugh that had the ring of sincerity. He held his liquor magnificently, even though he had consumed a full quart over a three-hour period.

"Al must have told you," he said, shortly after we walked in. "This time I mean to win. I've never felt as confident, and Al agrees that my chances are very good."

"What I meant, was the following," said Al Dix, looking at me a little ruefully. His rimless glasses gave him the look of an earnest school teacher as he began to play with the hotel silverware on the snow-white tablecloth. "Clint projects superbly, in person. Turn him loose to press the flesh and he communicates his integrity to every man, woman and child in the street. If we key him to talking about the issues that are in everyone's heart, he definitely could make it."

"I agree," I interjected. "But to put it bluntly, when Clint goes on television, he looks like any other self-conscious, shifty-eyed politician. And now that Congress has banned in-person campaigning, we're really in trouble."

Clint's face grew somber.

"I just don't feel natural in front of those cameras," he said.

I looked at Al Dix and he looked at me. We both sighed. Suddenly Clint brightened.

"We're not licked yet, boys," he said, pouring us each another round of drinks. "You'll come up with something. And you know why? Because there's too much money at the end of that rainbow."

For days thereafter, I ran over several possibilities in my mind, but prospects were bleak. Clint was not my only client, but he provided most of our bread. I was overfocused on his problem, so much so that I found it hard to concentrate on other matters. It could only have been for this reason that I agreed to visit a small East Side theater, to see a demonstration of a new approach to consumer polls.

As I entered the theater, I saw Al Dix coming up the aisle with a tall, handsome black man. We shook hands warmly.

"This is Sam Carsons," said Al.

"I know," I said, "Sam and I are old friends."

"It's been fifteen years," said Sam. "Are you still bugged on lizards?"

"It helps me relax," I said, and we both grinned at memories of chaotic desert field trips in another era. "How is Lillian?" I added. "And the kids?"

Sam shrugged.

"We're divorced." His fingers began to tremble, ever so slightly. It was an awkward moment, and Al solved it neatly.

"Let me tell you about Sam's new system," he said.

He sat me down in one of the center orchestra seats and fastened a small bracelet to my arm and a clip to my ear lobe.

"Sam has wedded an old idea to a new one. On your arm and ear are special sensors. They monitor your skin resistance, pulse rate, arterial pressure and blood gases, and tell us if you're angry, indifferent, happy, excited, and so on. This information is telemetered to a receiver backstage and processed by computer."

"Let me take over," said Sam. He looked at me with the beginning of a smile on his lips. "Would you like to see your father?"

I was jolted.

"My father?"

"We'll start," said Sam, "by projecting a three-dimensional image of a man onto stage center. It's done by a holographic process, and you might be fooled into thinking it was a real man. At first, he won't look a bit like your father. But I'll call out, *nose*. Depending on whether or not you think his nose is like your father's, it will begin to change until it is exactly like your father's nose. Then we'll go on to the eyes and so on."

I was intrigued but skeptical.

"Let's try it," I said.

The nose took form with surprising speed, then the eyes, the chin, ears, and hair styling. The complexion followed. Then I worked on the arms, posture, height and body shape. Within minutes my father looked out at me from the stage, big and frightening as he'd been in life.

"Uncanny," I said. My throat was choked and my heart was pounding.

"I developed this system," said Sam, "with the idea of selling it to the various Missing Persons Bureaus around the country. It seemed to me to be a hell of lot better than having an artist sketch from verbal description."

"Then," said Al Dix, "it occurred to him that he had a neat way of determining the best package for a perfume or a breakfast food. A computer stores all of the choices, and, depending on how the majority of the audience reacts, the package gets modified step by step to the most desirable form."

"It's a powerful idea," I said, still shaken by that man on stage who seemed to be my father. "What a pity it has no sound!"

"But it has!" said Sam. "Let's take your Dad one step further."

I was startled as the image began a rambling statement on the weather, in high-pitched falsetto. Then the voice began to deepen as I reacted. It shifted an octave lower. Next it developed a slight quaver, ultimately arriving at a thickening of the esses, adopting a New England twang, and my shock was complete. The total reproduction of my father in form and voice was unnerving.

"It's witchcraft," I told Sam, and he grew inches taller.

Al Dix was beaming as we shook hands all around. I looked at him for a moment and then a new connection suddenly went through.

"It's here," I said. "We've got the key to Clint Speare's problem right in this auditorium."

Al looked at me, puzzled.

"Don't you see," I said, grabbing his arm with ferocious intensity. "By using representative audiences, we can find out exactly what Clint must say to please them. We can film these sessions, cut it into edited one-minute tapes, and spot them on television."

Al caught the idea immediately.

"It's wild," he said. "But it might work."

"Wait a minute," said Sam. "I'd like to know what's going on."

I told him the truth, but not all of it. I didn't think it expedient, yet. Sam was reluctant.

"It's not what I had in mind," he said. "I figured on packaging products, not people."

"Give it a try," I said. "I want a six-month option. At the end of the time, you'll have the right to veto the entire project if you want to. And I'll pay you well, more than you ever dreamed of."

"Let me think it over," said Sam.

I walked outside with Al Dix, and I sketched out some of the things I wanted to do with this system. Al added some of his own ideas, and our excitement began to build even further. After a suitable time, I reentered the auditorium. Sam was still sitting there, but on stage was Lillian, Sam's ex-wife, as lovely as I'd remembered her. The deep brown skin had a lustrous sheen. I backed out of the auditorium, waited a few minutes longer, and then called out before going inside. Lillian was offstage, now, although in another sense her image hadn't been on it. Having met her several times, I knew that she was white.

"I still have my doubts," said Sam, "but as long as I hold full rights to withdraw my system after a six-month trial, I'll take a chance."

We shook hands on the deal.

Our first live audience of two hundred viewers was made up of carefully chosen members of the suburban middle class. I can still see the pseudo Clint Speare as he appeared on stage. His voice was affirmative, strong, and his gaze level and direct. His ideas at first were vague, shapeless, with just a hint of something concrete underlying each point. He attacked crime in the streets, poverty, corruption in high places, disrespect to elders, the high cost of living, unfaithful allies, and the bankrupt policy of the current National Administration.

But then he began to heat up. His statements became more biting and he began to attack minority elements by name, his voice became passionate and the audience was aflame with excitement. I watched the real Clint Speare at my side, and it was amazing to see how he mimicked the projection on-stage. The audience had narrowed the nostrils of the speaker slightly, and Clint Speare narrowed his. In some incredible way, he was adapting his facial muscles to the set of those of the pseudo Clint Speare. And he began to mutter, sotto voce, right along with the speaker, the words and phrases paralleling what came through to the audience. Afterwards, he was elated.

"Did you see that?" he kept saying. He was too excited to sit down.

"Remember," I warned. "That rousing ovation wasn't really for you. They were applauding themselves. And left to themselves they might abolish welfare, legislate restrictive housing, segregated schooling, the works."

"I intend to give them what they want," said Speare.

"Don't be a fool," I said. "There are other audiences. You've got to be something more than the man we saw on stage tonight."

Sam had said nothing but now he opened up.

"It was sickening," he said. "I was skeptical about this deal when it started, and I didn't know the half of it then. I'm pulling out."

"You missed the point," said Clint. "I'm no bigot. I'll satisfy *all* of the people."

"Sam," I said, "don't be hasty. You still have the right to withdraw after six months. But I have another test planned that I think you'd enjoy seeing. I want to set up our next speech before *an all black audience.*"

They were restive at the beginning until Clint Speare seemed to appear on stage. His appearance began to alter in subtle but important ways. The nostrils were broader, the skin a little darker, the hair more curly. The actions became broader, the voice intoned more rhythmically, and an impassioned plea for equal treatment under the law, in housing, schooling and jobs came from the mouth of the pseudo Clint Speare. At my side, the real Clint had taken on the look of the reconstructed stage figure, and was going along vocally with everything the speaker said. The close of the speech was greeted with an impassioned standing ovation that practically lifted us all out of our seats.

Afterward, Sam asked Clint how he had reacted to the audience.

"How do you feel about today's speech as compared to the last one?"

"I stand behind everything the man said on stage," said Clint. Sam was nonplussed.

"How can you? A certain amount of hedging is normal, but outright contradictions don't make sense. If one of these groups gets wind of what you're saying to the other, they'll cut you to pieces."

"That will never happen," said Clint. "I don't need that man on stage. I can sense what people want to hear. I'd like to go up there on my own, next time, with an audience that represents everybody."

"Not yet," I said. "You'd be getting ahead of the game."

"It won't wash for me," said Sam. "I never meant to create a human chameleon. I'm going to exercise my option to kill this deal."

"Don't knock chameleons," I said. "Besides, this system has gotten too big for petty squabbles. I'll be glad to pay you a fortune in royalties if you stay with us. But if you pull out, I still won't let go. You're a pretty sharp man, but I can buy all the brains I need to keep this thing going, and I will."

"You'd be infringing on my patent rights and breaking our agreement," said Sam. "I'd beat you in court."

I laughed.

"Go ahead," I said. "And in fifteen years I'd be forced to give you what I would have paid you anyway. And that's only if you win. Do you have the time and the money to buck my high-powered lawyers?"

He was silent. I thought of the time, seventeen years back, when Sam and I had been at college together. We'd held the Dean's office for three days and nights before the bust.

"Be smart, Sam," I said. "I don't want to do this. But I will if I have to. Don't make me, for old times' sake."

"Old times' sake," he snorted and walked out of the auditorium.

"What's he going to do?" said Al Dix.

"He'll stick," I said. "But I don't trust him any longer. I want another programmer put on this project right away. I want every move that Sam makes checked and double-checked. I don't want anybody or anything sabotaging our next meeting."

"What kind of a meeting is that going to be?" said Clint Speare.

"We're going to run one more test with two hundred people chosen to match the entire national voting population. Let's see how our system works then!"

It was clear that we could no longer count on Sam's help. He rarely appeared at the office, and when he did, he confined himself to biting remarks about amateur zoologists playing with human specimens. But he came to the key meeting. The audience was strikingly different from those we'd used before, weighted perfectly for income, age, color, and religion. Clint Speare was more jittery than I'd ever anticipated he could be.

And then, suddenly, I lost control. Just before the speech began, I became nauseated from the tension and had to leave the auditorium. I spent ten painful minutes turning myself inside out. When I came back, the air had filled with shock, and the figure of the pseudo Clint Speare on stage was immobile and silent.

I grabbed Al Dix's arm.

"What's going on?" I cried.

"That's *really* Clint up there," he said. "The damn fool ran on stage. He wanted to prove that he'd caught the true feelings of the entire nation. But when he got up there, he just seemed to freeze, as if all the crosscurrents of divided emotions were tearing him apart, inside."

"Get him off the stage!" I said. "Get him off at once!"

We did, but it was too late. Clint had gone through a nervous shock that had disintegrated all of his controls. It was clear that he would probably require hospitalization and extended treatment. As he was carried out to a waiting ambulance, I noticed that Sam was one of the stretcher bearers. When he came back, I stopped him.

"I guess you won out, after all," I said.

"I didn't win a goddam thing," he said. "I never hated Clint, personally, although it was clear that he wasn't fit for any office, let alone President. But you're the lizard man. You should have had the foresight to see what might happen."

"Foresight? To see what?"

"To visualize," said Sam slowly, "what happens when you put a chameleon on a plaid."

Evidence

ISAAC ASIMOV

"Evidence" is one of the best science-fiction stories ever written about an electoral contest and the charges, countercharges, and mudslinging that often accompany this type of competition. The charge leveled against the protagonist in the story is a serious one — What would you do if your opponent claimed that you were a machine? — M.H.G.

"But that wasn't it, either," said Dr. Calvin thoughtfully. "Oh, eventually, the ship and others like it became government property; the Jump through hyperspace was perfected, and now we actually have human colonies on the planets of some of the nearer stars, but that wasn't it."

I had finished eating and watched her through the smoke of my cigarette.

"It's what has happened to the people here on Earth in the last fifty years that really counts. When I was born, young man, we had just gone through the last World War. It was a low point in history — but it was the end of nationalism. Earth was too small for nations and they began grouping themselves into Regions. It took quite a while. When I was born the United States of America was still a nation and not merely a part of the Northern Region. In fact, the name of the corporation is still 'United States Robots —.' And the change from nations to Regions, which has stabilized our economy and brought about what amounts to a Golden Age, when this century is compared to the last, was also brought about by our robots."

"You mean the Machines," I said. "The Brain you talked about was the first of the Machines, wasn't it?"

"Yes, it was, but it's not the Machines I was thinking of. Rather of a man. He died last year." Her voice was suddenly deeply sorrowful. "Or at least he arranged to die, because he knew we needed him no longer. — Stephen Byerley."

"Yes, I guessed that was who you meant."

"He first entered public office in 2032. You were only a boy then, so you

wouldn't remember the strangeness of it. His campaign for the Mayoralty was certainly the queerest in history—"

Francis Quinn was a politician of the new school. That, of course, is a meaningless expression, as are all expressions of the sort. Most of the "new schools" we have were duplicated in the social life of ancient Greece, and perhaps, if we knew more about it, in the social life of ancient Sumeria and in the lake dwellings of prehistoric Switzerland as well.

But, to get out from under what promises to be a dull and complicated beginning, it might be best to state hastily that Quinn neither ran for office nor canvassed for votes, made no speeches and stuffed no ballot boxes. Any more than Napoleon pulled a trigger at Austerlitz.

And since politics makes strange bedfellows, Alfred Lanning sat at the other side of the desk with his ferocious white eyebrows bent far forward over eyes in which chronic impatience had sharpened to acuity. He was not pleased.

The fact, if known to Quinn, would have annoyed him not the least. His voice was friendly, perhaps professionally so.

"I assume you know Stephen Byerley, Dr. Lanning."

"I have heard of him. So have many people."

"Yes, so have I. Perhaps you intend voting for him at the next election."

"I couldn't say." There was an unmistakable trace of acidity here. "I have not followed the political current, so I'm not aware that he is running for office."

"He may be our next mayor. Of course, he is only a lawyer now, but great oaks—"

"Yes," interrupted Lanning, "I have heard the phrase before. But I wonder if we can get to the business at hand."

"We *are* at the business at hand, Dr. Lanning." Quinn's tone was very gentle, "It is to my interest to keep Mr. Byerley a district attorney at the very most, and it is to your interest to help me do so."

"To *my* interest? Come!" Lanning's eyebrows hunched low.

"Well, say then to the interest of U.S. Robot & Mechanical Men Corporation. I come to you as Director-Emeritus of Research, because I know that your connection to them is that of, shall we say, 'elder statesman.' You are listened to with respect and yet your connection with them is no longer so tight but that you cannot possess considerable freedom of action; even if the action is somewhat unorthodox."

Dr. Lanning was silent a moment, chewing the cud of his thoughts. He said more softly, "I don't follow you at all, Mr. Quinn."

"I am not surprised, Dr. Lanning. But it's all rather simple. Do you mind?" Quinn lit a slender cigarette with a lighter of tasteful simplicity and his big-boned face settled into an expression of quiet amusement. "We have spoken of Mr. Byerley—a strange and colorful character. He was unknown three years ago. He is very well known now. He is a man of force and ability, and certainly the most capable and intelligent prosecutor I have ever known. Unfortunately he is not a friend of mine—"

"I understand," said Lanning, mechanically. He stared at his fingernails.

"I have had occasion," continued Quinn, evenly, "in the past year to investigate Mr. Byerley—quite exhaustively. It is always useful, you see, to subject the past life of reform politicians to rather inquisitive research. If you knew how often it helped—" He paused to smile humorlessly at the glowing tip of his cigarette. "But Mr. Byerley's past is unremarkable. A quiet life in a small town, a college education, a wife who died young, an auto accident with a slow recovery, law school, coming to the metropolis, an attorney."

Francis Quinn shook his head slowly, then added, "But his present life. Ah, that is remarkable. Our district attorney never eats!"

Lanning's head snapped up, old eyes surprisingly sharp, "Pardon me?"

"Our district attorney never eats." The repetition thumped by syllables. "I'll modify that slightly. He has never been seen to eat or drink. Never! Do you understand the significance of that word? Not rarely, but never!"

"I find that quite incredible. Can you trust your investigators?"

"I can trust my investigators, and I don't find it incredible at all. Further, our district attorney has never been seen to drink—in the aqueous sense as well as the alcoholic—nor to sleep. There are other factors, but I should think that I have made my point."

Lanning leaned back in his seat, and there was the rapt silence of challenge and response between them, and then the old roboticist shook his head. "No. There is only one thing you can be trying to imply, if I couple your statements with the fact that you present them to me, and that is impossible."

"But the man is quite inhuman, Dr. Lanning."

"If you told me he were Satan in masquerade, there would be some faint chance that I might believe you."

"I tell you he is a robot, Dr. Lanning."

"I tell you it is as impossible a conception as I have ever heard, Mr. Quinn."

Again the combative silence.

"Nevertheless," and Quinn stubbed out his cigarette with elaborate care, "you will have to investigate this impossibility with all the resources of the Corporation."

"I'm sure that I could undertake no such thing, Mr. Quinn. You don't seriously suggest that the Corporation take part in local politics."

"You have no choice. Supposing I were to make my facts public without proof. The evidence is circumstantial enough."

"Suit yourself in that respect."

"But it would not suit me. Proof would be much preferable. And it would not suit *you,* for the publicity would be very damaging to your company. You are perfectly well aquainted, I suppose, with the strict rules against the use of robots on inhabited worlds."

"Certainly!" — brusquely.

"You know that the U.S. Robot & Mechanical Men Corporation is the only manufacturer of positronic robots in the Solar System, and if Byerley is a robot, he is a *positronic* robot. You are also aware that all positronic robots are leased, and not sold; that the Corporation remains the owner and manager of each robot, and is therefore responsible for the actions of all."

"It is an easy matter, Mr. Quinn, to prove the Corporation has never manufactured a robot of a humanoid character."

"It can be done? To discuss merely possibilities."

"Yes. It can be done."

"Secretly, I imagine, as well. Without entering it in your books."

"Not the positronic brain, sir. Too many factors are involved in that, and there is the tightest possible government supervision."

"Yes, but robots are worn out, break down, go out of order — and are dismantled."

"And the positronic brains are re-used or destroyed."

"Really?" Francis Quinn allowed himself a trace of sarcasm. "And if one were, accidentally, of course, not destroyed — and there happened to be a humanoid structure waiting for a brain."

"Impossible!"

"You would have to prove that to the government and the public, so why not prove it to me now."

"But what could our purpose be?" demanded Lanning in exasperation. "Where is our motivation? Credit us with a minimum of sense."

"My dear sir, please. The Corporation would be only too glad to have the various Regions permit the use of humanoid positronic robots on inhabited worlds. The profits would be enormous. But the prejudice of the public against such a practice is too great. Suppose you could get them used to such robots first — see, we have a skillful lawyer, a good mayor, — and he is a robot. Won't you buy our robot butlers?"

"Thoroughly fantastic. An almost humorous descent to the ridiculous."

"I imagine so. Why not prove it? Or would you still rather try to prove it to the public?"

The light in the office was dimming, but it was not too dim to obscure the flush of frustration on Alfred Lanning's face. Slowly, the roboticist's finger touched a knob and the wall illuminators glowed to gentle life.

"Well, then," he growled, "let us see."

The face of Stephen Byerley is not an easy one to describe. He was forty by birth certificate and forty by appearance—but it was a healthy, well-nourished, good-natured appearance of forty; one that automatically drew the teeth of the bromide about "looking one's age."

This was particularly true when he laughed, and he was laughing now. It came loudly and continuously, died away for a bit, then began again—

And Alfred Lanning's face contracted into a rigidly bitter monument of disapproval. He made a half gesture to the woman who sat beside him, but her thin, bloodless lips merely pursed themselves a trifle.

Byerley gasped himself a stage nearer normality.

"Really, Dr. Lanning . . . really—I . . . I . . . a robot?"

Lanning bit his words off with a snap, "It is no statement of mine, sir. I would be quite satisfied to have you a member of humanity. Since our corporation never manufactured you, I am quite certain that you are—in a legalistic sense, at any rate. But since the contention that you are a robot has been advanced to us seriously by a man of certain standing—"

"Don't mention his name, if it would knock a chip off your granite block of ethics, but let's pretend it was Frank Quinn, for the sake of argument, and continue."

Lanning drew in a sharp, cutting snort at the interruption, and paused ferociously before continuing with added frigidity. "—by a man of certain standing, with whose identity I am not interested in playing guessing games, I am bound to ask your cooperation in disproving it. The mere fact that such a contention could be advanced and publicized by the means at this man's disposal would be a bad blow to the company I represent—even if the charge were never proven. You understand me?"

"Oh, yes, your position is clear to me. The charge itself is ridiculous. The spot you find yourself in is not. I beg your pardon, if my laughter offended you. It was the first I laughed at, not the second. How can I help you?"

"It could be very simple. You have only to sit down to a meal at a restaurant in the presence of witnesses, have your picture taken, and eat." Lanning sat back in his chair, the worst of the interview over. The woman beside him watched Byerley with an apparently absorbed expression but contributed nothing of her own.

Stephen Byerley met her eyes for an instant, was caught by them, then turned back to the roboticist. For a while his fingers were thoughtful over the bronze paper-weight that was the only ornament on his desk.

He said quietly, "Don't think I can oblige you."

He raised his hand, "Now wait, Dr. Lanning. I appreciate the fact that this whole matter is distasteful to you, that you have been forced into it against your will, that you feel you are playing an undignified and even ridiculous part. Still, the matter is even more intimately concerned with myself, so be tolerant.

"First, what makes you think that Quinn—this man of certain standing, you know—wasn't hoodwinking you, in order to get you to do exactly what you are doing?"

"Why it seems scarcely likely that a reputable person would endanger himself in so ridiculous a fashion, if he weren't convinced he were on safe ground."

There was little humor in Byerley's eyes, "You don't know Quinn. He could manage to make safe ground out of a ledge a mountain sheep could not handle. I suppose he showed you the particulars of the investigation he claims to have made of me?"

"Enough to convince me that it would be too troublesome to have our corporation attempt to disprove them when you could do so more easily."

"Then you believe him when he says I never eat. You are a scientist, Dr. Lanning. Think of the logic required. I have not been observed to eat, therefore, I never eat Q.E.D. After all!"

"You are using prosecution tactics to confuse what is really a very simple situation."

"On the contrary, I am trying to clarify what you and Quinn between you are making a very complicated one. You see, I don't sleep much, that's true, and I certainly don't sleep in public. I have never cared to eat with others—an idiosyncrasy which is unusual and probably neurotic in character, but which harms no one. Look Dr. Lanning, let me present you with a suppositious case. Supposing we had a politician who was interested in defeating a reform candidate at any cost and while investigating his private life came across oddities such as I have just mentioned.

"Suppose further that in order to smear the candidate effectively, he comes to your company as the ideal agent. Do you expect him to say to you, 'So-and-so is a robot because he hardly ever eats with people, and I have never seen him fall asleep in the middle of a case; and once when I peeped into his window in the middle of the night, there he was, sitting up with a book; and I looked in his frigidaire and there was no food in it.' "

"If he told you that, you would send for a straitjacket. But if he tells you, 'He *never* sleeps; he *never* eats,' then the shock of the statement blinds you to the fact that such statements are impossible to prove. You play into his hands by contributing to the to-do."

"Regardless, sir," began Lanning, with a threatening obstinacy, "of whether you consider this matter serious or not, it will require only the meal I mentioned to end it."

Again Byerley turned to the woman, who still regarded him expressionlessly. "Pardon me. I've caught your name correctly, haven't I? Dr. Susan Calvin?"

"Yes, Mr. Byerley."

"You're the U.S. Robot's psychologist, aren't you?"

"*Robo*psychologist, please."

"Oh, are robots so different from men, mentally?"

"Worlds different." She allowed herself a frosty smile, "Robots are essentially decent."

Humor tugged at the corners of the lawyer's mouth, "Well, that's a hard blow. But what I wanted to say was this. Since you're a psycho — a robopsychologist, *and* a woman, I'll bet that you've done something that Dr. Lanning hasn't thought of."

"And what is that?"

"You've got something to eat in your purse."

Something caught in the schooled indifference of Susan Calvin's eyes. She said, "You surprise me, Mr. Byerley."

And opening her purse, she produced an apple. Quietly, she handed it to him. Dr. Lanning, after an initial start, followed the slow movement from one hand to the other with sharply alert eyes.

Calmly, Stephen Byerley bit into it, and calmly he swallowed it.

"You see, Dr. Lanning?"

Dr. Lanning smiled in a relief tangible enough to make even his eyebrows appear benevolent. A relief that survived for one fragile second.

Susan Calvin said, "I was curious to see if you would eat it, but of course, in the present case, it proves nothing."

Byerley grinned, "It doesn't?"

"Of course not. It is obvious, Dr. Lanning, that if this man were a humanoid robot, he would be a perfect imitation. He is almost too human to be credible. After all, we have been seeing and observing human beings all our lives, it would be impossible to palm something merely nearly right off on us. It would have to be *all* right. Observe the texture of the skin, the quality of the irises, the bone formation of the hand. If he's a robot, I wish U.S. Robots *had* made him, because he's a good job. Do you suppose then, that anyone capable of paying attention to such niceties would neglect a few gadgets to take care of such things as eating, sleeping, elimination? For emergency use only, perhaps; as, for instance, to prevent such situations as are arising here. So a meal won't prove anything."

"Now wait," snarled Lanning, "I am not quite the fool both of you make me out to be. I am not interested in the problem of Mr. Byerley's humanity or nonhumanity. I am interested in getting the corporation out of a hole. A public meal will end the matter and keep it ended no matter what Quinn does. We can leave the finer details to lawyers and robopsychologists."

"But, Dr. Lanning," said Byerley, "you forget the politics of the situation. I am as anxious to be elected as Quinn is to stop me. By the way, did you notice that you used his name? It's a cheap shyster trick of mine; I knew you would, before you were through."

Lanning flushed, "What has the election to do with it?"

"Publicity works both ways, sir. If Quinn wants to call me a robot, and has the nerve to do so, I have the nerve to play the game his way."

"You mean you—" Lanning was quite frankly appalled.

"Exactly. I mean that I'm going to let him go ahead, choose his rope, test its strength, cut off the right length, tie the noose, insert his head and grin. I can do what little else is required."

"You are mighty confident."

Susan Calvin rose to her feet, "Come, Alfred, we won't change his mind for him."

"You see," Byerley smiled gently, "You are a human psychologist, too."

But perhaps not all the confidence that Dr. Lanning had remarked upon was present that evening when Byerley's car parked on the automatic treads leading to the sunken garage, and Byerley himself crossed the path to the front door of his house.

The figure in the wheel chair looked up as he entered and smiled. Byerley's face lit with affection. He crossed over to it.

The cripple's voice was a hoarse, grating whisper that came out of a mouth forever twisted to one side, leering out of a face that was half scar tissue, "You're late, Steve."

"I know, John, I know. But I've been up against a peculiar and interesting trouble today."

"So?" Neither the torn face nor the destroyed voice could carry expression but there was anxiety in the clear eyes. "Nothing you can't handle?"

"I'm not exactly certain. I may need your help. *You're* the brilliant one in the family. Do you want me to take you out into the garden? It's a beautiful evening."

Two strong arms lifted John from the wheel chair. Gently, almost caressingly, Byerley's arms went around the shoulders and under the swathed legs of the cripple. Carefully, and slowly, he walked through the rooms, down the gentle ramp that had been built with a wheel chair in mind, and out the back door into the walled and wired garden behind the house.

"Why don't you let me use the wheel chair, Steve? This is silly."

"Because I'd rather carry you. Do you object? You know that you're as glad to get out of that motorized buggy for a while as I am to see you out. How do you feel today?" He deposited John with infinite care upon the cool grass.

"How should I feel? But tell me about your troubles."

"Quinn's campaign will be based on the fact that he claims I'm a robot."

John's eyes opened wide, "How do you know? It's impossible. I won't believe it."

"Oh, come, I tell you it's so. He had one of the big-shot scientists of U.S. Robot & Mechanical Men Corporation over at the office to argue with me."

Slowly John's hands tore at the grass, "I see. I see."

Byerley said, "But we can let him choose his ground. I have an idea. Listen to me and tell me if we can do it—"

The scene as it appeared in Alfred Lanning's office that night was a tableau of stars. Francis Quinn stared meditatively at Alfred Lanning. Lanning's stare was savagely set upon Susan Calvin, who stared impassively in her turn at Quinn.

Francis Quinn broke it with a heavy attempt at lightness, "Bluff. He's making it up as he goes along."

"Are you going to gamble on that, Mr. Quinn?" asked Dr. Calvin, indifferently.

"Well, it's your gamble, really."

"Look here," Lanning covered definite pessimism with bluster, "we've done what you asked. We witnessed the man eat. It's ridiculous to presume him a robot."

"Do *you* think so?" Quinn shot toward Calvin. "Lanning said you were the expert."

Lanning was almost threatening, "Now, Susan—"

Quinn interrupted smoothly, "Why not let her talk, man? She's been sitting there imitating a gatepost for half an hour."

Lanning felt definitely harassed. From what he experienced then to incipient paranoia was but a step. He said, "Very well. Have your say, Susan. We won't interrupt you."

Susan Calvin glanced at him humorlessly, then fixed cold eyes on Mr. Quinn. "There are only two ways of definitely proving Byerley to be a robot, sir. So far you are presenting circumstantial evidence, with which you can accuse, but not prove—and I think Mr. Byerley is sufficiently clever to counter that sort of material. You probably think so yourself, or you wouldn't have come here.

"The two methods of *proof* are the physical and the psychological. Physically, you can dissect him or use an X-ray. How to do that would be *your* problem. Psychologically, his behavior can be studied, for if he *is* a positronic robot, he must conform to the three Rules of Robotics. A positronic brain can not be constructed without them. You know the Rules, Mr. Quinn?"

She spoke them carefully, clearly, quoting word for word the famous bold print on page one of the "Handbook of Robotics."

"I've heard of them," said Quinn, carelessly.

"Then the matter is easy to follow," responded the psychologist, dryly. "If Mr. Byerley breaks any of those three rules, he is not a robot. Unfortunately, this procedure works in only one direction. If he lives up to the rules, it proves nothing one way or the other."

Quinn raised polite eyebrows. "Why not, doctor?"

"Because, if you stop to think of it, the three Rules of Robotics are the essential guiding principles of a good many of the world's ethical systems. Of course, every human being is supposed to have the instinct of self-preservation. That's Rule Three to a robot. Also every 'good' human being, with social conscience and a sense of responsibility, is supposed to defer to proper authority; to listen to his doctor, his boss, his government, his psychiatrist, his fellow man; to obey laws, to follow rules, to conform to custom—even when they interfere with his comfort or his safety. That's Rule Two to a robot. Also, every 'good' human being is supposed to love others as himself, protect his fellow man, risk his life to save another. That's Rule One to a robot. To put it simply—if Byerley follows all the Rules of Robotics, he may be a robot, and may simply be a very good man."

"But," said Quinn, "you're telling me that you can never prove him a robot."

"I may be able to prove him *not* a robot."

"That's not the proof I want."

"You'll have such proof as exists. You are the only one responsible for your own wants."

Here Lanning's mind leaped suddenly to the sting of an idea, "Has it occurred to anyone," he ground out, "that district attorney is a rather strange occupation for a robot? The prosecution of human beings—sentencing them to death—bringing about their infinite harm—"

Quinn grew suddenly keen, "No, you can't get out of it that way. Being district attorney doesn't make him human. Don't you know his record? Don't you know that he boasts that he has never prosecuted an innocent man; that there are scores of people left untried because the evidence against them didn't satisfy him, even though he could probably have argued a jury into atomizing them? That happens to be so."

Lanning's thin cheeks quivered, "No, Quinn, no. There is nothing in the Rules of Robotics that makes any allowance for human guilt. A robot may not judge whether a human being deserves death. It is not for him to decide. *He may not harm a human*—variety skunk, or variety angel."

Susan Calvin sounded tired. "Alfred," she said, "don't talk foolishly. What if a robot came upon a madman about to set fire to a house with people in it. He would stop the madman, wouldn't he?"

"Of course."

"And if the only way he could stop him was to kill him—"

There was a faint sound in Lanning's throat. Nothing more.

"The answer to that, Alfred, is that he would do his best not to kill him. If the madman died, the robot would require psychotherapy because he might easily go mad at the conflict presented him—of having broken Rule One to adhere to Rule One in a higher sense. But a man would be dead and a robot would have killed him."

"Well *is* Byerley mad?" demanded Lanning, with all the sarcasm he could muster.

"No, but he has killed no man himself. He has exposed facts which might represent a particular human being to be dangerous to the large mass of other human beings we call society. He protects the greater number and thus adheres to Rule One at maximum potential. That is as far as he goes. It is the judge who then condemns the criminal to death or imprisonment, after the jury decides on his guilt or innocence. It is the jailer who imprisons him, the executioner who kills him. And Mr. Byerley has done nothing but determine truth and aid society.

"As a matter of fact, Mr. Quinn, I have looked into Mr. Byerley's career since you first brought this matter to our attention. I find that he has never demanded the death sentence in his closing speeches to the jury. I also find that he has spoken on behalf of the abolition of capital punishment and contributed generously to research institutions engaged in criminal neurophysiology. He apparently believes in the cure, rather than the punishment of crime. I find that significant."

"You do?" Quinn smiled. "Significant of a certain odor of roboticity, perhaps?"

"Perhaps. Why deny it? Actions such as his could come only from a robot, or from a very honorable and decent human being. But you see, you just can't differentiate between a robot and the very best of humans."

Quinn sat back in his chair. His voice quivered with impatience. "Dr. Lanning, it's perfectly possible to create a humanoid robot that would perfectly duplicate a human in appearance, isn't it?"

Lanning harrumphed and considered, "It's been done experimentally by U.S. Robots," he said reluctantly, "without the addition of a positronic brain, of course. By using human ova and hormone control, one can grow human flesh and skin over a skeleton of porous silicone plastics that would defy external examination. The eyes, hair, the skin would be really human, not humanoid. And if you put a positronic brain, and such other gadgets as you might desire inside, you have a humanoid robot."

Quinn said shortly, "How long would it take to make one?"

Lanning considered, "If you had all your equipment — the brain, the skeleton, the ovum, the proper hormones and radiations — say, two months."

The politician straightened out of his chair. "Then we shall see what the insides of Mr. Byerley look like. It will mean publicity for U.S. Robots — but I gave you your chance."

Lanning turned impatiently to Susan Calvin, when they were alone. "Why do you insist — "

And with real feeling, she responded sharply and instantly, "Which do you want — the truth or my resignation? I won't lie for you. U.S. Robots can take care of itself. Don't turn coward."

"What," said Lanning, "if he opens up Byerley, and wheels and gears fall out. What then?"

"He won't open Byerley," said Calvin, disdainfully. "Byerley is as clever as Quinn, at the very least."

The news broke upon the city a week before Byerley was to have been nominated. But "broke" is the wrong word. It staggered upon the city, shambled, crawled. Laughter began, and wit was free. And as the far off hand of Quinn tightened its pressure in easy stages, the laughter grew forced, an element of hollow uncertainty entered, and people broke off to wonder.

The convention itself had the air of a restive stallion. There had been no contest planned. Only Byerley could possibly have been nominated a week earlier. There was no substitute even now. They had to nominate him, but there was complete confusion about it.

It would not have been so bad if the average individual were not torn between the enormity of the charge, if true, and its sensational folly, if false.

The day after Byerley was nominated perfunctorily, hollowly—a newspaper published the gist of a long interview with Dr. Susan Calvin, "world famous expert on robopsychology and positronics."

What broke loose is popularly and succinctly described as hell.

It was what the Fundamentalists were waiting for. They were not a political party; they made pretense to no formal religion. Essentially they were those who had not adapted themselves to what had once been called the Atomic Age, in the days when atoms were a novelty. Actually, they were the Simple-Lifers, hungering after a life, which to those who lived it had probably appeared not so Simple, and who had been, therefore, Simple-Lifers themselves.

The Fundamentalists required no new reason to detest robots and robot manufacturers; but a new reason such as the Quinn accusation and the Calvin analysis was sufficient to make such detestation audible.

The huge plants of the U.S. Robot & Mechanical Men Corporation was a hive that spawned armed guards. It prepared for war.

Within the city the house of Stephen Byerley bristled with police.

The political campaign, of course, lost all other issues, and resembled a campaign only in that it was something filling the hiatus between nomination and election.

Stephen Byerley did not allow the fussy little man to distract him. He remained comfortably unperturbed by the uniforms in the background. Outside the house, past the line of grim guards, reporters and photographers waited according to the tradition of the caste. One enterprising 'visor station even had a scanner focused on the blank entrance to the prosecutor's unpretentious home, while a synthetically excited announcer filled in with inflated commentary.

The fussy little man advanced. He held forward a rich, complicated sheet. "This, Mr. Byerley, is a court order authorizing me to search these premises for the presence of illegal . . . uh . . . mechanical men or robots of any description."

Byerley half rose, and took the paper. He glanced at it indifferently, and smiled as he handed it back. "All in order. Go ahead. Do your job. Mrs. Hoppen"—to his housekeeper, who appeared reluctantly from the next room—"please go with them, and help out if you can."

The little man, whose name was Harroway, hesitated, produced an unmistakable blush, failed completely to catch Byerley's eyes, and muttered, "Come on," to the two policemen.

He was back in ten minutes.

"Through?" questioned Byerley, in just the tone of a person who is not particularly interested in the question, or its answer.

Harroway cleared his throat, made a bad start in falsetto, and began again, angrily, "Look here, Mr. Byerley, our special instructions were to search the house very thoroughly."

"And haven't you?"

"We were told exactly what to look for."

"Yes?"

"In short, Mr. Byerley, and not to put too fine a point on it, we were told to search you."

"Me?" said the prosecutor with a broadening smile. "And how do you intend to do that?"

"We have a Penet-radiation unit—"

"Then I'm to have my X-ray photograph taken, hey? You have the authority?"

"You saw my warrant."

"May I see it again?"

Harroway, his forehead shining with considerably more than mere enthusiasm, passed it over a second time.

Byerley said evenly, "I read here as the description of what you are to search; I quote: 'the dwelling place belonging to Stephen Allen Byerley, located at 355 Willow Grove, Evanstron, together with any garage, storehouse or other structures or buildings thereto appertaining, together with all grounds thereto appertaining' . . . um . . . and so on. Quite in order. But, my good man, it doesn't say anything about searching my interior. I am not part of the premises. You may search my clothes if you think I've got a robot hidden in my pocket."

Harroway had no doubt on the point of to whom he owed his job. He did not propose to be backward, given a chance to earn a much better—i.e., more highly paid—job.

He said, in a faint echo of bluster, "Look here. I'm allowed to search the furniture in your house, and anything else I find in it. You are in it, aren't you?"

"A remarkable observation. I *am* in it. But I'm not a piece of furniture. As a citizen of adult responsibility — I have the psychiatric certificate proving that — I have certain rights under the Regional Articles. Searching me would come under the heading of violating my Right of Privacy. That paper isn't sufficient."

"Sure, but if you're robot, you don't have Right of Privacy."

"True enough — but that paper still isn't sufficient. It recognizes me implicitly as a human being."

"Where?" Harroway snatched at it.

"Where it says 'the dwelling place belonging to' and so on. A robot cannot own property. And you may tell your employer, Mr. Harroway, that if he tries to issue a similar paper which does *not* implicitly recognize me as a human being, he will be immediately faced with a restraining injunction and a civil suit which will make it necessary for him to *prove* me a robot by means of information *now* in his possession, or else to pay a whopping penalty for an attempt to deprive me unduly of my Rights under the Regional Articles. You'll tell him that, won't you?"

Harroway marched to the door. He turned. "You're a slick lawyer — " His hand was in his pocket. For a short moment, he stood there. Then he left, smiled in the direction of the 'visor scanner, still playing away — waved to the reporters, and shouted, "We'll have something for you tomorrow, boys. No kidding."

In his ground car, he settled back, removed the tiny mechanism from his pocket and carefully inspected it. It was the first time he had ever taken a photograph by X-ray reflection. He hoped he had done it correctly.

Quinn and Byerley had never met face-to-face alone. But visorphone was pretty close to it. In fact, accepted literally, perhaps the phrase was accurate, even if to each, the other were merely the light and dark pattern of a bank of photocells.

It was Quinn who had initiated the call. It was Quinn who spoke first, and without particular ceremony, "Thought you would like to know, Byerley, that I intended to make public the fact that you're wearing a protective shield against Penet-radiation."

"That so? In that case, you've probably already made it public. I have a notion our enterprising press representatives have been tapping my various communication lines for quite a while. I know they have my office lines full of holes; which is why I've dug in at my home these last weeks." Byerley was friendly, almost chatty.

Quinn's lips tightened slightly, "This call is shielded — thoroughly. I'm making it at a certain personal risk."

"So I should imagine. Nobody knows you're behind this campaign. At least, nobody knows it officially. Nobody doesn't know it unofficially. I wouldn't worry. So I wear a protective shield? I suppose you found that out when your puppy dog's Penet-radiation photograph, the other day, turned out to be overexposed."

"You realize, Byerley, that it would be pretty obvious to everyone that you don't dare face X-ray analysis."

"Also that you, or your men, attempted illegal invasion of my Rights of Privacy."

"The devil they'll care for that."

"They might. It's rather symbolic of our two campaigns, isn't it? You have little concern with the rights of the individual citizen. I have great concern. I will not submit to X-ray analysis, because I wish to maintain my Rights on principle. Just as I'll maintain the rights of others when elected."

"That will no doubt make a very interesting speech, but no one will believe you. A little too high-sounding to be true. Another thing," a sudden crisp change, "the personnel in your home was not complete the other night."

"In what way?"

"According to the report," he shuffled papers before him that were just within the range of vision of the visiplate, "there was one person missing—a cripple."

"As you say," said Byerley, tonelessly, "a cripple. My old teacher, who lives with me and who is now in the country—and has been for two months. A 'much-needed rest' is the usual expression applied in the case. He has your permission?"

"Your teacher? A scientist of sorts?"

"A lawyer once—before he was a cripple. He has a government license as a research biophysicist, with a laboratory of his own, and a complete description of the work he's doing filed with the proper authorities, to whom I can refer you. The work is minor, but is a harmless and engaging hobby for a—poor cripple. I am being as helpful as I can, you see."

"I see. And what does this . . . teacher . . . know about robot manufacture?"

"I couldn't judge the extent of his knowledge in a field which I am unacquainted."

"He wouldn't have access to positronic brains?"

"Ask your friends at U.S. Robots. They'd be the ones to know."

"I'll put it shortly, Byerley. Your crippled teacher is the real Stephen Byerley. You are his robot creation. We can prove it. It was he who was in the automobile accident, not you. There will be ways of checking the records."

"Really? Do so, then. My best wishes."

"And we can search your so-called teacher's 'country place,' and see what we can find there."

"Well, not quite, Quinn." Byerley smiled broadly. "Unfortunately for you, my so-called teacher is a sick man. His country place is his place of rest. His Right of Privacy as a citizen of adult responsibility is naturally even stronger, under the circumstances. You won't be able to obtain a warrant to enter his grounds without showing just cause. However, I'd be the last to prevent you from trying."

There was a pause of moderate length, and then Quinn leaned forward, so that his imaged-face expanded and the fine lines on his forehead were visible, "Byerley, why do you carry on? You can't be elected."

"Can't I?"

"Do you think you can? Do you suppose that your failure to make any attempt to disprove the robot charge—when you could easily, by breaking one of the Three Laws—does anything but convince the people that you *are* a robot?"

"All I see so far is that from being a rather vaguely known, but still largely obscure metropolitan lawyer, I have now become a world figure. You're a good publicist."

"But you *are* a robot."

"So it's been said, but not proven."

"It's been proven sufficiently for the electorate."

"Then relax—you've won."

"Good-by," said Quinn, with his first touch of viciousness, and the visor-phone slammed off.

"Good-by," said Byerley imperturbably, to the blank plate.

Byerley brought his "teacher" back the week before the election. The air car dropped quickly in an obscure part of the city.

"You'll stay here till after election," Byerley told him. "It would be better to have you out of the way if things take a bad turn."

The hoarse voice that twisted painfully out of John's crooked mouth might have had accents of concern in it. "There's danger of violence?"

"The Fundamentalists threaten it, so I suppose there is, in a theoretical sense. But I really don't expect it. The Fundies have no real power. They're just the continuous irritant factor that might stir up a riot after a while. You don't mind staying here? Please. I won't be myself if I have to worry about you."

"Oh, I'll stay. You still think it will go well?"

"I'm sure of it. No one bothered you at the place?"

"No one. I'm certain."

"And your part went well?"

"Well enough. There'll be no trouble there."

"Then take care of yourself, and watch the televisor tomorrow, John."
Byerley pressed the gnarled hand that rested on his.

Lenton's forehead was a furrowed study in suspense. He had the completely unenviable job of being Byerley's campaign manager in a campaign that wasn't a campaign, for a person that refused to reveal his strategy, and refused to accept his manager's.

"You can't!" It was his favorite phrase. It had become his only phrase. "I tell you, Steve, you can't!"

He threw himself in front of the prosecutor, who was spending time leafing through the typed pages of his speech.

"Put that down, Steve. Look, that mob has been organized by the Fundies. You won't get a hearing. You'll be stoned more likely. Why do you have to make a speech before an audience? What's wrong with a recording, a visual recording?"

"You want me to win the election, don't you?" asked Byerley, mildly.

"Win the election! You're not going to win, Steve. I'm trying to save your life."

"Oh, I'm not in danger."

"He's not in danger. He's not in danger." Lenton made a queer, rasping sound in his throat. "You mean you're getting out on that balcony in front of fifty thousand crazy crackpots and try to talk sense to them — on a balcony like a medieval dictator?"

Byerley consulted his watch. "In about five minutes — as soon as the television lines are free."

Lenton's answering remark was not quite transliterable.

The crowd filled a roped off area of the city. Trees and houses seemed to grow out of a mass-human foundation. And by ultra-wave, the rest of the world watched. It was a purely local election, but it had a world audience just the same. Byerley thought of that and smiled.

But there was nothing to smile at in the crowd itself. There were banners and streamers, ringing every possible change on his supposed robotcy. The hostile attitude rose thickly and tangibly into the atmosphere.

From the start the speech was not successful. It competed against the inchoate mob howl and the rhythmic cries of the Fundie claques that formed mob-islands within the mob. Byerley spoke on, slowly unemotionally —

Inside, Lenton clutched his hair and groaned — and waited for the blood.

There was a writhing in the front ranks. An angular citizen with popping eyes, and clothes too short for the lank length of his limbs, was pulling to the fore. A policeman dived after him, making slow, struggling passage. Byerley waved the latter off, angrily.

The thin man was directly under the balcony. His words tore unheard against the roar.

Byerley leaned forward. "What do you say? If you have a legitimate question, I'll answer it." He turned to a flanking guard. "Bring that man up here."

There was a tensing in the crowd. Cries of "Quiet" started in various parts of the mob, and rose to a bedlam, then toned down raggedly. The thin man, red-faced and panting, faced Byerley.

Byerley said, "Have you a question?"

The thin man stared, and said in a cracked voice, "Hit me!"

With sudden energy, he thrust out his chin at an angle. "Hit me! You say you're not a robot. Prove it. You can't hit a human, you monster."

There was a queer, flat, dead silence. Byerley's voice punctured it. "I have no reason to hit you."

The thin man was laughing wildly. "You *can't* hit me. You *won't* hit me. You're not a human. You're a monster, a make-believe man."

And Stephen Byerley, tight-lipped, in the face of thousands who watched in person and the millions who watched by screen, drew back his fist and caught the man crackingly upon the chin. The challenger went over backwards in sudden collapse, with nothing on his face but blank, blank surprise.

Byerley said, "I'm sorry. Take him in and see that he's comfortable. I want to speak to him when I'm through."

And when Dr. Calvin, from her reserved space, turned her automobile and drove off, only one reporter had recovered sufficiently from the shock to race after her, and shout an unheard question.

Susan Calvin called over her shoulder, "He's human."

That was enough. The reporter raced away in his own direction.

The rest of the speech might be described as "Spoken but not heard."

Dr. Calvin and Stephen Byerley met once again — a week before he took the oath of office as mayor. It was late — past midnight.

Dr. Calvin said, "You don't look tired."

The mayor-elect smiled. "I may stay up for a while. Don't tell Quinn."

"I shan't. But that was an interesting story of Quinn's, since you mention him. It's a shame to have spoiled it. I suppose you knew his theory?"

"Parts of it."

"It was highly dramatic. Stephen Byerley was a young lawyer, a powerful speaker, a great idealist — and with a certain flair for biophysics. Are you interested in robotics, Mr. Byerley?"

"Only in legal aspects."

"*This* Stephen Byerley was. But there was an accident. Byerley's wife died; he himself, worse. His legs were gone; his face was gone; his voice was gone. Part of his mind was — bent. He would not submit to plastic surgery. He retired from the world, legal career gone — only his intelligence, and his hands left. Somehow he could obtain positronic brains, even a complex one, one which had the greatest capacity of forming judgments in ethical problems — which is the highest robotic function so far developed.

"He grew a body about it. Trained it to be everything he would have been and was no longer. He sent it out into the world as Stephen Byerley, remaining behind himself as the old, crippled teacher that no one ever saw—"

"Unfortunately," said the mayor-elect, "I ruined all that by hitting a man. The papers say it was your official verdict on the occasion that I was human."

"How did that happen? Do you mind telling me? It couldn't have been accidental."

"It wasn't entirely. Quinn did most of the work. My men started quietly spreading the fact that I had never hit a man; that I was unable to hit a man; that to fail to do so under provocation would be sure proof that I was a robot. So I arranged for a silly speech in public, with all sorts of publicity overtones, and almost inevitably, some fool fell for it. In its essence, it was what I call a shyster trick. One in which the artificial atmosphere which has been created does all the work. Of course, the emotional effects made my election certain, as intended."

The robopsychologist nodded. "I see you intrude on my field—as every politician must, I suppose. But I'm very sorry it turned out this way. I like robots. I like them considerably better than I do human beings. If a robot can be created capable of being a civil executive, I think he'd make the best one possible. By the Laws of Robotics, he'd be incapable of harming humans, incapable of tyranny, of corruption, of stupidity, of prejudice. And after he had served a decent term, he would leave, even though he were immortal, because it would be impossible for him to hurt humans by letting them know that a robot had ruled them. It would be most ideal."

"Except that a robot might fail due to the inherent inadequacies of his brain. The positronic brain has never equalled the complexities of the human brain."

"He would have advisers. Not even a human brain is capable of governing without assistance."

Byerley considered Susan Calvin with grave interest. "Why do you smile, Dr. Calvin?"

"I smile because Mr. Quinn didn't think of everything."

"You mean there could be more to that story of his."

"Only a little. For the three months before election, this Stephen Byerley that Mr. Quinn spoke about, this broken man, was in the country for some mysterious reason. He returned in time for that famous speech of yours. And after all, what the old cripple did once, he could do a second time, particularly where the second job is very simple in comparison to the first."

"I don't quite understand."

Dr. Calvin rose and smoothed her dress. She was obviously ready to leave. "I mean there is one time when a robot may strike a human being without breaking the First Law. Just one time."

"And when is that?"

Dr. Calvin was at the door. She said quietly, "When the human to be struck is merely another robot."

She smiled broadly, her thin face glowing. "Good-by Mr. Byerley. I hope to vote for you five years from now—for co-ordinator."

Stephen Byerley chuckled, "I must reply that that is a somewhat far-fetched idea."

The door closed behind her.

I stared at her with a sort of horror, "Is that true?"

"All of it," she said.

"And the great Byerley was simply a robot."

"Oh, there's no way of ever finding out. I think he was. But when he decided to die, he had himself atomized, so that there will never be any legal proof.—Besides, what difference would it make?"

"Well—"

"You share a prejudice against robots which is quite unreasoning. He was a very good Mayor; five years later he did become Regional Co-ordinator. And when the Regions of Earth formed their Federation in 2044, he became the first World Co-ordinator. By that time it was the Machines that were running the world anyway."

"Yes, but—"

"No buts! The Machines are robots, and they are running the world. It was five years ago that I found out all the truth. It was 2052; Byerley was completing his second term as World Co-ordinator—"